T0158879

The *Horse* HOLDER

A NOVEL OF THE CIVIL WAR

ROBERT W. CALLIS

iUniverse

THE HORSE HOLDER

iUniverse books may be ordered through booksellers or by contacting:

iUniverse
1663 Liberty Drive
Bloomington, IN 47403
www.iuniverse.com
1-800-Authors (1-800-288-4677)

Because of the dynamic nature of the Internet, any web addresses or links contained in this book may have changed since publication and may no longer be valid. The views expressed in this work are solely those of the author and do not necessarily reflect the views of the publisher, and the publisher hereby disclaims any responsibility for them.

Any people depicted in stock imagery provided by Thinkstock are models, and such images are being used for illustrative purposes only. Certain stock imagery © Thinkstock.

ISBN: 978-1-5320-0302-8 (sc)
ISBN: 978-1-5320-0303-5 (e)

Library of Congress Control Number: 2016911930

Print information available on the last page.

iUniverse rev. date: 07/22/2016

AUTHOR'S NOTE

The characters and events in this book are fiction. Any similarity to real persons, living or dead, is coincidental and not intended by the author.

During the early years of the American Civil War the cavalry arm of the Union Army was far inferior to their Confederate counterparts, but by 1863 they had become a force to be reckoned with. Unlike their European counterparts, the Union Army cavalry were taught to fight like light infantry. The horse gave them swift mobility when the cavalry were used as scouts and raiding parties, but when they encountered strong opposition, they dismounted and fought on foot.

The basic unit of the Union cavalry was a group of four horsemen. When they dismounted to fight on foot, three of the cavalrymen advanced as part of a skirmish line, while the fourth cavalryman took all four horses and went to the rear of the skirmish line where he held the horses for his comrades. The other three depended on this horse holder to have their horses available for them, should they need to advance or to retreat.

Thus the fourth cavalryman or the horse holder had to be someone the other three could trust to not abandon them at a time when it mattered most. This story is about the kind of trust it took to be a horse holder in the face of great danger.

DEDICATION

This story is dedicated to my great-grandfather William Main, who served as a private in Company I, 102nd Illinois Volunteer Infantry Regiment from 1862 to 1865.

He served under General Sherman from Chattanooga to the end of the war, including Sherman's famous March to the Sea.

PROLOGUE

Altona Presbyterian Church
Altona, Illinois
1915

Mrs. Chambers walked quickly from the small clapboard house the church provided to her and her husband. Benjamin Chambers was the minister of the Altona Presbyterian Church, and as his wife, Lydia had certain duties to support her husband in various church activities. The morning worship service had gone smoothly, and the members of the congregation had been in good spirits.

The fall harvest was going well, and the crops were unusually bountiful. Since most of the congregation consisted of area farmers and the workmen and shopkeepers who provided the farming activity with support, everyone was in a good mood. As Lydia paused on the steps of the church before opening the front door, she looked up at the warm and sunny October sky. A few clouds hung overhead but not enough to keep the warmth of the sun from caressing her face.

She quickly opened the front door and swept into the entry of the solidly built brick church. The church building was fairly new. While it was plainly appointed, it was well constructed, right down to the heavy oak pews that dominated the worship area. For a small town of about five hundred souls it was an impressive church. The tall, imposing steeple seemed to demand attention while the large stained glass windows gave out a glow of color and serenity.

Lydia hurried to the back of the church where a small group of churchwomen had gathered awaiting her arrival. Lydia had helped prepare the church for funeral services before, but this funeral was for one of the most prominent members of the church. William Gunn had been a man who was well known and respected in the entire county. She was determined the funeral service would go smoothly and reflect well on her husband and to a lesser degree, herself.

By 2:15 everything was ready. The flowers were in place and the basement reception room was set up with coffee, punch, and cookies ready to be served. Lydia leaned against a nearby table and paused to go over the checklist she had in her mind. Satisfied she had missed nothing, she hurried upstairs. The service was to begin at 2:30 and she was to be part of a ladies' quartet who would sing at the service.

As she emerged into the worship area, she saw her husband standing by the altar and she gave him a nod to let him know everything was ready. Then she hurried to her designated seat in the choir loft where the other three ladies were already seated.

Benjamin Chambers was watching the people file into the church for the service. It was a large turnout, which was not surprising, considering the deceased was so well known. William Gunn had been not only a successful and prosperous farmer, but he had also been a man known for his kindness and generosity to his neighbors. Benjamin looked to his left, and seated in the front pew he saw the widow,

Anna Gunn, her son and two daughters and their spouses and children.

At 2:30 people were still filing into the church so Benjamin decided to delay the start of the service until everyone had arrived. A few minutes later, everyone was seated and the crowd grew respectfully silent.

Benjamin was about to give the organist the signal to begin the prelude music when the front door few open and three men entered the church. All three men were fairly tall and dressed in dark colored pants, white shirts with leather vests, and black dusters. All of them wore cowboy hats and cowboy boots complete with spurs that jangled as they walked. The men were all old, but they walked with backs ramrod straight, and they moved with a grace that belied their age. Benjamin let out an involuntary gasp as he saw all three men were armed with gun belts and holsters filled with Colt revolvers. The three men paused and each removed their cowboy hats.

The appearance of the three men had the same effect on the entire congregation as they sat unmoving in silent shock. The exception was Anna Gunn, the widow of the deceased. She rose from her seat in the front pew and ran to the three men, each of whom took their turn to receive a warm and enthusiastic hug from the widow. After a few whispered words were spoken, Anna led the three men to the front pew and her family made room for them to sit. When everyone was seated, Anna turned and looked directly at Benjamin and gave him a nod to begin the service. A stunned Benjamin recovered from his initial shock and began the service, which amazingly ran very smoothly after the surprise interruption.

After the service was concluded, the congregation gathered in the basement of the church for the reception and Anna held up her hands and asked for the crowd's attention.

"I would like to introduce some friends of the family, who have come all the way from Colorado to pay their respects to my husband. These three gentlemen rode with my husband in the Civil War. They served together in the 22nd Illinois Cavalry. This is Tom, Ted, and Tuck McMaster. They are brothers from Bent's Fort, Colorado."

Each member of the congregation came forward in a line and shook hands with the visitors. The three brothers were polite but had little to say and were sparse with their answers to people's questions.

After personally introducing the brothers to her family, Anna invited them to the farm for supper. The brothers tried to protest, telling Anna they only wanted to pay their respects and did not want to cause Anna any trouble. They further explained they had rooms at the hotel in Galesburg, but Anna would not hear of it and insisted they come to the farm.

After the internment of her husband in the Altona cemetery, Anna got on the horse-drawn buggy with her son and his family and led the buggies with the rest of the family, along with the three brothers on horseback, for the four-mile trip to the farm.

After dinner was over, the brothers, Anna and her children and their spouses retired to the large front parlor of the two-story Gothic white farmhouse.

"William never spoke much of what he did in the war," said Anna. "I knew about part of it, of course, but whenever I would ask a question, he would just smile and change the subject."

Tom McMaster looked at Anna's eyes, which were full of questions, and he made a decision.

"My brothers and I just brought a load of cattle to the stockyards in Chicago and since we were out East, we decided to stop in and pay old Billy a visit. We took the train to

Galesburg and found out about the funeral. We rented horses at the livery and rode to Altona. I thought we had plenty of time, but we were almost late, and I'm sorry about that," said Tom.

"Don't be sorry. I'm just glad you all are here."

"It's good to see you again, Anna. The years have been kind to you," said Tom.

"It's been a long time since you've seen me," laughed Anna. "If I'm not mistaken it's been about fifty years."

"Fifty years is a long time. You asked about the war. Maybe it's high time you knew what happened back then. I guess you and your children are entitled to hear about what took place. I tell you what, you have one of your children get me a mug of hot coffee, and I'll tell all of you a story about your father I'm pretty sure you've never heard." With that said, Tom paused to fill his pipe with tobacco and light it. Soon, the sweet smell of pipe tobacco filled the air in the parlor.

CHAPTER ONE

1864

William Gunn, private in Company I of the 102nd Illinois Infantry, could not believe his good luck. His company and two others had been selected to become mounted infantry on a temporary basis. The 102nd was in a winter camp near Lavergne, Tennessee, just east of Nashville. The company's job was to use mounted patrols to help guard the railroads from attacks by the rebels. Unlike many of the men in his company, Gunn was used to riding horses and caring for them. He did not look forward to the day they had to return to being regular infantry, but he knew it would happen sooner or later.

Gunn enjoyed riding horses and he enjoyed caring for them. Unlike many of his fellow infantrymen in I Company, he had plenty of experience with both draft horses and riding horses and he was comfortable working with them. He was also thrilled to exchange his muzzle loading long rifle for the new Spencer repeating carbine and the Colt 1860 Army revolver. He knew the rebels hated the seven shot Spencer and called it the rifle you could load on Sunday and shoot all week long. The added firepower of the Colt along with the ability to fire it while still in the saddle was another plus in his mind.

Two weeks later Gunn was busy cleaning the new Spencer repeating rifle he had been issued, when he was interrupted by the sudden appearance of Sergeant Nystrom. Nystrom was the same age as Gunn and from a small town near Gunn's home town of Altona, Illinois. Where Gunn was of medium height, Nystrom was a relatively tall fellow of stocky build, which could at least partially be due to his pre-war occupation as a blacksmith.

"I got a Sergeant Townsend lookin' for you Gunn. You in some trouble I don't know about?"

Gunn smiled at Anderson. "I ain't been in no trouble, Sergeant. How about you?"

Nystrom flushed at Gunn's challenge. Both men had enlisted together at Knoxville, Illinois. Nystrom had proved to be popular with the other newly enlisted soldiers and had been elected to the post of sergeant. Elections were the common way to select officers and some non-commissioned officers as well at the start of the war.

Gunn made Nystrom nervous. Gunn was quiet and kept to himself, but he had quickly proved to be one of the best soldiers in the company. During a recent mounted skirmish with the rebels attacking a train, Gunn had taken leadership of the company when the officers, including Captain Watson were nowhere to be found. He had led the men in a successful mounted attack to both surprise and then rout the rebel train raiders. Several men in the company said Gunn could ride like an Indian.

Nystrom was still a young farm boy. He was a little on the heavy side. He was strong, but a little clumsy like a young calf. He was still quite unsure of himself as a sergeant in the 102nd.

By contrast, Gunn was hard and lean. His hair and skin were dark and his eyes were black as night. He seldom smiled and always seemed to command a form of respect from those around him.

"Where is this mysterious Sergeant Townsend, Sergeant?"

Nystrom was relieved to get a question that he had an answer to. "Follow me private," said Nystrom.

With that, Sergeant Nystrom turned on his heel and began to walk swiftly away from Gunn. William quickly rose to his feet and followed after his sergeant. Gunn made no effort to catch up with him. Gunn was content to keep his own pace and follow a distance behind the sergeant.

After about a fifteen-minute walk both men arrived at the wood pole corral that housed I Company's horses. Nearby sheds held hay and grain used to feed the horses and also served as the tack room for all their saddles, bridles, horse blankets, and other gear.

Standing by the gate to the corral were several soldiers. One of them was Captain Watson, the company commander. Gunn recognized two of the men as lieutenants in the company, while a fourth man was a stranger. The stranger wore the uniform of the Union Cavalry. He had on a kepi like Gunn wore, but this one had crossed sabers on the front unlike the crossed rifles on Gunn's kepi. The man also wore the tight short cavalry jacket instead of the long woolen blouse Gunn wore. His pants were sky blue with a yellow strip on the outside of each leg. He also wore black riding boots with spurs and carried a Colt revolver in a holster on his belt.

As Gunn got closer, he could see the stranger wore sergeant stripes on his sleeves. He was a short man with a wiry build, and he sported a droopy moustache. His face was hard looking and he had the air of a man who took no nonsense from soldiers like Gunn.

Nystrom and Gunn stopped a respectful distance from the four men and came to attention and saluted.

"Sergeant Nystrom reporting, sir. I have collected Private Gunn as you requested, sir." With that statement, Nystrom executed an about face and quickly walked away. Dealing with officers always made the sergeant nervous. He never knew how they were going to react and dreaded getting another unpleasant assignment.

Captain Watson acknowledged Gunn's presence with a nod of his head, and then he turned to the cavalry sergeant. "This is the man you requested, Sergeant. Do with him as you will." With that the Captain and the lieutenants left Gunn alone with the sergeant.

The sergeant looked Gunn up and down and then spoke. "My name is Sergeant Townsend of the 22nd Illinois Cavalry. I am here to look over the men in the three companies of mounted infantry in the 102nd to see if there are any candidates for the regular cavalry. I asked your captain to show me the best riders in I Company, and he sent me you.

The sergeant looked Gunn up and down again and then he looked down at the ground and spat out a wad of phlegm. "Frankly everyone I have looked at in your company has been a piss poor example of a cavalryman. Most of them don't seem to know one end of a horse from the other. Riding a horse and not falling off seems to be a major accomplishment in your outfit. I have a question for you, Private Gunn. Can you ride?"

"Yes sir. I can ride."

"You don't call sergeants sir in the cavalry, son. That nonsense is for officers. You address me as sergeant. Do you understand that private?"

"Yes Sergeant."

"That's better. Now let's see you pick out a horse from this bunch of nags and show me you can actually saddle one."

"What then, sergeant?"

"How about we take one step at a time private. Most of your fellow soldiers had trouble getting a saddle on properly and never got to the riding part. Let's see if you can saddle a horse. Then I'll want to see if you can ride it. I'll give you instructions on what to do if you can manage to get in the saddle."

"Yes, Sergeant."

Gunn walked to the tack shed and collected his government- issue McClellan saddle, bridle, and saddle blanket. He also went to a bucket in the corner and took out an apple. He cut the apple in half and placed the halves in his pants pocket.

Returning to the corral Gunn placed the blanket and saddle over the top pole of the corral and held the bridle in his left hand. He then opened the corral gate and slipped inside, latching the gate behind him. He saw the horse he wanted, a black gelding, and slowly walked toward it. He talked softly to the horse as he walked and reached inside his pants pocket and removed one of the apple halves. As he approached the horse he extended his open hand to reveal the half apple. The gelding moved his ears straight up and began to move toward Gunn. As the horse took the piece of apple, Gunn slipped his right arm around the horse's neck and quickly slipped the bridle over the gelding's head and fastened it in place. Then he led the horse over to the pole fence where the saddle and blanket were. He placed the blanket on the horses back, being careful to lay it on smoothly. Gunn knew an uneven blanket would quickly produce saddle sores on the horse's back. Then he placed the saddle on the gelding, and placing his knee in the horse's side, he tightened the girth strap.

After checking the bridle and saddle, Gunn mounted the gelding in one easy motion and gently nudged the horse in the ribs with the heels of his boots. The gelding moved forward and Gunn rode him over to where the sergeant was standing.

"What now, Sergeant?"

Sergeant Townsend was taken by surprise and snapped out, "Walk him around the corral perimeter."

Gunn rode the gelding around the edge of the corral fence at a walk. He moved easily with the motion of the horse.

"At a trot," yelled Sergeant Townsend.

Gunn urged the gelding to a trot with his boot heels and again he moved in perfect concert with the movements of the horse.

"At a gallop," yelled Townsend.

Again Gunn urged the horse forward with his heels and again the horse responded. Riding at a full gallop Gunn's body was in perfect harmony with the now charging gelding.

As Gunn approached where the sergeant was standing, he saw the sergeant raise his right hand in the signal to halt. Gunn brought the speeding horse to a quick stop right in front of the sergeant.

"Dismount," ordered Townsend and Gunn quickly dismounted and moved next to the horse's head. Gunn came to attention while holding the horse's reins in his right hand.

"I think you'll do, Private Gunn. I'll have transfer orders in the hands of your regiment within a week. You're dismissed."

With that Townsend turned on his heel and walked off leaving a grinning Gunn to unsaddle his horse and stow away his gear.

CHAPTER TWO

Actually it was almost three weeks before orders transferring Gunn to the 22nd Illinois Cavalry were finally received at the 102nd Illinois regiment headquarters. As it turned out he was the only soldier from Company I chosen by Sergeant Townsend.

After signing the transfer papers and giving them back to Sergeant Nystrom, Gunn asked what he was supposed to do next.

"I ain't got no idea what the hell you're supposed to do, Gunn," said the sergeant. "Personally I think you're crazier than a loon to transfer to the cavalry. All I know is you're supposed to git yourself on over to Nashville to the supply depot and hitch a ride with one of the wagon trains heading down to Sherman's camp on the Chattahoochee River. The 22nd Illinois is supposed to be camped near someplace called Sandtown Ferry."

Nystrom extended his right hand and Gunn reached forward and shook his hand. "Good luck, Gunn. You're gonna need it."

"Thanks Sergeant. See you when we both get back to Knox County."

"God willing," replied the sergeant.

Gunn walked through his former company's camp, carrying his orders and gear in his saddlebags which he had slung over his shoulder. His Colt was in the holster on his belt along with his ammunition pouch and he carried his precious Spencer carbine in his right hand. He nodded to the soldiers he had known for almost two years as he passed them and finally he reached the main road on the edge of the 102nd's encampment. As he walked west on the road in the direction of Nashville, he wondered just how far it was to the Nashville supply depot.

After about an hour of walking an army freight wagon pulled by four mules pulled up next to him and came to a stop.

"You need a ride, soldier boy?"

The driver was a short, but wiry old man with a full grey beard and a jaw full of chewing tobacco. He was dressed like a farmer with a slightly battered straw hat.

"Much obliged," said Gunn as he pulled himself up next to the driver. Gunn placed his saddlebags and his rifle under the crude wooden seat, and the driver cracked his whip and the mules moved forward propelling the wagon and its two occupants towards the supply depot in Nashville.

"You headed to the supply depot?" asked the driver.

"Yes sir," replied Gunn.

"You don't sir me, young fella. I ain't in the army. I just work for them. I'm a civilian and damn glad of it."

Gunn extended his right hand which the old man shook. "My name is William Gunn."

"Ned Necaise, formerly of Mt. Pleasant, Iowa, and I'm hoping to get back there soon. Damn tired of this here war. Why you heading to Nashville? Getting out of the army?"

"Not exactly. I been transferred from the 102nd Illinois Infantry to the 22nd Illinois Cavalry, and I need to get to their camp down by Atlanta."

"I hear there's lots of fightin' goin' on by Atlanta. I want no part of that. I'm happy to haul supplies to outposts like Lavergne and Franklin. I just dropped off a load and am heading back to the depot for the next job."

Gunn looked behind him and saw that the wagon was indeed empty of any cargo.

"How long till we get to the supply depot?" asked Gunn?

"We'll git there in about three hours, maybe less. How you gettin' to Atlanta from the depot?"

"I hope to hitch a ride on a supply wagon like this one."

"Well, sonny, this is your lucky day. I got friends running freight wagons down to Sherman's men outside of Atlanta, and I'll direct you to them once we git to the depot."

"I'd really appreciate that Mr. Neicase."

"No one calls me Mr. Necaise, sonny. Call me Nate."

"All right. Nate it is."

Nate was true to his word. Once they reached the supply depot, Gunn helped Nate unharness the mules and led them to the livestock corral where they fed and watered them. Once they were finished, Nate led Gunn to the small tent encampment where the civilian teamsters, who worked for the army, were staying.

"There won't be any wagons headed south to Atlanta yet today. It's too late in the day. You can bunk in one of the empty tents, and I'll get you lined up with a wagon in the morning. I'll stop back for you in an hour and show you the way to the mess tent for dinner. If you got a plate and cup, be sure to bring 'em."

After showing Gunn to an empty tent, Nate left to head over to his bunk tent.

Gunn found himself in a Baker tent with high sidewalls and a wooden floor of rough cut planks. "This beats the hell out of sleeping on the ground," thought Gunn to himself.

There was a pile of straw filled pallets at the back of the tent. Gunn picked the best pallet of the lot and moved it to a spot by the front of the tent. He then pulled his blanket off his saddlebags and laid it on the pallet along with his saddlebags and carbine.

About an hour later, Nate showed up and led Gunn to the mess tent. A canvas fly extended from the large tent and under the fly was a series of long tables that held containers of hot food and coffee. Soldiers in once white aprons worked as servers to a long line of men, some in uniform and some dressed like Nate. The men in the line held out their metal plates and cups and moved down the line as they were served their rations. When Gunn reached the end of the line, he had a plate full of potatoes, beans, and some kind of ham along with a chunk of hardtack. His last stop was to get his cup filled with hot coffee. It was one of the best meals he'd seen in over a year.

Gunn joined Nate and some other teamsters sitting down on a series of sawed up logs. As Gunn ate his dinner, Nate introduced him to the other teamsters.

"This here is Nine-Fingers Frank. He's headed to Atlanta in the morning and he'll give you a ride."

"They call me Nine-Fingers Frank 'cause I lost a finger to a damn nasty mule. The son-of-a-bitch bit my finger off," said a short heavy-set older man with mutton-chop sideburns and a droopy mustache. He held out his right hand which was minus one finger, and Gunn shook it.

"Nate said you need to get to Sandtown Ferry. I'll be driving down toward it on my way to Sherman's supply depot. Glad to have you come along, especially if you're carrying a Spencer and a Colt. Have you seen any action?"

Gunn nodded affirmatively to Frank. He never liked to discuss what he had seen and done so far in the war. Frank's question brought back the image of the horseback fight with the rebels during their raid on the railroad. It had been at night and it had been hard to see who was who or what was what. The flashes from the muzzles of firearms had created small flashes of light that created short lived cones of daylight.

He had suddenly found himself riding up behind a group of Confederate horsemen. As he rode past them, he emptied his Colt. He saw three of the rebels fall from their saddles before his horse carried him past them. That action had unnerved the rest of the rebels, and they broke off their attack and fled into the darkness.

When the fight was over and he returned to the scene of his personal attack, he could clearly see that he had killed all three of the rebel soldiers. They lay on the ground, their blood soaked bodies twisted in unnatural disarray. He did not enjoy the sight then or remembering it now.

Their meal finished, the men cleaned their plates, cups, and utensils and put them away. Gunn headed back to his tent and was immediately fast asleep.

Chapter Three

"Rise and shine, soldier boy. It's time to skedaddle."

Gunn rolled off the pallet to see the outline of Nine-Fingered Frank outlined in the doorway of the tent. Gunn was quickly up and pulled on his boots and grabbed his kepi. He buckled on his gun belt and grabbed his saddlebags, blanket, and his Spencer.

Five minutes later he was up on a wagon seat with Frank and they were headed out of the supply depot and the wagon turned south on a main road.

"Sorry you missed breakfast, but maybe this will help," said Frank. He handed Gunn a hunk of cooked ham in a not so clean piece of cloth. "You got your cup handy?"

Gunn pulled his cup out of his saddlebags and held it out as Frank produced a large metal flask from under his seat. He unscrewed the top and poured hot black coffee into Gunn's cup.

"Thanks," said Gunn.

"You're welcome. I'm just happy to have an armed guard with me. Where we're goin' these rebels can be real pesky."

They rode slowly as the heavily loaded wagon slipped and lurched on the crude, rutted roadway. After almost two hours, the sun was coming up and Gunn found himself enjoying the warmth of the sun's rays.

"Sun feels good, don't it," said Frank. "Enjoy it now cause in a few hours it will feel like it's cookin' you. It gets damn hot down here. I just can't get used to it."

"Where are you from?" asked Gunn.

"I hail from Minnesota, and the sooner I get back there I'll never complain about the cold again."

Gunn laughed out loud.

"Where are you from, soldier boy?"

"I'm originally from Scotland and now from Illinois."

"I never been there. I heard they have pretty good farm land. Is that true?"

"Knox County is where I'm from, and they have great soil for crops."

"I guess they grow lots of stuff here, but I ain't fond of their soil. They seem to have lots of this damn red clay that sticks to everything and practically sucks your boots off."

"I've walked through plenty of it, and you're right about the damn clay. We learned to hate it."

Gunn finished his hunk of ham and then finished off his coffee. He used the dirty cloth to wipe out his cup and then tossed the cloth under the wagon seat and slipped his cup back into his saddlebags.

Frank had been dead on in his prediction of the heat as the day progressed. The higher the sun rose in the sky the hotter it got. Gunn took off his kepi and used his sleeve to wipe the sweat off of his forehead.

"Heat getting' to you, sonny," said Frank with a grin.

"I thought I was used to the heat since I've been in Tennessee, but this is more than I thought it would be."

"It's close to midday here and the sun is straight overhead. In about three hours the sun will drop enough that the trees will shield it from us. Tall thin pine trees lined both sides of the road and the trees grew so thickly that

13

they were all one could see from the seat on the freight wagon.

A half hour later they came to a wooden bridge over a small stream. After crossing the bridge, Frank pulled the wagon over to the side of the road.

"It's time for a water break, sonny," said Frank as he tied the reins to the mules off against the hand break.

"Come on down and make yerself useful, soldier boy," said Frank as he used the front wheel of the freight wagon to help himself down off the wooden seat and to the ground.

Gunn dismounted from the wagon. Frank promptly handed him a collapsible canvas bucket. "Fill this up and start watering the mules," said Frank.

Gunn gingerly slipped down the slope from the road to the stream and filled the bucket with cold, clear water. He carefully made his way up the slope, being careful not to spill the bucket and walked to the front of the mule team. He placed the bucket under the muzzle of the front left mule and let him drink his fill. When he was finished, Gunn went to the trailing mule and the animal drank the bucket dry.

As Gunn turned to refill the bucket he could see that Frank was checking the hooves of the mules and making sure the harnesses were all tight. Gunn smiled to himself. Old Frank knew his business, despite all his bluster. Gunn refilled the bucket and watered the other two mules. By the time he was finished, Frank was up in the driver's seat. Gunn handed him the bucket and was surprised to see Frank hand him two canteens.

"Fill these up and make sure to get good, clear water. I don't like walking in this state's damn mud and I'll be damned if I have to drink it."

Gunn laughed as he took the canteens and then carefully filled them from a clear pool by the edge of the stream. He returned the canteens to Frank and swung himself up to the wagon seat. He was no sooner in his seat when Frank cracked his whip and wagon lurched forward. They were back on the road.

Each man took a canteen and took a long swig of the cool water before placing them back under the wagon seat.

"How much longer before we get to the Sandtown Ferry?" asked Gunn?

"Me and my wagon ain't goin' to the Sandtown Ferry," said Frank.

"What the hell do you mean?" said a suddenly angry Gunn.

"Didn't Nate explain this to you?" asked Frank.

"Explain what?" said an exasperated Gunn.

"I'm taking you to the next depot. When we git there you spend the night and then hitch a ride with another wagon till you get to the next depot. Then you take a train ride down to a depot just north of the Chattahoochee River, courtesy of the former Georgia and Southern Rail Road. I'm pretty sure they won't charge you for the trip. Than you make your way to Sandtown Ferry which I think is about six miles from the train depot. You got all that?"

"Yeah, I got it," said a still surprised Gunn.

"Sonny, it would take me and this here team more than a week to get to Atlanta and you're gonna do it in three days. Yer almost flyin' to Atlanta," laughed Frank.

Gunn just shook his head.

CHAPTER FOUR

As Frank had predicted, the sun slipped behind the tall pine trees to their right and the temperature began to cool. It was still hot, but by comparison it was almost pleasant.

After they rounded a fairly sharp curve in the road they came to a small clearing. Set back against the back of the clearing was a small shack with a small dilapidated building behind it.

"We stop here, soldier boy. Keep your carbine ready in case we ain't welcome."

Gunn pulled out his Spencer and after checking to see that a round was in the chamber, he cocked it and eased himself down off the wagon to the side opposite of the shack. Frank was already on the ground and walking slowly toward the shack.

"Hello the house. We is friendly and looking to buy some lunch," yelled Frank.

Gunn positioned himself behind the front of the wagon and aimed the Spencer in the direction of the shack.

The old door to the shack slowly creaked open and a large black woman peeked outside at the approaching Frank. Frank held both arms out at his sides as he slowly approached the shack.

The woman stepped outside and stood in front of the door with her arms crossed defiantly in front of her. Gunn could see she held nothing in her hands. When Frank finally reached a spot a few yards in front of the woman, he came to a stop. The two began talking, but did so softly enough that Gunn could not hear what was being said.

Finally, the woman turned and went back into the shack and Frank turned and walked back to the wagon.

"Lunch will be served shortly, soldier boy. You can put your rifle down."

"What do you mean lunch will be served?"

"This place is the home of Miss June. I bin here before. She'll make us a lunch. It'll be better than you might think. She's one hell of a cook."

"You been here before?"

"I told you I bin here before. I bin here many times. Miss June worries about thieves, but she knows I pay for my food so she is happy to make us a lunch. Relax, soldier boy."

With that Frank led Gunn behind the shack where an old, crude wooden table sat under the shade of a large pine tree.

"Grab a stump, soldier boy," said Frank, pointing to several large chunks of tree trunk that had been cut and stacked for future firewood. Both men picked up a sizeable stump and placed it in on either side of the table. In about fifteen minutes the black woman reappeared and she had food on a large wooden tray.

Frank had been telling the truth. They had a lunch of ham-hocks, collard greens, beans, and hot coffee. Frank had supplied Miss June with the coffee beans from a sack he kept under the wagon seat. Miss June pounded the coffee beans with a small hammer she produced and swept the results into an old tin cup. She poured the contents of the cup into an old battered tin coffee pot and filled it with water. She took the pot and disappeared into the shack. She was back in ten minutes with a pot of fresh, hot coffee.

When they had finished their lunch they thanked Miss June and Frank gave her a couple of Yankee greenbacks. They climbed up on the freight wagon and were quickly on their way.

"Have you been stopping at Miss June's place often," asked Gunn?

"I bin stoppin' at her place for the past two months. Before that there was some other old gal staying there and I bought lunch from her. A couple times I stopped and no one was there. The place was abandoned."

"If you knew Miss June was there, why were you so cautious when we arrived?"

"In this country you don't know nothin' for sure, soldier boy. I'm too damn old to be taking foolish chances. Plus, one time I got a little surprise when I stopped."

"What happened?"

"Couple of rebel deserters tried to bushwhack me. They had the old black woman tied up and they tried to jump me. They had one small problem."

"What was that?"

"They was armed with was knives."

"What happened?"

"Never bring a knife to a gun fight, soldier boy."

Frank flicked his whip to urge the mules to a faster pace. "I want to get to the depot before it gets too dark. Bad things can happen when it gets dark in this here country."

Gunn nodded and recognizing that was all he was going to get out of the old teamster, he let the subject drop. As he turned to look behind them, he saw an object stuck between two supply sacks directly behind Frank's seat. He quickly recognized the object as a double barreled shotgun. Gunn smiled to himself. His questions had been answered.

They stopped twice more at small streams and he watered the mules while Frank checked the harnesses and the freight wagon's load of supplies. It was late in the afternoon when they were suddenly challenged by a Union sentry. Frank brought the wagon to a halt.

"You with the Colt. Keep your hands up where I can see 'em," said the sentry.

Gunn was pretty sure there was more than one sentry, and sure enough two more soldiers emerged from the trees behind the wagon. All three sentries were armed with rifles.

The first sentry checked Frank's dog-eared paperwork, while the one of the other two checked the freight wagon's load. The third sentry stayed on alert with his rifle at the ready. Gunn was impressed. The sentries were good, and they had obviously done this many times before.

"All right, driver. Move on into the depot," said the first sentry.

Frank took back his paperwork and stuffed it in his pants pocket. Then he picked up the reins and snapped them, so the mules began to move forward.

They traveled about a quarter of a mile, and as they turned through a sharp curve, a large clearing opened up in front of them. Part of the clearing was a natural meadow, but much of it was land recently cleared of timber. Off to one side of the clearing were large piles of timber. Inside the clearing were several crude log buildings, the wood showing signs of being freshly cut. There were large wall tents and also large canvas shelters made with locally cut poles and large sections of canvas stretched tight with ropes and stakes and held up by the poles. Under these homemade shelters were piles and piles of supplies and material on top of rough plank flooring.

Gunn estimated the depot was guarded by at least two companies of infantry. There was also one battery of artillery almost hidden in the edge of the trees that surrounded the depot on three sides. The open end of the depot was contained with a log pole fence. In the middle was a gate with a guardhouse.

To a Confederate scout, the precautions that had been made by the Union soldiers meant an attack on the depot might be very costly. That was obviously the intention of the Union officer in command of the supply depot.

Frank drove his team through the gate and was stopped by two soldiers. After checking Frank's paperwork and the load on his freight wagon, they directed him to a canvased roofed area with rough wooden plank floors. After Frank pulled his wagon up next to a wooden dock, a team of six men appeared and began unloading the wagon. As each item was unloaded, an officer with a checklist noted items unloaded from the wagon as each man on the unloading team passed him. In fifteen minutes the freight wagon was completely empty. Then Frank was directed to another canvased loading dock where empty barrels stood waiting.

Frank drove his mule team up next to the correct dock and after tying off the reins, he jumped down from the wagon. Gunn quickly followed.

"Them boys is goin' to load them empty barrels on the wagon for the return trip," explained Frank. "As soon as the wagon is loaded, we'll take it over to the wagon lot and unhitch the mules. We take the mules over to the corral and the boys there will feed and water them. Once we got that done, we'll head over to the mess tent and git us some supper."

Gunn nodded his head in understanding.

As soon as they had unharnessed the mules and led them into a huge pole corral, Frank led the way to a large canvased roof area with a long wall tent on one side. "This here is the mess tent, soldier boy. We should eat pretty good as the cooks here buy a lot of food from the farmers in the area."

"You mean rebel farmers?"

"Yup. Rebels need the money. Their money is almost worthless. Yankee dollars will buy them a lot more."

Gunn carried his saddle bags and his Spencer and followed Frank into the mess tent area. This time there were rough sawn plank tables with benches made of the same material. Considering most of his previous experience in the Union army, Gunn found this place pretty luxurious.

They left their gear at one of the tables and both of them pulled out their tin plates and cups and headed to the cook line. Dinner was a thick beef stew with potatoes and carrots and a large chunk of hard tack. Each man also had his cup filled with hot coffee. Gunn and Frank attacked their food and were soon finished and sipping their hot coffee.

Frank put down his cup and looked over at Gunn. "I'll find out who you can hitch a ride with to the train depot and let you know. You go find us an empty tent to bunk in for the night. Gunn nodded his agreement and Frank stuck his plate and cup in his knapsack and disappeared in the crowd of soldiers and teamsters who had filled up the mess tent. Gunn walked off in the direction of a line of tents that looked to house the teamsters and civilian workers. After finding an empty tent he set out two of the better straw filled pallets and placed his gear on one. Then he found himself a comfortable place on the ground in front of his tent and sat down to watch all the activity in the supply depot.

He hadn't been sitting there more than twenty minutes when Frank appeared with a young teamster with flaming red hair. "This here is Red Gamble. He'll be givin' you a ride to the train depot in the morning. We'll meet him at breakfast at five tomorrow morning and you'll be on your way, soldier boy."

Gunn shook hands with young Red and thanked him for offering to give him a lift to the train depot. Red promptly left, and both Gunn and Frank flopped down on their pallets and were soon sound asleep.

CHAPTER FIVE

"Up and at 'em, soldier boy. It's time for chow."

Gunn was quickly up and packed. He and Frank stepped out of the tent and into the still dark cool of the morning. They hurried down the line of tents and soon could see the lights of the mess area.

As soon as they stepped into the pool of light cast on the ground by the flickering kerosene lanterns hung on the mess area's poles, they were surrounded with hungry men in both uniforms and civilian dress. They stashed their gear near one of the poles. After grabbing their plates and cups, they quickly made their way to the end of the serving line. Once again Gunn was surprised by both the quality and the quantity of food being served. He had biscuits and gravy, bacon, and scrambled eggs along with a cup full of hot, steaming coffee.

Gunn had followed Frank in line, and Frank made his way to a table in one of the corners of the mess area. Gunn and Frank sat down and joined Red and four other teamsters. The men shook hands and quickly introductions were made.

"These boys here are Jed, Thomas, Isiah, and Shorty," said Red. "They're teamsters like me, and all of them will be in our train this morning'."

"How many wagons will there be in the train today," asked Gunn?

"I ain't rightly sure cause they kinda decide without askin' me," said Red with a big smile.

"Who is they," asked Gunn?

"Army officers," answered Red. "They may not be too smart, but they is officers."

The other teamsters roared with laughter.

"We usually have about twenty wagons in a train," said Shorty. "Red's just havin' fun with you."

"We also have a small escort on these trips to the train depot," said Red. "The rebs get kinda nasty from time to time and try to ambush our train."

"Have you lost any wagons in these raids," asked Gunn?

"We've lost a couple, but they was burned up by the rebs. They'd killed the mules so there weren't no way to move the wagons. That was real smart of them."

"What kind of escort does the army provide?"

"Our escort is usually one soldier on each wagon and maybe four on horseback. It ain't always the same," replied Red.

Having finished his breakfast, Red rose and said, "Let's roll, boys, we got freight to move."

Gunn quickly cleaned off his plate and stuffed it and his cup into his saddlebags. He grabbed his saddlebags and the Spencer and followed Red through the camp. Although it was still dark, there was enough light to see Red's brightly colored red hair. It was like following a lantern.

In a few minutes they had reached Red's wagon. Gunn stood to one side as Red skillfully checked his four mule team and made sure all the harnesses were in proper alignment. When he was satisfied with the mules, Red climbed into the freight wagon and checked the supply load and its rigging. Finally, he climbed down from the wagon's bed and began to check the wheels, pulling on each one to make sure there was no excess give.

Red pointed up to the wagon seat, and he and Gunn climbed up and made themselves comfortable. Gunn placed his saddlebags under the seat and took the Spencer in both his hands. He pulled out the spring-loaded magazine and made sure it was loaded and then he replaced the magazine and slid the Spencer butt first under the seat.

The other wagons in the train were still getting ready when several armed soldiers appeared out of the darkness and began climbing on board the other freight wagons. Finally, four soldiers on horseback appeared. Gunn noted they were mounted infantry, not regular cavalry. A sergeant was one of the four mounted soldiers. The horsemen moved to the front of the line of wagons and in a few minutes Gunn heard a distinct shout cut through the darkness. "Wagons Ho!"

One by one the wagons fell into a long column with about twenty feet of space between the lead mules and the back of each wagon.

Red clucked to his mules and flicked his reins and generally ignored his passenger. The wagon train lurched forward and after a while it began to assume a steady pace and the wagons moved southeast in a rough, but steady rhythm.

They rode in silence with nothing but the sound of the mules' feet striking the ground, the creaking of the harness and the wagon, plus the occasional crack of a teamster's whip.

After an hour the sun was making an appearance and the sky became much lighter. The road was rutted dirt. It was narrow, with its boundaries set by the thick growth of tall pine trees on either side.

Red reached inside his ragged jacket and pulled out a small pouch with a draw-string and then a small paper box. While still holding the reins, he expertly pulled a thin paper out of the box and held it in his left hand. Then he used his teeth to open the bag and used his rein hand to pour a small amount of tobacco on the paper. He used his teeth to tighten the bag and slipped it back into his jacket. He licked one edge of the paper and expertly rolled it up into a cigarette. Red produced a match from inside his jacket and struck it on the side of the wagon seat. After lighting the cigarette, he tossed the dead match down on the road and looked over at Gunn.

"Sorry, I forgot to ask if you wanted one."

"No thanks, I don't smoke," said Gunn.

"I didn't either till I got this job, and now I can't seem to get along without a little tobacky," replied Red.

Gunn just smiled and stared ahead at the line of wagons in front of them. The wagons stopped after about four hours when they came to a stream. One by one, the wagons stopped and the mules were watered with the same collapsible buckets Gunn had seen before.

Once again the sun made its presence known. From the cool of the morning, the teamsters and their escorts suffered from the ever increasing heat as the sun rose higher in the sky. Shortly after noon the road turned into a clearing and the wagons stopped to rest the mules and teamsters dismounted their wagons to check on the mules and the wagons. The soldiers got down off the wagons and sought shade from any nearby trees and even the wagons themselves. Gunn noticed that only a few of the soldiers bothered to take their rifles with them. He dismounted the wagon with his Spencer in hand and began to carefully scan the pine woods surrounding the clearing.

Gunn could see nothing. He sniffed the air, but all he could smell was the sweat from the mules and the smell of wet leather harness. Then he realized what was wrong. He could hear nothing, no birds, no insects, nothing. To Gunn that meant something or someone was hidden in the woods and was moving toward the wagon train.

From where Gunn stood he could not see anything. He walked out from the side of the wagon to get a better angle, but all he could see was the mule team on the point wagon.

Red had finished his inspection of the mules and he looked at Gunn and saw the concern on his face.

"What's wrong," asked Red?

"I think we got unwelcome visitors. Rebs! Get under the wagon, Red."

Red took a quick look around. "I don't see nothin' but trees."

Before Gunn could reply, shots rang out and suddenly armed horsemen dressed in grey seemed to spring from the edge of the woods into the clearing. Pistol shots rang out, punctuating the blood-chilling sound of the rebel yells from at least two dozen throats.

Gunn dropped to one knee and brought the Spencer up to bear. He flipped the sights up and through them he could see four rebels charging toward his section of the wagon train. They were about sixty yards away. When the four horsemen were forty yards distant, Gunn fired and one of the rebels flew out of the saddle with his hands in the air. Gunn fired three more times in rapid succession, pulling down on the rifle's lever to eject a spent shell and insert a live one and then cocking the gun before firing again. Quickly there were four horses without riders still running toward him. Gunn stood up and grabbed the reins of the horse that was nearest to him.

Gunn pulled the horse to a stop, turned him around, and mounted him. He urged the horse forward toward the front of the wagon train. Two more rebels were shooting at one of the wagons directly in front of him. He reined the horse to a stop and slipped off the saddle to the ground and held the reins under his right foot. Gunn brought the Spencer up to his shoulder and flipped up the sight. He fired twice and again watched two riders drop from their saddles. Two of the rebels located toward the front of the train had seen their fellow raiders fall and they were riding hard to find out what had happened. Gunn paused and then shot one of the rebels from a range of thirty yards. He realized the Spencer was now empty of ammunition, so he dropped the rifle and pulled out his Colt and shot the second rebel who fell from his saddle at a range of fifteen yards. Gunn returned the Colt to his holster, then reached down and grabbed the Spencer.

Gunn mounted the horse and quickly tied the now empty rifle to a leather strap on the side of the rebel saddle. He again urged the horse forward. As he reached the front of the train, three of the rebels had captured the front two wagons and shot the teamsters and the two soldier escorts. The rebels had dismounted and were climbing up on the front freight wagon.

Gunn pulled out his Colt Army revolver and brought his horse to a stop directly being the three rebels. At a range of ten yards, he shot all three in rapid succession. Then he turned his horse toward far end of the clearing where he could see a fight between the mounted Union soldiers and five more rebels. Two of the Union soldiers were wounded and were lying on the ground. The other two were fighting for their lives. Only one of the mounted rebels appeared to be wounded. The rebels were intent on finishing off the Union soldiers and had their horses standing still while they attempted to aim and shoot.

Gunn rode up behind them and before they were aware of his presence, he had shot two of them in the back. As they tumbled from their saddles, the other three rebels looked on in shock and then quickly turned their horses to make their escape from the suddenly deadly clearing. Soon they were urging their horses on to greater speed with their quirts. A

Union soldier with sergeant stripes fired his Colt revolver and one more rebel fell from the saddle.

Gunn brought his horse to a halt and dismounted. The sergeant he had seen was one of the two unwounded soldiers.

"I don't know who the hell you are, soldier, but you got here just in the nick of time. You saved our bacon today," said the sergeant as he extended his hand to Gunn.

'I'm Private William Gunn headed to join up with the 22nd Illinois cavalry at Sandtown Ferry. I was riding with one of the wagons in this train when the rebs attacked it," said Gunn as he took the sergeant's hand.

"Well, thank God for that," said the sergeant. "I'm Sergeant Ben Van Dyke. I'm in charge of the escort for this supply train, or what's left of it."

"I don't think they got any wagons, Sergeant, but I think we may have lost some people," replied Gunn.

"I've got two badly wounded men here," said Van Dyke. "Let's go see what the rest of the damage is."

Van Dyke and Gunn rode back to the wagon train, while the remaining soldier stayed with his two wounded comrades.

After a thorough head count Van Dyke and Gunn determined two of the teamsters and two of the soldiers had been killed. Three more teamsters and four soldiers had been wounded, including the two mounted soldiers who had been in the front with Van Dyke. That totaled four killed and seven wounded.

Van Dyke quickly got things reorganized and room was made on the wagons for the dead and the wounded. The wounded were treated with what little they had in medical supplies and made as comfortable as possible. Soldiers from the escorts were converted into teamsters. Two of the lesser wounded teamsters refused to ride in the wagons and insisted in continuing in their role as teamsters. Van Dyke did not argue with them. He wanted to get out of the killing ground as fast as he could.

Luckily, none of the mules had been killed or wounded. After getting the wagon train reorganized, Van Dyke rode up to Gunn, who remained mounted on the now confiscated rebel horse.

"I'd like you to ride up front with me, Private Gunn," said Van Dyke.

Gunn nodded his assent and the two men rode to the front of the column. In short order Van Dyke had the train back on the move, heading to its train depot destination.

Van Dyke looked over at Gunn as they led the column down the narrow dirt roadway. "You said you were headed to join up with the 22nd Illinois Cavalry, but you're wearing an infantry uniform?"

"I was in the 102nd Illinois Infantry up at Lavergne, Tennessee, and got transferred to the 22nd," replied Gunn.

"Well, I don't care if you're cavalry or infantry, Gunn, but I could sure use someone like you in my outfit. By my count you killed three men, grabbed one of their horses and then killed six more. That's pretty deadly shootin' in my book."

"Sorry, Sergeant. I've been ordered to join up with the 22nd and that's where I'm headed. I'm from Illinois, and like the idea of fighting alongside men like me."

"Well, I'm sorry to hear that, but I'll keep the offer open just in case you change your mind, Private."

"Thank you, Sergeant."

CHAPTER SIX

Just before dark they reached the train depot. The depot had been built by the army in a clearing they had made much larger by cutting down vast amounts of timber. They had used the timber to build fairly substantial log buildings, and they were supplemented by numerous large tents. The area was enclosed by dirt and log walls, and the depot was full of activity. There were lots and lots of soldiers everywhere Gunn looked. As they rode into the depot, he saw at least three batteries of artillery that provided more firepower to the depot's defense.

The wagons carrying the dead and wounded split off from the rest of the wagon train and headed toward a large tent that served as the hospital for the train depot. Gunn and Van Dyke accompanied those wagons and helped to carefully unload the wounded and carry them into the hospital tent.

When they were done, Van Dyke grabbed Gunn by the elbow and said, "Follow me."

"Where are we headed," asked Gunn?

"We're goin' someplace to get a stiff drink," replied the smiling sergeant.

Gunn willingly followed the sergeant, who seemed to know his way through the maze of tents.

They stopped at a wash tent, and Gunn found himself in front of a tin basin of water. As he began to wash his hands, Gunn became aware that his hands, his arms and much of his uniform were covered with dried blood. The water in the basin soon turned to a pale pink.

After the two men had done their best to clean up, Van Dyke led Gunn to a large and formidable looking log building near the center of the depot. The front door of the building was open, in deference to the heat, but two armed soldiers stood guard on either side of it.

Van Dyke led the way up to the two guards, who stepped forward to challenge him. Van Dyke stated his business and one of the guards went inside. He returned shortly and told Van Dyke he was cleared to enter. As Gunn started to follow Van Dyke through the door, the soldier placed himself with his rifle at port arms in front of Gunn, blocking his way.

"You can enter, soldier, but without that Spencer. No rifles are allowed in the headquarters building."

Gunn looked the young soldier in the eye. "Where I go, my Spencer goes," he said.

The young soldier wilted under Gunn's hard gaze and a second look at Gunn's blood spattered uniform eroded his resolve.

"Very well. You can pass, soldier."

"Thank you very kindly," said Gunn in a sarcastic tone.

He followed Van Dyke into the building and after reaching a desk manned by a soldier with sergeant's stripes, they came to a halt.

"You and the private may enter," said the sergeant. "The colonel is expecting you."

The sergeant opened a large wooden door and ushered Gunn and Van Dyke into a sizeable room that was well lit by several large windows facing the south side of the building and freely let in the welcome rays of sunlight.

A surprisingly young man in a colonel's uniform sat behind a large rough wooden plank desk. The desk was flanked by a large American flag standing proudly from a brass floor base.

The young colonel, who was clean shaven and wearing an immaculate uniform, looked up from his work and motioned the two soldiers to approach.

Both soldiers came to attention. Sergeant Van Dyke spoke. "Sergeant Van Dyke and Private Gunn reporting, sir."

"At ease men," said the colonel.

Both soldiers complied and came to parade rest.

"I understand the supply train ran into some trouble. Do you have a report, Sergeant?"

"Yes, sir. We were attacked by about two dozen mounted rebels about fifteen miles south of here," replied Van Dyke.

"What happened, Sergeant?"

"They hit us while we were in a rest area in a clearing. They must have been following us and waited until we had our guard down and then they attacked, sir."

"What were our losses?"

"We had two KIA and four WIA, sir. We also had two teamsters killed and three of them wounded."

"Did we lose any wagons or supplies?"

"We did not lose any wagons or supplies, sir."

The colonel turned his gaze to Gunn. "What role did you have in this action, private?"

Gunn hesitated. He was unaccustomed to being addressed by anyone as high ranking as a colonel and wanted to carefully choose his words. "I was a passenger on one of the wagons, sir. I was hitching a ride to this depot so I could catch a train ride to my new outfit, sir."

"What outfit is that, Private?"

"The 22nd Illinois Cavalry, sir."

"But you're dressed in an infantrymen's uniform, pPrivate?"

"Yes, sir. I was with the 102 Illinois Infantry regiment and just got transferred to the 22nd Illinois Cavalry."

"I see," said the young colonel, although the look on his face indicated that clearly didn't.

"Sergeant, "said the colonel; "I will expect a report on this action on my desk by first thing tomorrow morning."

"Yes, sir."

"You are dismissed."

"Yes, sir."

Both soldiers came to attention and saluted, holding their salutes until the young colonel raised his hand in a dismissive salute.

Van Dyke and Gunn quickly exited the colonel's office and headed out the front door of the building.

Van Dyke led the way to the Sutler's cabin and soon the two soldiers were enjoying an overpriced, but welcome cool beer in the shade of the Sutler's roofed back porch.

"That colonel seem awful darn young to you," asked Gunn?

"This here war has made all kinds of folks end up in all kinds of jobs they don't seem suited to," replied Van Dyke.

"You did real well in there, Gunn. I make it a point to say as little as possible to officers. I've seen a lot less trouble that way."

Gunn nodded his head in agreement.

"He seemed more concerned about the supplies and wagons than he did about the dead and wounded men."

"That didn't surprise me one bit," replied Van Dyke.

As they finished their beers, Gunn looked around him with curiosity.

"What ya' lookin' for, Gunn?"

"I'm trying to figure out where I need to go to hitch a ride on the next train that will take me down to the 22nd," replied Gunn.

"See the white building across the way there? The one over by the railroad tracks?"

Gunn looked where Van Dyke was pointing with his finger and saw a small clapboard building with faded and peeling white paint that seemed to standout amid all the larger unpainted wood frame buildings surrounding it.

"Why is it painted white and nothing else here is painted," asked Gunn?

"It was a train station long before the army got here and built a supply depot. Them boys over there will get you on the next train."

Van Dyke and Gunn got to their feet and shook hands. "Good luck, Private. Yer gonna need it where yer headed. Say howdy to them Johnny Rebs for me."

Gunn smiled. "I'll be sure to do that, Sergeant. Good luck to you as well."

Gunn shouldered his saddlebags and his Spencer and walked over to the train station.

A short chat with the station agent determined that there would be a southbound train arriving in three hours. The train would stop for about an hour to refuel and have supplies loaded for the trip south. Gunn thanked the agent and went looking for the mess hall. He followed his nose with the smell of food cooking and after a hot meal accompanied with several cups of coffee, Gunn returned to the station.

He found a space on the track side of the building and made himself and his gear comfortable. Gunn had learned to never waste the opportunity to take a nap since he had joined the army.

Gunn was awakened from his slumber by a distant train whistle. The sun had gone down and it was dark except for the light escaping from the train station window directly above him.

Minutes later the small steam engine pulled into the supply depot towing ten boxcars and several flatcars behind it. Steam escaped from the engine's boiler as it idled on the tracks by a long wooden warehouse and under an elevated wooden water tank.

Gunn watched as the train crew lowered a spout on the water tank and added water to the engine's boiler. Other crew men loaded wood to the existing supply on the tender located behind the engine. Large hand wagons were pulled up to the train by Negroes directed by white foremen. The wagons were pulled up next to the waiting train and supplies were loaded from the wagons to several of the boxcars and flatbed cars.

The station agent came outside and seeing Gunn, he motioned for Gunn to come to him. Gunn rose and grabbed his gear and the Spencer and joined the agent alongside the tracks.

"Follow me, soldier," said the agent.

Gunn followed the agent to the caboose at the rear of the train. As he walked along the train he began to see that there were armed guards on the flatbed cars and in the boxcars that he had not seen before because of the darkness.

The caboose was illuminated by light coming out through the windows of the train car. The agent led Gun to the landing at the rear of the caboose and motioned for him to stay put. The agent climbed up on the landing and went through a door into the caboose. He soon returned with a soldier with sergeant stripes on his sleeves. The agent motioned for Gunn to join them on the landing. As soon as he was up even with the two men, the agent introduced Gunn to Sergeant Sutton and then he stepped off the platform and walked back to the station.

Sergeant Sutton and Gunn shook hands and the sergeant led him into the caboose.

"Find a spot for you and your gear and get as comfortable as you can. We got a ten-hour trip ahead of us and we'll make a couple of stops for water and fuel."

"Thanks, Sergeant. I appreciate the ride."

"Glad to have another gun on the train, especially a man with a Spencer. We have had some trouble with rebel attacks, but usually it's just some militia taking pot shots at us as we go by them," replied Sergeant Sutton.

Gunn found an empty corner of the caboose and pulled a half empty grain sack over to provide him with a softer back rest. Ten hours on a train might be a long trip, but it beat riding a freight wagon on a rutted road.

Ten minutes later, Gunn was fast asleep.

CHAPTER SEVEN

Gunn was rudely awakened when the train engineer applied the brakes and the braking effect rippled through the train cars including the caboose. The effect of the sudden braking had tossed Gunn onto his side where he lay sprawled out on the floor of the caboose.

"Grab your weapons, men and exit the caboose," yelled Sergeant Sutton.

Gunn scrambled to his feet and grabbed his Spencer. He quickly followed the sergeant out the door at the rear of the caboose.

Gunn dropped off the platform and went into a crouch. It was dark and all he could hear was the steam escaping from the train engine. He waited for his night vision to return and carefully sniffed the night air. It smelled of the steam and smoke from the train and little else.

He rose to his feet and moved carefully toward the front of the train. While he moved, Gunn was careful to keep his Spencer in both hands. As his night vision returned, Gunn was soon moving past other soldiers who were stumbling about in the dark of the night. When Gunn arrived at the front of the train he could see a small knot of figures standing there. Among them were the engineer and the fireman from the train engine.

Gunn stopped when he was next to the group, and he looked ahead to see what was being discussed. He could see long dark shapes across the tracks in front of the train. Gunn moved closer to the shadows until he realized they were trees having been cut down to block the train tracks.

Gunn returned to the edge of the small group of men who were discussing their current predicament. He could hear Sergeant Sutton arguing with the engineer. He decided to step back and lean against the train engine until the people in charge decided what to do.

Finally, the group broke up and Gunn caught up with Sergeant Sutton who was walking back toward the train.

"What's the plan, sergeant," asked Gunn?

"We got some tools including some axes back in the caboose. I'll get a detail to cut up those trees and get them off the tracks."

"Do you have a block and tackle among those tools," asked Gunn?

"I'm pretty sure we do. Why do you ask?"

"If we've got enough rope, we could put the block and tackle on a large tree to the right of the train. Then run the rope from one of the trees across the tracks through the block and tackle and back to the train," said Gunn.

"I see what you mean. Then we back up the train and pull the tree off the tracks," said Sergeant Sutton.

"Seems to me it would be a lot faster and a lot easier," said Gunn.

"You got that right, soldier. Thanks for the idea."

Within minutes the block and tackle and some long rope were brought forward from the caboose. Gunn grabbed the block and tackle and quickly attached it to a sizeable tree that was sufficiently distant from the tracks. Sutton had a long rope secured around the first downed tree and run the rope through the block and tackle and then secured it to the cowcatcher on the front of the train's engine. Twenty minutes later the downed trees had been removed, and the train had resumed its journey.

Gunn returned to his half empty grain sack in the corner of the caboose and promptly fell back asleep.

When Gunn awoke, the pale light of dawn was seeping through the windows of the caboose. He sat up and rubbed his eyes as he recognized his surroundings. There was a small potbellied wood stove in the back of the caboose and Sergeant Sutton was standing by it, his body swaying slightly with the movement of the caboose over the train tracks. Gunn slowly got to his feet.

"Good morning, sunshine. How're you feelin'," said Sergeant Sutton.

"I feel like I been rode hard and put away wet," replied Gunn.

"This here will fix you right up," said the sergeant as he handed Gunn a tin cup full of hot coffee.

Gunn gratefully took the cup of coffee and began to sip the hot beverage. He was careful to match his attempts to drink it with the swaying of the caboose floor beneath his feet.

"This tastes great. Thanks Sergeant."

"It's the least I can do for someone smart enough to figure out how to git them trees off the tracks in a hurry," said Sutton.

"It's just an old farm trick," said Gunn.

"Farm trick or not, it was just what we needed. The longer we stayed stopped last night the more likely we were to get jumped by some rebs. I was surprised they didn't stick around and try to pick us off when we were stopped," said Sutton.

"They can't see any better in the dark than we can," said Gunn. "I ain't never seen an attack at night by them or us while I been in the army."

"I guess that's probably right. Come to think of it I can't remember a night attack either."

"How long until we get to Sherman's lines," asked Gunn?

"With the delay and all I ain't sure how long, but it'll be at least four to five more hours. We got a stop for water coming up pretty soon."

Sutton had no longer finished speaking than the two men felt the train begin to slow down. Soon they felt the brakes being applied to bring the train to a stop.

Gunn stepped out the back door of the caboose with his Spencer in his arms. The train was stopped in a large clearing and there was a small shack, a wooden water tower, and several rows of army tents stretched out from the tracks toward the edge of the clearing.

Gunn hopped off the caboose platform and walked toward the shack. It felt good to stretch his legs after sleeping on the hard wooden floor of the caboose. Walking past the shack, his nose caught the small of bacon frying. Gunn turned and followed his nose to one of the larger tents where breakfast was being served to the troops who were guarding the station area. He grabbed some bacon and hardtack, and he made a rude sandwich which he quickly devoured. Gunn made a second pass through the mess tent and emerged with a second sandwich.

He walked back to the caboose with the second sandwich and retrieved the tin cup Sutton had handed him. He filled the cup with hot coffee from the coffee pot on the stove and sat on the caboose platform, enjoying his breakfast in the cool morning air.

Shortly after he finished his coffee, the train whistle blew and Gunn pulled himself up and re-entered the caboose as the train began to resume its journey south.

Gunn found space on a rough wooden bench attached to the side wall of the caboose and made the space as comfortable as possible. He stretched his feet out and tried to grab some sleep.

He was sound asleep when he awoke to the sound of glass breaking and he felt fragments of the caboose window fall on his chest. He lurched to his feet just as he heard the sound of gun shots coming from outside the caboose. He grabbed his Spencer and moved to the side of the window on the opposite side of the caboose where the glass had been broken out.

Carefully Gunn eased closer to the edge of the window and peered outside. The train was going up a steep grade and had eased to a slow speed. The grade was a sizable hill populated with a few sparse pine trees. Gunn could see several men clad in grey and butternut, kneeling behind trees, rocks, and bushes firing at the train. He could see no horsemen.

Gunn pulled back on the lever of his Spencer to chamber a round, and then he cocked the hammer. He pulled up the folding sight and brought the rife up and rested the barrel on the frame of the window. When he could see grey filling his sight, he pulled the trigger and the rifle fired. Gunn felt the recoil in his shoulder.

Gunn pulled the lever down again and ejected the spent round and chambered another. Then he cocked the rife and searched for another target from the slow moving train.

Again he found grey in his sight and he pulled the trigger. Gunn pulled the lever down and repeated the sequence and again found grey in his sight. Gunn shot again and this time he saw the figure in grey fall backward, as Gunn absorbed the recoil.

Suddenly bullets were flying through the window of the caboose as the rebels become aware of the threat that Gunn had posed with his accurate and rapid fire.

Gunn ducked down and waited for a few seconds. Then he carefully rose up and stood next to the side of the window.

He carefully peered out from the top of the window and again slipped the barrel of the Spencer out through the now thoroughly broken window. He could see in his sight a grey clad figure trying to reload a muzzle loading rifle. Gunn carefully squeezed the trigger, and the figure fell over.

As Gunn was loading another round in the Spencer's chamber, the shooting from the rebels stopped just as suddenly as it had started. The train had reached the top of the hill and was now picking up speed.

Gunn slid down to the floor and sat there, breathing heavily. As soon as he realized that the danger had passed, he pulled out the magazine from the butt of rifle's stock and replaced the rounds he had fired with new bullets from the bullet pouch on his belt. When he had finished he replaced the spring loaded magazine back inside the stock and turned it so it was properly locked in place. While he had been reloading the Spencer, he could now hear the gun fire of Union soldiers on the train firing back at their rebel attackers. As he listened he could hear the firing start to slacken until he could only hear an occasional shot.

He looked back into the caboose and he could see that one of the soldiers who had been sharing space in the caboose was wounded. Sergeant Sutton was trying to stop the bleeding from a wound in the man's shoulder.

"Can I help," asked Gunn?

"I think I got this taken care of. See if you can get him some water," said Sutton.

Gunn found the water barrel with a spigot and filled a nearby tin cup he found hanging on a wooden peg. He brought the cup of water to Sutton who helped the wounded soldier drink from it. Gunn got to his feet and grabbed a tin pot and filled it with water from the barrel. When the pot was almost full, he placed it on the top of the hot pot-bellied wood stove.

"Sergeant, when that water boils, take it off the stove and use it to clean his wound," said Gunn to Sutton. Sutton nodded his understanding as he held the now bloodied cloth tight against the soldier's wound to try to stop the bleeding.

As Gunn was returning to the now glassless window, he felt the train slowing until it finally came to a lurching stop. He quickly slipped out the back door of the caboose and crept to the edge of the rear platform.

He could see nothing at first, but as his gaze moved to the area behind the caboose, Gunn could see several grey clad bodies lying on the ground downhill from where he stood.

Gunn slipped down onto the ground and moved slowly in a half crouch toward the bodies with his Spencer at the ready.

A quick inspection of the fallen rebels found two of them dead and one wounded. The wounded rebel was very young. He looked to be a teenager with his dirty blonde hair and beardless smooth chin. The boy was crying and moaning with good reason. He had been gut shot. Gunn had seen it before. In his experience no man had survived being gut shot. It was an awful way to die. He collected the three men's weapons and ran back to the train. When he reached the caboose, the wounded Union soldier had been joined by another who had been wounded in the attack. His head had been creased by a rebel bullet and while the impact had knocked the soldier unconscious. His wound was no worse than a hard blow to the side of the head. The skin was broken and bleeding, but the wound was not life threatening.

Three more Union soldiers had crowded around the rear of the caboose's platform and were talking excitedly among themselves. Looking through the open door of the caboose, Gunn could see Sergeant Sutton had his hands full, but he now had the assistance of a corpsman. The corpsman had been part of the train's company in one of the boxcars.

Gunn grabbed one of the three soldiers by the arm to get his attention. "Are there any other wounded on the train," he asked?

The befuddled soldier shook his head from side to side and looked at Gunn with panic-stricken eyes.

A disgusted Gunn let go of the man's arm and proceeded to move from car to car as he made his way to the front of the train. At each car he checked with any soldiers he found to inquire about any wounded and by the time he had reached the engine he had found no more wounded Union soldiers. He found a Sergeant Snyder in the boxcar located right behind the tender and reported to him what he had seen.

"So you found two dead rebs and one wounded," asked the sergeant?

"Yes, Sergeant. I also saw that we had two wounded; one fairly badly, and one not so much."

"We were lucky no one got killed, Private. It could have been worse. They do this all the time. They hit us from hiding, and then they run away. Damn their hides!"

Gunn excused himself and left the sergeant and moved quickly back to the caboose. By now the soldier grazed in the head had a bandage on his head and was sitting up on the bench in the caboose. Sergeant Sutton had succeeded in stopping the bleeding of the soldier wounded in the shoulder and corpsman had gotten the wound cleaned with the hot water and bandaged the wound with fresh bandages.

Sergeant Sutton turned to look at Gunn. Sutton's hands and the sleeves of his uniform were spotted with blood. He was a gruesome sight. His eyes looked weary, like the eyes of a much older man.

"What happened out there, Private Gunn?"

"The rebels lost two killed and one wounded. These two appear to be our only casualties, Sergeant."

"Where's the wounded reb?"

"He was gut shot. I left him where he was. There's nothing we can for him. I collected their weapons and left them over there in the corner," said Gunn as he pointed to far corner near the bench.

Sutton nodded his approval. He walked over to the bench and sank down on it like a man who had lost his ability to stand.

"Do you have any orders for me, Sergeant?"

"Git up to that engineer and tell him to git this train moving and get us the hell out of here," said Sutton.

"Yes, Sergeant." Gunn hurried out the door. Soon he had returned and the train was moving forward once again.

CHAPTER EIGHT

Gunn woke up with a start, his hands quickly reaching for his Spencer. Then he realized the train had lurched to a stop and caused him to fall over onto his side on the hard wooden floor of the caboose. He heard no shooting or shouting and he quickly got to his feet in the now motionless caboose. Gunn moved to the rear platform and looked around him.

The train had stopped at a watering and refueling station that was guarded by a company of Union troops.

His nose told him there was some bacon frying and coffee brewing and he jumped down from the caboose platform and swiftly walked toward one of the canvas roofed open areas using his nose as his guide.

He joined a line of hungry men and quickly made a couple of bacon sandwiches with two chunks of hard tack he cut in two with his knife. He "borrowed" a spare tin cup and got it filled with hot coffee and made his way back to the caboose. Once seated in the caboose, he wolfed down the two sandwiches and drained the coffee like a man who was dying of thirst.

The wounded men had been unloaded while he was absent and he found himself alone in the caboose. He was quickly joined by Sergeant Sutton who had a plate full of bacon, hard tack and scrambled eggs in one hand and a tin cup filled with hot coffee in the other.

"Good morning, Private Gunn. Glad to see you're still among the living," said a smiling Sergeant Sutton.

"Good morning to you, Sergeant. Where in the hell did you find scrambled eggs?"

"Sergeants have a special way about them, Private. We know everything and that includes where they're serving scrambled eggs. I got a surprise for you, Private."

Sutton reached in his coat pocket and pulled out two sizable hunks of smoked ham.

"I saved one for you as a reward for your hard work today," laughed the Sergeant. "Enjoy it cause it's likely the only reward you're likely to get from this man's army."

Gunn gratefully accepted the ham. This time he ate slowly, savoring every bite. His hunger satisfied he wiped his hands on his pants and walked over to the now glassless window.

"You must be fallin' down on your job, Sergeant. This here window seems to be broken."

Both men roared with laughter. The tension of the previous encounter with the rebel gunman was now dissipated.

"Any more stops before we get to where I get off," asked Gunn?

"Not unless we run into another mess of rebels," replied the Sergeant.

"How much longer to my stop?"

"I'd say maybe less than two hours depending on our speed," replied Sutton.

"What's the name of the place I'm supposed to get off," asked Gunn?

"Your stop will be a place called Vining's Station. From there you'll need to ask directions to the place where your outfit is located. If I were you I'd try to hitch a ride, or else you might have yourself a nice walk in the woods."

Gunn returned to his seat on the wooden bench. "Don't let me sleep through my stop, Sergeant."

"I won't have to, Private. The train stopping there will probably toss you out on the floor," said Sutton with a grin.

Gunn actually awoke just before the train pulled into Vining's Station. He looked out the broken window as the small wooden frame station came into view. The building was small, dilapidated, and badly in need of paint. Even the sign on the front of the building denoting it as "Vining's Station" was faded and almost unreadable.

The train came to a halt and Gunn rose to his feet. He grabbed his saddle bags and his Spencer and headed for the caboose door. He stopped by the now standing Sergeant Sutton who had his hand extended. Gunn shook his hand and stepped back.

"You're a hell of a soldier, Private Gunn. Feel free to ride on my train anytime," said a smiling Sergeant Sutton.

Gunn touched the brim of his kepi in salute to the sergeant and quickly exited the caboose where he had seen so much action in so little time. It is often said that a soldier's life is one of days of boredom punctuated by moments of pure terror. Such had been the case on this journey for Private Gunn.

Gunn made his way into the small station building which was crowded with soldiers and others awaiting a chance to get on the train and return to the north. Many of the soldiers Gunn saw had been wounded and were probably returning north for treatment or rest.

Gunn saw one of the men with captain's bars on his uniform. He made his way through the crowd and brought himself in front of the captain.

"Captain, sir," said Gunn, who stood at attention and saluted.

The officer looked up at the private standing before him. He could not help but notice that the man had blood spatters on his uniform and that he smelled of gun smoke. The Captain returned Gunn's salute.

"What can I do for you, Private?"

"Sir, I've just arrived here after being transferred to the 22nd Illinois Cavalry and would beg the Captain's indulgence to inform me where I might find the regiments location," asked Gunn?

The Captain paused for a moment and then looked up at Gunn. "I believe the 22nd Illinois is encamped near Defoors Ferry on the Chattahoochee River. That would be about six miles south of here. Just follow the road next to the railroad tracks south and you should run into their encampment, Private."

Gunn saluted the captain and said, "Thank you, sir." The captain returned the salute and Gunn turned and made his way out of the station.

Once he had made his way outdoors, Gunn made his way over to the side of an empty loading dock. There he carefully disassembled his Colt and Spencer and using an oily rag from his saddle bags, he carefully cleaned both weapons and reassembled them. Then he reloaded both weapons. Satisfied with his gear, he made his way to a wash area and used a basin of water to wash his hands and face. He dried them with a nearby hanging piece of cloth.

Gunn wanted to make sure he was prepared to defend himself during his trip to Defoors Ferry. He preferred to arrive at his new regiment looking more like a soldier and less like a refugee.

Chapter Nine

As Gunn reached the edge of the depot grounds, he noticed a second encampment. This one was rough and ragged and very primitive. He quickly realized that it was a camp of suddenly freed slaves. The former slaves had now become camp followers for the Union army and they were making themselves available for any kind of work that would lead to being provided with food. He could see the camp was quite large and probably contained about five hundred Negroes of all types and ages.

As he neared the Negro encampment, silence seemed to descend on the camp like a large blanket falling. As Gunn walked by, he could see men, women, and children who had stopped what they were doing to stare at this passing white soldier in a blue uniform as though they had never seen one. Gunn knew that was silly. Of course they had seen white Union soldiers, but maybe they were seeing him through the eyes of a free people for the first time. He could smell the smoke of their cooking fires and the distinct odor of meat frying over an open fire. Gunn looked over at the silent children, and he smiled and waved at them. They instantly broke into big, bright smiles and waved back at him.

Gunn grinned to himself and kept on walking.

He stopped after about an hour and drank from his canteen. The water was warm, but welcome in the humid heat pouring down on him from the relentless sun overhead. Occasionally a freight wagon pulled by mule teams thundered past in a hurry to get somewhere, but none of them slowed to offer him a ride.

His nose detected the water first. He could smell the river, although he could not yet see it. Another twenty minutes of walking, and he could now hear the river over the background humming noise of countless small flying insects.

Another fifteen minutes of walking passed, and he came upon a solitary sentry dressed in Union blue. The sentry guarded the entrance to a medium sized camp of Union infantry. Gunn stopped to chat with the sentry, who welcomed a break from what appeared to be a hot and boring duty.

"What outfit is this?" asked Gunn.

"This here is the 78th Ohio," replied the infantryman guard.

"You wouldn't happen to know where the 22nd Illinois Cavalry is camped, would you?" asked Gunn.

"If I recollect correctly, the 22nd Illinois is about a mile down the road and on your right," replied the sentry.

"Thank you kindly," said Gunn, and he continued on down the road.

In about twenty minutes he reached the outskirts of the camp of the 22nd Illinois Cavalry. He was stopped by two sentries, who gave him directions to Sergeant Townsend's tent.

Gunn thanked the sentries and after carefully following their directions, he found himself in front of a somewhat weathered Sibley tent.

Gunn was not sure exactly what he was supposed to do so he came to attention in front of the tent and announced himself.

"I'm looking for Sergeant Townsend," said Gunn with as much authority as he could muster in his voice.

"Who the hell wants Sergeant Townsend in the middle of his afternoon nap?" came the snarling reply from inside the tent.

"Private Gunn from the 102nd Illinois Infantry reporting as ordered, Sergeant," replied a nervous Gunn.

"Great jumpin' gophers," said the voice within the tent. Sergeant Townsend burst from the tent like a cannonball and stood almost nose to nose with Gunn.

Townsend looked Gunn up and down before he spoke again. "You sure took your damn time gettin' here, Private Gunn. What the hell took you so long?"

"I ran into a little trouble with some rebs on the way down here, Sergeant."

"I don't like excuses, Private Gunn, but one of the few good excuses in my book is fightin' rebs, so I'll let this one slide."

Sergeant Townsend stepped back to take a better look at Gunn. "Is that blood on your uniform, Private?"

"Yes, Sergeant."

"Ours or theirs, Private?"

"A little of both, Sergeant."

"Well, it's time to get you signed up and into a proper uniform. Did you bring your weapons?"

"Yes, Sergeant. I brought my Colt and my Spencer."

"Outstanding, Private. There may be hope for you yet. Follow me and we'll take you to the company clerk and then the quartermaster, and get you squared away into the 22nd Illinois."

Without another word Sergeant Townsend started walking quickly to his right and Gunn scrambled to catch up with him. Townsend took him to the company clerk and gave the clerk instructions. Then he turned to Gunn.

"When you are finished with all this foolishness, bring your gear and report to my tent."

"Yes, Sergeant."

The next couple of hours were kind of a blur to Gunn. He was officially enrolled into the 22nd Illinois Cavalry by the company clerk. At the quartermaster's tent he was issued an entire uniform including boots and spurs. The quartermaster clerk took note that Gunn had his own weapons, but he was also issued a cavalry saber and scabbard.

The quartermaster clerk directed Gunn to the wash tent, and he had his first bath in over a month, although it was cold water coming down on him from an elevated barrel with holes in the bottom of it. Nevertheless, Gunn felt better than he had in months. He dried himself off with rough towels that were provided and then donned his new uniform. He tossed his old ragged and bloodstained infantry uniform in a trash barrel. Gunn picked up the rest of his new gear along with his saddlebags, gun belt, and his Spencer, and made his way back to Sergeant Townsend's tent.

"Sergeant Townsend, Private Gunn reporting as ordered."

Sergeant Townsend emerged from his tent to find Gunn standing at attention with his equipment stacked in front of him.

Townsend glanced down at the pile of equipment and then looked back up at Gunn. "Did you obtain all of your required equipment, Private Gunn?"

"I believe so, Sergeant."

"If that be so, where is the gear for your mount?

"I failed to obtain it, Sergeant."

"Get your ass back to the quartermaster's tack room and get the rest of your gear, Private. When you have everything you are supposed to have, then you report back to me. Is that clear, Private?"

"Perfectly clear, Sergeant."

"Well then, what the hell are you doing still standing in front of me? Get your ass moving, Private."

Gunn saluted and executed an about face and began running back to the quartermaster's area of the camp.

Gunn quickly found the tack tents in the quartermaster's area and was issued the following items by a grizzled old soldier in a cavalryman's uniform:

1. A McClellan Saddle
2. A blue with orange border saddle blanket
3. A nose bag
4. A Curry comp
5. A horse brush
6. A picket pin and length of rope.
7. A halter
8. A thimble (used to attach to the saddle and hold the carbine.

Gunn refused the saddlebags, explaining that he already had saddlebags.

After he had placed all the horse tack in an acceptable pile, Gunn gathered them up and made his way back to the Sergeant's tent at the double quick.

"Sergeant Townsend. Private Gunn reporting as ordered."

Again Sergeant Townsend emerged from his tent to find Private Gunn at attention with the horse tack now stacked next to his other gear. Townsend took his time checking off the items on a mental checklist and finally looked up at Gunn who was standing at attention the entire time.

"At ease, Private. You appear to have acquired everything required to equip a cavalryman in the 22nd Illinois. Get all your gear together, and I'll have Corporal Patterson take you to your new assignment with I Troop.

Gunn remained at attention while Sergeant Townsend bellowed out with a voice that could be heard for a great distance, "Corporal Patterson, front and center."

Less than a minute passed and a tall, broad-shouldered man with the build of a blacksmith appeared out of nowhere. He wore a cavalryman's blue uniform with corporal stripes on his sleeves. His uniform was worn and faded, indicating he was no newcomer to the cavalry.

"Corporal Patterson, this is Private Gunn, newly assigned to the 22nd Illinois. Take him down to his new assignment with I Troop."

"I Troop, Sergeant?" asked Corporal Patterson with a strange look on his face.

"Do yah have mud in your ears, Corporal. I Troop is what I said, and I troop is what I meant."

"Yes, Sergeant Townsend, I troop it is," replied the corporal.

Patterson turned to face Gunn. "Grab your gear and follow me, Private."

Gunn reached down to gather his gear and when he stood up, Corporal Patterson was already headed down a line of tents. Gunn hurried to catch up with the rapidly walking corporal.

They walked at a fast pace. Gunn observed the rows upon rows of tents all aligned in orderly lines with small alleyways of beaten down grass in front of each row. All around him were soldiers cleaning weapons or repairing gear while others sat around small cooking fires and smoked pipes and cigarettes.

They walked about half a mile and Patterson brought them to a halt just before a new row of tents to their left.

"Stay here, Private. I'll find the troop sergeant and bring him back to take charge of you," said Corporal Patterson.

Patterson started to walk away and then he stopped and turned to face Gunn. "I got no idea who you are Private, but you should know this troop has a real nasty reputation. I hope you're tough, because you're gonna need to be to survive in I Troop." With that, Patterson turned and continued on his way until he turned to his left and disappeared from Gunn's view.

Gunn looked around him and saw several troopers in front of their tents cleaning their weapons. Patterson appeared to be right about one thing, thought Gunn. The men he could see looked hard-bitten and battle worn. None of their uniforms were new and most were in need of replacement or patching. On the other hand, he observed that they all seemed to take excellent care of their weapons. Every weapon he saw looked well cared for.

Gunn was getting tired of carrying all of his gear and was about to set the pile down on the ground while he waited when Corporal Patterson suddenly appeared walking out from behind a tent about thirty yards away. He was accompanied by a lean looking trooper with sergeant's stripes on his sleeves. The sergeant had flaming red hair and a full beard to match.

As the two non-commissioned officers reached Gunn, the private came to attention.

"At ease, Private Gunn. This here is Sergeant Mann. He's the troop sergeant of I Troop, and I'm turning you over to him."

With that Corporal Patterson turned to walk back the way he and Gunn had come. Once again he paused and turned to face Gunn. "Good luck, Private. You're gonna need it." Patterson turned for the final time and hurried away from an area he obviously was not comfortable with.

Gunn looked to his new sergeant and waited for him to speak.

"You new to the cavalry, Private?" asked Mann.

"Yes, Sergeant. I've served two years with the 102nd Illinois Infantry."

"What the hell are they doing sending me an infantryman?" asked Mann.

"I spent three months as mounted infantry in Tennessee and was recruited here by a Sergeant Townsend, Sergeant."

"Sergeant Townsend. He's a real hard ass, Private. You say Townsend recruited you to the 22nd Illinois?"

"Yes, Sergeant."

"If Townsend recruited you, then I'm pretty sure you proved to him that you can ride a horse better than most. Is that so, Private?"

"I can ride a horse pretty well, Sergeant."

"We'll see how well you can ride pretty soon, Private. How are you at getting along with assholes, Private?"

"Assholes, Sergeant?"

"Yes, Private, I said assholes. You're familiar with assholes, Private."

"Yes, Sergeant. I am familiar with assholes. I've known a few and try to avoid them if possible."

"I repeat, Private. Can you get along with assholes?"

"Yes, Sergeant. I can get along with assholes."

"Well that's a comfort, Private, because I'm assigning you to a group of four where the other three are brothers."

"Yes, Sergeant."

"These three brothers are the meanest assholes I have ever known. They hate everyone and sometimes they even hate each other. Nobody in I Troop likes them and the feeling is mutual."

"I don't understand, Sergeant."

"There's not much to understand, Private. The three brothers are assholes, but they are also the best fighters and horsemen in the 22nd Illinois. I need to warn you that they're very close knit and every other trooper I've tried to assign to their group of four has asked for a transfer because they wanted no part of him and drove out every trooper I assigned. I need someone to be the fourth trooper and in this case the horse holder and I'm assigning you to be that mam. Do you understand, Private Gunn?"

"Yes, Sergeant."

"All right, Gunn. Grab your gear and follow me over to their squad area."

"Yes, Sergeant."

Chapter Ten

Gunn followed Sergeant Mann as he led the way through rows of two man wall side tents. As they passed the tents, Gunn noticed most of the tents had wooden floors which placed the inhabitants and their possessions up out of the ever present mud.

Mann suddenly came to halt in front of an empty tent. The tent had a wooden floor and contained nothing but two empty cots.

"This here is your new home, Private Gunn. Get settled in, and I'll see if I can round up your squad mates," said Mann.

"Yes, Sergeant," responded Gunn.

Mann quickly walked away and Gunn began arranging his gear on one side of the tent. He was almost done when his labors were interrupted by a loud voice with an unfriendly tone to it.

"Who the hell are you and what the hell are you doing in this tent?" came to Gunn's ears loud and clear.

Gunn turned to face the speaker and found himself face to face with a tall, lean man with a bushy moustache and angry eyes. The man's skin was browned by the sun, and his face was one that had seen a lot of outdoor activity in all kinds of weather. The man would have been handsome, if it were not for the dark scowl on his face.

Gunn hesitated before he answered, and the man took it for fear.

"I asked you a question, trooper."

"My name is Gunn, and I've just been transferred to I Troop. I was assigned to this tent by Sergeant Mann."

"Sergeant Mann? Where the hell is he?"

"He told me he was looking for the rest of this squad to let them know I was here."

"Well, you done found one of the squad, bub."

Gunn stepped forward and looked the intruder straight in the eyes. "I told you who I am, trooper. How about you introduce yourself or get the hell out of my tent."

Gunn saw a moment of hesitation in the man's eyes. He had been surprised by Gunn's reaction.

The trooper stepped back a pace to put some space between him and Gunn. "I'm Tom McMaster, Private, I Troop of the 22nd Illinois Cavalry and this is my squad area. You stay put while I find out what's going on here from Sergeant Mann," said McMaster.

With that, McMaster turned and walked away. Gunn returned to his chore of storing his gear. When he was finished, he sat on his bunk and waited.

It wasn't long before McMaster returned with two other troopers who looked very similar to McMaster, right down to the scowl. They were accompanied by Sergeant Mann.

"Step out here, Private Gunn," said Mann.

Gunn stood and stepped out of the tent where he was facing the three McMaster brothers with Sergeant Mann between them as though he were a referee in a wrestling match.

"Private Gunn, these here are the McMaster brothers. This here is Tom, who you've already met. This one is Ted, and this one on the end is Tuck. I've assigned Gunn to your squad to be the fourth trooper. Gunn is new to the cavalry and to the 22nd. He'll be getting some training to bring him up to our standards. Before you three boys start getting any ideas, Gunn was recruited from the infantry by Sergeant Townsend, and he intends for Gunn to be the horse holder in your squad."

"Gunn's training starts tomorrow morning. You boys show him the ropes for your squad. You boys need to get along, and I'm here to make sure that you do. I know that you three have forced out every trooper assigned to your squad. That ain't gonna happen this time."

"Word is that something big is up and we're gonna be moving on Atlanta real soon. I need every man is this regiment ready to ride. Our enemy is the rebs, not each other. Besides, a squad without a horse holder is like a boar hog with tits. Worthless."

Sergeant Mann paused and looked each of the three brothers in the eye.

"You boys have any questions?"

There was silence from the three McMaster brothers and from Gunn. Sergeant Mann took that for no questions and he turned and walked swiftly away from the squad area, breathing a sigh of relief as he did so.

When the sergeant was gone, Tom McMaster spoke. "You ain't welcome, Gunn or whatever your name is. Me and my brothers don't want no man we can't trust riding with us. You won't last here, and you can make it easy on yourself by getting out now."

Gunn looked at all three brothers. They were all tall, lean and tough looking. Tom was the oldest and obviously the leader of the three. Gunn looked in their eyes and saw only dislike and distrust.

"I was assigned here, and as a soldier I'm here to do my duty for the army and my country. I don't give a shit what you boys like or think. I spent the last two years killing rebs, so any plan to scare me off ain't gonna work. I'm here to stay. You boys best get used to it."

With that Gunn turned and entered his tent and sat down on his cot. He pulled out his Colt and began to disassemble and clean it as though he was no longer aware that the three brothers were still standing just outside the tent.

Tom looked at Ted and Tuck and nodded at them and the three walked over to the neighboring two tents that they shared. When they reached Tom's tent, they went inside and sat on the two bunks.

"He's got some sand, I'll say that," said Tuck.

"I agree. But he has to show us he's tough enough to stand and fight and he has to prove to me that we can trust him when things might go against us," said Tom.

"I say we treat him just like we did the others and see what his true colors are," added Ted. The other two brothers looked up and nodded their agreement.

The next morning found Gunn up early and sitting on his bunk waiting for Sergeant Mann to appear. The three brothers had made breakfast over a cook fire in their squad area and had made no effort to encourage Gunn to join them. He had fished his tin cup out of his saddlebag and walked over to them and picked up the coffee pot and poured himself a cup of coffee. They had ignored him, and he had ignored them in return.

Sergeant Mann appeared outside Gunn's tent without any warning, but Gunn had heard him approaching and he was standing when Mann stuck his head inside the tent.

"Are you ready to become a cavalryman, Private Gunn?"

"Yes, Sergeant."

"Grab all your horse tack and follow me, Private."

Gunn had anticipated this and picked up his carefully arranged pile of gear from his bunk and followed the sergeant as he made his way through the small city of tents.

They soon arrived at a log corral and Gunn was directed to put his gear on the ground. Gunn took the saddle, saddle blanket, and bridle and hung them over the corral fence.

Inside the corral were half a dozen horses. Gunn could tell by the ears on the horses that they were wary of the men, and it told him that the horses were probably fairly green and not fully broken. He was pretty sure that was standard for breaking in new recruits. He was to be tested in more ways than one in providing how well he could ride a horse.

"Pick yourself out a mount, Private," said Sergeant Mann.

Gunn spotted a lariat looped around one of the corral's fence posts and he retrieved it and then opened the corral gate, slipping inside it and then closing it behind him.

Gunn picked out a good looking mare and slowly approached it. As he approached the mare, he began talking softly to it. He kept the lariat in his left hand and held his right arm by his side. As Gunn got within about six feet of the mare, she snorted and moved her ears back. Gunn stopped where he stood, but he continued to talk softly to the mare. Finally, the mare's ears returned to an upright position and Gunn began to slowly move closer, still talking softly as he did.

The mare was wearing a halter and when Gunn was within two feet of the horse he slowly raised his left hand with the lariat to get the mare's attention. At the same time, he slowly slipped his right arm up and secured the halter with his hand. He did not jerk the halter nor did he make any sudden moves. Still talking softly to the horse he took the halter in his left hand and slowly began to stroke the mare's neck with his right hand. All this time he continued to talk softly to the horse. The mare had twitched when he first took ahold of the halter but now Gunn could both see and feel the horse was relaxing.

Once Gunn was sure the horse was sufficiently comfortable with him, he began to slowly lead the horse around the corral using the halter. After he had made three circuits of the corral, he turned the mare around and made three more circuits of the corral going the opposite direction. Then Gunn led the horse over to the corral fence where he had left his gear.

Gunn grabbed the bridle from the fence, while holding on to the horse's halter. He then slipped the bridle over the horse's head. He placed the bit in the mare's mouth and secured the bridle. Then he used the reins to tie the mare to the corral fence. Then he took the saddle blanket and placed it on the mare's back. He followed that with flipping the saddle on top of the blanket. Then he placed his knee in the mare's side and tightened the girth strap, making sure the mare could not keep pumped full of air to make the saddle less than secure.

Gunn checked the bridle and the saddle and then untied the reins from the corral fence and placed his left foot in the mare's left stirrup and swung himself into the saddle. Then Gunn sat in the saddle and used his left hand to hold the reins, while he stroked the mare's neck with his right hand, still continuing to talk softly to the horse.

Gunn looked at his surroundings. In addition to Sergeant Mann, there were about twenty on-lookers, including the McMaster brothers. No doubt they had all gathered to see the greenhorn from the infantry get tossed off a green horse. He studied their faces. They looked both confused and surprised. This was not the entertainment they were expecting.

Gunn leaned forward in the saddle and whispered something in the mare's ear. The horse turned to look at his rider. Gunn smiled. He flicked the reins and lightly flicked the mare's sides with his boot heels and the mare moved forward smoothly into a walk. The walk was followed by a fast walk, then a trot, and then a gallop. Gunn followed that performance with a series of quick turns and stops and then had the horse back up. Satisfied with his mount, Gunn rode the mare over to where Sergeant Mann stood and brought the mare to a halt.

"What is it you would like me to do, Sergeant Mann?" asked a smiling Gunn.

Sergeant Mann had to suppress a grin before he could reply.

"I'll run you through the basic horseback drills, Private Gunn. When we're done with them, I'll have a bugler give you the bugle calls and have you and your horse respond to them. Is that clear?"

"I'm not familiar with the cavalry bugle calls, Sergeant."

"I'm sure you're not, but you will be by supper time," said a now smiling Sergeant Mann.

It was a tired and dusty Private Gunn who returned to his tent burdened with all his gear. Sergeant Mann had worked him hard and by the time the day was over, Gunn had mastered every drill Mann had put him through. Gunn was now more than familiar with all the cavalry bugle calls. The mare had performed well and when the drills were over, Gunn had fed and watered the horse and rubbed him down, then used his curry comb until the mare's coat shone.

The McMaster brothers were cooking supper over the squad cook fire, and they ignored Gunn when he appeared. Gunn placed his gear in his tent and then grabbed his cup and tin plate and without a word he stepped between the brothers and filled his plate and cup from the stew pan and coffee pot on the cook fire.

Gunn stepped back and returned to his tent without as much as a word to the brothers. They returned the favor.

The following morning was a repeat of the first day of training. This time it went much more quickly and Gunn smoothly performed all of the drills that Sergeant Mann ordered. This time there were few spectators at the corral. Gunn noted that the McMaster brothers were still present, as if waiting for him to fall on his face. If they were, they were disappointed. It became obvious to any observer, including Sergeant Mann, Gunn was an accomplished rider. Again he returned to his tent tired and sore, and again he was ignored by his three squad mates.

After two more days of riding drills, Sergeant Mann appeared at Gunn's tent early in the morning. Again Gunn was waiting for him.

As Gunn turned to pick up his horse tack, Sergeant Mann put up his hand.

"No horse tack today, Private. I think we've had enough horse drill. Today we find out if you can shoot as well as you can ride. Bring your Colt and your Spencer and sufficient ammunition and follow me."

Gunn buckled on his belt, holster, and ammunition box. He placed the Colt in the holster, grabbed his Spencer, and then followed the sergeant back through the city of tents.

After a few minutes, they came to the main road. Gunn followed the sergeant when they turned to the right on the road and walked for another fifteen minutes. They came to a break in the trees that bordered the road and Gunn could see a well- worn path through the trees on the right side of the road. The sergeant turned onto the path, and they walked until they came to a large clearing. At the far end of the clearing was a small hill. The base of the hill had been dug out. Now it served as a backstop for several wooden target butts that had been erected to hold paper targets.

The sergeant led Gunn to the butts where he produced a paper target printed with ever decreasing circles with a solid black circle in the very middle.

Sergeant Mann tacked the target to a wooden butt and then he turned and walked off about fifty paces and came to a stop. Gunn followed him.

"Let's see how much damage you can do at fifty yards, Private. Unsling that Spencer and start with two rounds from a standing positon, then two rounds from a kneeling positon and then three rounds from a prone positon. Is that clear, Private?"

"Yes, Sergeant. It's perfectly clear."

Gunn brought his Spencer rifle up with both hands. He extracted the magazine from the butt stock of the rifle and checked to make sure the magazine was full with seven rounds of ammunition. Satisfied, he replaced the magazine. He brought the rifle up to his shoulder, squared his body to the target and flipped up the sights. Satisfied with the rifle, Gunn pulled down on the lever and then up, placing a round in the rifle's chamber.

Gunn turned and looked at the Sergeant. Mann nodded and said, "Fire when ready, Private. Two rounds, please."

Gunn turned back to face the target and then cocked the Spencer. He acquired the paper target in his sight, then took a deep breath, let half of it slowly out and squeezed the trigger. The Spencer barked loudly and smoke slipped from the barrel. Gunn effortlessly pulled down the rifle's lever and re-cocked it before quickly firing a second time. Again the rifle barked and more smoke slipped from the rifle's barrel.

Gunn brought the gun to a port arms positon and waited.

Sergeant Mann had his binoculars up and was focusing in on the paper target fifty yards distant.

"I think you got a bulls-eye and a complete miss, Private," said Mann.

"I think you should have someone check the target, Sergeant Mann," replied Gunn.

Sergeant Mann turned to one of the privates who manned the shooting range. "Retrieve the target, Private and bring it to me," said the sergeant.

The private leaped to his feet and ran down to the target butts, pulled down the paper target and ran back to the Sergeant.

The private came to a stop in front of the Sergeant and silently handed him the paper target.

"I'll be damned," said Sergeant Mann.

The paper target he was holding had two bullet holes side by side in the bulls-eye section of the target.

"Private, place a new paper target on the target butt," said Mann.

The private raced down the range to the target butt and placed a new paper target on it and ran back to the Sergeant.

"All right, Private Gunn. Assume a kneeling positon and on my signal, fire two rounds at the target," said a slightly flustered sergeant.

Gunn went to one knee and loaded a fresh round into the Spencer. He brought the rifle to his shoulder and adjusted the sight. Satisfied with the rifle he turned to face the Sergeant.

"Fire two rounds when ready, Private."

Gunn turned back to the target and after sighting in on the paper target, he fired the Spencer, quickly reloaded and fired a second time. He then rose to his feet and held the Spencer at a port arms positon.

Mann didn't even bother with his binoculars. He motioned to the range private to secure the target. When Mann had the new target in his hands he saw the same result, with the bullet holes overlapping as they were even closer together than the first effort.

The rifle range private had secured a new paper target while he was retrieving the second one in anticipation of what would be next.

Sergeant Mann made no comment on what he saw in the second target.

He looked to Gunn and said, "Three rounds from the prone positon and you may fire when ready, Private."

Gunn reloaded and slipped down to a prone positon. He made himself as comfortable as he could and when he was satisfied with his sight position, he fired, reloaded, fired, reloaded, and fired a third time. He had fired and reloaded so fast it was if he had fired three times with barely a second between shots.

The echo of the report of his Spencer had barely faded away before the range private had raced down to the target butts and retrieved the paper target. He returned and handed the target to Sergeant Mann.

Mann was incredulous. The target had three overlapping holes in the bullseye. They were so close together that the three holes were like one hole with three different round edges.

Sergeant Mann turned to Gunn, who was now standing and holding his Spencer at port arms.

"That was good shooting, Private. How are you with the Colt?"

"I'm an all right shot with the Colt, Sergeant, but I need to be a lot closer."

Sergeant Mann could not help smiling at Gunn's answer. Most men could not shoot a Colt accurately at ten yards.

The sergeant directed the range private to place a new target on the target butts. Then he and Gunn walked closer to the butts until they were within fifteen yards of the paper target.

"Is this close enough, Private Gunn?" asked Sergeant Mann.

"This distance will be fine, Sergeant."

Sergeant Mann stepped to a positon that was behind and to the left of Gunn.

"Draw your weapon and shoot the paper target six times, Private. Fire when ready."

Gunn turned to face the paper target. He placed his feet squarely under his shoulders for balance and dropped his hands to his sides.

"When you want me to draw and shoot, just say now, Sergeant."

"Now!"

Gunn's right hand flashed to his side and he drew his Colt and brought it up to where his eyes were focused on the paper target. His left hand flashed up to pull back on the hammer while the trigger finger on his right hand squeezed the trigger back. Each time his left hand pulled and released the hammer the Colt fired and bucked in his right hand. The Colt fired six times in rapid succession and smoke poured from the end of the barrel.

As soon as he had fired the last round, Gunn had returned the Colt to his holster and had his hands up in the air signaling that he was finished shooting.

Mann stepped up to the paper target. Three of the rounds had gone through the bulls-eye. The other three were right on the edge of the bulls-eye.

Mann tore down the target and looked at it closely. He had never seen anyone shoot a Colt that fast and that accurately. He carefully folded the paper target and put it in his pocket.

He turned to face Gunn. "Do you always shoot this well, Private?"

"Most of the time, Sergeant," replied Gunn.

"I think we're done here, Private. Let's head back to camp," said Mann.

"Yes, Sergeant."

Chapter Eleven

Sergeant Mann was silent as they walked back to the 22nd Illinois' encampment. As they neared Gunn's squad area, Mann turned and looked directly at Gunn.

"Can you shoot on horseback?"

"Yes, Sergeant."

"Can you shoot as well on horseback as you did today?"

"Pretty close, Sergeant."

"Report to me at the corral first thing in the morning. It's time we found out if you have any skill with a cavalry saber, Private."

"Yes, Sergeant."

"You're dismissed, Private."

"Yes, Sergeant."

Sergeant Mann turned on his heel and quickly walked away. Gunn sat down on the wooden floor of his tent and began to clean his guns. He had finished the Spencer and was cleaning the Colt when a shadow fell across his hands.

He looked up and there was the somewhat nervous figure of Tuck McMaster, the youngest of the three brothers.

"Nice looking Colt you got there, Gunn," said Tuck.

Gunn stopped cleaning the Colt and looked up at Tuck. "Thanks," he replied.

"I need to talk to you about something, Private," said Tuck.

"Go ahead," answered Gunn.

"Our troop still doesn't have a mess tent, so each squad has to fix their own meals. In our squad, Tom goes to the quartermaster every day and draws our rations. Ted does the cookin' and since I'm the youngest I get stuck with cleanin' things up."

"I see," said Gunn.

"The thing is, now that you're in our squad, I think it's only fair that you help me clean up."

Gunn could see that making this little speech was hard for Tuck. He was obviously very nervous.

"Sounds only fair to me," said Gunn.

"It does?" said a surprised Tuck.

"What do you want me to do?"

"Well, I thought we could start out together so I could show you how we do it and then maybe we could switch off. You know, like you clean up one day, and then I clean up the next."

"That works for me, Tuck."

"That's great," said an obviously relieved Tuck. "When we're done with lunch today, I'll show you the ropes."

"See you at lunch," said Gunn.

Tuck turned to go and then stopped himself and turned around to face Gunn. "Gunn."

"Yes?"

"Thanks." With that Tuck had finished his dreaded mission, and he fled in the direction of his tent.

Gunn put his head down to try to hide his smile.

When lunch time arrived, Gunn appeared at the squad cook fire with his tin cup and plate. Ted was hunched over the fire. He was stirring a small pot suspended over the fire by a tripod made of green tree branches stripped of all leaves. The branches were lashed together and a short rope hung from the tripod with a metal hook tied at the end. The pot hung from the hook.

"We could use some more wood," said Tom to Tuck.

Tuck stood up and motioned for Gunn to follow him. Gunn followed Tuck out of the camp, and they walked into the nearby woods.

"Look for dry, dead wood, not too thin and not too thick," said Tuck.

Gunn smiled to himself and began gathering pieces of dry, dead wood until he had a sizeable armful. He walked up to Tuck, who had also accumulated a sizeable amount of firewood.

"That'll do," said Tuck as he looked approvingly at the bundle in Gunn's arms. Tuck headed back to the squad cook fire with Gunn in tow.

As they reached the cook fire, Tuck placed his pile of firewood on a spot next to the cook fire and Gunn followed suit.

The cook fire was surrounded with sizeable flat rocks. At each end of the cook fire the rocks were pushed closer together. Ted had a coffee pot placed on the rocks at one end and a black iron skillet filled with strips of bacon frying at the other end.

When the bacon was done, Ted removed the bacon with a fork and laid the bacon strips on a flat rock. There he used a knife to cut the bacon into chunks. He took the chunks and tossed them into the stew pot over the fire. Then he placed pieces of hardtack in the bacon grease in the frying pan and placed the pan back on the end of the cook fire.

Gunn understood what Ted was doing. Hard tack was the bread issued to the army and it was notoriously hard and difficult to break up, much less chew on. By placing the hard tack in the bacon grease, the bread was softened and partially soaked in the bacon grease making it not only edible, but fairly tasty.

"Time to eat," announced Ted and each of the four men filled their tin plates with stew and hard tack and filled their tin cups with coffee from the coffee pot.

The four men sat on the ground and ate their lunch in silence. When they were finished, Tom and Ted got up, leaving their cups and plates on the ground. The two brothers walked off without a word to Tuck or Gunn.

"Ready to clean up?" asked Tuck.

"I was born ready," replied Gunn.

Tuck grabbed two canvas buckets and handed one to Gunn. "Follow me," said Tuck.

Gunn followed Tuck down to the edge of the river where they filled both buckets. They returned to the cook fire and Tuck poured water in the now empty stew pot. He rinsed the stew pot out and then refilled it with water. Tuck replaced the stew pot over the cook fire. In a few minutes the water was boiling. Tuck emptied the remains of the contents of the coffee pot and then washed the coffee pot and the tin cups and plates along with some spoons and a knife. Tuck emptied the stew pot and he and Gunn used more water to rinse off the stew pot, coffee pot, the cups and plates, and the few utensils. The rinsed items were placed on nearby rocks to air dry.

Tuck grabbed the black iron skillet and an empty canvas bucket and Gunn followed him back to the river. On the banks of the river, Tuck carefully scrubbed the black iron skillet with sand from the river's edge. When he was finished he rinsed the frying pan in the river and had Gunn refill the empty canvas bucket with river water.

They walked back to the squad area and Tuck placed the frying pan on a rock by the other items to air dry. Tuck took the bucket from Gunn and placed it next to the cook fire.

"Tom likes to have water ready to make coffee or to put out the fire if we have to move out," explained Tuck.

Gunn nodded his understanding.

Both men stood. Tuck awkwardly stuck out his right hand. "Thanks for helping me, Gunn."

Gunn took his hand and shook it. "Thanks for the lesson in cleaning up. You do a damn fine job."

Tuck seemed to blush with embarrassment. "I'm just doing what we learned to do back home."

"Just where is home?" asked Gunn.

"Some place you never heard of," replied Tuck.

"Try me. I think I know most of the places in Illinois," said Gunn.

"We ain't from Illinois." Said Tuck

"But you're part of the 22nd Illinois Cavalry?"

"Our Pa was born and raised in Illinois. When he growed up he went out west and started a ranch"

"Where out west?"

"We got us a good sized ranch near a place called Bent's Fort in the Colorado Territory. You ever heard of it?"

"Can't say that I have," replied a puzzled Gunn.

"I told you it was some place you never heard of."

"Well you were right about that. Just where is Bent's Fort?"

"It's on the old Santa Fe Trail on the banks of the Arkansas River in the northeast part of the territory. You'd need a map to find it," laughed Tuck.

"So why did you come east to enlist in the army?" asked Gunn.

"Back in Colorado they have organized militia to protect the territory from Indians. Pa wanted to fight the rebs, so he brought us back to Illinois to enlist."

"So, the three of you are here. Where's your Pa?"

Tuck seemed to become suddenly uncomfortable and he hesitated before giving Gunn an answer to his question.

"Pa's an officer with a different Illinois outfit. The three of us wound up here in the 22nd," replied Tuck with a voice full of uncertainty.

Gunn nodded his understanding.

"Well, I got to be goin'. See you at supper, Gunn."

With that Tuck turned and headed in the direction of his tent. This time he walked normally, not like he was escaping from something.

CHAPTER TWELVE

Supper was a repeat of lunch. Ted had made another stew that included some potatoes as well as a couple of rabbits Tom had managed to procure from somewhere other than the quartermaster.

When they had finished dinner, Tom and Ted got to their feet, leaving their plates and cups on the ground and they walked back to their tent without saying a word to Gunn or Tuck.

This time the clean-up went faster and more smoothly as now Gunn knew what Tuck expected of him. When they were on the banks of the river, rinsing out the stew pot and filling the canvas bucket, Gunn decided to take a chance.

"So your brothers have a problem with me?" he asked Tuck.

A change seemed to come over Tuck. His face got hard as he emptied out the river water from the stew pot and got to his feet, ignoring Gunn's question. Tuck began walking swiftly back to the squad camp, trying to put as much distance as possible between him and Gunn.

Gunn shrugged his shoulders. He followed Tuck, keeping a reasonable distance between them. When he got to the squad camp, Tuck had left the pot on the rocks to air dry and had disappeared into his tent. Gunn placed the canvas bucket of river water next to the fire and retired to his tent.

He had no idea what the problem was, and he was no closer to finding out.

At dawn the next day, Gunn was waiting at the corral when Sergeant Mann strode up.

"Well Private, are you ready to learn something about the cavalry saber this morning."

"Yes, Sergeant."

Mann disappeared into a nearby shed and when he emerged, he was carrying a cavalry saber encased in a scabbard. With a bit of an exaggerated motion, Sergeant Mann drew out the sword and flashed it from his left to his right. When he stopped, the sword was pointing directly in front of the sergeant.

"This, Private Gunn, is the sharp teeth of the cavalry. When your guns are empty or broken, this is a weapon that will never fail you. It is a weapon that no infantryman wants to see unsheathed."

With that said, Mann proceeded to explain the various thrusts to be made in combat with the saber.

"You must remember, Private Gunn, because you are right handed the scabbard is worn on the left side to allow the trooper to draw it out of the scabbard with his right hand and draw it across his body so it ends up in his right hand on his right side."

"It is also important to understand that before you attempt to use the saber, you must have not only pictured your opponent in your mind, but also to have determined exactly where you want the blow of the saber to fall. Slashing with the saber is preferred as an attempt to penetrate through the opponent with the saber can result in getting the blade stuck in the opponent and suffering the embarrassment of having the saber ripped from your grasp. Is this clear to you, Private Gunn?"

"Yes, Sergeant."

"Very well, Private, buckle the saber and scabbard on and let's see how well you listened to me."

Gunn buckled on the scabbard and made a few adjustments for his size. When he was satisfied, he stood straight, his feet directly under his shoulders and with his left arm at his side. Gunn reached across his body with his right arm and placed his right hand on the hilt of the saber. With one motion he drew the blade from the scabbard and moved it across his body to his right side with the point of the saber held straight up. He was surprised at the metallic singing noise the blade made exiting from the scabbard.

"Well, you seem to have step one down, Private. Let's see how you do with the various thrusts as I call them out. Are you ready, Private?"

"Yes, Sergeant."

"Let's proceed." For the next fifteen minutes Sergeant Mann would call out a thrust and Gunn would attempt to execute it. When Gunn made a mistake, Mann would correct him and then have him repeat the thrust at least ten times until he was satisfied.

"Do you think you understand all of the saber thrusts now, Private Gunn?" asked Sergeant Mann.

"Yes, Sergeant."

"Unbuckle the saber and hand it to me, Private."

"Yes, Sergeant."

Sergeant Mann took the belt, scabbard and saber from Gunn and disappeared back into the nearby shed. When he emerged he held a wooden saber that was exactly the same size as the steel saber.

"Take this back to your camp and practice all of the thrusts you learned this morning. Make sure you get all of them right. I want you to react by instinct to a command without having to think about it. Can you do that, Private?"

"Yes, Sergeant."

"Be back here promptly at one o'clock and bring your horse tack. When you arrive I want you to acquire a mount and have him ready to ride by a quarter after one. Is that clear, Private?"

"Yes, Sergeant."

Sergeant Mann turned on his heel and headed away from the corral. Gunn headed back to his squad area.

Lunch followed the same pattern that had already been established. Only this time Tuck had joined his brothers in shunning Gunn, and all four men ate in silence. When Gunn picked up the cavass buckets and turned to head to the river, he found his way blocked by Tuck.

"You do the clean-up today, and I'll do it tomorrow," said Tuck. His voice was hard and his look was cold. Then Tuck spun on his heel and walked to his tent.

Gunn shrugged his shoulders and went about completing the lunch clean-up. When he was finished he sat the canvas bucket down next to the cook fire and went to his tent. There he gathered his horse tack and the wooden saber, and he headed down to the corral for his meeting with Sergeant Mann.

Gunn had a horse saddled and ready before Sergeant Mann made his appearance. Gunn stood next to the horse with the reins in his left hand and the wooden saber in his right.

The Sergeant carefully looked Gunn and the horse over and then nodded for Gunn to follow him. They walked past the corral and down to a field that had been cleared of all trees and brush. Six-foot-high poles had been placed upright in several places in the field. Attached to the poles were what looked like scarecrows. On closer inspection, Gunn could see that the scarecrows were figures of burlap filled with straw.

The figures had distinct arms reaching out from their straw filled bodies. Some of the figures were even wearing old battered hats of various types.

Sergeant Mann led them down to one end of the field. When they reached the edge of the field of straw figures, the sergeant pointed to the figures and said, "What do you see out there in the field, Private Gunn?"

"I see straw figures, Sergeant."

"You're wrong, Private. Those are rebs. Those figures you see are the enemy, and they are here to kill you and your fellow troopers. Is that clear, Private?"

"Yes, Sergeant."

"I'm going to go out in the field and stand by one of those reb figures and raise my right arm in the air. I want you to climb into the saddle with the wooden saber in your right hand. Is that clear, Private?"

"Yes, Sergeant."

"When I drop my right arm, I want you to charge this figure. When I yell out where I want you to strike the reb figure; you are to do so with the correct thrust while at a full gallop. Is that clear, Sergeant?"

"Yes, Sergeant."

The sergeant walked out to the middle of the field and stood to the left of a straw figure. He turned and looked directly at Gunn. The sergeant raised his right arm in the air. Gunn leaped into the saddle and took the reins in his left hand and the wooden saber in his right hand.

Once in the saddle, Gunn looked out at the sergeant. The sergeant's right arm fell and Gunn dug his heels into the ribs of his horse, urging him into a full gallop. The horse quickly gathered speed, and Gunn approached the straw figure from his right. As he approached the figure, he heard the Sergeant yell, "Right arm, Gunn."

As Gunn and his horse flashed by the straw figure he slashed down at the protruding straw right arm. When he passed the figure, he pulled back on the reins and brought the horse to a halt. He turned the horse and trotted back to where the sergeant and the straw figure awaited him.

As he drew near, Gunn could see that the straw right arm of the figure was untouched. He had missed the target entirely.

"It's not as easy as it looks, Private," said the sergeant.

"What did I do wrong, Sergeant?"

"You took your eye off the target, Private. You need to focus on the point of attack and strike swiftly with the saber. Then make sure you follow through with your saber stroke. Let's try it again."

Gunn was red faced when he rode back to his original starting point. He wheeled the horse until he was facing the sergeant again. This time he waited with the sword in his right hand as the sergeant raised his right arm. When the sergeant's arm dropped, Gunn quickly had his mount into a full gallop. This time he leaned forward slightly in the saddle as he approached the straw figure. He heard the sergeant yell out, "Strike the head."

This time, Gunn kept his eyes on the figure which grew larger and larger as he drew closer. As he flashed by the straw figure, Gunn brought the saber forward and down with a swift stroke. As soon as he was past the figure, Gunn brought his horse to a halt and wheeled it around. Then he trotted over to where the sergeant and the straw figure were waiting.

The figure was now headless. A few tufts of straw remained where the head had previously been located.

"That's more like it, Private," said Sergeant Mann. "Now let's try it again on another figure."

Gunn touched his wooden saber to his kepi in salute to the sergeant and trotted back to his starting point.

After three hours, both Gunn and his mount were tired. His right arm ached from the impact of the wooden saber and the straw figures that he had ravaged. As the afternoon wore on, Gunn became better and better at wielding the wooden saber. The proof of his effort was in the field. None of the straw figures had heads or right arms. All had fallen victim to Gunn's right arm.

Sergeant Mann finally held his hand up to stop the drill. "See me at the corral with your horse tack and wooden saber first thing in the morning, Private. Is that clear?"

"Yes, Sergeant."

When the sergeant called the drill over, Gunn led his horse back to the corral where he wiped it down with an old blanket and used a curry comb until he was satisfied with the horse's appearance. He fed and watered the horse, and then picked up his horse tack and made his way back to his squad area.

Ted was preparing supper and this time Tom was helping him. Tom had acquired some chunks of beef along with potatoes, carrots, and onions. The smell was delicious. Gunn noticed the stew pot was full to the brim. When Ted announced that supper was ready, all four men filled their tin plates and dug in. For once there was enough for seconds, and Gunn participated along with the three brothers. The delicious supper was accompanied with the usual silence. When they were finished, all three brothers got up and went to their tents, leaving their plates and cups on the ground.

Gunn smiled grimly. He was determined to do his job and endure what he must to get along with them. Assholes were what the sergeant had called them and he had been right on the money with that remark. Gunn quickly finished his clean-up chores and headed to his tent and a welcome night's sleep.

CHAPTER THIRTEEN

Dawn found Gunn at the corral with his horse saddled and ready to ride. His wooden saber hung loosely from his right hand. His right arm was still stiff from the previous day's exercise, but he was anxious to see what Sergeant Mann had in store for him.

The sergeant arrived at the corral with two troopers and their horses in tow.

"Good morning, Private Gunn. Are you ready for some sword play?"

"Yes, Sergeant."

"Outstanding, Private. I've brought some helpers for today's lesson. This is Trooper Whitehouse and Trooper Jones. They will be your opponents this morning."

"Opponents, Sergeant?"

"Today's lesson is some mock battle with wooden sabers, Gunn."

"Yes, Sergeant."

Gunn noticed that both of the troopers were carrying wooden sabers identical to the one he held in his right hand.

"Follow me, men," said Mann.

The sergeant led them down to the field with the posts and the straw figures. When they reached the edge of the field, he turned to face the three troopers.

"Troopers Whitehouse and Jones will ride to the other end of the field. Private Gunn, you will remain on this end of the field. I will raise my right arm. When I drop my arm, Trooper Jones will gallop towards us and trooper Gunn will gallop towards Jones. When you meet in the middle of the field, each of you will attempt to unhorse the other utilizing your wooden saber."

When the first mock combat is concluded, then trooper Gunn will return to this side and we will repeat the process with trooper Whitehouse replacing trooper Jones. Is that clear, gentlemen."

"Yes, Sergeant," replied the three troopers in a loose chorus.

Gunn looked over his two adversaries. Whitehouse was the larger of the two and probably had thirty pounds on Jones. Both of them had a smirk on their faces as they expected to make short work of the newcomer.

"Move to your stations, gentlemen," said Mann.

Whitehouse and Jones rode to the opposite end of the field and wheeled their horses, so they were facing the sergeant and Gunn.

Sergeant Mann looked over at Gunn. "Are you ready, trooper?"

"Yes, Sergeant. I was born ready."

"Bold words, trooper. Let's see if you can back them up."

The sergeant raised his right arm and after making sure both riders were ready, he dropped his arm.

Both troopers quickly brought their mounts to a gallop and thundered across the field directly at each other.

As he approached the other rider, Gunn crouched low in the saddle as he tried to give his opponent as small a target as possible.

Upon seeing Gunn crouch down, Jones could not keep the smile off his face. He knew Gunn was making a classic novice's mistake. From that low a position Gunn could not wield his saber effectively and would be an easy target for Jones.

Just as the two mounted troopers began to close, Jones brought his saber up to strike a downward blow to Gunn's head. At the last second, Gunn raised his wooden saber vertically to his position and when Jones struck his blow, it was parried by an upright wooden saber held firmly in Gunn's right hand.

Both riders came to a halt and each wheeled their mounts around to engage their opponent.

Jones was surprised to see that this time Gunn was setting erect in the saddle and holding the saber with the tip pointed at the sky.

Both mounted troopers moved next to each other to attack with their sabers. Jones brought his saber down at Gunn, who parried the blow and then tried to launch a blow of his own. Jones easily parried the attempt by Gunn, and then Jones tried to slice at Gunn's head with his saber.

Gunn ducked under the blow and dropped his reins. Using his free left hand, Gunn grabbed Jones' wrist holding the saber and pulled on it. A surprised Jones found himself being propelled out of his saddle and he followed his wooden saber all the way down to the hard ground of the field.

Gunn simply grabbed his mount's reins and rode back to the end of the field where Sergeant Mann stood with a look of disbelief on his face.

A sore and embarrassed Trooper Jones caught his horse, mounted, and returned to the far side of the field.

Sergeant Mann was surprised at Gunn's victory. Jones was a veteran and a bit of a hard ass and Mann had picked him as a tough test for Gunn. He knew Whitehouse was also a combat veteran and a big man with a cruel streak. Gunn had been lucky with Jones, but the sergeant was sure Gunn would be learning a hard and painful lesson from Whitehouse.

Sergeant Mann could see Whitehouse was ready so he turned to look at Gunn.

"Are you ready, Private Gunn?"

"Yes, Sergeant."

The sergeant raised his arm and checked to see both riders were ready. When he was satisfied, he dropped his arm.

Again both mounted troopers galloped at each other. As they neared each other, Gunn again crouched down in his saddle. Whitehouse had watched the encounter with Jones carefully, and he had a surprise in store for the newcomer.

As the riders drew next to each other, Gunn again brought his wooden saber upright and this time Whitehouse started to bring his saber down against Gunn's, but then brought it back and leveled an angled blow that glanced off Gunn's right shoulder.

The blow hurt Gunn, and he felt both the pain and a numbness that extended from his shoulder down his right arm. He was afraid he would drop his wooden saber, but somehow he managed to hang on to it.

Both horses had come to a halt, and the troopers wheeled them around until they were side by side.

Whitehouse moved in for the attack and slashed his saber down at Gunn's head. Gunn brought his saber up to parry the blow. The movement caused pain to shoot through his right shoulder and arm. Whitehouse slashed at Gunn two more times and each time Gunn managed to parry the blows. Whitehouse noticed each time Gunn was slower to get his saber in a positon to parry, and he grinned to himself. He could see that Gunn's sword arm was weak from the blow he had taken.

Whitehouse faked a saber stroke and then struck a hard stroke at Gunn's head. Gunn had somehow anticipated the move and he ducked and the blow missed him. Whitehouse was outraged at his miss and he dropped his reins and took the wooden saber in both hands and prepared to bring it down in Gunn with all the force he could muster.

Gunn brought his wooden saber up to block the blow, but the force of the strike was so strong, it broke Gunn's wooden saber in two.

Gunn looked down at the much shorter saber in his right hand and then looked over at Whitehouse. Whitehouse was supposed to yield when something like this happened, but the trooper was so enraged with Gunn, he was preparing to deliver another two handed blow to the defenseless Gunn.

Gunn dropped the useless broken wooden saber and wheeled his horse away from Whitehouse. When he was thirty yards distant, Gunn again wheeled his mount and spurred the horse into a gallop. Gunn's mount rammed into the side of Whitehouse's horse and the impact caught Whitehouse with both hands on his wooden saber and no reins to control his horse. Whitehouse's mount lurched suddenly to the right, and Whitehouse found himself flying through the air until he made contact with the hard ground of the practice field.

Gunn sat on his horse and took a long hard look at Whitehouse lying on the ground. Then he wheeled his horse and rode slowly back to the end of the field where Sergeant Mann waited.

Gunn brought his horse to a halt by the sergeant and dismounted. He stood by the horse with the reins in his right hand.

"Sergeant, I am sorry to report that I lost my wooden saber."

"Where the hell did you learn how to do something like that, Private?"

"I had no saber and my opponent had no visible control of his mount so I used what I had, my horse."

"Well, Private Gunn. I think we've given you about all the training you need. You're dismissed."

Gunn slowly walked his horse back to the corral, rubbing his sore right shoulder as he walked.

When he reached the corral, he watered and fed his horse and wiped him down with an old saddle blanket. Then Gunn thoroughly used a curry comb on the horse until he was satisfied that he had done all he could do to thank the beast for helping him survive the day's training.

Gunn then searched through the tack shed until he found what he was looking for. A bottle of what was known as horse liniment. He took off his shirt and opened the bottle. Gunn poured a small amount out into his left hand. Then he applied the liniment to his right shoulder and began rubbing it in. After about five minutes he stopped and put his shirt back on. He gathered his horse tack and headed back to his squad area. As he walked, he could feel that liniment begin to work and the pain slowly seemed to seep out of his shoulder. He was glad the training was over, but he knew he had probably made two new enemies in Jones and Whitehouse. The last thing he needed was more enemies while dealing with three asshole brothers, but he looked at the training incident as a fair fight, and Whitehouse had been way out of line in attacking him when he was defenseless.

As he was walking he noticed a large crowd of soldiers gathered around a large canvas fly that had not been there when he had passed by early that morning. He went up to one of the troopers standing at the back of the crowd and touched him on the shoulder.

The trooper turned to see who had touched him and Gunn took the opportunity to ask him a question.

"What's going on here?" asked Gunn.

"We're finally getting' a mess tent," said the trooper with a smile on his face. "No one in my squad can cook worth a shit. I heard that they'll be serving supper tonight," said the excited trooper.

Gunn continued on his way with a smile on his face. That was good news. No more having to put up with the silent treatment at every meal. He increased his pace and noted that the pain in his shoulder had diminished greatly.

CHAPTER FIFTEEN

Gunn spooned his lunch onto his tin plate when the food was pronounced ready by Ted. He took the plate and his tin cup of coffee back to his tent. When he was finished, he walked back to where the three brothers sat and dropped his plate and cup on the ground with a flourish and then disappeared back into his tent. He had made his point with the brothers, as it was Tuck's turn to clean-up and he wanted to rest his still sore arm. He lay down on his cot and was soon fast asleep.

After a short nap, Gunn awoke and was pleased to see his shoulder felt better. He pulled out his gear and began to clean his Colt. When he finished, he carefully inspected the Colt. When he was satisfied with his work, he replaced the Colt in his holster and pulled out his Spencer. He carefully cleaned the rifle and inspected it. Satisfied, he placed it back under his bunk. Since they never talked to him, Gunn had no idea if the brothers knew about the mess tent. He decided that it was not his problem whether they knew or not.

He walked out into the woods and began looking for firewood. He knew he didn't need to, but he knew he was still part of the squad and even if the fire wasn't needed as a cook fire, there was always a need for a fire to make coffee. He gathered up a large armful and walked back to the squad area. There he deposited the wood next to the fire pit. After grabbing his plate and cup from his tent, Gunn headed back to where he had seen the canvas fly that was serving as the mess tent for I Troop.

A crowd had already gathered at the newly erected mess tent as hungry troopers stood in line, each of them carrying their tin plates and cups.

Gunn got in line behind a short, skinny trooper who looked to be no older than teenager. Gunn grinned to himself. He was making judgement on some youngster when he was a grizzled veteran at the age of twenty.

Finally, Gunn reached the serving line. There were ham steaks, boiled potatoes with some sort of brown gravy, and beans. At the next serving station came the big surprise. There was freshly baked bread with real butter. No hard tack! This was truly a feast for the hungry soldiers.

Gunn filled his cup with hot coffee and took his cup and plate piled heavy with food, and found a spot under a nearby tree. The tree shaded him from the still present sun, and his shoulder felt good resting against the tree trunk.

After he finished his hearty meal, Gunn sipped on his still hot coffee and looked around at his surroundings. He could see several familiar faces, including the three McMaster brothers and Sergeant Mann. He saw no sign of Jones or Whitehouse, but he wasn't sure they were in I Troop. Maybe Sergeant Mann had recruited them from a different troop. Gunn didn't really care, but in his short time in the army he had learned to keep track of anyone he considered unfriendly.

Having finished his coffee, Gunn headed to the river to wash off his plate and cup. He made his way through the gathering dusk to the bank of the river at a place where he could easily clean off his utensils. He went to one knee and started to wash off his plate, when he felt, more than saw, a movement to his right. Instinctively he rolled to his left just in time to hear and feel the hiss of a large club passing close to his right ear.

Gunn continued rolling and then leaped to his feet. He had dropped his plate and had only his tin cup in his left hand. Standing in front of him and moving forward was an angry Whitehouse with Jones close behind him.

"Let's see how you fare without Sergeant Mann to protect you, mama's boy," sneered Whitehouse. He held a club upright with both hands. Jones stood behind him with an evil grin on his face.

Gunn knew they had skipped the supper meal at the mess tent so they could watch him and then follow and ambush him. All he had was a tin cup in his hand.

Whitehouse stepped closer to Gunn who was standing with a tree behind him and the river on his left. He had nowhere to retreat.

Gunn faked a move to his right as though to try to run that way and then came back to his left until he was literally standing in the shallow edge of the river.

Whitehouse had shifted his body to his left to match Gunn's first move and was off balance. Gunn quickly bent down and filled the cup with river water with one hand and grabbed a handful of river mud with the other.

He arose and rushed forward, coming straight at a surprised Whitehouse. Jones was too close behind Whitehouse to maneuver. Gunn got close to the two men and tossed the cup of river water in Whitehouse's face and eyes. Then he slammed the handful of river mud into Jones' eyes.

Gunn dropped his cup and then delivered a still muddy right fist into Whitehouse's nose. The sound of crunching bone followed and blood quickly flowed from Whitehouse's face. Gunn then grabbed a mud-blinded Jones by the neck and drove his head into the trunk of a nearby tree. Jones went down like a sack of wet flour.

Gunn turned back to the badly bleeding Whitehouse who was bent over in pain and kicked him squarely in the balls. Whitehouse let out a scream and fell to the ground, his hands cupping his privates.

Gunn went back to the river and washed the mud and blood off his hands. Then he retrieved his tin plate and cup and washed them in the river. He arose and calmly walked back up the river bank to the campground like nothing had happened.

Gunn's heart was beating like he had just run for two miles, but he walked slowly until his heartbeat had returned to something that resembled normal.

He hoped the two troopers would learn from this encounter that messing with Gunn would be more trouble than it was worth. But he also knew that an enemy was an enemy and that usually never changed. He would have to be wary of them.

When he arrived at the mess tent, it was still crowded with several soldiers of I Troop. Gunn looked around and could see no sign of the three McMaster brothers or Sergeant Mann. It was just as well that nobody knew what had happened down by the river, other than the two assailants and himself. He returned to his tent and laid down on his cot. Within minutes Gunn was fast asleep.

Gunn was awakened by Tuck shaking his still sore shoulder.

"Get up, Gunn. It's boots and saddles time," said an excited Tuck.

Gunn leaped off the cot and was dressed and ready in minutes. When he raced out of his tent with his horse tack and Spencer, he found the three McMaster brothers and Sergeant Mann waiting for him.

"Git your horses and git mounted. We got rebels raidin' the ferry crossing. Meet me just north of the corral." Mann turned and all Gunn could see was his retreating backside.

Gunn and the three brothers raced to the corral and joined other troopers trying to catch and saddle mounts. Gunn saw the mare he had ridden before and easily slipped up to the mare's side and quickly had her saddled and ready. He slipped the Spencer into the leather thimble attached to his saddle and rode to where the sergeant was waiting. They were quickly joined by the three McMaster brothers and several other troopers. There were about twenty troopers gathered at the spot Mann had indicated. Gunn took a look around at the faces of the troopers. He saw the three McMaster brothers, but no sign of Whitehouse or Jones. That was a relief., Mann led them at a fast trot to the bank of the river where the ferry was located.

The ferry was ready and waiting for them. Mann and the twenty troopers dismounted and led their horses onto the ferry and the ferryman began the short journey across the Chattahoochee River. As soon as the ferry touched the other bank, the men and horses quickly disembarked. Once off the ferry, the troopers mounted their horses and followed Sergeant Mann in the early light of dawn.

They quickly came upon a squad of Union infantry who had been serving as pickets to protect the southern approach to the ferry. Several of the soldiers were wounded.

Mann slipped off his horse and quickly conferred with the sergeant who was in charge of the infantry squad. After a short exchange, Mann returned and mounted his horse.

"Rebs were here about fifteen minutes ago. Maybe thirty of them. Let's go!"

The Mann led riders moved to a full gallop and thundered down the barely lit rutted dirt road. After about ten minutes at a gallop, Sergeant Mann raised his right hand in the air to signal a halt.

The small column stopped, and the men rested in their saddles. Gunn strained his ears to hear something besides the heavy breathing of their mounts and the whispering of some of the troopers.

Gunn raised his hand and said, "Silence," in a semi-loud voice. All the troopers stopped their chatter. Gunn could hear some faint voices and more importantly he could hear the clink of metal against metal as soldier's gear collided.

"They're close, Sergeant. Sound carries, but I'd say they are less than half a mile ahead of us," said Gunn.

Mann nodded. "Move forward at a fast walk, men. Get your weapons at the ready." he whispered. The sergeant then motioned his right arm forward and the small column of troopers moved forward with as little noise as possible.

The troopers rode forward in the slightly brightening light of dawn. The only sound was the horses' hooves on the dirt road. Fortunately, the ground was soft from a recent rain and that muffled some of the noise.

The sergeant halted the column when he could distinctly hear the sound of the rebels located just to the front of them. He turned in his saddle and motioned to Tom McMaster to come forward to him. Tom moved his horse forward and reined in when he was next to the sergeant.

"Take one of your brothers and scout ahead and let me know what we're up against," whispered Mann.

Rather than risk alerting the enemy of their presence by replying, Tom touched the brim of his kepi and turned and motioned to Ted to join him. Both troopers moved quietly ahead and moved into the nearby trees where they were quickly lost to sight by the others.

Ten minutes later, the two brothers returned as quietly as they had departed. Both brothers stopped when they reached the sergeant.

"It looks to be about thirty men, give or take a couple," whispered Tom.

"What are they up to?" whispered the sergeant.

"They stopped because they have a couple of wounded, and it looks like two or three of the horses are hurt as well," whispered Tom.

"We'll advance on foot and surprise them on two sides. You take half the men and block the road, Tom. I'll take the rest and set up on their left flank. Let's move out," whispered Mann.

Tom touched his finger to the brim of his kepi in reply, and he and Ted returned to the column and whispered instructions.

The men dismounted with the horse holders each taking control of four horses.

Tom handed his reins to Gunn and then paused. "Do your job, Gunn. These horses better be here when I return, or I'll hunt you down and kill you," whispered Tom.

Gunn looked him straight in the eyes. "Me and the horses will be here when and if you get back, Tom," he whispered in reply.

Tom bristled at Gunn's reply, but he said nothing. He and Ted and Tuck took their Spencer rifles and joined the sergeant and the others. The sergeant took seven troopers and maneuvered to get to the left of the rebels. Tom, Ted, and Tuck, and five other troopers moved silently up the road to block the rebels.

Gunn and the four other horse holders stood just off the road, each man holding the reins of four horses. The horses sensed something was up, and they snorted and nervously stomped their hooves on the ground.

Gunn didn't like not knowing what was going on, and he was determined to be ready if something went wrong. He had been in numerous clashes with the rebs. Something almost always went wrong, and he sensed that this time it would be no different. He moved the reins to his left hand and pulled the Colt out of his holster with his right hand. He listened intently, but all he could hear was the sound of some crickets and the heavy breathing of the horses along with the occasional hoof stomping the ground.

Suddenly the silence was broken by the sound of gunfire, lots of it. Then Gunn could hear men yelling and screaming. Then he could hear the sound of terrified horses, and finally he could hear the sound of horses' hooves as they thudded against the dirt of the road in front of him.

"Get back off the road," ordered Gunn to the four other troopers. "Get ready for an attack," he practically shouted at them.

The words were no sooner out of his mouth when two mounted rebs suddenly appeared in the road heading for them at a full gallop. The rebs were trying to look behind them and failed to immediately see the troopers and the horses held in front of them.

Gunn gripped the reins in his left hand tightly and then sighted in on the lead rebel rider with his Colt.

When the rider was thirty yards in front of him, Gunn shot him twice with the Colt. The reb fell backwards off his saddle like he had been pulled there with a rope. Gunn shifted his sights to the other rider and shot him through the head at fifteen yards. The reb's horse raced by Gunn and his horses and disappeared down the road.

Gunn looked at his surroundings. There were no other riders. The first reb's horse had stopped and was grazing on the side of the dirt road. The shooting from down the road at the site of the Union attack had ceased.

The other troopers had been standing by the side of the road in shock. Finally, one of them recovered and leading his horses he approached Gunn who still had his Colt in his hand.

"Man, that was some shootin'! I never saw nothin' like that before," he said to Gunn.

"I was lucky," said Gunn.

"I seen shootin' before and that didn't look like no luck to me," said the disbelieving trooper.

Gunn just shrugged his still sore shoulder. He handed the reins of his horses to the trooper and moved forward with his Colt still drawn to check the bodies of the fallen rebels to make sure they were dead and not wounded. Both rebels were dead. He dragged the bodies off the one side of the dirt road. Gunn checked their pockets and gear for any papers, but found none. Satisfied, he stood up and returned to the trooper holding his horses.

"Are they dead?" asked the trooper, whose name was Barnes.

Gunn took a closer look at Barnes. He was younger than Gunn, but his eyes were clear and his voice was normal. He was no longer frightened. Gunn knew that was a good sign.

"They both made their last rebel yell," said Gunn.

Gunn and the other horse holders waited for about another fifteen minutes when they again heard men and horses moving their way from the direction of the fire fight.

The sky was getting lighter as the sun began to rise in the east, but the wall of tall pine trees on both sides of the road kept their positon in the shadows.

Gunn could see dark forms down the road that soon morphed into Sergeant Mann and the rest of the troopers. Mann signaled a halt with his right arm and the column came to a ragged halt in front of the horse holders.

Mann looked tired and he had the smell of gun smoke on him. The troopers were unusually silent. Gunn was pretty sure he knew why. This was probably the first combat for many of them and the reality of death is a telling force.

Gunn could see two of the troopers were wounded. One trooper was wounded in the arm and another in the shoulder. Both wore makeshift bandages. The last three troopers in the column were leading horses that bore the bound figures of three rebel raiders.

"How did it go, Sergeant?" asked Gunn.

"We surprised them, but they put up a good scrap and we had two wounded. We killed five of them and captured three. I'm not sure about wounded. The rest of them ran off like rabbits. I think two of them were headed this way, but we didn't find them."

"You mean these two, Sergeant?" said Gunn as he pointed to the two bodies that lay sprawled on the side of the road.

"It looks like they picked the wrong road, Private Gunn. Nobody here got hurt?" asked the sergeant.

"We got them before they had a chance to do any damage," replied Gunn.

Mann dismounted and strode over to where the two bodies lay on the edge of the road. He quickly searched the bodies for any papers, but found nothing. He returned to his horse and faced his troopers.

"All right men, let's mount up and get back to camp," said Mann.

The three McMaster brothers took their horses reins from Gunn without a word or a glance in his direction. Gunn just shrugged his shoulders and then felt the slight pain in his right shoulder. He gingerly mounted the mare and joined the column as they made their way back across the river to their camp.

Once back at the corral, Gunn rubbed down the mare and fed and watered her. He spent about fifteen minutes with the curry comb and then realized how hungry he was.

He made his way to the mess tent where they were still serving breakfast. Gunn was surprised to see eggs and bacon and flapjacks being served. He filled his plate and grabbed a tin cup of hot coffee. He looked for a place to sit down and ended up on the ground with his back to the same tree he had used before.

Gunn attacked his plate of food and when he was finished, he surveyed his surroundings as he sipped his hot coffee. He was surprised by movement to his left and turned to see trooper Barnes plop down on the ground next to him.

Gunn watched as the young Barnes attacked his food with the same gusto Gunn had.

Barnes paused his attack on his plate and looked up at Gunn. "Fightin' makes me hungry. I ain't sure why."

Gunn grinned at the young trooper. "It surely does, Barnes, it surely does."

CHAPTER SIXTEEN

That evening, Sergeant Mann appeared in the troop mess tent during supper. He called all the men to attention and all chatter stopped. Even the cooks and servers paused, so there was no clanking of pots and pans or other noise.

"I Troop is to conduct a patrol across the river tomorrow morning. You are to be mounted and ready to ride at three o'clock in the morning. Is that clear, men?"

"Yes, Sergeant!" came the chorus of response from eighty-five men's throats.

Satisfied, Sergeant Gunn slipped out of the mess tent. As soon as he was gone, the buzz of speculation on where they were going filled the mess tent.

Gunn walked back to his tent and took out both the Colt and the Spencer and began cleaning them. He looked up as a shadow crossed the opening to his tent. Standing in front of Gunn was Tuck. He looked a little nervous, but not like he had before when he seemed to be on a mission he would rather not have been assigned.

"You done good today, Gunn. Thanks for keeping our horses safe."

Tuck turned and strode away in the direction of his tent.

"Wonders never cease," said Gunn to himself.

When he was finished with his guns, he checked his horse tack and lastly he took out the cavalry saber. He drew the saber from its scabbard and looked carefully at it. He hoped he never got down to where the saber was his last resort, but it was comforting to know it would be there if he did need it.

Three o'clock in the morning found the troop formed up outside the corral. Normally the troop marched in columns of four, but because the roads they had encountered in the South were so narrow, they now formed up and rode in columns of two.

Gunn found himself next to Tuck. Ahead of them were Tom and Ted McMaster.

At the head of the column were Captain Dexter and Lieutenant Blust. There were three other sergeants in the column that Gunn did not know. Trailing the column were two pack mules led by mounted troopers. The packs contained extra ammunition and medical supplies.

The column moved out and soon reached the ferry crossing of the Chattahoochee River. It took over two hours to get the entire column over the river and then reformed. The column moved past the outpost that had been attacked the night before. Gunn noted the number of soldiers at the outpost had been almost doubled in number.

Around mid-day, the column stopped to rest and Sergeant Mann was ordered forward. Soon he came riding back and he pulled his mount to a halt when he reached the McMaster brothers.

"McMaster, Whitmore, your squads are to serve under me as scouts. Follow me!"

Mann wheeled his horse and headed to the front of the column with the eight troopers of two squads trailing him. They rode past the captain and lieutenant who touched the brim of their hats in salute to the sergeant, and then moved up the road ahead of the column at a trot.

When they were out of sight of the column, Mann called them to a halt.

"McMaster, I want you and one of your squad to move out to the left side of the road and make sure we have no surprises ahead of us. Whitmore, I want you to do the same to the right side of the road. The rest of the troopers remain with me. Is that clear?"

"Yes, Sergeant," said the two troopers in unison.

"Move out!" said the sergeant.

Within minutes, neither set of riders could be seen from the road. Mann had sent two of his most experienced troopers to scout ahead of him. He was well aware that getting surprised in rebel country could be both unforgiving and deadly.

The sergeant and his remaining four troopers continued forward on the road at a trot. They had been riding for almost an hour when he could see Ted McMaster riding back on the road towards him at a gallop.

Ted McMaster brought his horse to a sliding stop next to the sergeant. "There's a small rebel outpost about two miles up the road. Looks to be about a dozen of them. They's hunkered down and looks to be eatin' breakfast. What are your orders, Sergeant?"

Mann turned to one of the troopers riding with him. "Ride back to the column and tell Captain Dexter about the outpost. Request orders on how we are to proceed. Is that clear, trooper?"

"Yes, Sergeant," said the trooper who then wheeled his horse, and after jabbing at the horse's flank with his spurs, was soon thundering back down the road at a full gallop.

"What do we do now, Sergeant?" asked Ted?"

"We do what all good soldiers do, McMaster. We wait."

Fifteen minutes later the trooper was back with three more squads totaling twelve riders.

The trooper reined up next to the sergeant.

"The Captain says to take all five squads and to attack the outpost on horseback and attempt to take prisoners, Sergeant."

"Very good, Trooper," said the sergeant.

"McMaster, you go ahead and gather up the other scouts and wait for us about half a mile from this outpost."

"Yes, Sergeant," said McMaster and he turned his horse and galloped off.

"No talking in the ranks. We need to surprise them," said the sergeant to his remaining troopers.

Using his right arm as a silent signal, the sergeant moved it forward to order the small column to move forward.

The cavalrymen rode forward at a fast walk, doing their best not to make any unnecessary noise, but the creaking of leather and the occasional banging together of metal gear along with the sound of the horse's hooves on the dirt road were hard to ignore. Sergeant Mann just hoped it wasn't noticeable to the men in the rebel outpost.

Finally, they caught sight of Tom McMaster on foot, standing just behind the cover the pine trees lining the road provided. Tom had his back to a tree and was holding up both his arms as a signal to stop.

The sergeant brought his horse to a stop and dismounted, handing the reins to the trooper next to him. He walked forward until he reached Tom's hiding place and slipped behind the tree next to Tom.

"Did you learn any more about the rebel position, Tom?" asked the sergeant in a whisper.

"Nothing has changed. There are about a dozen rebels having breakfast with their horses on a picket line. Something seems strange, Sergeant."

"What seems strange?"

"I know they're on their side of the river, but they have no sentries out and that seems awful careless this close to our lines."

"Anything else bother you, Tom?"

"I don't understand what are they doing here? Are they guarding something? If so, what the hell are they guarding? This just don't feel right to me, Sergeant."

"The captain wants us to attack and try to take some prisoners," said Mann.

"I don't like the idea of walkin' into an ambush, Sergeant."

"How do we find out if we are, Tom?"

"I'd like to take one other trooper and slip around behind them and make sure there aren't more of them in the trees where we can't see 'em."

"Take one man and scout their rear. I'll hold the men here. Don't take too long, Tom. I don't want them discovering us, and we wind up empty handed. The captain would have my ass for that."

"I'll take Ted, and we'll be quick," said Tom.

Mann had learned that the McMaster brothers had a lot of experience fighting Indians out west, and they were probably the best scouts in the regiment. He had a lot of faith in Tom's judgement.

The sergeant hadn't waited more than ten minutes when Tom and Ted came running carefully through the pine trees. Tom was slightly out of breath when he arrived next to the sergeant. When he could talk, he whispered what he had seen to the sergeant.

"There are about three companies of rebel infantry camped about a hundred yards behind that rebel outpost. That's why they feel so damn safe. We hit that outpost, and we'd run smack dab into a hornet's nest. I ain't interested in getting' stung, Sergeant."

The sergeant thought for a minute while he tried to peer into the dark woods that McMaster had just emerged from.

"My mama didn't raise no fools, McMaster. Let's gather up the men and get the hell out of here and back to the column. We'll let the captain decide what to do."

"Sounds good to me, Sergeant. I'll get the rest of the scouts."

Very shortly Sergeant Mann and his small column of riders had rejoined the I Troop column and the sergeant had reported the situation to the captain.

After a heated, but short discussion between the captain and the lieutenant, the captain gave orders to retreat, cross the river and return to camp.

CHAPTER SEVENTEEN

I Troop's camp was full of unhappy men that evening. They had embarked on a patrol and been given the opportunity to engage the enemy, only to have it yanked away at the last minute. The way they looked at it, they had signed up with the army to fight, not run away. There were lots of arguments and not a few fist fights before the night was over.

Sergeant Mann knew how his men felt, but unlike them, he had already seen plenty of combat, and he knew better than to risk the lives of his men against a superior force. He knew that would be a hard argument to sell to his men on that night. He also knew they would simmer down by morning.

Gunn lay on his cot thinking about the missed encounter. His experience told him that cavalry charging entrenched infantry that outnumbered the cavalry by better than three to one was not a good idea. He also knew there would be plenty of other chances to fight rebs and hopefully they would be opportunities where the odds were in I Troop's favor. Tomorrow was another day.

Tom McMaster also knew the wisdom in retreating in the face of superior numbers, but he also had an idea he wanted to see if he could get the sergeant to approve. He made his way to Sergeant Mann's tent and carefully announced himself.

"Enter," came the reply from within the sergeant's tent.

"A little late to be socializing, ain't it McMaster?" asked the sergeant with a frown on his face.

"I got an idea and I'd like you to consider it, Sergeant," said McMaster.

"Let's hear it so I can git me some sleep."

"If I were to take my brothers with me, we could head out about three o'clock tomorrow morning and sneak up on that outpost we found. We should be able to slip in and snatch one of the sentries as a prisoner. I think we can pull it off, and I'm pretty sure it would be worth the risk. If we're successful, it was your idea and if we're not, you knew nothing about it. What do you say, Sergeant?"

Mann thought for a moment and then he turned to face McMaster. "I'll agree to this scheme on one condition."

"What's the condition, Sergeant?"

"You take Gunn along. You're a squad of four and anything less is not acceptable to me."

"We don't need Gunn. We can do this by ourselves."

"I don't give a shit what you need, McMaster. You take Gunn or you don't go."

"This is a crappy deal, Sergeant."

"Take it or leave it, McMaster. Gunn goes or nobody goes."

"All right, Sergeant. Gunn goes with us."

"Good luck, McMaster and make sure you are back before dawn. The less anyone knows about this stunt the better."

"Yes, Sergeant."

Tom McMaster left the sergeant's tent and in twenty minutes he had managed to wake up his two brothers and Gunn and explain the plan. All of them had agreed to go.

Shortly before three o'clock the next morning, the four men were quietly leading their saddled horses down the road to the ferry crossing. They had to wake up the ferryman before they could cross the river. Once across, they rode hard at a gallop until they were within one mile of where they believed the rebel outpost stood.

They walked their horses as quietly as they could until they could see a campfire burning in the middle of the rebel position.

Tom whispered his plan to the others. "Ted and I will slip up on the outpost and find a sentry. We'll jump him and knock him out and then drag him back here. Tuck, you and Gunn hold the horses and be prepared to cover us if we come runnin' back with a passel of rebs chasing us."

Both Tuck and Gunn silently nodded their agreement with Tom's plan. They dismounted and Tuck and Gunn each held two horses, while Tom and Ted slipped into the dark shadows in the surrounding pine trees.

Neither Tuck nor Gun spoke, but each of them took time to check both their Colts and their Spencer rifles. They waited in the darkness for about twenty minutes, but it seemed much longer.

Finally, Tom emerged from the pine trees. Ted was behind him and he was carrying a fairly small rebel soldier on his back. When he reached the horses, he let his human burden slip to the ground. Tom and Ted mounted their horses. Tuck held his horse and Gunn's while Gunn picked up the rebel and lifted his limp form up and over the front of Tom's saddle. Gunn noted the rebel soldier was young and fortunately, fairly small.

Gunn took his horses reins from Tuck and both men mounted their horses. Tom signaled that he was ready and the four of them moved back onto the road and kept their horses to a walk as they made their way back to the river. They remained at that pace until they were about a mile from the rebel outpost. Once they felt they had come far enough, they urged their mounts to a trot. They were challenged by the sentries of the Union outposts by the river and after a short wait for the ferry, they were soon across the river and heading back to their camp.

They slipped back to the corral and unsaddled their horses, making sure to feed and water them. Their captive had regained consciousness during this time, and he was not happy about his situation. He started to cry out and Tom promptly backhanded the young lad into silence. They promptly bound his hands behind him and gagged his mouth to keep him quiet.

The three McMaster brothers and Gunn force walked their prisoner to Sergeant Mann's tent.

Tom McMaster slipped into the sergeant's tent and whispered to awaken him.

"What the hell is going on, McMaster?" sputtered the sleepy sergeant.

"We got a little present for you, Sergeant," said Tom.

"Mann got up from his cot and stepped outside to see the four cavalrymen holding onto their rebel captive. All three brothers and Gunn were sporting huge grins. Mann gawked at the prisoner in obvious surprise. Then he realized what he was looking at.

"Sentry!" bellowed the sergeant. "Sentry!"

The sentry on duty arrived in a hurry with his rifle at port arms. "Yes, Sergeant. What is it?" said the sentry.

"We have a rebel prisoner, sentry. Escort him to the sergeant of the guard and have him take custody of the prisoner. Tell the sergeant that I will be down to see him as soon as I am dressed."

"Yes, Sergeant," The sentry took charge of the prisoner and led him by the arm away into the early morning darkness.

Mann turned and looked at the four soldiers standing in front of him. "Good job, men. You're dismissed."

The McMaster brothers and Gunn retired to their tents and tried to get some sleep, but none was forthcoming as they were all too excited about what they had just done.

Dawn found Gunn and the McMaster brothers walking down from their squad area to the mess tent. None of the brothers spoke to Gunn as they walked. That was fine with Gunn. He was getting used to the silent treatment. He knew he had done well on the last two clashes with the rebs, and he knew the brothers knew it too.

Gunn took his filled plate and cup from the serving line and took his accustomed seat at the base of the nearby tree. He was promptly joined by young Barnes.

"Good morning, Gunn. Mind if I join you?" said Barnes.

"It's a free country, Barnes. Sit where you want."

"I heard you and the McMaster boys brought in a prisoner last night. Is that true?"

"You'd have to ask the McMaster brothers, Barnes."

"I'm askin' you, Gunn."

Gunn had to give young Barnes credit. He wasn't afraid, and he wasn't bashful. Gunn decided he was entitled to an answer.

"Me and the McMaster brothers took a little ride last night and managed to scoop up some small fry reb we found out in the dark. We didn't know what to do with him, so we turned him over to the sergeant. That's all I know, Barnes," said Gunn with a straight face.

Barnes seemed satisfied with the answer and he proceeded to attack his breakfast with gusto. Gunn finished his breakfast and sat his plate down on the ground and sipped the still hot coffee from his tin cup. He carefully surveyed his surroundings as he sipped his coffee.

He could see the McMaster brothers setting together, but he didn't see Sergeant Mann or Whitehouse or Jones. He wasn't sorry not to see them, but he knew Whitehouse and Jones were vicious bastards, and he needed to stay watchful in case they decided to try something else. Gunn had hoped the last encounter had proved painful enough that they would wise up and leave him alone. Somehow he didn't think that was going to happen.

Then he saw Sergeant Mann enter the mess tent and walk over to where the McMaster brothers were sitting. Gunn saw the sergeant asking questions, and finally Tuck pointed over to where Gunn sat.

The sergeant turned to face Gunn and motioned for him to join them. Gunn reluctantly picked up his empty plate and slowly walked over to join Mann and the three brothers.

When Gunn joined the group, Mann did not waste any time. "I want the four of you to serve as a scouting party. I want you to leave after lunch and scout the road past the ferry. If you see rebels, you are to avoid any contact. I want you to keep scouting until you reach a place called Latimer's Crossroads. You are to remain out of sight and make no contact with the rebels. You are to note any rebel forces you see, and I want an accurate count of their numbers. I especially want to know if they are infantry or cavalry and make sure to note the location and number of any artillery. Is that clear, gentlemen?"

"Yes, Sergeant," replied the four troopers in unison.

"Report to me when you get back, even if it's in the middle of the night."

"Yes, Sergeant," came the response.

"You boys are dismissed."

Tom McMaster stood up and faced Gunn. "You be at the corral at one o'clock and be saddled and ready." With that he turned and began walking back to the squad area.

The other two McMaster brothers quickly got to their feet and followed their brother. Gunn just shook his head and headed down to the river to clean his plate and cup.

CHAPTER EIGHTEEN

At exactly one o'clock the four troopers left the corral and soon arrived at the ferry over the Chattahoochee River. As soon as they were across, they put their horses in a trot and moved quickly down the road until they came to the Union outpost. They stopped and identified themselves to the sergeant in charge, and then resumed their journey.

Every fifteen minutes, Tom McMaster called a halt to the scouts and they paused to look, listen and smell the air for any sign of the enemy. Sound carries, and Gunn grudgingly acknowledged that this was a smart strategy.

As they neared the site where they had kidnapped the young rebel, they stopped and moved into the trees on the side of the road. Tom pointed at Ted, who slipped from his horse, handing his reins to Gunn.

Ted walked carefully into the woods and promptly disappeared from their sight.

Ten minutes passed, and Ted reappeared from the pine trees.

"Their camp is still up ahead and there looks to be about twenty rebs in it," said Ted to Tom.

"What about that infantry we saw last time?" asked Tom.

"I couldn't see' em, smell 'em, or hear 'em, so I reckon they've hightailed it," replied Ted.

"We'll move into the trees on the left side of the road and lead our horses and go around the outpost," said Tom.

The other three troopers nodded their understanding, and the troopers slowly walked their horses across the road and into the tree line. There they dismounted and followed Tom in single file.

Twenty minutes later they were successfully past the outpost, and they led their horses out onto the road and mounted them. They moved down the road in a column of twos and kept to their pattern of stopping every fifteen minutes to check for any signs of the enemy.

After almost two hours, Tom halted the scouts. "I smell smoke," said Tom.

By then the other three scouts had also detected the smell of wood smoke.

"Ted, you slip on ahead and see who's making the smoke," said Tom.

Ted again slipped from the saddle and handed the reins of his horse to Gunn. Ted moved quietly into the woods and was soon lost from sight.

He was back in about ten minutes. He took the reins from Gunn and mounted his horse.

"It's a small farm. I could see a couple of women, but no men or soldiers," he said to Tom.

"Can we get around it?" asked Tom.

"If we go through the woods on the right side of the road, they'll never see us," replied Ted.

"You lead the way, Ted," said Tom.

Ted rode his horse into the woods on their right and after a short ride he stopped and dismounted. The other three troopers did likewise. Then they followed Ted in single file as they glided through the dark forest of pine trees in silence.

Finally, Ted led them out to the road, and they all mounted their horses. Tom took the lead and they resumed their journey. Tom continued to stop about every fifteen minutes, and then he held up his right hand as a signal to halt.

Tom turned in his saddle to face the other three troopers. "Can you hear that?" he whispered.

The others strained to hear and sure enough the sounds of voices and metal objects being employed reached their ears.

"Ted, go see what this is all about," said Tom

Once again Ted slipped into the tree line on their right and vanished.

He returned about fifteen minutes later, and he was breathing hard.

"Well I think I found where that infantry went. They are camped up on the left side of the road in a clearing. There must be at least three hundred of them."

"Do they have sentries out?" asked Tom

"Sure do, Tom. I saw at least five sentries plus two on the road. They ain't real alert. Two of them looked to be having a tough time stayin' awake."

"What's the best way around them?" asked Tom.

"We move through the pine trees to our right and go Indian style and we should be fine," said Ted.

"What's Indian style?" asked a bewildered Gunn.

Tom looked at him scowl on his face.

"Indian style means we lead our horses and we move very slowly. You put down the toes of your foot every time you take a step and then slowly lower your heel. Make sure you don't snap a twig or make some sound that the rebs might notice," said Ted, much to his brother Tom's disgust.

"Let's go, then," said Gunn.

They dismounted, and Ted led them slowly into the woods on the right side of the road.

It took almost an hour of slow motion movement for the four troopers to skirt around the edge of the sizeable rebel camp without being detected. When Ted finally led them back to the road, they all paused. A combination of the difficult trek, along with the fear of discovery, had drained their energy.

Once they were rested, they mounted their horses and continued on their dangerous scout. They had to skirt two more farms and one smaller encampment of rebel cavalry. When they moved around the rebel cavalry, they took the precaution of keeping their hands over their horses' mouths to prevent them from making or receiving greetings from the rebel cavalry horses that were collected in a rude log corral.

Finally, they reached the outskirts of Latimer's Crossing. They observed that a small detachment of rebel infantry camped at the crossing. Ted thought they numbered less than fifty. He also noted they had seen no artillery since they left the Chattahoochee River.

The four troopers rested in a small clearing they found that was hidden from the road. There they found a small stream where they watered their horses and filled their canteens. They ate hardtack and drank water from their canteens and prepared for the long trek back to their camp.

Gunn went over to where Tom McMaster sat on a log and was drinking from his just refilled canteen. He waited until McMaster finished drinking before he spoke.

"I think we should wait until supper time or dusk to head back," said Gunn.

McMaster looked up at Gunn. Then he looked away and took another drink from his canteen. He paused and then looked back at Gunn.

"I think you could be right. Sentries will be less alert if they're waitin' to be relieved for supper and the dusk makes us much harder to see. We'll wait till just before supper and then start back."

McMaster got to his feet and let his two brothers know of the new plan, before he returned to the stream to refill his canteen.

CHAPTER NINETEEN

The four cavalrymen rested in the shade of the trees at the edge of the clearing for the next two hours. During that time, they heard no sounds from the road, nor did they see anyone on the road.

Finally, Tom McMaster said, "Saddle up," and all four men quickly mounted their horses. They made their way out to the road and began at a walk in single file. Tom McMaster took the point and Gunn brought up the rear of their small column.

They had ridden for almost an hour with only one interruption. Tom had heard a distant set of hoof beats and had directed his men off the road and into the woods. One rider had thundered past at a gallop, and he looked to be a rebel courier headed back to Latimer's Crossing.

Another advantage of traveling at dusk was sound seemed to travel much farther and more clearly than in the heat of the day. Tom McMaster heard the small rebel cavalry encampment long before he saw it.

Tom signaled a halt and using his arm as a silent signal, he sent Ted ahead in the woods to find them a safe route past the cavalry camp.

Ted quickly returned, and they dismounted and led their horses in single file as they followed Ted into the dark woods on their right. All three brothers and Gunn were walking Indian style and carefully leading their horses. After about twenty minutes, Ted led them back to the road, where they mounted their horses and resumed their walking pace.

Time passed slowly and the men maintained as much silence and quiet as possible. The only sound audible was the faint noise of the horses' hooves striking the soft dirt road. They had by-passed one of the small farms by going into the woods and following Ted, and now they were approaching the second small farm.

The silence of the approaching darkness was shattered by screams coming from the direction of the farm. Tom turned to Ted.

"Find out what the hell is going on, but don't let anyone see you," whispered Tom.

Ted nodded his understanding, and he dismounted and handed his reins to Gunn. Then he slipped into the woods and out of sight.

The screams and yelling and loud voices continued, but they were muffled enough by the woods so anything being said could not be heard clearly. It sounded like women screaming and men yelling.

"This can't be good," thought Gunn. In anticipation, he pulled out his Colt and checked to see it was fully loaded and ready for action. Satisfied, he replaced it in his holster.

Ted returned and motioned the others to join him and all three men dismounted and moved to make a small circle around Ted.

"I ain't totally sure of what's goin' on, but it looks like some rebel deserters or outlaws are raidin' this farm for food and valuables. I could see three women, one older and two younger and they was trying to stop these four men from stealin' their food, valuables, and such. I didn't see no menfolk there. I did see an old darkie man, but the rebs had him down on his knees and he looked scared to death," whispered Ted.

"This ain't our problem," whispered Tom. "With all this commotion, we should be able to slip by unnoticed."

"Why isn't it our problem?" asked Gunn.

"It ain't our problem 'cause we ain't rebs and those people ain't our people," replied an annoyed Tom.

"I ain't so sure it ain't our problem, whispered Tuck. "Back home in Colorado we wouldn't stand for men to harass and steal from women, even if we didn't know them."

Tom was even more annoyed now that his youngest brother had sided with Gunn, and he pointed his finger at Tuck. "You ain't got no vote in this."

Tuck did not back down from his big brother. "I ain't gonna just ride on and let this happen, Tom. I don't give a shit what you do, but I'm gonna put a stop to it."

Before Tom could formulate a retort to his newly insubordinate younger brother, Ted spoke up.

"I'm sorry Tom, but I agree with Tuck and Gunn. Pa didn't raise us to let something like this happen and not do something about it," Ted whispered.

"Shit," said Tom as he realized he was now outvoted by three to one.

Gunn broke the ensuing silence by speaking up. "How should we handle it, Tom?" he asked.

Tom took a look at Gunn and his two brothers and then paused to take off his kepi and run his fingers through his thick brown hair.

He replaced the kepi on his head and after a few seconds of thought, he spoke softly to the other three men.

"I ain't rightly sure what would work best. Do you boys have any suggestions, 'cause I'm plumb out?"

"I suggest we walk our horses in and get to the edge of trees that surround the clearing the farm is in and have one of us hold the horses, while the other three use the darkness to slip up to the farmhouse and surprise those yahoos," replied Ted.

"Works for me," said Gunn and Tuck nodded his agreement.

"All right, then that's the plan," whispered Tom. "Gunn, you hold the horses."

"Normally I'd agree with you, Tom," answered Gunn. "But I'm pretty sure I've had a lot more experience with a gun than Tuck has. I think he should hold the horses."

Before Tom could protest Gunn's idea, Tuck spoke up.

"I think Gunn's right. I'll hold the horses," whispered Tuck.

"Do you agree, Ted?" asked Tom.

"I agree," answered Ted.

"Let's move out with Ted in the lead," whispered Tom.

Ted led them silently through the woods and they were quickly at the edge of the farm clearing. A two- story farmhouse that was in need of paint and had seen better days was nearest the road. Behind the farm house was a sizable barn in fairly good condition. There were also two smaller out buildings. Tuck took the reins of the four horses and one by one, Tom, Ted, and then Gunn slipped through the clearing to the back wall of the farm house. Ted peered into a window and then dropped back down to where Ted and Gunn were crouched.

"There's three of them in the house. One of them just knocked the older lady down 'cause she didn't want to let them know where their valuables was hid. I think the other one is out front," whispered Tom.

"Ted, you take out the one in front of the house. Me and Gunn will slip in through this back porch."

Ted nodded his approval and slipped to the front of the house, He made no noise as he approached edge of the house.

He dropped to his knees and carefully peered around the corner. The fourth rebel outlaw was sitting on the front porch, smoking a pipe. He had a rifle lying across his lap. Ted pulled out his Colt and quietly slipped up onto the porch and slowly made his way behind the smoking outlaw.

When he was directly behind the rebel, Tom tapped him lightly on the right shoulder. When the outlaw turned to the right to see who was there, Tom nailed him with the butt of the Colt across the man's left temple. The outlaw fell to floor of the porch without a sound.

Then Ted slipped in the front door with his Colt ready to fire. He could hear the yelling and screaming going on in the next room, and he moved behind a high-backed chair and waited for Tom and Gunn to make their move.

Tom and Gunn had carefully opened the door from the back porch to the farmhouse. When it was open enough for Tom to look into the room, he could see this was the kitchen. He could see the three outlaws. The biggest one had a huge beard and he was slapping the older of the three women with one large hand while he held on to her by grabbing the front of her homespun dress with the other.

The other two outlaws were standing with their backs to Tom, watching the beating being administered with undisguised glee. To Tom's left were the two younger women. They were standing in the corner of the kitchen, crying and hugging each other for comfort.

Tom slipped aside and let Gunn take a look inside the kitchen. When Gunn pulled back, Tom whispered, "Let's take the bastards. If they resist, kill them."

Gunn nodded his agreement. Both men stood up and drew their Colts. After a nod from Tom, he and Gunn burst into the kitchen with guns drawn.

"Hands in the air, you sons of bitches," yelled Tom.

The outlaws were stunned by the sudden appearance of two armed Union soldiers. The big outlaw released his grip on the older woman, and she fell to the floor. Then one of the other two outlaws went for his pistol. Gunn shot him between the eyes and the outlaw dropped like a rock to the kitchen floor. His gun falling from his now dead hand.

The other two outlaws quickly raised their hands. "Don't shoot. Don't shoot," yelled the big outlaw.

"Get their pistols, Gunn," said Tom. "I'll cover you."

Gunn moved his Colt to his left hand and moved quickly next to the smaller outlaw and snatched his pistol from his belt. Then Gunn moved to the large outlaw and relieved him of his pistol.

By this time Ted had appeared in the doorway to the front room with his Colt in hand. Gunn handed the pistols to Ted. Then he turned and punched the large outlaw in the nose, the sound of crunching bone and blood spurting was loud in the sudden silence that overtaken the once noisy kitchen.

The impact was fierce and it knocked the large outlaw to his knees. "What did you do that for?" said the outlaw. "I gave you my gun."

"That's for hitting a defenseless woman, you asshole," shouted Gunn in the man's face.

After a short discussion between Tom, Ted, and Gunn, they tied up the surviving three outlaws and drug them out to the front of the house. There they tied each of them to separate trees. Then they carried the dead man out to the front of the house and laid him on the ground in front of the now tightly bound trio of outlaws.

By now the older women and her two daughters had recovered and were standing on the front porch, watching with intense interest the treatment of the outlaws.

The older women came forward and addressed Tom McMaster.

"I take back every bad thing I ever sad about Yankee troops. I owe you my life, suh. I cannot tell you all how deeply we appreciate your help. I thought we were safe here in Georgia, even with our menfolk gone."

"Goodness gracious, where are mah manners? I'm Melinda Calhoun and these are my two daughters, Suzanne and Anna. We are forever in your debt, suh."

Tom was a little overwhelmed by outburst by the older southern lady, but he quickly recovered.

"Private Tom McMaster of the 22nd Illinois Cavalry, at your service, ma'am. This is my brother Ted McMaster and the young man holding our horses is my other brother, Tuck McMaster. The other gentleman is William Gunn."

"You owe us nothing, ma'am. These outlaws are scum. I'm sure if Rebel soldiers were in the north and found a similar situation, they would have done the same. We're soldiers, ma'am, not outlaws. You flag down the first rebel troops that pass by and let them take care of this scum."

"I intend to do just that, Mr. McMaster. I'll send Teddy to fetch the sheriff," said Mrs. Calhoun as she pointed to the elderly darkie who had appeared behind her.

Mrs. Calhoun and her two daughters each came forward and shook hands with the four troopers. When Anna Calhoun got to Gunn, she shook his hand and held on to it.

"I concur with what my mother said. In addition, Mr. Gunn, I would like to add that I'm glad you all killed that outlaw. He was threatening to ravage me and I had no idea how I was going to stop him."

"He went for his gun, ma'am. I had no choice," replied a suddenly tongue-tied Gunn.

Anna continued to hold his hand. Her hand was small in his. He could feel the smoothness of her skin. She was a dark haired beauty. She had flashing brown eyes that seemed to sparkle when she smiled up at him.

When he began to release his hand from hers, she held on. "Will I see you all again, Mr. Gunn?"

"I'll be back, Miss Calhoun," said Gunn.

"I'll be waiting, Mr. Gunn," she said with a smile and she finally released his hand.

The three McMaster brothers had not failed to notice the extended hand shake between Gunn and Ann Calhoun. All three of them were smiling as they each took their horses and mounted them.

"Let's move out," said Tom and the four troopers returned to the road and headed back north. Tom led the small column and Gunn brought up the rear. He turned in his saddle to look back at the slowly diminishing farm house. Mrs. Calhoun and Suzanne had returned to the front porch of the farm house. Anna still stood in the yard, waving her hand to Gunn. Gunn returned the wave and kept looking back at her until she finally disappeared behind a bend in the road.

CHAPTER TWENTY

Once they were out of sight of the farm house, Ted and Tuck started to rib Gunn about his encounter with Anne Calhoun. Tom listened to the ribbing for a few minutes and then he spoke.

"This scout ain't over and any rebs we run into ain't goin' to give a shit about what we just done here. Keep your yaps shut and remember, we still got a good piece to go. We need to be careful if we're to have any chance of getting back to camp in one piece."

The subdued brothers lapsed into silence and the small column continued its way back to the north and safety.

They kept a steady pace with the horses moving at a walk in the darkness of the night. After an hour, Tom held up his right hand to signal the other three troopers to halt.

Tom turned in his saddle to face the other three men. "That big encampment is just ahead of us. I can smell it. Ted, you lead us around it like we did before," he whispered.

Ted and the others dismounted and with Ted in the lead they moved single file into the even darker woods.

They moved slowly in Indian style with as little noise as possible. After what seemed like hours, but in reality was only about thirty minutes, Ted led them back out to the road. The four troopers had heard sounds from the rebel camp, but they had seen no one. They had moved in almost absolute silence and were now past the enemy camp. They mounted their horses and resumed their single file column. Stars had come out in a sky void of clouds and there was a half-moon that provided a little light in what was a dark night.

It was almost midnight when they approached the location of the first farm they had encountered on their scout to the south. They halted on the road and Ted dismounted and moved ahead on foot. Gunn was amazed at Ted's ability to not only move in almost complete silence, but how gracefully he seemed to move. Ted seemed to slip into the woods and disappear.

After a few minutes, Ted reappeared from the pine trees. He slipped up next to Tom. "I saw no signs of life. I think we can use the road and walk the horses by the farm," he whispered.

Tom nodded his agreement and whispered his instructions to Tuck and Gunn.

The four troopers moved forward, leading their horses and keeping a hand near their mount's noses to keep them from whinnying when they might smell other horses from the farm.

After a few minutes they had successfully passed the farm. They mounted their horses and the small column continued its' march north to safety.

They slipped past the small rebel outpost that stood between them and the Union lines. It was about two hours before dawn when they reached the ferry across the Chattahoochee River. They crossed the river in silence. Each man felt exhausted. The combination of a hard physical ride and the intense emotional strain of operating behind enemy lines on a scout had taken its toll.

Gunn was tired, but he felt a genuine sense of relief when they led their horses off the ferry and onto the north bank of the river. They quickly mounted up and rode into the 22nd's camp. They left their horses in the corral after feeding and watering them. Gunn and Tuck stayed behind to wipe down and curry comb the horses, while Tom and Ted went to Sergeant Mann's tent to report.

Mann was seated on a log in front of his tent. He was smoking a pipe. He had not slept much that night, as he was anxious for his scouts to return. Each passing hour had only increased his concern. He knew the scout was dangerous, but he knew he had picked the best men in the regiment for the job. He knew from experience even good men died in a war that neither distinguished which men would die nor cared.

The sergeant saw Tom and Ted approaching through the gloom of an early dawn and he rose to his feet and extinguished his pipe, tapping it against his hand to force the remaining ashes out of it.

Both Tom and Ted came to attention in front of the sergeant.

"Private McMaster reporting, Sergeant," said Tom.

"At ease, men. What did you find on your scout to Latimer's Crossing, Mr. McMaster?"

Tom carefully recounted all the details of their scout including their run-in with the outlaws at the farm house.

Sergeant Mann listened carefully and asked few questions. "Why didn't you bypass the farmhouse with the outlaws. Surely no one would have heard you with all that ruckus goin' on?"

Tom explained how the decision was made. "I was against it, but I got outvoted by my brothers and Gunn. After it was over, I realized they were correct. We felt It was the right thing to do."

"Officially, I can't agree with you, McMaster, but unofficially I would have done the same thing," replied the sergeant.

"Good job, men. A good report. The captain will be pleased to hear it. He will be especially pleased that you saw no evidence of artillery during your scout. Take your men to the mess hall and get something to eat. All four of you have tomorrow off to sleep in. Or should I say all of today off," said the sergeant as he looked out at the slowly rising sun.

"Yes sergeant," said the two brothers. They quickly headed back to the mess hall, picking up Tuck and Gunn as they went.

The mess hall was almost empty, as the cooks were getting ready for breakfast, but they quickly made up a hot breakfast for the weary troopers.

The brothers and Gunn sat together for the first time. Each man had a plate full of eggs, ham, and best of all, fresh baked biscuits instead of hard tack. They ate in silence, washing down their breakfast with several cups of hot coffee.

Ted looked up from his cup of coffee to face Tom. "I'm sorry about votin' against you back at the farm house, but I agreed with Tuck. Pa would have stopped to help those ladies."

"Nothing to be sorry about, Ted. I was wrong, and you boys were right. I'm glad we stepped in. When we do somethin', we do it as family, except for Gunn, of course."

"Gunn may not be family, but now I feel he's one of us," said Tuck.

"I agree," said Ted. "He's got sand, and he shot that son of a bitch who tried to pull leather on Tom."

Tom looked over at Gunn, his face void of emotion. Then he extended his hand to Gunn and his face broke into what, for him, passed for a smile. "Welcome to the squad, Billy Gunn."

Gunn shook Tom's hand and then did the same with Ted and Tuck.

"Now that we got that crap over with, what you gonna do about that southern belle that seemed so taken with you, Billy Gunn?" said a smirking Tuck.

"Why are you all callin' me Billy? I've been William all of my life."

"Back where we come from, you'd be a Billy so to us that sounds a hell of a lot better than William. William sounds like you was a preacher or a judge."

"Billy it is then," said a smiling Gunn.

"Now getting back to that little southern belle who took a shine to you, Billy. Just what was that all about?" said Tuck with a grin.

"None of your damn business," replied Gunn as he tried to keep a straight face as he said it.

All three of the brothers broke into loud laughter.

From that moment on, things were different in the squad. Gunn now belonged and the three brothers had adopted him as part of their family of brothers.

The four troopers finished their breakfast and walked back to their squad area. All of them immediately went to their cots and soon the only sound from their squad area was a chorus of loud snoring.

CHAPTER TWENTY-ONE

In the following week some unusual things began happening in the camp of the 22nd Illinois Cavalry. Supply wagons kept arriving at the camp. Worn out uniforms were exchanged for new ones. Any worn or slightly worn piece of horse tack was replaced. New Spencer rifles were issued to those Troopers who still had the Sharps single shot carbines. Boxes of fresh ammunition were unloaded and stacked in the regiment's supply tent. None of this went unnoticed by the troopers of the 22nd.

"It looks like we're headed for a big push to take Atlanta," said Tom one night while they were sitting around the mess tent having supper.

"Well, we can't sit here on this side of the Chattahoochee River forever," answered Ted.

"The sooner we take Atlanta, the closer we are to getting this here war over with," said Gunn.

"I'd like to head back to Colorado Territory and our ranch," offered Tuck.

"We'd all like to go home, but that ain't gonna happen until we beat these rebel sons of bitches so bad they finally give up," said Tom.

Their conversation was interrupted by the sudden appearance of Sergeant Mann.

"Jesus Christ! You boys are cacklin' like a bunch of old maids. Ain't you got nothin' better to do?" said the sergeant.

"We are at your service, Sergeant," said Tom lazily from where he sat on the ground and making no effort to stand up.

"Bunch of lazy slackers, that's what you are," said Mann.

"What is it you want us lazy slackers to do, Sergeant?" asked Tom.

"The captain wants a scouting party to go back across the river and make sure nothing has changed with the rebs over there."

"So why us, Sergeant?" asked Ted.

"I chose you slackers because you happen to be the best scouts in the regiment and probably in all of Sherman's army. You leave at dawn. Ride all the way to Latimer's Crossing and back. This time try not to shoot anyone. Is that clear?"

"Yes, Sergeant," came the reply from the throats of all four troopers.

"Oh, I almost forgot. These are for you," said the sergeant as he tossed a set of corporal stripes to Tom McMaster. "You been promoted. Them officers up in regiment must be dumber than a box of rocks."

Tom caught the chevrons in his hand and looked at them. "I don't want to be no corporal, Sergeant."

"The army don't give a shit what you want. They decided that you're a corporal, and now you're a corporal, Corporal." Mann then laughed out loud.

"Serves you right, you damn slacker," he said and then he laughed louder and turned and walked away from the troopers.

As the four of them made their way back to their squad area, Ted, Tuck and Gunn gave Tom a good natured bad time about his promotion.

Dawn found the four of them waiting for the ferry at the north bank of the river. Gunn noticed that Tom, despite all his protesting, had sewed the corporal's chevrons on the sleeves of his uniform jacket.

Once they led their horses off the ferry and were mounted, they headed down the now familiar road at a gallop. They passed the Union outpost without bothering to stop and let the sergeant of the guard know who they were or where they were going. No one at the outpost made an attempt to stop them.

When they approached the locations where they had seen rebs before, they simply dismounted and followed Ted single file through the pine tree forest bordering the rutted, dirt road.

In about three hours they had made it to the outskirts of Latimer's Crossing. This time there were no rebel troops at the crossing. They retraced their steps back north for about an hour, and then they slipped into a nearby clearing to rest their horses and have a short lunch break. Lunch consisted for hard tack and water.

After about twenty minutes, Tom ordered them to return to the road. They did so and mounted their horses as they emerged from the woods. Tom led the troopers' column in single file. Gunn was amazed. Since they crossed the Chattahoochee River no words had been spoken. All orders had been given with hand signals. They had managed a scouting trip almost devoid of noise.

Finally, they were approaching the location of the Calhoun farm. Tom motioned for Gunn to move up next to him. When Gunn pulled his horse next to him, Tom whispered to Gunn, "I think we should stop and see how the ladies are doin'. Do you agree?"

Gunn blushed and nodded his agreement.

"A beau shouldn't go callin' on his gal without some sort of present, Gunn," said a smiling Tom as he motioned back to Tuck. Tuck rode up and produced two small sacks from his saddlebags and handed them to Gunn.

"What's this?" whispered Gunn.

"Tuck here is a little light fingered, and he managed to pay the mess tent supply area a visit last night. In them bags is a little coffee, a little sugar, a little flour, some salt, some bacon and some potatoes. Consider it the 22nd Illinois Cavalry's present to you to pass on to your gal," said a still smiling Tom.

Gunn was stunned at the gift from the brothers. He shook his head in wonder as he stuffed the bags into his saddle bags and resumed his place in line. Tom led the scouts forward and soon they were trotting into the clearing that housed the Calhoun place.

The old darkie was working in a large garden located on the far side of the farm house. When he first sighted the troopers, he reacted in a panic. Then he saw who the riders were and he stopped in his tracks. Then the old darkie broke loose and ran into the farmhouse.

By the time the four troopers had reined in their horses in front of the farmhouse, Mrs. Calhoun and her two daughters had burst through the front door and onto the front porch.

"Good day, Mrs. Calhoun," said Tom McMaster as he removed his kepi.

"Good day, Mr. McMaster. Oh, wait. I see now it is Corporal McMaster. Congratulations on your promotion," said Mrs. Calhoun.

"We thought we would stop by and see how you ladies were doin'," said Tom.

"We've been doing fine, sir. We thank you all again for saving us from those filthy wretches."

"I see those wretches have disappeared. I do hope it was in the custody of the local sheriff," said Tom.

"Indeed it was, Corporal McMaster. He herded them off like shorn sheep," replied Mrs. Calhoun. "Thank you again for all your help."

"We were pleased to be of service, ma'am. If it isn't too much trouble, Billy Gunn here would like a word with your daughter, Anna."

"We'd be honored to have Mr. Gunn address Anna, Corporal."

By now Gunn's face was beet red from blushing. He was thoroughly embarrassed by Tom's words, but he soon lost his fear as Anna stepped forward and looked up at him. Her eyes shone and they seemed to penetrate straight into his heart.

Gunn dismounted and handed his reins to Tuck. He reached into the saddle bags and took out the two sacks. Holding a sack in each hand, Gunn stepped forward and faced Anna.

He tried to speak to her, but nothing came out. His mount and throat were as dry as the dirt road he had traveled here on.

Anna saved him by speaking first. "Is that something you all brought for me, Mr. Gunn?" she asked.

"Yes, ma'am," choked out a befuddled Gunn. "We thought you and your family could use these." With that he held out the sacks for her inspection. Anna looked into the bags and almost squealed in delight.

"My goodness. There's coffee, sugar, bacon, flour, salt, and potatoes. How can we ever thank you all!"

Anna turned and handed the sacks to her mother and her sister. Then she turned to face a still red-faced Gunn.

"I'm glad you all came back and thank you all again for the gifts. We can certainly use them. Coffee and sugar are so dear in these times."

"You're very welcome, Miss Anna."

Anna stepped closer to Gunn. "Will you be coming back, again, Mr. Gunn?" she said in a low throaty voice.

"Like I told you before, Miss Anna. I'll be back. I promise," said Gunn.

"Like I said before, Mr. Gunn. I'll be waiting." With that Anna stepped back next to her mother and sister.

"Mount up Gunn, we're burning daylight," said Tom.

Gunn took the reins from Tuck and mounted his horse. Tom turned his horse and led the others out of the farm yard and back to the road. Gunn was the last in the single file line and he turned to look back at the farm house, he could see Anna waiving at him. This time she blew him a kiss. His throat and mouth dried up all over again.

The scout party reached the ferry in the mid-afternoon. Tuck, Ted and Gunn headed to the mess tent to get an early supper, while Tom trudged on to Sergeant Mann's tent to make his report.

Apparently it was a short report, because Tom joined them in less than twenty minutes. The four men savored their supper and sat on the ground next to the mess tent drinking hot coffee and discussing the day's scout. No one mentioned the stop at the Calhoun farm. The three brothers respected Gunn and they were a little envious of the lovely Anna's attraction to Gunn. It was hard to forget they were fighting a war, but today had been a welcome ray of sunshine in what was both a dark and dangerous time in their young lives.

Chapter Twenty-Two

Gunn was sound asleep in his tent when an urgent bugle call pierced the quiet of the dark night. His brain registered the importance of the music before the rest of him did.

Gunn rolled out of bed and jumped into his uniform. He slipped his boots on and grabbed his Colt and placed it in his holster. He reached down under the bed and snatched his Spencer and then dashed out of his tent.

Gunn had no idea why the bugle call for assembly was being sounded in the dark of night, but he reached the I Troop parade ground and fell in line with his squad mates who had somehow beat him there.

Captain Dexter strode to the front of the assembled troop. He spoke in a loud and clear, but urgent voice.

"It's boots and saddles, men. The supply train has been attacked just two miles west of the depot. We ride to attack the rebels!"

Sergeant Mann then stepped forward and yelled for all to hear," Get to your damn horses and be ready to ride in ten minutes. Assemble just south of the coral. Now move!"

The ninety-three troopers of I Troop quickly ran to the corral and began saddling horses. Within ten minutes every man was mounted and assembled in columns of twos.

Captain Dexter appeared at the front of the column along with Lt. Blust and after raising his right arm, he brought it forward and shouted, "Forward ho!"

I Troop moved out and once on the road paralleling the Chattahoochee River they moved at a fast walk. When they had passed all the other Union encampments along the river road, they broke into a trot.

Gunn knew the standard order for Union Cavalry was to move at a walk, but he understood the need for more speed if they were to get to the site of the attack in time to do any good.

When the column got near the site of the attack on the supply train, they could hear gunfire. They could see the flashes of rifles and pistols resembling fireflies in the darkness of the night.

The column came to a halt at the signal of Captain Dexter. "Sergeant Mann!" he yelled.

"Yes, sir," replied Mann.

"Get your scouts forward and find out what the hell is going on and where the enemy is located," ordered Dexter.

"Yes, sir. Corporal McMaster, your squad to the head of the column," he bellowed out.

Quickly Tom, Ted, Tuck, and Gunn had ridden to the front of the column and turned their horses to face the sergeant.

"Scout ahead and find out what's going on and where the rebels are. See if you can find the best way to hit them."

"Yes, Sergeant," replied Corporal McMaster. Tom gave a short hand signal and he and the other three troopers swung their horses in the direction of the attack and were soon at a full gallop.

When the four riders were within four hundred yards of the train attack, Ted called them to a halt.

"Ted, you and Gunn circle around to the left and see what's there. I'll take Tuck and we'll move to the right. Do it quick and meet back here as fast as you can, boys."

The other three troopers nodded their agreement and rode off into the darkness.

Ten minutes later, the four men had returned to their original starting point.

"I saw about two dozen rebs riding around the rear of the train, shooting it up. What did you and Tuck see, Ted?" asked Tom.

"We saw about a dozen of them rebs by the front of the train. They piled what looks like tree trunks on the tracks to stop the train. The boys in the train are holdin' their own and givin' the rebs a good scrap."

"Let's head back to the captain," said Tom. He turned his horse and galloped off with the other three troopers in close pursuit.

Tom pulled his horse to a halt right in front of Captain Dexter. He saluted the captain. "Corporal McMaster reporting, sir. We got a train stopped by a blockade on the tracks. About two dozen rebs are attacking the back of the train and about a dozen more are attacking the engine and the front of the train. Our boys are fightin' back and givin' a good account of themselves, sir."

Captain Dexter turned to Sergeant Mann. "Sergeant, do you have any suggestions?"

"With the Captain's permission, I would take half the troop and come in behind the rebs at the rear of the train and charge them. Have the other half of the troop attack from the front and drive the bastards into themselves while the boys in the train are shooting at them from their flank."

"Excellent suggestion, Sergeant. Lieutenant Blust, you take half the troop and attack from the front of the train. I'll take the sergeant and the other half of the troop and attack from the rear of the train. Wait for the bugle call and then charge the rebels. Is that clear, Lieutenant?"

"Yes sir," replied Lieutenant Blust.

Within a few minutes the two sections of I Troop had separated and were moving quickly to their assigned start positions.

When Captain Dexter was positive Lieutenant Blust had enough time to get into position, he ordered the troop bugler to signal "Charge."

The bugle call reached the ears of the rebel raiders even amid the crashing sounds of rifles and pistols being fired at close range. Before it dawned on them what the bugle call meant, waves of blue clad mounted troopers emerged from the darkness. Their pistols fired and the resulting flashes lit up small cones of daylight in the middle of the dark night. Just as planned, the rebels retreated from the mounted attacks and ended up running into each other near the middle of the stalled supply train.

The pistol shots from I Troop were joined by the rifle fire from the Union troops riding on the supply train. The rebels had only one avenue for escape. They had I Troop to the front and rear and to the north was the train filled with Union soldiers firing their rifles. Those rebels who were still in the saddle turned to the south and raced into the darkness as they fled for their lives.

The men of I Troop followed in rapid pursuit of the fleeing rebel horsemen. Two of the closest pursuers were Tuck and Gunn. Gunn noted several of the rebel horses were without riders. As he and Tuck drew closer to the fleeing rebels, Tuck took aim at a rebel and missed. Close behind him rode Gunn and when he fired, the rebel threw up his hands and fell from his saddle. His body made a hard sounding thump as he hit the hard ground.

Suddenly the bugle sounding "Recall" pierced the night. Both Gunn and Tuck reined their horses to a halt.

"Dag nab it. We almost had 'em," said a disgusted Tuck.

"We ain't seen the last of Johnny Reb, Tuck. You'll get plenty more chances to tangle with them. Be careful what you wish for. We had the advantage tonight because the captain was smart enough to ask the sergeant for advice and then he was smart enough to use it. When I was in the infantry, I seen more than a few officers who got no business giving orders in a fight. I don't aim to get killed just 'cause some greenhorn officer thinks he's smarter than a wily old veteran sergeant."

"I suppose you're right, but we were so close, Billy."

"Close don't count, Tuck. Hittin' the nail on the head counts. Second place don't cut it."

The two troopers wheeled their horses and headed back to where I Troop was assembling. It was still dark, so Captain Dexter had a group of troopers helping the train crew and the train guards remove the tree trunks from the tracks. The troopers used their horses and ropes to help drag the trees off the tracks.

Once the track was clear, the supply train resumed its trip to the train depot. Captain Dexter had I Troop make a temporary camp at the attack site. He wanted to wait until daylight to collect the dead and wounded rebels along with any weapons.

The train guards had suffered two killed and seven wounded. All of them had been loaded into a boxcar and were headed to the supply depot.

The troopers of I Troop picketed their horses using their picket pins and proceeded to make small campfires to add some light. A few enterprising souls had produced coffee pots and coffee and were busy preparing their treasured brew.

Captain Dexter and Lieutenant Blust sat on their haunches next to a small fire a trooper had prepared for them. Sergeant

Mann entered the ring of light provided by the campfire, and he came to attention and salted the captain.

"Sergeant Mann reporting, Captain."

Dexter returned Mann's salute. "At ease, Sergeant. Let's hear your report."

"We had two troopers slightly wounded, sir. There were no other casualties in I Troop."

"Excellent, Sergeant. How about the rebels?"

"We've found eleven dead and nine wounded, sir. I don't' think two of the wounded are goin' to make it, sir."

"Good job, Sergeant. Where are the rebel prisoners and dead?"

"We loaded the dead on the train, sir. We have the prisoners tied up and under guard. We'll herd them back to camp in the morning and turn them over to the Provost Marshall, sir."

"Very good, Sergeant." The Captain paused and then looked back at the sergeant. "You gave me good advice, Sergeant. I appreciate it."

"Yes, sir," replied Sergeant Mann.

"You're dismissed, Sergeant."

'Yes, sir," replied Sergeant Mann. Mann then turned and disappeared back into the darkness when he stepped outside of the circle of light cast by the small camp fire.

McMaster's squad had made a small campfire and it had attracted other troopers as well as their own. Tuck and Gunn had picketed the squad's four horses nearby and they were contentedly grazing on what grasses grew close to them.

The troopers gathered around the small camp fire were surprisingly quiet considering they had just come from engaging the enemy in combat at night.

One of the other troopers took a harmonica out of his shirt pocket and began to softly play. He played simple songs at first and then as he gained confidence, he began to get bolder in his choices. When he began to play the *Battle Hymn of the Republic,* the troopers began to join in with song. The first time though the song, saw the singing grow in force and volume as other nearby troopers joined in. The other troopers at the fire urged the musician to play it again. He did and this time over fifty men nearby joined in the singing of the Union army's favorite song. The night air carried the sound, and it floated over the battle area like a message from the gods. The harmonica player took requests of songs he knew how to play and he finished up with *Tenting tonight.*

Finally, the sun began to rise and the darkness of the night gave way to the faint rays of the dawn. Troopers rose from their resting spots on the ground and sought their mounts. The troop sergeants, including Sergeant Mann, began getting their men organized, and finally I Troop was on the road in columns of two and ready to ride.

Sergeant Mann rode out to where Captain Dexter and Lieutenant Blust were astride their horses.

"The troop is all present and accounted for and ready to proceed at your order, Captain," said the sergeant.

The captain and the lieutenant rode to the head of the column. Once there, Captain Dexter raised his right arm and then brought it forward with the command, "Forward ho!"

I Troop rode back to their camp at the army dictated pace of a walk. Once they reached the corral, they were dismissed and the troopers began the job of feeding and watering their horses as well as wiping them down and curry combing them.

As soon as the troopers of I Troop finished with their horses, they quickly made their way to the mess tent for breakfast. The troopers stood in line and took as much food on their plates as they could convince the cooks to give them. That didn't stop many of them from coming back for seconds.

Nothing makes a trooper hungrier than surviving a night battle. I Troop was no exception to the rule.

After they finished their breakfast, the McMaster brothers and Gunn retreated to the solitude of their tents and the comfort of their cots.

Gunn found himself to be restless and sleep eluded him. He sat in his bunk and rummaged through his saddle bags. After a thorough search, he found some paper and a pencil. He sat on his cot and tried to write a letter to his father. He had difficulty trying to tell his father on paper what he had experienced. He gave up trying and just told his father that he was well and now in the 22nd Illinois Cavalry, so if his father chose to write him, the army would know where to deliver the letter.

When he was finished, he thought about Anna Calhoun. He thought about writing her, but he had no idea of how to address such a letter. In addition, he was clueless about what to say to her. He knew places like plantations in the south had names. He was pretty sure the farm house he had seen was hardly a plantation, but other than Anna's last name, he knew little about her. She had a mother and a sister. Gunn wondered if she had a father or brother, and if they were in the Confederate Army. Would he find himself fighting against the father or brother of the woman who now constantly filled his mind?

Gunn gave up on the letter writing idea and laid down on his cot. In just a few minutes, he was fast asleep.

Gunn woke up about noon because Tuck was shaking his shoulder. "Get up, sleepy head. It's time for lunch. Time to go."

Gunn had not even undressed, so he put on his boots, slipped the Colt into his holster, and he was ready to go. He joined the McMaster brothers, and they walked down to the mess tent.

After the four men had been through the mess tent line, they gathered under a nearby tree for shade and sat on the ground to eat their lunch.

"Before we eat, I think we should take a moment to thank the lord that we came through last night's fight without any harm coming to any of us," said Ted.

"Amen to that," said Tom.

"Anybody want to say some words?" asked Ted.

Tuck surprised his brothers and Gunn by speaking up. "Thank you lord for looking out for my brothers Tom and Ted and my friend, Billy Gunn."

"Amen," said the other three men in chorus.

After they had finished their lunch, the four men sat in the shade of the tree and sipped their hot coffee.

"Wonder why the rebs tried to hit the supply train so close to the camps. That don't make good sense," said Ted.

"It might be that the rebs are having a hard time getting' supplies and were just desperate enough to try to hit the train where it's close to the river. They probably know enough fords to get across without us seein' them," said Tom.

"Either way, it was not a smart move, and they really paid for it. Last night was like shooting fish in a barrel," said Gunn.

"The guy I shot was totally surprised to see me riding at him," said Tuck.

"Surprise was on our side last night," said Tom.

"If we had used ten troopers as a blocking force between the rebs and the river, we would have wiped them out," said Gunn.

"I wonder why the captain didn't do that?" asked Ted.

"It was night, we had to organize quickly, and we weren't sure what we were up against," said Tom. "The captain went with what he thought was best at the time."

"I'm just glad he asked Sergeant Mann for advice," said Gunn. "We coulda' just rode in there and shot it out and ended up getting shot by our own men."

"That's why I hate having to fight in the dark," said Tom. "You can't be sure of anything and like Billy said, you could get shot accidentally by our own."

"I'm just glad it's over and none of us got hurt," said Tuck.

The other three men nodded their agreement. The little coffee left in their cups had cooled and they tossed the remains out on the ground.

The foursome got to their feet and made their way down to the river where they washed out their plates and cups. They headed back to their squad area, carrying their dinnerware.

They were halfway back to their area when two troopers stepped from behind a tent and blocked their way.

Standing in front of the four men were two troopers armed with sabers in their right hands. Gunn recognized Whitehouse and Jones. He had almost forgotten about them with all that had happened. He realized they must have been with the troop in the attack on the train raiders last night, although he did not remember seeing them.

"We got no beef with you and your brothers, McMaster. It's Gunn we got a bone to pick with," said Whitehouse, his face red with rage and twisted with anger.

"Billy's part of my squad. You got a problem with him, you got a problem with me and my brothers," responded Tom.

A look of shock and surprise came over the faces of Whitehouse and Jones. This was something they obviously had not expected.

"But we heard you didn't trust Gunn and were doing your best to force him out of your squad like you done with everyone else that got assigned to you," said a bewildered Jones.

"Well, you heard wrong. Now get the hell out of our way or we'll beat the shit out of you," said Tom.

"We just had our breakfast and we could use a little exercise to work it off," said Ted with an evil smile on his face.

"Good way to start the day is to beat the crap out of a couple of cowards," chimed in Tuck.

"This is my fight," said Gunn. "You boys stay out of it. The day I can't handle a couple of hombres like these two is the day I hang up my guns."

Tom and his brothers stepped back to see how Gunn was going to handle this.

"So what were you boys planning to do?" said Gunn. "Were you planning to cut me up with them sabers you're carryin'?"

"Let me give you two a little advice. Never come to a gun fight with a knife or a saber," said Gunn as he pulled the Colt out of his holster. "Which of you wants it first?" he said.

Neither Whitehouse nor Jones had expected Gunn to be armed and both men began backing away in the face of having to look down the barrel of Gunn's Colt.

"This ain't over, Gunn," said Whitehouse. "We'll deal with you later."

With that he and Jones began to back away and when they were behind the tent, they turned and ran as fast as they could.

Gunn and Tuck and Ted broke into laughter. Tom did not join in. He had a grim look on his face.

"You don't think those two are funny?" asked Tuck

Tom did not answer immediately. The grim look did not leave his face. "Those two are stupid. You can knock them down and they'll get up and ask for more. That makes them dangerous. They aren't smart enough to know when they are overmatched. In the end there is only one way to deal with them," said Tom.

"What way is that?" asked Tuck.

"Kill them," said Tom grimly.

"Killing them two bumkins would get us a firing squad," said an astonished Ted.

"There's other ways of killing assholes like that," retorted Tom.

"What other ways?" persisted Tuck.

"With any luck, the rebs will do the job for us," said Tom. "But if they don't, we might just stand by and refuse to support them."

"I know they're assholes, Tom, but I don't think I could do that. They may be assholes, but they're our assholes," said Gunn.

"Maybe so," said Tom, "But I think those two will force you to change your mind, Billy."

The four men continued on their walk and soon were back in their squad area. All four headed to their tents to make up for a lost night of sleep. Soon their snoring dominated the sounds in their squad area.

Dawn the next day brought heavy rain and most of I Troop remained in their tents, grateful for the chance to stay dry. They donned their slickers for their trips to the mess tent and the need to meet nature's calls. Otherwise they sat in tents and talked and played cards.

The rain stopped early in the evening. Shortly after the rain ended, Sergeant Mann appeared in the squad area. He stopped in front of Tom and Ted's tent and motioned for Tom to come out and join him.

Once Tom emerged from the tent, Mann began slowly walking towards the nearby pine tree line that surrounding the squad area clearing. When he got to the tree line he stopped and turned to face Tom.

"I've been ordered to assemble my best scouts for a patrol up the river. The mission is to check all the crossing points from here to the east. The captain wants to know rebel strength and activity at every crossing. You are to lead the scout and add another squad to yours. We also want to know if there are any hidden fords that we are unaware of. Is that all clear, Tom?"

"Yes, Sergeant."

"Very good, Tom. I know you don't need me to tell you this, but be very careful. Don't get into any scrapes with the rebs. Your job is to observe and not be seen. Is that clear?"

"Yes, Sergeant."

"One more thing, Tom. Rumor has it that Sherman has ordered a series of large cavalry raids behind the Confederate lines to destroy the railroads that are supplying Atlanta. He wants to cut them off and force Hood out of his trenches around Atlanta. I heard the captain talkin' to the lieutenant and the 22nd Illinois would be one of nine regiments of cavalry assigned to General Stoneman."

"How many troopers would that be, Sergeant?"

"By my guess it would be about five thousand troopers plus support wagons."

"On those narrow, rutted, dirt roads! I can't imagine how long that line of cavalry would be. Why it could be miles from the front to the rear of that line."

"My thoughts, exactly, Tom. Maybe the country gets more open to the east, but I ain't sure."

Tom had been as far south as Latimer's Crossing and he had seen very little open country that would be more suitable to cavalry operations.

"There's one more thing to the rumor that I heard and I think you should know," said Sergeant Mann.

"What's that, Sergeant?"

"The objective is to cut the Macon and Western Railroad, but after that's done, Stoneman has permission to move south at his discretion, whatever the hell that means."

"Why would we move south? That's deeper into rebel territory. The purpose of a raid is to get in and get out."

"Apparently General Stoneman has decided that we should move south to Macon and capture the town and liberate the Union officers held in the prison there. I think that name of the place is Camp Oglethorpe."

"That's one hell of an ambitious plan. How many Union officers are being held in that prison?"

"The number I heard was around fifteen hundred."

"If we were lucky enough to get to Macon and take the city and the prison, how the hell would we get back through the reb lines with fifteen hundred freed prisoners?

"I ain't got no idea, but that's why I wear sergeant's stripes and not officer bars," said an exasperated Mann.

Tom looked at Sergeant Mann with a shocked expression on his face. "Unbelievable," he muttered.

"Well, I probably told you more than I should, but I figure you got a right to know since you're gonna be stickin' you neck out on this trip, same as me."

With that the sergeant turned and started walking back toward the long line of tents. Tom followed behind the sergeant. His mind was racing at a mile a minute. He knew they were planning on an attack, but cavalry raids behind the rebel lines with a force larger than he could have imagined was a complete shock to him. Add to that the idea to extend the raid to Macon and the prison there was almost beyond his comprehension.

It was boots and saddles for the eight troopers the next morning. They met at the corral and were soon mounted and ready to begin their scout up the north bank of the Chattahoochee River.

Tom's rank as a corporal put him in charge of the scout. He decided to have Ted and Gunn scout ahead of the patrol. They moved out in the dark of the night at the Union army approved pace of a walk.

CHAPTER TWENTY-THREE

The eight horsemen made their way north traveling on the road paralleling the bank of the Chattahoochee River. After about an hour of riding through the darkness of the night in relative silence, the scouting party reached Pace's Ferry.

The two lead scouts reached the ferry about fifteen minutes ahead of the rest of the scouting party. Ted and Gunn found the Union sentries alert and the ferry secured to their side of the river. A short conversation with the sergeant of the guard at the ferry confirmed they had seen no activity from the rebels across the river other than the occasional movement of a sentry. They had heard no unusual noises or any increased activity from the rebel side of the river.

Ted and Gunn waited at the ferry for the rest of their party to arrive. When they did, Ted informed Tom of what they had learned from the sergeant of the guard at the ferry. After Tom had heard Ted out, he motioned for them to resume their scout.

Ted and Gunn spurred their horses and quickly disappeared into the darkness engulfing the river road. Tom then had the rest of his scout follow at a slower pace.

Another hour on their scout brought Ted and Gunn to Power's Ferry. Again they found the Union sentries alert and were challenged when they approached the ferry. Ted talked to the sergeant of the guard and heard almost an exact duplication of what he had heard at Pace's Ferry. After a few minutes wait, Ted and Gunn were joined by the rest of the scouting party. Ted gave his report to Tom, and then he and Gunn again turned and galloped into the darkness shrouding the river road.

As Ted and Gunn rode, the approaching heat of the day had caused fog to rise from the edges of the river. Now they had fog and darkness to contend with. Ted slowed their pace to make sure they didn't suddenly come upon sentries who might shoot first and ask questions later when they were surprised in the dark while on guard duty.

Soon they reached Cochran's Ford. Here they discovered the two sentries were sitting on the ground with their backs resting against the trunks of large cypress trees. Both soldiers were fast asleep.

Ted slipped from his saddle and handed his reins to Gunn. He slipped up next to the two sleeping soldiers and drew his Colt. Keeping the Colt in his right hand, Ted used his left hand to jostle the shoulder of the closest sentry. The soldier suddenly awoke and gasped as he saw the barrel of the Colt pointed at him.

"Wake up your partner, soldier," said Ted. "You're damn lucky I'm not a reb. If I was, you'd have your throat cut by now."

The soldier scrambled to his feet and grabbed his still sleeping companion by his shoulder until he awoke. Both soldiers were scared and apologetic to Ted.

"Don't be sucking up to me, boy. I ain't your sergeant. Where is your sergeant of the guard?"

The soldier ran down to the edge of the river and turned to his right as he disappeared into the bushes that lined the river bank. He soon reappeared with a sleepy sergeant in tow.

"What the hell is going on here?" bellowed the sergeant when he caught sight of Ted and the still mounted Gunn.

Ted holstered his Colt and looked at the blustering sergeant. "Both your boys were asleep on duty, Sergeant. I'd make sure that didn't happen again if I were you," said Ted.

The sergeant blustered a bit and then had the good sense to shut up. Ted asked him about rebel activity and the sergeant told him that there had been no activity at all for the past two days.

Ted thanked the sergeant and mounted his horse. He and Gunn rode back on the road the way they had come for about a hundred yards. There they halted and waited for Tom and the rest of the scout to arrive. When they did, Ted told Tom what had happened and what the sergeant had said about rebel activity.

"Them boys are lucky they're still alive," said Tom. "Head on out to Johnson's Ferry, Ted."

Ted touched the brim of his kepi in reply, and he and Gunn wheeled their horses and moved quickly back on the river road to continue their scout.

As they rode through the foggy darkness, Gunn could make out stars above him in patches where there was little or no fog. Ted put up his right hand to signal a halt and Gunn moved his horse next to Ted's when they both were stopped.

"Johnson's Ferry should be just ahead," said Ted.

"How can you be sure?" asked Gunn.

"I smell the smoke of their campfire," replied Ted.

Gunn sniffed the air, and he too caught the scent of wood smoke.

The two horsemen kept their mounts to a slow walk, and soon they could see the ferry through the fog.

The sentries at Johnson's Ferry were alert and they challenged the two horsemen. After Ted and Gunn identified themselves, one of the sentries led them to their sergeant of the guard.

Ted asked the sergeant about rebel activity and the sergeant told him that the rebels had been very quiet, too quiet in his estimation.

Ted inquired if they had done any probing across the river to see why it was so quiet.

"Mister, I been shot at too many times in this here war to be stupid enough to ask to get shot at. I'm just happy the damn rebs are being quiet at my post," replied the sergeant.

Ted stifled a laugh and thanked the sergeant for his information. He and Gunn returned to the road and waited for Tom and the rest of their scout to arrive.

When they did appear out of the fog and darkness, Ted filled Ted in on what he had learned from the sergeant. Tom just nodded as he listened to Ted's report.

"What's next?" asked Tom

"Our last stop is a place called Shallow Ford. Once we get there, our scout is over and we can head for home," said Ted.

"Get us to Shallow Ford and we can end this foolish scout. I ain't heard nothing that sounds like it was worth this trip," said Tom.

Ted's answer was to touch the brim of his kepi with his finger, and then he and Gunn were racing off into the fog and darkness of river road.

After about a mile, Ted slowed the pace to a trot and he pointed to the east with his finger and smiled at Gunn. Gunn looked where Tom had pointed and he could see the beginning of some light on the horizon. Dawn could not be that far away. Gunn looked forward to the sun. He did not care for the heat it brought, but it would quickly burn off the fog that kept confounding their vision.

About half an hour later, the eastern skyline was getting even lighter. Ted brought their pace down to a walk, and Gunn slowed his horse to the same pace.

Ted raised his right arm in a silent signal to halt. Gunn complied and the two horsemen stopped on the river road. They were side by side and Ted leaned over to Gunn and whispered, "Do you see anything wrong?"

Gunn swiveled his head around slowly as he took in all their surroundings. The fog has dissipated somewhat, but he could see nothing. He sniffed the air and could only detect the smells he associated with a river. He listened and all he could hear with the heavy breathing of their horse.

Gunn shook his head from side to side in a silent answer to Ted.

Ted whispered to Gunn. "This time of morning the birds would be stirring. I don't hear nothin'. Not even bugs. That ain't right."

Ted dismounted and motioned for Gunn to do the same. They walked slowly and quietly forward, leading their horses as they moved in single file with Ted in the lead.

Both men moved Indian style to keep any noise to a minimum. When Ted could make out where the road split off to the ford over the river, he stopped and handed Gunn his reins.

Ted moved into the brush on the river side of the road and quickly disappeared from Gunn's sight. After a couple of minutes, he reappeared and walked silently over to where Gunn stood, holding the horses.

"The sentries are dead," whispered Ted. "Both of them have their throats cut. I found the tents of the rest of the ford guard, and all four of them are dead as well. Bodies are still warm, so whoever did it ain't far from here."

"Did you see anyone else?" whispered Gunn.

"Nope. I saw fresh tracks. They were still wet with water from crossing the ford over the river. They headed north. I think it was a raiding party of rebs."

"What do we do?" asked Gunn.

"We go back up the road and meet Tom and the rest of the scout. I think he'll want to set up an ambush and catch these bastards when they try to cross back over the river," said Ted.

Gunn nodded his agreement, and both men mounted their horses and headed back the way they had come.

When Ted and Gunn found Tom and the rest of the scouts, they had a hurried conference about what Ted and Gunn had found at the ford.

"I think Ted is right about setting up an ambush for those rebs when they return to cross the river. Any thoughts on the best way to do it?" asked Tom.

There was a minute or two of silence as each man tried to think of the best way to ambush the rebels. Gunn was the first to speak up.

"I ain't sure about how to set up an ambush in the cavalry, but in my time in the infantry we would set up an L-shaped ambush."

"What in blazes is an L-shaped ambush?" asked Tom.

"We set up a line of four men in the brush against the river and then the other four men on a line from the river that makes a right angle with the line of men on the river. That way there is no danger of any of us shooting at our own men. It creates what my old sergeant called a kill zone," explained Gunn.

"That makes good sense to me," said Ted.

"Me too," chimed in Tuck.

"Any of you boys got a problem with this plan?" Tom asked the other four troopers. They were all in agreement with the plan.

Ted asked a question that had been on Gunn's mind as well. "What do we do with the dead sentries, Tom?"

"We leave them were they are. We do anything else and the rebels will know something is wrong."

"Where do you want us positioned, Tom?" asked Gunn.

Tom thought for a moment and then spoke to the men. "Me, Gunn, and my brothers will make the line coming from the river and you four boys will be in the brush along the banks of the river where the ford crosses it. Everyone in agreement?"

The other seven troopers nodded.

"All right. Everyone get into position. No smoking, no talking, and no sleeping. Stay in position and keep alert. When the rebels are in the kill zone, I'll fire first and then the rest of you join in. Is that clear?" said Tom.

"Yes, Corporal," replied the other seven troopers in an uneven chorus.

"We'll picket the horses back in the trees, about two hundred yards back," said Tom.

"Why so far back?" asked Tuck.

"Less chance of anyone finding them or of anyone hearing them," said Tom. "A little walk will do you good, little brother," Tom said with a wry smile on his face.

The scouts led their mounts back into the woods about two hundred yards and used picket pins to secure them. Then they returned to the ford.

Tom helped the four troopers find good spots along the river bank that lay in line with the ford. Then he took Gunn and his brothers out away from the river on a line from the position of the last man he had placed on the river bank. He positioned them every fifteen yards from the river bank. Now the men's hidden positions conformed to the L-shape he wanted.

Gunn lay on the cold, damp ground with his Spencer in his right hand. The night was still fairly dark although the fog had lessened. He moved around on the ground to try to find the most comfortable positon. He was worried about chigger bites. He hated chiggers. Soon it was apparent that chiggers were not his only worry. Swarms of mosquitoes located him and buzzed about his face and ears as well as his hands. He managed to remain quiet, but he passed the time by capturing and killing as many mosquitoes with his fingers as he could.

After almost an hour had passed, Gunn felt the urge to take a piss. He knew that wasn't possible in his current situation. The rebs could show up at any time and he had no desire to be standing there with his dick in his hand instead of his rifle. He fought back the urge and tried to occupy his mind with other things. The image of Anna Calhoun drifted into his mind, and he forgot about his swollen bladder.

Gunn's sensitive ears heard something beside the buzzing of pesky mosquitoes. He heard muted voices and the sounds of horses' hooves coming down the road. He peered through the few early rays of daylight preceding the dawn. His eyes adjusted, and soon he could make out a group of riders. He watched them approach the ford. He could make out seven riders and all of them wearing a combination of grey and butternut. They were the reb raiders headed for the ford.

Gunn pulled back on the hammer of his Spencer, cocking it, and brought the barrel up so he could get a rebel rider in his rifle sights. He held his breath and waited for the rebels to get in the trap and for Tom to take the first shot.

Without warning a shot rang out breaking the silence of the night. Gunn thought he heard a muffled yell, "It's a trap."

With that shot all hell broke loose. The rebel raiders were on the edge of the kill zone and they brought their horses to a halt and began to mill around and shout.

Tom had not fired and he quickly realized the rebels had left a guard hidden at the crossing and he and his men had missed finding him. Now the hidden rebel guard had managed to warn the raiders about their ambush.

"Nothing works out the way you plan it," thought Tom and he opened fire on the raiders with the Spencer.

He saw the raider nearest him fall from the saddle. Then everyone began shooting. Flame shout out from the muzzles of the rifles and pistols being fired and for brief seconds, the darkness was replaced in small areas with the flash of gunpowder producing light.

Three of the raiders laid the quirt to their horses and made a dash for the ford across the river. The other three managed to get their frightened horses under control enough to follow their fellow raiders to the ford.

This was the worse decision the raiders could have made as now they were in the center of the kill zone Tom had set up.

The Union scouts fired their repeating Spencer rifles and the result was five more raiders being shot from their saddles. Their horses continued across the ford over the river and back to the Confederate lines.

The surviving raider followed the fleeing rider less horses to the ford and he was halfway across the river when Gunn's Spencer fired and dropped the rebel from his saddle. His body made a huge splash in the river and then it disappeared under the flowing water.

"Be careful," shouted Ted. "That damned rebel guard is still out there. Stay where you are. Ted and I will flush him out."

Tom motioned to his brother Ted, and they slipped through the brush, Tom on one side of the ford and Ted on the other. Before they reached the ford, a shot rang out and then a scream. Both the shot and the ensuing scream had come from the banks of the river.

As Ted reached his side of the ford, a figure burst from a clump of bushes and attempted to run across the ford to the other bank. Ted recognized the butternut colored shirt the man was wearing, and shot him in the back with his Spencer. The man let out a grunt and pitched forward into the river. He too, soon disappeared under the surface of the river.

"Stay put," shouted Ted. "We ain't done checking for other reb guards."

After Tom and Ted had carefully checked the brush around the river ford, Tom called out to the others.

"All clear. Come on out and let's see what we got here," said Tom.

Gunn, Tuck, and three of the other troopers arose from their hiding places. A quick check by Ted discovered the other trooper had been shot in the back by the rebel guard. The trooper was dead.

"This was my fault," said Tom. "I shoulda had us check the area for a possible guard. God damn it."

"Even then we coulda missed him," said Ted. "He managed to stay hidden real good. I didn't hear him or smell him and part of this is on me."

"Sometimes bad things happen, no matter how good your plan," said Gunn. This ambush was my idea."

"Maybe so, Billy," said Tom. "But it was a damn good idea and for the most part it worked. Still I hate losing a man."

A pall of silence fell on the seven troopers. There wasn't much any of them could think of to say and privately they were all glad the dead trooper wasn't them.

"Tuck, you and Billy go get the horses. We'll tie our casualty to his horse and take him back to camp," said Tom.

"His name was Ben, Ben Sawyer," said one of the other three troopers. Gunn recognized him as Trooper Barnes.

"I'm sorry, Trooper. I didn't know his name," said an embarrassed Tom.

"With the Corporal's permission, I'll take care of his body. I'll tie it to his horse and lead it back to camp," said Barnes.

"I'd be pleased if you would. Thank you, Trooper Barnes," said Tom.

Barnes stayed with the body of the dead trooper while Gunn and Tuck went back into the woods and returned with the horses. Gunn helped Barnes lift the lifeless body of his friend Ben over the saddle of his horse and assisted with tying him to his saddle.

Meanwhile, Tom and the others checked the bodies of the slain rebel raiders for any papers. When they were finished, they pulled the bodies to the side of the road and laid them out, side by side.

Then they did the same with the bodies of the dead Union guards. Ted then rode up the rode to where he thought the campsite of the river ford guards was located.

Ted returned about half an hour later with a Union patrol from the camp. The sergeant of the guard talked with Tom and thanked him for avenging his men. He then took charge of the bodies.

Tom and the remaining scouts mounted their horses and slowly made their way back the way they had come on the river road. Barnes brought up the rear leading his dead friend's horse with its sad burden.

Chapter Twenty-Four

It was well past dawn when the scouts returned to the camp of the 22nd Illinois Cavalry. All seven troopers were exhausted. The long ride coupled with the adrenaline rush of a night combat had drained them physically and emotionally.

Tom and Trooper Barnes left their horses at the corral and led the horse bearing the body of Ben Sawyer back to his squad area. Ted, Tuck, Gunn and the other two troopers fed and watered all of the horses. Then they rubbed them down and curry combed them.

When they were finished, they stopped by the mess tent and while some of them filled their plates with a hot breakfast, Ted, Tuck, and Gunn had only coffee and some fresh biscuits. They were still too tightly wound up to eat. Gunn had learned combat did that to a man. It took you to a place unfamiliar, and you had to allow your body and mind to return to normal before you had an appetite.

Soon they were joined by Tom and Trooper Barnes. They too only had coffee and biscuits. The troopers sat in the shade of an old oak tree and sipped their coffee and nibbled on their biscuits. No one spoke. The only sound from their group was the sound of thirsty men slurping hot coffee.

They had not been there long before Sergeant Mann appeared. He motioned for Tom to join him and they moved away from the group. Mann led Tom to a couple of empty wooden packing crates that sat on the other side of the mess tent.

"How did it go, Corporal?" asked the sergeant.

"I made a mess of it, Sergeant."

"How so?"

"We found our guards at Shallow Ford dead, and fresh tracks leading from across the river. I decided to set up an ambush, but I neglected to thoroughly search the river banks for a lookout."

"What happened?"

"We set up the ambush and just before the rebels moved into my kill zone, the lookout fired a shot and yelled to warn them."

"Did they get away?"

"No, they didn't. They panicked and made a run for the ford, and we shot all seven of them. The lookout shot one of my troopers in the back and killed him."

"Did he escape?"

"No, Sergeant. Gunn shot him trying to cross the ford."

The sergeant said nothing. He reached into his jacket pocket and produced a briarwood pipe. It was a simple pipe that his father had given him years before. He produced a small pouch of tobacco and diligently occupied himself with filling the pipe. Satisfied with his work, the sergeant put the pouch away. He fished around in another pocket and produced a match. He struck the match against the wooden crate he was sitting on and carefully lit his pipe. Soon he had the pipe lit and the fragrant aroma of pipe tobacco filled the air around the two seated men.

"In my experience Corporal, losing one man and killing eight of theirs is considered good odds."

"Try telling that to Trooper Sawyer's family. It was my fault, Sergeant."

"Maybe it was and maybe it wasn't, Corporal. Very little goes as planned in a war. Every plan I have ever seen since I've been in this army has gone to hell in a handbasket as soon as the shooting starts."

"I should have searched harder for a lookout, Sergeant."

"Yes, Corporal, you should have, but you didn't and you still brought back all but one of your men. In my book, that's quite an accomplishment. Stop beating yourself up, Corporal. War is all about killing and the best we can hope for is to survive it. You and six of your men survived a night fight. Next time it will probably be worse."

"Maybe so, Sergeant, but it's still my mistake."

"It is your mistake, Corporal. Learn from it and stop feeling sorry for yourself. It could just as easily have been your body strapped to a horse when your scout came back to camp."

The sergeant got to his feet, turned and walked away from Tom.

Tom sat there for a few minutes, thinking about what Sergeant Mann had told him. He looked up at the morning sky and took a deep breath. He had made a mistake, and he was still lucky in the outcome. He took another deep breath. It was good to be alive. He got to his feet and rejoined his brothers and the others.

A few miles away from where Tom drank coffee with the other troopers of his scout, a different kind of meeting was going on.

General George Stoneman was meeting with his senior staff in a large walled tent near Peachtree Creek. Stoneman stepped to the front of the tent and addressed his cavalry commanders.

"Gentlemen, General Sherman has ordered us to raid east into Confederate territory. We are to rendezvous with

General McCook's forces at a place called Latimer's Crossing on July 28th. Then our combined forces will move east to reach the Macon and Western Railroad at Lovejoy Station. Once there, we will destroy five miles of track, all telegraph lines, and any other material of war that we shall encounter. Once finished we will be free to return to the Union lines from whence we started."

"One of our objectives is to try to draw General Hood's Confederate army out of the trenches around Atlanta. If that is successful, the city of Atlanta will fall to us."

At that point, Stoneman paused, letting the facts he had just imparted have their full impact on his commanders. He could feel the tension in the room and he could hear some hoarse whispering. When he was sure he had everyone's undivided attention, he continued.

"We will advance with a combined force of about six thousand, five hundred troopers. You will each be given a copy of these orders along with the order of march as you leave this meeting."

Stoneman paused again, this time for a longer period. He knew that this portion of the orders would be both surprising and upsetting to some of his staff.

"General Sherman has also given me the discretion to make adjustments to the plan. After we have destroyed the Macon and Western Railroad, I intend to turn south, rather than return to the Union lines. I intend to march to Macon and seize the city and the prison there. Our mission will be to free the fifteen hundred Union officers being held at Camp Oglethorpe."

This time there were noticeable murmurings coming from his seated staff.

Stoneman waited for the room to become quiet again. When it did he continued. "Then I intend to march further south and free the thirty thousand Union soldiers imprisoned at Andersonville."

An audible gasp came involuntarily from the mouths of many of Stoneman's staff. Andersonville was more than one hundred and sixty miles south of their present location.

Stoneman paused again and looked carefully over stunned looks from his seated staff.

"You are dismissed, gentlemen," said Stoneman with authority, deliberately not allowing any questions.

It was as though Stoneman had dropped a cannon shell in the middle of the walled tent. Even though Stoneman had dismissed them, most of his staff were so shocked they remained in their seats. Some of Stoneman's staff had known in advance, but most of them had not.

When the general's staff had cleared out of the wall tent, some of them gathered in small groups outside of the tent to discuss what they had just heard from the general.

In one small group, Colonel Thomas Butler of the 5th Indiana Cavalry talked with Colonel James Biddle.

"If I were you, Colonel Biddle, I'd write a letter to my wife and let her know you are going on a long ride and will be gone a very long time because you are liable to spend the rest of this war in a Confederate prison," said Colonel Butler."

"Why do you say that?" asked Biddle.

"Because I have no faith in General Stoneman to carry out such a raid. In addition, in the rare chance that we were successful at Macon, how would we transport fifteen hundred sick and hungry men back through the rebel army to reach our lines safely? This plan of Stoneman's is lunacy, sir."

Biddle just shook his head in disbelief.

By the next day it was obvious to the lowliest private in the Union cavalry that something big was up. Every trooper available was being pressed into a state of readiness. Even the regimental hospital was scoured for the possibility of able bodied troopers in some state of recovery.

I Troop of the 22nd Illinois Cavalry was no exception to the rule. Weapons, ammunition, and gear was checked and rechecked as every trooper endured countless inspections of themselves and their equipment. The countryside was also combed for horses and mules. Blacksmith's and farriers were kept busy shoeing horses and making sure all available mounts were ready for travel.

Sergeant Mann met with Corporal McMaster to pass on his orders.

"It turned out the rumors were mostly true for a change, Corporal. We should be movin' out sometime on July 27th. I am to be in charge of flanking scouts for the 22nd. That means you will be in charge of a scouting party of sixteen troopers, including yourself. Is that clear, Corporal?"

"Yes, Sergeant."

"This here raid will be dangerous and dirty work, Corporal. If we make a mistake, we'll likely wind up dead or in Andersonville. If it was up to me I'd choose dead over Andersonville."

"I'll cross that road when I come to it, Sergeant. I got no intention of losing to the rebs," said Tom.

"No one ever does, Corporal. No one ever does. See to your men, and I'll have the other squads I selected come in to meet with you."

"How good are the troopers you selected, Sergeant?"

"I'm givin' you the best scouts in the regiment, Corporal. You take care of them for me."

"I will, Sergeant," replied McMaster.

CHAPTER TWENTY-FIVE

The order for boots and saddles came at three o'clock in the morning for the men of the 22nd Illinois Cavalry along with the men of eight other cavalry regiments. Altogether six thousand five hundred troopers were mounted and ready to ride half an hour after the order was issued.

Tom, his brothers, Gunn and twelve other troopers stood together on their horses in columns of two on the left flank of the 22nd Illinois Cavalry. Tom had met with the other squads and given them the same briefing he had been given and had passed on to Ted, Tuck, and Gunn. He was pleased to see Trooper Barnes in the group. Another plus was the presence of Corporal Ned Snyder, a veteran trooper who had distinguished himself well in the skirmish with the train raiders.

Somewhere in the front of the long column the order was given and the cavalry group began to move forward in columns of twos. In the darkness of the night the column seemed to stretch out forever. The narrow, rutted dirt road restricted the width of the cavalry column to two abreast. That meant five thousand six hundred mounted cavalrymen made a column stretching about three miles from the front of the column to the rear. The dust raised from the horses' hooves created a cloud that seemed to engulf the riders and did engulf their mouths, eyes, and noses. Many troopers pulled their neckerchiefs up to protect themselves from the dust.

After about an hour, they reached the site of DeFoors Ferry. Union army engineers had been there most of the night and had laid no less than three pontoon bridges over the Chattahoochee River. Army engineers directed traffic and every ten riders were directed to a separate pontoon bridge. Even so, it took until dawn to get all fifty-six hundred troopers across the river. When the column reached far banks of the river, they halted to get reorganized. Gunfire broke out just down the road from the pontoon bridges. General Stoneham ordered the troopers into a defensive positon and general chaos ensued as troopers armed with Spencer rifles hurried forward while the horse holders quickly led four horses back to the area of the pontoon bridges.

A movement forward by scouts determined whoever fired the shots had fled and the horse holders brought the mounts forward. The officers fought to get the troopers organized and back into proper order in the column.

When order was finally restored, the column began their march. In the pale light of early morning, the troopers could see the road was thickly lined with tall pine trees and only the sunlight from above the trees filtered through to the column.

Occasionally, they passed a few weather-beaten farm houses with rambling out buildings in run-down condition. They saw no sign of life, except for the occasional fenced in area containing a few pigs or cows.

Gunn determined they seemed to be following the trace of the Georgia Rail Road. He could tell from the position of the sun that they were heading east. He was puzzled by that as he knew their goal was the rail road by Jonesboro. He had seen Sergeant Mann's map and Jonesboro was to the west. Gunn assumed that since Stoneman was a general, he knew what he was doing and Gunn's job was to follow orders, not question the wisdom of his superior officers.

As they rode on into the mid-morning sun, they began to pass more prosperous farms and even some large plantations. Groups of troopers designated as foragers or "bummers," as the enlisted men in the army called them, left the column to forage from the farms and plantations. They returned leading horses and mules and carrying sacks of bacon, hams, and corn tied around their saddle horns.

This practice was new to Gunn, but it was well established by the Union army of the west as foraging both supplemented the supply lines of the army and reminded the rebel families that starting a war with the Union had consequences.

The long, dusty column of horsemen continued east at a slow walk. They saw no rebel troops nor did they meet with resistance of any kind, other than the unpleasant looks they got from the old men, women, and children they passed on the road.

Finally, the cavalry column halted for lunch. The troopers fed and watered their horses and made quick fires for their coffee, wolfing down chunks of bacon and hardtack.

As soon as their brief lunch was finished, the troopers mounted up and the column continued. They reached Latimer's Crossing about noon. There they halted and tended to their horses.

General Stoneman was waiting for General Gerrard and his column of cavalry raiders to arrive. Gerrard was to provide protection for Stoneman's right flank. Gerrard and his men arrived at Latimer's Crossing about one o'clock. The two generals had lunch together, and General Gerrard led his troops out. Shortly thereafter, Stoneman's column mounted up and rode east.

They were on the Georgia Rail Road near the tiny hamlet of Lithonia. As soon as the column had crossed bridges over the Yellow River, they burned and destroyed the bridges.

Gunn sat on his saddle and watched the destruction of the once sturdy bridges. The smoke added to his discomfort, and he felt sad at the destruction of something he was sure the people of the area found both useful and necessary.

Tom McMaster was disgusted. His scout unit was supposed to scout the flanks of the 22nd Illinois, but so far they had been kept in the column with the rest of the troopers.

Finally, Sergeant Mann rode over to him while the bridges were burning and reined in next to Tom.

"Time to get out and scout, Corporal," said Mann.

"Yes, Sergeant," replied Tom and he quickly gathered his troopers and led them away from the main column. All of the scouts were glad to get away from the dust and monotony of the main column. They rode slowly and carefully through the thick growth of pine trees that seemed to encase the narrow dirt road. After about half an hour, the trees began to thin and they were able to spread out and make better time.

Other than sighting a few small deer and some song birds, the scouts saw no living thing beside themselves.

The scouts could not see the column, but they could hear it and they could see the clouds of dust that rose higher than the tops of the pine trees. They passed a few run-down shacks, but none of them looked like they had been lived in.

The sun went down and as the darkness grew in depth, the scouts were forced to move even slower and more carefully. Occasionally, Tom would send one of the scouts back to the column to report to Sergeant Mann. He did this diligently even if there was nothing of substance to report, just to let Mann know the scouts were still out there doing their job.

Finally, the scouts came to a river that blocked their progress. They searched for a ford or bridge, but were unable to find one. Tom led the scouts back to the column. When they arrived, they found the column was crossing the river over what was known to the locals as Brown's Bridge. The entire column including Tom and his scouts were across the bridge by midnight.

Troopers then returned to the bridge and used lamp oil to set it ablaze. The tinder dry wood of the bridge was fully engulfed with flame within minutes. The troopers watched as the flaming bridge timbers crashed into the river below, sending steam and smoke skyward.

The column was then brought to a halt and camped for the night. Tired and weary troopers tended their picketed horses, ate a quick supper of coffee and hardtack. After spreading their blankets on the ground, the troopers were quickly asleep except for their sentries.

At dawn the troopers were back in the saddle. They had camped two miles southwest of the town of Covington. This was the first rebel community of any size they had encountered. It was not pleasant for the unsuspecting residents.

The head of the column arrived in Covington during breakfast. The men, women, and children of the community appeared shocked at the sudden appearance of the dreaded Yankee horse soldiers.

Stoneman failed to exercise strong control over the regiments under his command. Part of this was due to the fact some regiments had only be assigned to him for this raid. The first regiment to enter the town immediately headed to the nearest bar and got thoroughly drunk. This was hardly the mark of a well-disciplined army.

Gunn and the rest of Tom's scouts had been deployed on the flanks when the cavalry column approached the edge of Covington. After the initial shock by the local citizenry, more than a few of the residents attempted to leave town as quickly as possible with as many of their valuables as possible. Horse-drawn buggies and wagons crammed with people and material came down a side rode directly at Tom and his scouts. Tom put up his hand and the scouts backed off the road and let the fleeing southerners pass without interference.

Meanwhile, the undisciplined soldiers of many of the regiments began to plunder the homes of private citizens. As one southern man put it later, "They stole everything that wasn't nailed down."

As Tom and his scouts rode into town, they were shocked to see troopers carrying women's dresses and hats as well as silverware, fine china, and other valuables.

"What they hell are they gonna to do with women's dresses," thought Tom.

"This is bullshit," said Gunn in a loud voice.

"You're right, Billy," said Tom. With a wave of his arm, he led the scouts to the front of two sizeable homes where several women, both young and old, were trying to prevent pillaging troopers from entering their homes.

Tom rode right through the open gate of the home's fence and up to the front porch. He reined in his horse to a halt and pulled out his Colt. He reached down the jammed the muzzle of the barrel into the ear of the nearest pillager.

"I'll shoot the first man who tries to enter this lady's house," yelled Tom in a voice that gave no doubt to the sincerity of his words.

The resulting effect was electric. The other pillaging troopers froze in their tracks as the rest of the scouts rode forward with the Colts drawn up as they backed up their Corporal.

"Move out, assholes," said Gunn as he brought the barrel of his Colt down on the head of a trooper who had started to voice his protest at this intrusion.

The trooper dropped to the ground like he had been poleaxed. Within minutes Tom's mounted scouts were lined up in front of both houses, facing the street. All of them had their Colts drawn.

It didn't take much longer for the word to spread and soon there were no pillagers on that street. Nearby homes were not so lucky, but Tom had decided none of that shit was going to happen where he had control and sixteen armed mounted troopers proved to be quite a discouragement to any potential pillagers.

Disgusted officers of several cavalry regiments began to take control of their unruly men and order was finally restored.

Tom and his scouts waited until the cavalry column had reformed and began to ride out of town before they moved from their defensive positons in front of the two houses.

The frightened women of the two houses were huddled on their front porches. Tom turned his horse and walked it over to face the women.

"Ladies, I apologize for the actions of my fellow troopers. We are soldiers, not brutes and outlaws. Please accept my apology."

One of the older women stepped forward. "Thank you all, suh, we accept your apology. It is a pleasant surprise to see that some Yankees are gentlemen."

Tom doffed his kepi to the women and then led his men to join the column that was still heading east.

When Tom and his scouts caught up with Sergeant Mann and the rest of the 22nd Illinois Cavalry, he sent them ahead to scout the front of the entire column.

All of the scouts, including Gunn, were pleased to be away from the column once more. They passed the head of the column and galloped down the narrow road. Once they were out of sight, Tom had the scouts slow to a walk.

As they rode, Gunn saw an old, hand-painted sign indicating they were traveling on Monticello Road. When they were three miles out of Covington, a courier riding at a gallop caught up with them.

"Corporal McMaster?" asked the courier.

"Yes, trooper," answered Tom.

"Colonel Boyle's compliments, Corporal. You are to halt and wait for the column to join up with you, Corporal."

"Very good, trooper. Ride back to the Colonel and inform him we will remain here until joined by the column."

'Yes, Corporal."

With that the courier wheeled his horse back the way he had come and left at a gallop.

The column arrived shortly after. Due to illness, lame horses, and other issues, the column was now down to five thousand troopers.

General Stoneman called a hasty meeting of his staff and commanders. They dismounted and gathered under the shade of a nearby large pine tree. Stoneman waited until all of his men were present and then he spoke.

"Gentlemen, we are just outside a small hamlet called Starrville on what is called the Monticello Road. I want Colonel Capron to take a detachment of his choosing and backtrack on this road and to destroy the bridge over the Alcovy River once our rear guard has crossed. I also wish him to burn Henderson's Mill, and the cotton mill called Newton Factory. When he is finished, he and his men are to rejoin the column. We will continue on to Monticello. You are dismissed gentlemen." Once more Stoneman did not ask for questions or offer any more explanation.

Colonel Capron and one regiment of Union cavalry left the column and headed back the way they had come. The main column assembled and continued their march to the east.

Tom McMaster and his fifteen scouts moved quickly to the head of the long column and galloped past it. Once again they slowed to a walk once they were out of sight of the column.

Tom noticed the forest of pine trees bordering the narrow dirt road were thinning. He directed Ted to take Tuck and flank the road to the left, and Gunn and Trooper Barnes to flank the road to the right. He and the remaining eleven troopers remained on the narrow dirt road.

As they rode, they passed more prosperous appearing farms and some large plantations. It was broad daylight and their passage was noted by curious groups of white southerners and their Negro slaves. No one spoke to them or acknowledged them in any way. Gunn could feel the hate emanating from the white southerners. The slaves just looked confused.

As the scouts continued to ride east on Monticello road, they could hear strange noises coming from their rear in the direction of the column. Then they heard some gunshots.

Tom sent Corporal Snyder and two troopers back to make sure the column had not run into an ambush.

Corporal Snyder and his troopers returned at a gallop about fifteen minutes later. Snyder reined in his horse next to Tom.

"You ain't gonna believe this, Corporal McMaster," said Snyder.

"Try me, Corporal," said Tom

"Our troopers are looting every farm and plantation that we've passed. And the officers ain't doin' nothin' about it! They is just sitting on their horses watchin' like everything was just peachy. I never seen nothin' like it. Has the army gone crazy?"

Tom sighed. He took off his kepi and ran his fingers through his hair.

"I ain't got no idea what's goin' on or why," said Tom. "What I do know is whatever is happenin' back there is way over my pay grade."

"What are we supposed to do?" asked Snyder.

"We do what we been doin'," said Tom. "We do what we was ordered to do and right now that means we got orders to scout this country. Let's move out and do our jobs,"

"Yes, Corporal," replied Snyder.

Tom and his scouts turned their horses east and resumed their scout. Tom was amazed they had seen no rebel soldiers, not even a home guard of old men. He wondered how long their luck would hold.

As dusk approached, the scouts neared the town of Monticello. Tom halted his men and called in his flankers. The small group of scouts dismounted and waited for the main column to arrive. While they waited, they remained on the alert for a possible surprise attack from the rebels.

It was almost an hour before they column finally arrived, and it took almost another two hours for the rear of the column to reach to reach the spot where the scouts had halted.

CHAPTER TWENTY-SIX

General Stoneman and his staff dismounted and made their way to the nearby shade of a clump of pine trees.

The General got right to the point.

"Colonel Adams and his brigade were supposed to meet us here and they have not yet arrived. We will camp here and wait for them. As soon as they arrive, we will move through Monticello. I want better discipline from our men regarding the property of private citizens. Burning and destroying property of military value to the enemy is our objective. Stealing from private citizens is not. Is that clear?"

There was no response from his stony-faced subordinates.

The General continued. "We are now on the east side of the Ocmulgee River. I intend to use bridges available in the area of Seven Islands to cross to the west side. Once over the river, we will turn north and march to Lovejoy Station where we will join up with General McCook's column. Together we will march on Jonesboro and destroy the Macon and Western Rail Road junction located there."

General Stoneman paused to see that all of his staff were paying close attention. Satisfied, he continued with the explanation of his plans.

"Once we have destroyed the Macon and Western facilities there, we will split away from General McCook's forces. He will swing to the north and divert the Confederate forces to him. We will turn to the south and move along the western banks of the Ocmulgee River until we arrive at Macon. Once there, we will take the city and free the Union officers held prisoner at Camp Oglethorpe. Estimates of the number of Union officers held there are approximately fifteen hundred men. We shall commandeer horses, mules, and wagons in Macon to transport the freed prisoners back north to Union lines. Are there any questions?"

Because the plans had already been made public to most of the staff, there was little to no surprise at the general's announcement, but there was a strong undercurrent of serious concern among the staff.

The general swept his gaze over the silent group of officers and satisfied there were no questions, he dismissed his staff.

General Stoneman had been assured by Sherman's staff there were at least three bridges over the Ocmulgee River in the area of Seven Islands. Seven Islands was about ten miles southwest of Monticello. Once over the Ocmulgee River, Stoneman and his men would be only a good day's ride north to Lovejoy Station.

General Stoneman was not aware the Confederates in Georgia had been alerted about the raids being led by he and General McCook. Word of the raids had been spread throughout Georgia by telegraph and courier. The rebel forces in Macon were in a state of panic. Calls of alarm had gone out, and small groups of militia and volunteers from the area were swarming into Macon to help with the defense of the city.

The Confederate regular forces were also sending available troops and supplies to Macon by train from as far as Charleston, South Carolina. The rebels in charge of the defense of Macon had pleaded for help via telegraph to

General Hood in Atlanta. He was powerless to help, as he was charged with the defense of the city against Sherman's surrounding army.

The Confederates received orders for the removal of the Union officer captives held at Camp Oglethorpe. Arrangements were then underway to move the fifteen hundred captives by train to Charleston, South Carolina.

It was midnight before Colonel Adams and his Brigade of cavalry arrived at Stoneman's camp outside of Monticello. After Adams's men were allowed time for a hasty breakfast, the order for boots and saddles was given, and very shortly the entire column of Stoneman's cavalry had resumed their march into Monticello.

The citizens of Monticello awoke in the pre-dawn light to the sounds of hundreds of horsemen and the shouts of officers and sergeants. Many of them rushed to the windows and front porches of their homes to a sight they could never had imagined. Over two thousand Union cavalry were moving through their once quiet and serene town.

Several key government buildings in Monticello were burned along with any supplies and documents they contained. This work was supervised by Stoneman's officers. Unfortunately for the citizens of Monticello, several large groups of Stoneman's troopers ignored the orders of their officers and sergeants, and they began to loot the homes of private citizens. They took food, whiskey, silverware, and valuables of all types. They looted stores and shops and generally terrorized the citizens of the town. There were few men of military age in Monticello, and most of them were crippled veterans who had been sent home from the war.

Gunn and the McMaster brothers along with the rest of the 22nd Illinois Cavalry had moved into a nearby stockyard on the edge of Monticello. The move kept the 22nd Illinois away from the rest of Stoneman's column. The stockyard also allowed Gunn and the rest of the men of the 22nd Illinois to use forage at the stockyard to feed and water their horses.

Gunn and the rest of the men in the 22nd Illiniois finished feeding and watering their horses and unsaddled them to rub them down. When they were finished, they drank hot coffee that Trooper Barnes had managed to produce from a shed next to the stockyard.

Tom sipped hot coffee and watched the chaos erupting from troopers storming through private homes and looting valuables while terrorizing the occupants.

"No army operating a raid behind enemy lines can afford to be this stupid," he said.

"We're wasting time and just pissing people off for no good reason," said Gunn.

"I wouldn't want to get captured and have to face these people," added Tuck.

"Me neither," said Ted.

"I don't plan on us getting captured," said Tom. "We got things to do that need doin', and that don't include robbin' and stealin'".

Ted and Tuck nodded their heads in agreement with Tom. Gunn was puzzled at Tom's statement, but he let it pass. What he saw in Monticello sickened him. If this had happened to his friends and neighbors back in Altona, Illinois, it would have enraged him. He tossed out the remains of his coffee from his cup and rinsed it off. He was anxious for the officers to get control of this nonsense and get them on the road.

It took several hours for Stoneman's officers to bring order to the chaos they had allowed to erupt, and finally they had all the troopers mounted and organized into a column.

After questioning several leading citizens, Stoneman's officers informed him of some disturbing news. According to the locals, there were no existing bridges over the Ocmulgee River at Seven Islands. Nor were there any bridges anywhere on that stretch of the river. There were three small ferries near Seven Islands.

Stoneman called together his officers for a hasty conference. He told them the news about the bridges and the ferries. All of them agreed to use the ferries to cross the Ocmulgee River would take too long and leave their column too exposed to a rebel attack. That left two options. They could turn back and retreat to the Union lines. That would be a hazardous trip with every rebel unit in Georgia looking for them. Or they could continue south to Macon, cross the Ocmulgee River there, and take the city and free the men in Camp Oglethorpe. After listened to his staff, General Stoneman decided to head south to Macon.

"Gentlemen, we shall ride to Macon and free our fellow officers at Camp Oglethorpe. We must move quickly, and I urge you to control your men. We cannot allow looting and thievery of the private citizenry. It is not only immoral, but it slows down our progress when we cannot allow ourselves to be anything but swift in our movement."

General Stoneman dismissed his commanders and within an hour the column had formed and moved south out of Monticello past the silent, but grim faced citizens of the town.

Once the column was south of the town, General Stoneman had his forces divide into two separate columns. Stoneman send a brigade to the right of the road to scout the county just east of the Ocmulgee River. The remainder of the column continued south on the road leading to Macon. Stoneman's plan was the two columns would meet and rejoin at the town of Clinton.

Tom and his scouts were ordered to scout ahead of the main column, and they galloped forward. Once out of sight of the main column, they slowed their mounts to a walk. All of them were glad to be clear of the dusty column and the chaos Stoneman's men had created back in Monticello. Once again, Tom had Ted and Tuck deploy to the left of the road and Gunn and Trooper Barnes were deployed to the right side.

After the scouts had traveled about six miles, they came to a very large and opulent plantation. This was the plantation of a southerner named Carden Goolsby. They admired the beautiful house and outbuildings of the plantation as they rode past. The long front porch of the home was occupied with several southern women of various ages along with several darkie house servants of both genders. None of them spoke or waved. The faces of the women were hard and angry looking.

When the main column of Stoneman's cavalry passed by the plantation, several troopers broke ranks and rode their horses onto the plantation grounds. They invaded the stately home and looted valuables and destroyed pictures, furniture, and dishes. They helped themselves to ripe apples, peaches, and watermelons. They discovered casks of peach brandy and filled their canteens. Soon many of them were drunk, only adding to the general disorder.

Several sergeants and officers were finally able to force the troopers out of the house and off the plantation property. The troopers were too drunk to care. Many of them had trouble staying in the saddle, let alone being able to keep in formation.

Tom raised his right hand as a signal to his scouts to halt. Approaching him from the right flank were Gunn and Trooper Barnes. They had five men walking sullenly in front of them. All of the five men wore some semblance of butternut colored clothing. None of them were armed and all had their hands tied in front of them.

"What in tarnation have you got there, Billy?" asked Tom.

"We found these boys trying to hide in the woods where they could watch the road," said Gunn.

"Where they armed?" asked Tom.

"Well they all had rifles, but none of them was holdin' one when me and Barnes surprised them," said Gunn.

"What the hell were they doin'?" asked Tom.

"One was watching the road, three was sleepin' and one was taking a piss," said Gunn.

"Did you seize their weapons?" asked Tom.

"They had a bunch of old, rusty smoothbores that didn't look like they'd ever been cleaned," said Gunn.

"Where are the guns?"

"We swung them against some pine trees and busted them into kindlin'," said Gunn with a grin on his face.

Tom left one of his scouts to guard the prisoners after they tied all five of them to separate pine trees. The column would come along and pick up the prisoners and the trooper could then catch up with the rest of the scouts.

Meanwhile Stoneman's column was moving slowly south on the road to Macon. As the column passed farms and plantations along the road, troopers were ignoring the orders of their sergeants and breaking ranks to loot and steal. The column kept moving south, but the lines of stragglers drunk and loaded with stolen valuables were getting longer and falling further behind.

Tom and his scouts passed through Hillsboro without incident, as the citizens of the town watched them ride by. The people were silent, but obviously distressed at the sight of armed Union cavalry in their quiet town.

When the main column arrived in Hillsboro, the officers were more successful in keeping order. One reason was the large number of disorderly troopers who had perpetuated much of the looting were both drunk and already had as much loot as they could carry. The column passed through Hillsboro with only a few minor incidents.

The long dusty column moved south past Round Oak and Sunshine Church. The looting and ransacking of farms and plantations continued and the line of stragglers continued to grow behind the column.

General Stoneman ordered the column to halt at noon when they were eight miles south of Hillsboro. The men were allowed to dismount and prepare a noon meal. A nearby stream provided water for the horses and men. Coffee was soon being prepared on dozens of small cook fires. Men sprawled on the ground and under pine trees to seek shade from the scorching overhead sun.

General Stoneman consulted his maps and then met with his staff. They convened in the shade of a small grove of oak trees. While they sipped cool stream water from their canteens, the general announced a new decision.

"Gentlemen, I am sending Major Carlson and five troops of the 22nd Illinois on a separate raid to Gordon. They are to ride there and destroy all the railroad facilities as well as create a diversion to draw the Confederates away from our main column. We will be reinforced by Adams' brigade when we reach Clinton and will then advance to Macon. Are there any questions?"

The officers looked at each other in surprise. A diversion was not a bad idea, but dividing their force in the face of the enemy of unknown strength did not appeal to many of them. In addition, Major Carlson's five troops would only amount to about one hundred and thirty men. It was enough men to make an effective raiding party, but too small to make an effective defense if they ran into a force of Confederates.

The worried glances between the officers resulted in no questions, much to the satisfaction of General Stoneman.

With the loss of Major Carlson's five troops, he would be down to slightly more than two thousand troopers, but he would gain men when he reached Clinton and was rejoined by Adams' brigade.

Major Carlson wasn't sure if he should laugh or cry. Leading an independent raid with his troopers was something he had always dreamed of, but not when he was a hundred miles behind enemy lines with only one hundred and thirty troopers. He had recovered from his shock at the general's decision to send him on a separate diversion raid. But after he recovered from his initial surprise he continued to wonder why the general had not given him any orders on how he was to proceed after he had conducted the raid on Gordon. He knew the general's plan to capture Macon and Camp Oglethorpe faced overwhelming odds. A thought came to the major. It just might be he had been given the chance to both disrupt the enemy supply lines and get his men safely back to the Union lines. He took off his kepi and scratched his head as he thought. Then he headed to where his troopers were located to inform them of General Stoneman's new orders.

Chapter Twenty-Seven

Tom, Tuck, Ted, and Gunn were seated around a small cook fire drinking coffee and eating hard tack. The hard tack was aptly named, as hard was the best way to describe it. It was the army's version of a biscuit, but to the troopers it was more like trying to eat a brick. The four of them were dunking their pieces of hard tack into their coffee cups to try to make the army biscuits soft enough to bite into.

They watched as Major Carlson strode into their area. He had a worried look on his face, and all four men knew that something was up.

Major Carlson called a hasty conference with his officers and after a few minutes, the conference ended and the officers hurried off to talk with their sergeants.

"Looks like something is up that affects us," said Tom.

"You mean other than scoutin'?" asked Ted.

"It looks like this affects the whole troop, maybe more," said Tom as he watched the interchanges between the regiment's officers and their sergeants.

It wasn't long before Tom and his scouts were gathered together by Sergeant Mann. Once the sergeant had all sixteen troopers around him, he put up his hand for silence. The troopers quickly complied.

"Men, we got new orders. I Troop and four other troops are being sent on a separate raid to destroy some rebel railroad facilities at a place called Gordon. I ain't got no idea what's in Gordon or how big the place is or how many rebs might be located there, but that's where we're goin'," said Sergeant Mann.

Silence and looks of surprise greeted the sergeant's news. Trooper Barnes broke the silence.

"When are we leavin' Sergeant?" he asked.

"We leave in half an hour. Check your weapons and your gear and be in the saddle in thirty minutes," replied Sergeant Mann.

"How many of us will there be on this here raid?" asked Ted.

"I ain't exactly sure about that. My best guess is between one hundred and twenty and one hundred and forty, Corporal."

"Don't that seem a mite small for a raiding party, Sergeant?" asked Gunn.

"A small raiding party can move fast and it's harder to find, Gunn," said the sergeant without a complete sound of confidence in his voice.

No one else raised a question, and the sergeant left as the men began to gather their gear and check their weapons. When the thirty minutes had passed, one hundred and thirty-two officers, sergeants, and troopers were mounted and ready to ride.

Major Carlson sat on his horse at the head of the small group of troopers in columns of two. The major was a young man of twenty-eight with a handsome face and white blonde hair and a thin moustache. He had been a school teacher before the war, but he had developed into a capable cavalry officer. He liked riding horse and he cared about his men. He had studied cavalry tactics from several army manuals in his spare time and had served in the 22nd Illinois for two years. He had seen enough of the war to lose any sense of glory. He knew fighting a war was a dirty and nasty business. He wanted to serve his country, win the war, and get back home to his young wife in Illinois. He knew to accomplish all of this, he needed to survive the war and not risk the lives of his men unnecessarily. He was both excited and frightened at the prospect of his new assignment.

When the other officers in his small command reported their troops were assembled and ready to ride, Major Carlson brought his right arm up and then forward as he shouted, "Forward, ho!" The small raiding party moved away from Stoneman's main column as they headed southeast on a side road in the direction of the small railroad center of Gordon.

Tom McMaster and his men were sent forward as scouts for Carlson's small column. Once again, Tom McMaster sent Ted and Tuck to the left side of the road and Gunn and Barnes to the right side. Once the scouts were out of sight of the column, they slowed their mounts to a walk. They moved slowly and none of them spoke as they made their way to the southeast under a hot and constantly present sun.

The land was rolling and contained less pine trees and more open areas of grass and brush. There were a few farms, but no plantations until they had traveled for over an hour and a half. Then they came to the plantation of Dr. Palacia Stewart. The plantation was huge. The main house was one of the largest buildings Gunn had ever seen, and that included barns from back in Illinois.

Major Carlson had the column halt at the plantation. He ordered McMaster's scouts to hold their positions about a half a mile down the road.

The major rode up to the main house and dismounted, tying his horse's reins to the iron ring on a cement post. He had no sooner finished his task, when a white-haired, older southern woman appeared on the front porch. The woman was well dressed and had an air of authority about her.

Major Carlson doffed his kepi and said, "Good afternoon, madam."

"Good afternoon to you, suh. May I ask the purpose of your visit to our home, suh?" she said.

"Yes, ma'am. I am Major Carlson of the 22nd Illinois Cavalry, and I wish to ask permission for my men to water their horses, ma'am."

The women paused as if studying both the major and his request. "The horse trough and well are behind and to the right of the house, Major. Your horses and men are welcome to as much water as you all need. Please see to it your men do not misinterpret this offer and try to avail themselves of any property of our plantation. The Doctor is not at home, but I am Mrs. Stewart. Mah name is Esther. I make this offer in the hope of your guarantee of the safety of our plantation as an officer and a gentleman."

"I thank you for your generosity and hospitality, ma'am," said Major Carlson. "You have my word that no harm will come to you or your fine plantation."

Esther turned and disappeared back into the enormous house. The major untied his horse and began to lead it back to the horse trough. His men followed, leading their horses in single file back to the well and the water trough. There was a pump handle over the well, which directed water into the trough. The men took turns watering their horses, washing themselves off, and filling their canteens. Major Carlson and his officers and sergeants had told the troopers of the 22nd Illinois they would not tolerate any undisciplined behavior, nor any looting or damage to the property of any civilians they encountered. It took almost an hour to get all the horses watered and all the canteens of the 22nd Illinois filled.

Tom and his scouts returned to the plantation, and they too watered their horses and filled their canteens. When they were done, they mounted their horses and rode out to get ahead of the small column to scout the road ahead. Soon, the entire column was assembled and headed on the road in a southwesterly direction.

Another hour and a half of riding brought Tom and his scouts to Salem Church. It was a small, white-washed one-story building that looked like it could use a fresh coat of white-wash. Tom had his scouts pause in the tree shaded area next to the old church. They dismounted and drank water from their canteens and rested.

Tom and Gunn walked a short distance down the road from the church. Both men listened carefully and sniffed the air. They could neither see, hear, nor smell anything that was not normal. They could hear the songs of the birds in the trees and hear the buzz of insects. The smell in the air was of pine trees and green grass. Satisfied, they returned to the old church and mounted their horses.

At Tom's arm signal, Ted and Tuck rode to the left of the road, while Gunn and Barnes rode to the right.

Tom led his scouts on the narrow, rutted dirt road as they continued their scout to the southeast. They soon crossed Commissioners Creek over a small bridge. They had not ridden much further when they heard shouting in the distance to their right.

Tom urged his mount to a gallop and the rest of his scouts followed closely behind. McMaster came around a sharp turn in the road that bent around a grove of tall pine trees and reined his horse to a halt. Directly in front of Tom were Gunn and Barnes. They were holding their Colts on two older farmers who were mounted on mules.

"What do we have here, Billy?" asked Tom.

"We saw these two jaspers sitting behind some bushes. They was watchin' the road. We kinda surprised them, and they tried to make a run for it. I never seen no one try to make a run for it on a mule," said a smiling Gunn.

Tom could see that Barnes held the reins to two saddled mules in his free hand. The two men were dressed as farmers and seemed a little old for military service, but when it came to rebels, Tom knew anything was possible.

Tom dismounted, handing his reins to Corporal Snyder. "I'm Corporal McMaster of the 22nd Illinois Cavalry. Who are you?"

The two farmers were reluctant to speak as they had a hard time taking their eyes off the barrels of the two Colts Gunn and Barnes were pointing at them.

"I'm Wilbur Pitts and this here is my neighbor, Malachi Woods. We have farms hereabouts."

"What were you doin' hiding and watching the road, Mr. Pitts. Are you spies for the Confederates?" asked Tom.

"Oh, no, suh. We was just bein' careful. We heard word yesterday the Yankees was comin' and when we see soldiers, we reckon we're better off not bein' seen."

Tom shifted his questioning. "So you two men farm the land around here?"

"Yes, suh. We both have farms hereabouts."

"Were both of you born and raised in these parts, Mr. Pitts?" asked Tom.

"Yes, suh. We was both of us born and raised hereabouts."

"So both of you know this country pretty well?"

"Yes we do. Why we know this country like the back of our hands, don't we Malachi," said Pitts.

"Then this is your lucky day, Mr. Pitts," said Tom.

"Why is that, suh?" asked Pitts.

"That's because you two have just been drafted as guides for the 22nd Illinois Cavalry," said a smiling Tom McMaster.

"We'll sure try to do the best we can to help you fellers," said Pitts in a weak voice.

"Billy get these two guides mounted on their mules, but keep their hands tied," said Tom.

"Yes, Corporal," said Gunn. He took the reins of one of the mules from Barnes and led the mule up to Pitts. Then he took the other mule and led it up to the farmer called Woods.

"You two boys mount up," said Tom. "I want both of you riding right up front next to me. Do you understand me?" said Tom.

Both Pitts and Woods nodded their heads that they understood, and Tom and the two farmers led the scouts down the road. Gunn and Barnes returned to the right flank of the scouting party.

After an hour's ride, they came to a crossroads. The crossroad was a larger road and in better shape than the one they had been traveling on. Tom halted the scouts at the crossroads.

"What road is this?" asked Tom of Pitts.

"This here road is Garrison Road," replied Pitts.

"Where does this Garrison Road lead to?" asked Tom.

"It goes south to Macon and north to the M&E Railroad," said Pitts.

"Are there any other towns between here and Macon," asked Tom.

"No, suh," replied a nervous Pitts.

"What's directly ahead of us on this road?" asked Tom.

"This road will take you all to Gordon," answered Pitts.

"How far is Gordon from here?" inquired Tom.

"Gordon is about twelve miles from here," said Pitts.

"Are there any towns between her and Gordon?"

"No suh. Just some farms and one big plantation."

"What plantation is that, Mr. Pitts.?"

"That would be the Choates Plantation, suh. It's the biggest place around these parts," said Pitts.

"Thank you, Mr. Pitts," said Tom.

The scouts rode on for about half an hour when they heard hoof beats on the road ahead of them. Suddenly Ted and Tuck rode into view at a full gallop.

Ted reined in his horse right next to Tom. When he caught his breath, he told Tom why they had ridden so hard.

"We saw a large plantation up about a mile from here, Tom. There's a small group of rebels resting there. They've been moving a sizeable herd of horses and mules and they were watering them at the plantation."

"How many rebels?" said Tom. "Were they cavalry or infantry?"

"They looked like militia to me," said Ted. "They was about six or seven of them. They was either pretty old or pretty young."

Tom turned in his saddle. "Corporal Snyder. Ride back to the column with all speed and bring Major Carlson up as quickly as possible."

Yes, Corporal," said Snyder and he turned his horse back up the road and spurred it into a gallop.

A few minutes passed before Snyder returned with Major Carlson and Captains Dexter and Warren. Tom saluted the officers, and they returned his salute.

"What is it, Corporal?" asked Major Carlson.

"Our scouts spotted a small group of six or seven militia herding a group of horses and mules. They're about a mile ahead of us watering the stock at a place called Choate's Plantation, sir," replied Tom.

"What opportunity do you see here, Corporal?" asked Major Carlson.

"Me and my boys can slip in there and surprise them rebs and capture the entire herd of horses and mules. I think we can use some remounts as some of the boy's horses are in pretty sad shape," said Tom.

"Do you need any more men than your scouts, Corporal?" asked the Major.

"No sir. But you could move the column up closer and have them surround the plantation, so we don't lose any of the stock in case there's any shootin'," said Tom.

"I have no doubt there will be some shooting," said the major. "Just make sure you and your men are doing the shooting. I do not wish to add any casualties."

"We'll do our best, sir," replied Tom.

Major Carlson and the two captains turned their horses and raced back to the main column.

Tom dismounted and motioned for his scouts, including Gunn and Barnes, to dismount and listen to his plan.

Once Tom had all his scouts gathered around him, he outlined his plan.

"I want you boys to move out quietly and have four of you on each side of them rebels. Four each from the north, south, east and west. You got that?"

All of the troopers nodded their heads.

"I will fire one shot, and you are to gallop in with your Colts out. I want each of you to fire one shot and yell your fool heads off. I want them rebs to think they are under attack by a whole brigade of cavalry. If we can catch them by surprise and fool them, I am pretty sure they'll throw their guns down and surrender," said Tom.

"Remember, nobody moves or fires until you hear my shot." Tom looked at his pocket watch. "I'll give you fifteen

Robert W. Callis

minutes to be in position. Make sure you aint' late to the party, boys," said Tom with a crooked smile.

The troopers were divided into groups of four. Tom led one group, while Ted, Gunn, and Ned Snyder each led another. The horsemen rode off at a trot and within fifteen minutes all of the troopers were in position.

After checking his watch to make sure fifteen minutes had passed, Tom pulled out his Colt and fired it harmlessly into the air. Then he and the three troopers with him spurred their horses into a gallop and began yelling at the top of their lungs. After a few seconds each of the three troopers riding with Tom had fired their Colts into the air.

As he galloped toward the plantation, Tom could hear the shots and yells of the other troopers as they too galloped toward the plantation, screaming like banshees as they rode.

Tom's prediction turned out to be correct. The four old men and three young boys of the local militia were so frightened by the surprise attack that two of the boys had wet themselves. As the Union troopers crashed into the yard around the plantation, the seven militia members threw down their rifles and raised their hands in surrender.

Tom's troopers quickly reined up their horses and dismounted. Two troopers scooped up the rifles of the rebels and stepped back from them.

"Tie these rebels up, Ted. Gunn, take three men and check out the house for any unpleasant surprises. You know how I hate surprises," said Tom.

"Corporal Snyder," said Tom.

"Yes, Corporal."

"Take some men and get all the horses and mules rounded up and put them in the corral with the plantation's stock. Also check out all of the outbuildings and see that no one is hiding there."

"Yes, Corporal," replied Snyder.

Some of the horses and mules had bolted due to the gunfire and yelling, but they had not gone far and were milling around close to the plantation's outbuildings.

Tom turned to his youngest brother. "Tuck, get mounted and ride back to the major and tell him to bring the column up."

"Yes, Tom," said Tuck as he swung himself back into the saddle. Tuck wheeled his horse around and spurred the horse into gallop.

While Tom's scouts were rounding up the loose stock, Gunn, Barnes, and one other trooper had ascended the steps to the spacious front porch of the huge plantation house. Gunn had sent the other trooper to the rear of the house to guard against someone trying to escape out the back door. Gunn grabbed the oversized, iron door knocker on the front door and rapped it against the huge walnut door three times.

The knocks were greeted with silence. Gunn waited for a minute and then rapped the door knocker another three times.

He put his ear to the massive front door and thought he could hear footsteps. Suddenly the door swung open and an older Negro woman in servant's dress stood in the doorway.

"Kin I hep you, suh," said the woman.

"Are the owners at home?" asked Gunn.

"No suh," answered the woman.

"I'll have to ask you to step aside ma'am," said Gunn. "We are going to search the house. I promise we will neither steal nor damage anything. We're looking for rebel soldiers."

The women did not respond. She simply stepped aside and made way for Gunn, Barnes, and the trooper.

Gunn turned to the trooper. "You stand guard here and make sure no one slips out behind us, Trooper."

Robert W. Callis

The trooper nodded he understood and took up his position by the front door with his Spencer at port arms.

Gunn had never been in a home so large and so palatial. The rugs on the floor, the ornate furniture, the art on the walls were almost overwhelming to his senses.

He had Barnes check out the rest of the main floor while he went upstairs and searched every room. He found no one on the second floor. Gunn returned to the main floor and found Barnes there guarding four Negro women including the one who had greeted them at the front door.

"I found these darkies in the kitchen, Gunn. They was cookin' somethin', but I didn't find anyone else," said Barnes.

Gunn questioned the other three women servants, but they knew nothing about the whereabouts of the owners of this fine plantation.

"Ain't it strange that nobody would be home in a fine place like this?" asked Barnes.

"They must have got word we were headed this way and are probably hiding out in the woods," said Gunn.

"Should we go look for them?" asked Barnes.

"What would we do with them, Barnes? We're lookin' for reb soldiers or anyone who would do us harm. I doubt that includes the owners of this plantation," said Gunn.

"I spose the last thing we need is prisoners," said Barnes.

"They'd just slow us down and cause problems," said Gunn. "We need to move fast and travel light."

"What do we do with these darkies?" asked Barnes.

"We leave them be to do what they was doin' when we got here," said Gunn.

"Was there anyone upstairs?" asked Barnes.

"Nope."

Gunn took a final look around the grandeur of the plantation house and led the way out the front door.

Gunn and his men returned to the yard by the outbuildings. By now the stock had been rounded up by Snyder and his men and collected in the corral with the plantation's stock. Gunn heard the nose of horses' hooves and turned around to see the major and the rest of the column coming down the entrance of the plantation from the road.

The major halted the column and he and Captain Dexter rode forward to where Tom and his scouts waited for them.

"Congratulations, Corporal. It looks like a job well done. Did you have any problems?"

"No, Major. We surprised them and all seven surrendered without a fight. They're militia. Old men and boys. We collected all the stock they were herding and the put them in the corral with the plantation stock."

"Is there anyone else about, Corporal?"

"My men found some darkie servants in the big house," said Tom.

"There were no owners or overseers present?" asked the major.

"No, sir. We think they heard that some Yankees were comin' down the road and they hightailed it for the woods to hide out until we left," answered Tom.

"Very good, Corporal." The Major turned in his saddle to face Captain Dexter. "Captain Dexter. Please take a trooper with you and enter the house and see if you can purchase whatever salt, sugar, coffee, and bacon that they can spare."

"Yes, Major," replied the captain. He dismounted and signaled to a trooper to dismount and join him. Both men soon entered the house and disappeared from view.

"What do you wish to do with the prisoners, Major?" asked Tom.

The major took a moment to look over the seven poor wretches seated on the ground with their hands tied in front of them.

"I can't decide whether to spank the young ones or scold the old ones," said a smiling Major Carlson. "We'll parole them and leave them here. Leave them tied up and lock them up in one of the outbuildings."

Tom smiled at the major's remark. "You heard the major, Gunn. Take the prisoners and lock them up in one of the outbuildings," he said.

"Yes, Corporal," said Gunn. He and Barnes helped the bound prisoners to their feet and led them away to a nearby corn crib. The seven prisoners were ushered into the crib and the door locked behind then with a spike through the iron hasp.

"Them two young boys smelled really bad," said Barnes.

"I think it's because they pissed their pants when we surprised them," said Gunn with a wide grin on his face.

"I have a feeling that after three days in the saddle and eatin' about a pound of dust a day, we don't smell like roses, Barnes."

The major had directed Tom and his scouts to sort through all the stock held in the corral and pick out the best looking horses and mules. Cavalry horses that had fared poorly during the march were exchanged for fresh mounts and healthy mules were moved out of the corral to be herded at the rear of the cavalry column.

When all the sorting was finished and new mounts had been selected and saddled, the major gave orders for the column to form up out on the road.

Captain Dexter and the trooper appeared from the plantation house carrying several sacks. The major saw them approach him and he smiled at the sight of the sacks.

"You were successful in your requisitions, Captain?" asked the major.

"Yes, sir. We were able to purchase coffee, salt, sugar, bacon, and some tea, said the captain.

"Excellent job, Captain. Let's get mounted and on our way."

As Ted led his scouts out of the plantation grounds and onto the road, he glanced at the waiting column and reined his horse to a halt.

"Major, something seems to be missing," said Tom.

"What is missing, Corporal?"

"I see Mr. Pitts, but where is Mr. Woods?"

The major looked around him and asked for the whereabouts of Mr. Woods. A quick search of the ranks did not produce any evidence of Mr. Woods.

"I'll be damned," said the Major. "The bugger must have slipped away in all the confusion."

A questioning of Mr. Pitts was fruitless. He said he saw nothing, and he heard nothing, to the surprise of no one.

"Do you want me to send a detail to find him, Major. He can't have gotten far on that mule," said Captain Dexter.

"Don't bother, Captain," said the major. "He's probably halfway to Atlanta by now. We still have Mr. Pitts and to date he has been a lot more talkative and helpful that Mr. Woods. Let's move out."

On hearing the major's order, Tom put his heels to his horse's ribs and led his scouts in a gallop as they moved rapidly down the road in front of the little column.

Once the scouts were out of sight, Tom had them slow their horses to a walk. He sent Ted and Tuck out to the left and Gunn and Barnes out to the right to serve as flankers.

They rode for over an hour and when they came to a small stream, Tom ordered a halt to water the horses and to fill their canteens. The men dismounted and led their mounts to the stream. The troopers let the horses water and munch on green grass growing on the stream bank. A dozen troopers collected canteens from the others and filled them upstream from where the horses were watering.

Ted, Tuck, Gunn, and Barnes had returned and they watered their horses and filled their canteens. When Tom, Ted, and Tuck were off by themselves, Tuck cornered his oldest brother.

"When are we gonna talk to Gunn?" Tuck asked.

Tom paused for a moment. He looked around to make sure no one was close enough to them to overhear what was being said. Satisfied, he turned to face Tuck.

"When we get to Gordon, the major is gonna have to decide where to go next. If he decides to head on down to Macon, we say nothing. If he decides to turn back north, then we need to talk to Gunn."

"Are you worried about what Gunn will do?" asked Ted.

"He'll do what he wants to do. I can't force him to do anything. He's a solid man and we need him, but he has to decide. If he don't, he don't. I can't do nothing about that."

"What do we do if he don't?" asked Tuck.

"We do what we gotta do. It'll be harder without Gunn, but we always thought it would get down to the three of us anyway."

Tom looked up as Corporal Snyder approached him with a handful of freshly filled canteens. "How good is the water, Ned?" asked Tom as though they had been discussing nothing more important than the weather.

After the horses had been watered and the canteens filled, Tom ordered the scouts back on the road and sent the flankers out to their respective sides.

Half an hour later, the sun had dropped just below the tops of the pine trees bordering the road. Tom and the rest of the scouts felt instant relief from the heat, as suddenly they found themselves riding in the shade. Marching through Georgia in late July left something to be desired.

Suddenly the relative silence of their surroundings was broken by the boom of a shotgun being fired. Almost immediately shouts were heard in the distance to the front of the scouts. Tom kicked his horse in the ribs and galloped ahead to the source of the noise. His scouts quickly followed. All of them, including Tom, had drawn their Colts.

As Tom and his scouts swept around a curve in the road they saw Gunn and Barnes on their horses with their Colts drawn. As Tom and the others drew closer they could see Ted and Tuck on the road with Tuck holding their horses. Tom was holding his Colt on a bearded old man in a battered hat. Lying on the ground at the feet of the old man was an ancient, rusty shotgun.

Tom reined in and quickly dismounted, handing his reins to Corporal Snyder.

"What happened here, Ted?" asked Tom.

"This old geezer stepped out of the trees and tried to bushwhack me in the back," snorted a very angry Ted.

"It looks like he wasn't much of a shot, Ted," said Tom.

"This ain't funny, Tom. Have some old fart try to shoot you in the back and see how you like it."

Tom turned and looked down at the old man sprawled on the side of the road. "What's your name, old timer?" he asked.

"Name's Rufus," growled the old man.

"Would you mind telling me why you fired on my trooper?" asked Tom.

The old man looked at Tom with eyes filled with hate. "I tolt my boy I'd shoot the first Yankee I saw," he said.

"Well you shot and you missed. So I don't suppose you would object if I let Ted here shoot you in the guts," said a stern faced Tom.

"You all Yankees will do what you're gonna do, no matter what I say," Rufus replied.

"What do you propose to do with this ancient assassin, Ted?" asked Tom with a faint smile on his face.

"I'd like to tie him to a tree and shoot his dick off," said a still angry Ted.

"I doubt he'd miss it much, at his age," said Tom.

"You got a better idea, Tom?"

"As a matter of fact, I do," said Tom.

"And what might that be?" asked an indignant Ted.

"I suggest we strip the old buzzard naked and burn his clothes. Then we turn him loose and let him make his way back to wherever he came from," said Tom.

"What about his shotgun," asked Tuck.

Tom stepped forward without a word. He picked up the decrepit weapon and promptly swung it against a tree and broke it into pieces.

"I think that takes care of the shotgun," said Tom.

All of the scouts were smiling and trying to keep from laughing and making Ted any madder than he already was.

"Fun is over," said Tom. "Let's mount up and continue our scout."

Everyone, including a still pissed off Ted, mounted their horses and returned to the road. Tom sent out his flankers, and the scouts resumed their ride.

CHAPTER TWENTY-EIGHT

Dusk was fast approaching as the scouts neared the railroad station and depot at Gordon. They passed the occasional shack and run-down farmhouse, as they neared the railroad town.

It was nine o'clock in the evening when the raiding party reached a place on the railroad line called Walden's Shanty. It was just a small way station and it was unoccupied. Major Carlson had the column halted and ordered a short rest. While the troopers dismounted, the major and his officers held a strategy meeting.

"I estimate we're about one mile from Gordon, said the major. "I propose that we sent McMaster and his scouts forward and get as much intelligence about the town and its fortifications as possible. Does anyone disagree or have another suggestion?" he asked.

None of the officers had any additional suggestions.

"Very good," said the major. "I suggest we have the rest of the men see to their horses. There's a small stream on the other side of the shanty. Have them water their horses by troop. Make sure they make no unnecessary noise and there must be no fires. This is to be a cold camp. If there are no further questions, you men are dismissed."

The officers left the meeting and hurried to their respective troops to get them organized. Captain Dexter walked over to where Tom McMaster and his scouts were seated on the ground.

Tom and the rest of the scouts jumped up from the ground and came to attention at the appearance of the captain. Tom snapped off a salute, and the captain returned it.

"Corporal McMaster. It is the major's wish that you and your scouts proceed on to the town of Gordon and scout the town and its possible fortifications and military strength."

"Yes, Captain. May I take only as many scouts as I believe I need, sir?"

"Of course, Corporal. Use your own discretion as to the size of your scout. Just get all the details you can and get back to me within two hours, if possible.

"Yes, Captain," said Tom as he then saluted the captain. The captain returned the salute and then turned and walked away.

"Listen up, men," said Tom. "This will be a small scout. I don't want too many of us moving around that town in the dark. The more of us there are, the more likely one of us will get noticed. Ted, I want you, Tuck, Gunn, and Barnes on this scout. The rest of you stay here with Corporal Snyder. Any questions?"

There were no questions.

"Get your horses and we move out now," said Tom.

Within minutes the five scouts were mounted and moving down the road toward Gordon. The night sky was fairly clear, and there was some light from the stars in the cloudless sky as well as from the moon. The air was hot and thick. The scouts moved in single file with Tom in the lead and Gunn bringing up the rear.

As the scouts got closer to the little railroad town of Gordon, they could see lights and hear noises. Tom turned his horse off the left side of the road and began to make his way through the pine trees and brush. The other four scouts followed almost noiselessly behind him in single file.

When they were about two hundred yards from the edge of Gordon, Tom dismounted and used his hand signals to tell the rest of the scouts to do the same.

Tom went to each man and whispered his instructions. "Leave your horse with Trooper Barnes. He'll be our horse holder tonight. Take your Spencer rifles and follow me. We move Indian style tonight."

Silently each scout handed the reins of his horse to Trooper Barnes and, Spencer in hand, they followed the lead of Tom McMaster. They moved slowly and silently through the darkness.

When Tom and his scouts had reached a spot that was just north of the railroad tracks, the stillness of the night was pierced by the shrill sound of a train whistle. All of the scouts soundlessly dropped to the ground, the raised railroad tracks shielding them from the lights of the small town.

A train was pulling into Gordon from the north. Tom slithered through the tall grass and reached a large pine tree. Once at the base of the tree, he slowly got to his feet, using the large trunk of the tree as a barrier between him and the arriving train.

Once he reached a standing position, Tom carefully peered around the tree. The train had slowed and was coming to a stop at the small depot in Gordon. Tom was shocked to see the train was filled with rebel militia. There must have been four hundred rebels on board the train. He knew this was not good. The Union raiding party would be outnumbered by almost four to one. They would have to wait until the troop train departed before they could attack.

As he was standing behind the tree, Tom got an idea. He motioned by hand signal to Tuck to have him come forward and join Tom.

Tuck carefully crawled forward through the tall grass until he reached the pine tree sheltering Tom. Tuck slowly stood up until he was standing next to Tom.

Tom pointed up at the pine tree. "Can you climb up this tree and not be heard?" whispered Tom.

Tuck looked up at the tree. While the tree was large, it had several large low hanging branches. Tuck looked at Tom and nodded his head up and down.

"Climb up the tree and see what else is in this damn town, besides this troop train," whispered Tom.

Tuck looked at his oldest brother and smiled. He had always been the best tree climber of all the brothers. He grabbed ahold of a large lower branch and effortlessly and silently swung himself up onto the branch. Once up on the branch, he began climbing higher up the tree. When he was about twenty feet high, he stopped and moved out to the side of the tree facing the town. He used large branches for support until he was comfortable and had an unobstructed view of the town of Gordon. He had a good view and even though it was dark out, there was light from the town as well as the available star and moon light from a cloudless night sky.

After about fifteen minutes, Tuck began to reverse himself and move to the backside of the tree. Once there, he began his descent. He was down the tree in much less time than it had taken him to climb it. When he reached the ground and stood next to Tom, Tuck touched Tom on the shoulder and pointed back to where the other scouts were waiting.

Tuck went down to the ground and began crawling back to the scouts' location. As soon as Tuck disappeared into the tall grass, Tom dropped to the ground and began crawling in the same direction. When Tom reached the rest of the scouts, he used hand signals to bring Ted and Gunn next to him.

"Circle around the edge of the town and see what you can discover. Don't be seen and meet us back here when you have come full circle," he whispered to Ted and Gunn.

Both Ted and Gunn nodded their understanding and began crawling east along the raised bed of the railroad track. In a few seconds they were out of sight. Although he listened intently, all Tom could hear was the sound of the wind in the trees and the tall grass.

Tuck then told Tom everything he had been able to see from his perch up in the tree. Tom and Tuck lay in the grass for almost an hour before Ted suddenly appeared with Gunn crawling closely behind him.

"Did you get all around the town?" whispered Tom.

"Does a bear shit in the woods?" whispered back a grinning Ted.

"Let's get the hell out of here," whispered Tom. Ted grinned and led the way as they slowly crawled back to where Trooper Barnes waited with the horses. Once there, Gunn and Ted told Tom what they had managed to see in the town.

Fifteen minutes later, they rode back into the temporary camp at Walden's Shanty. Tom rode directly over to where Major Carlson was talking with Captain Dexter. Tom slipped from his saddle and saluted the major as soon as his feet hit the ground.

"Corporal McMaster reporting, sir."

The major snapped a hasty salute back to Tom. "What did you learn, Corporal?" he asked.

"Let me show you as well as tell you, Major," said Tom.

Tom dropped to one knee and pulled his knife from his belt. Both the major and the captain joined him on one knee.

Using his knife in the dirt, Tom tried to draw what he was also explaining. "There is a sizeable depot and at least three large warehouses. We was surprised by the arrival of a troop train with about four hundred militias on it. They came from the north, and I think they are headed to Macon."

"That ain't good news," said Captain Dexter.

"I don't think they'll be stayin' long. We'll have to wait until they leave before we can attack," said Tom.

"What else did you see, Corporal?" asked the major

"We saw two passenger trains waitin' on sidings. One of them was full of passengers. All totaled, we counted eleven train engines, forty passenger cars, eighty boxcars, and twenty flatcars."

"This looks like a perfect target," said the major with a smile.

"I left Gunn to watch the town. When the troop train leaves, he'll ride back to let us know."

"Good work, Corporal. Did you see any telegraph lines?"

"Yes, I did, sir. They run along the railroad tracks," said Tom.

"Captain, send out two details. Send one to the east and one to the west of Gordon and have them cut the telegraph lines," ordered the major.

"Yes, sir," said the captain, and he hurried away to execute the major's orders.

"You are sure no one saw or heard you, Corporal?" asked the major.

"No one saw or heard us, Major," replied Tom.

"Very good, Corporal. Now, we need to get the men ready to ride. This will be a night the rebels will never forget."

Tom saluted the major and returned to get his scouts ready to ride.

CHAPTER TWENTY-NINE

Gunn sat under a pine tree next to his tethered horse. The noise from Gordon had become a dull hum in his ears. He struggled to stay awake. They had ridden hard all day, and he was tired, dusty, and hungry. He took a chunk of hardtack out of his shirt pocket and tried to nibble on it. The hardtack was as hard as a brick and when he did manage to break off a small piece of it and get it into this mouth, the thing tasted like sawdust. He took a swig of water from his canteen. The water was lukewarm, but it was wet and his parched throat welcomed every drop of it.

Despite his best efforts, Gunn found himself nodding off. He would awake with a start as his head would fall forward. He repeated this process a couple of time until he decided to stand up and get less comfortable. He had no sooner gotten to his feet when the night air was pierced by the sound of a train whistle. Gunn slipped around the tree and moved quickly to a vantage point where he could see the train tracks running through Gordon. As soon as he reached the vantage point, he could see the troop train moving as it picked up speed and headed west toward Macon.

Gunn turned to go back to his horse, when he was stopped by a second whistle. This time one of the passenger trains was also pulling out of Macon. It was following in the wake of the troop train heading west.

Gunn moved quickly, but carefully back to his horse. He grabbed the reins and swung up into the saddle. Soon he was over two hundred yards from the train tracks. Then he kicked his heels into his mount's ribs and urged the horse to a gallop. Gunn rode as fast as he could to Walden's Shanty.

When he reined in his horse at the shanty, Tom ran up to him. "The troop train and one of the passenger trains just left heading west to Macon," yelled Gunn.

Tom nodded and ran over to where the officers were gathered around the major.

"The troop train and one of the passenger trains just left Gordon. They're headed west to Macon," said a breathless Tom.

"You heard the man," said the major. "Get your men mounted. We're taking Gordon by surprise with a night cavalry charge."

The ensuing chaos quickly evolved into a disciplined column of twos as the raiding party left Walden's Shanty and headed for Gordon.

Tom and his scouts raced out ahead of the column to ensure no rebel surprises awaited them.

It was about two o'clock in the morning in Gordon. After the two trains had departed, most of the railroad crews had gone to bed. The other passenger train sat on a siding. The passengers were resigned to their fate of spending the night in a train car and had made themselves as comfortable as possible. Sleeping in a train car was still preferable to sleeping on the ground. The militia guards at the warehouse were struggling to stay awake and were looking forward to being relieved and the chance to get some much needed sleep.

At one minute past two o'clock that morning all hell broke loose in Gordon. The Union raiding party galloped into the small railroad town from both the east and west sides of town. The militia guards at the warehouse quickly threw down their rifles and raised their hands in surrender. Armed troopers rushed into every building in town and soon townspeople still in their nightshirts were herded out of their homes and into the streets.

The citizens sleeping in the passenger train were rudely awakened by armed troopers storming into the passenger cars and forcing them out into the night air.

The troopers quickly herded all of the civilians into the town square where ten troopers kept guard on them. The militia guards were herded into the depot where Captain Dexter began questioning them.

Two troops of cavalry invaded the three warehouses. They soon emerged with armloads of bacon, cornmeal, and flour. The foodstuffs were divided and crammed into individual trooper's saddlebags.

The major directed two sets of four troopers each to guard both the east and west ends of the railroad tracks on the outskirts of Gordon.

The major then gathered his officers for orders. "Divide your men into work parties. I want the railroad rails and ties torn up and burned. Destroy at least one hundred yards of the railroad tracks. You are to burn all the rolling stock including the passenger cars, boxcars, and flatcars. The operating controls of the engines are to be smashed. I want the warehouses searched and any useful items confiscated. Then I want this depot and all the warehouses burned to the ground. We do not have time to waste. Get your men organized and get busy burning this nest of rebels to the ground!" said the obviously excited major.

The efforts of the major's raiding party were largely successful. Not all of the fires they started managed to consume their targets and in the chaos and the darkness, some tasks were not completed. They did however, destroy twelve passenger cars and forty boxcars. They also managed to destroy the controls on seven train engines.

At the major's orders, the troopers set to work tearing up and destroying one hundred yards of track. They burned the railroad ties and when the fires were burning the hottest, they set iron rails on the fires until the rails were red hot. Then teams of troopers lifted the rails and wrapped them around telephone poles to make them useless. This method of destroying rails would become known throughout the South as "Sherman's neckties."

Trooper burned the railroad turntable in the center of the railroad yard. They also burned all three warehouses to the ground complete with their stores of foodstuffs and five hundred Enfield rifles.

Gunn and Tuck led a group of six troopers into the train depot. They seized the mail pouch they found in the trainmaster's office and Gunn directed a trooper to deliver the pouch to the major. Before they set fire to the depot, Tuck searched the trainmaster's office. He found something on the wall that brought a smile to his face. He tore the paper document off the wall and carefully folded it up. When he was finished, he slipped the document into his shirt pocket and went outside to join Gunn.

"is everyone out of the depot?" asked Gunn.

"I'm pretty sure I was the last one out," said Tuck.

"Did you find anything of value in the trainmaster's office?" asked Gunn.

"Nope," replied Tuck with a wisp of a smile on his face.

"Let's burn this place down," said Gunn and the other troopers began to set fires at the front corners of the depot.

While all of this activity was taking place, the townspeople, the train passengers, and the disarmed militia guards were all huddled in the town square. With all the fires burning around them it was like night had turned to day. Even the troopers guarding them had their backs to the captives as they watched the destruction of Gordon's railroad yard with wonder.

Major Carlson held a strategy meeting with his officers on the front porch of a nearby house.

"Gentlemen, thank you for all your hard work," said the major.

A compliment from their commanding officer at the height of a successful raid was in sharp contrast to what the officer's had endured during the initial part of their raid under General Stoneman.

"I want you to have your men prepare and eat a sumptuous breakfast from the stores we have confiscated here. Have them eat, check their weapons and gear, and see to their horses. If there are any problems with the horses, trade them out for horses we brought in the stock herd. In one hour we will be on the march," said the major.

"Are we headed to Macon to join General Stoneman?" asked Captain Wallace.

Major Carlson paused before answering the captain's question. He thought for a minute and then he responded.

"When the general ordered me to lead this raid, he gave me no instructions on what I should do after the raid was concluded. I have taken that to mean what we do at this point is up to my discretion. Part of the use of discretion is to adjust to the current situation.

Captain Dexter, would you be so kind as to inform the rest of the officers what you were able to learn from the militia we captured as well as what we learned from some of the townspeople and the trainmaster."

Captain Dexter stood up from the porch chair he had been sitting on. "While I am sure not everything we learned is reliable, enough of what we learned is as it was verified by more than one source we questioned. As all of you know the city of Macon lies on the west side of the Ocmulgee River. Both we and the forces under General Stoneman are on the east side of the river. According to the information we were able to extract, both wagon bridges over the Ocmulgee River to Macon are gone. One was washed away by a spring flood and the other was just burned by the rebels. The only remaining bridge over the river near Macon is a railroad bridge. Any crossing of that bridge would have to be in single file of horsemen. No wagons or artillery would be able to cross the bridge. The river turns south when it gets to the east of Macon and there are no bridges over the river for many miles."

"The prisoners told us many rumors they heard about the Yankee raid and while it sounds like Stoneman is approaching Macon, rebel forces of every kind are streaming to defend Macon. The trainload of militia we saw pull out of Gordon earlier is one of those groups. In addition, it sounds like General Wheeler has Confederate cavalry and infantry moving south from around the Atlanta area to attack General Stoneman from the rear."

"It would appear that if Stoneman is able to get to the banks of the Ocmulgee, he will have no way to get across the river into Macon or Camp Oglethorpe where the Union officers are held prisoner. In addition, Stoneman's ability to return his forces back to Union lines would require him to fight a running battle with Wheeler's forces of unknown size."

Finished with his report, Captain Dexter returned to his chair on the porch.

"Thank you for your detailed report, Captain Dexter," said the major. "As I said before, my decision is now discretionary. However, we are a force of a mere one hundred and thirty men who find ourselves one hundred miles behind enemy lines. Under these circumstances, I believe all of you are entitled to express your opinions before I make my decision. Does anyone have any thoughts on what we should do next?"

All of the officers present seemed to squirm in their seats and each of them took turns looking at each other as if they needed some sort of guidance before they expressed themselves.

To the surprise of all of the officers, Lieutenant Swanson rose to his feet. Swanson was only twenty-one years old and his face was clean shaven, making him look even younger. He was a short slim man with jet black hair. He seldom spoke at officer meetings and kept his own counsel and listened to his more experienced officers with deference.

As he stood before the major the rest of the officers, Swanson's cheeks became flushed. He took a deep breath and began speaking. "Major, it would seem to me that we have fulfilled our orders from General Stoneman with the successful completion of this raid on Gordon. We have been fortunate to have suffered no casualties and our small unit is still intact. I believe we have a duty to our men and to the army to find a way to safely return to the Union lines to the north so we may live to fight another day. I have no desire to spend the rest of the war in Andersonville." Somewhat embarrassed at his outburst, the lieutenant quickly resumed his seat on the porch.

"Anyone else?" asked Major Carlson.

No one else spoke. It seemed that the lieutenant had spoken well for all of them.

"Very well. Return to your troops. Pass on my orders to your sergeant and have your troops ready to march in one hour. We will march southeast parallel to the north side of the Central Railroad at a distance of no less than one half mile.

We will head for the town of McIntyre. You are dismissed," said the major.

The officers quickly disbursed and soon they were passing on the major's orders to their sergeants and men. The news was well received by almost all of the troopers, and they quickly set about cooking a robust breakfast and getting their horses, weapons, and gear in order.

CHAPTER THIRTY

Sergeant Mann had just finished passing on the major's orders to Tom McMaster and his scouts. He was surprised at Tom's reaction to the news. The sergeant had been pleased to hear of the major's decision to lead the raiding party back to the Union lines. He was almost positive a decision to march on Macon would result in most of the raiding party being killed, wounded, or ending up as prisoners in Andersonville.

Most of the scouts had been delighted with the decision. Tom, Ted, and Tuck had seemed somehow disappointed in the news. That didn't make any sense to the sergeant. He knew Tom and his brothers were smart men and had proven to be highly skilled at surviving in a very dangerous war. He walked away from the group of scouts feeling very puzzled.

Tom waited until the sergeant had left before he grabbed his brother Ted. "Get Tuck and Gunn and let's set up our own cook fire over there past them trees," said Tom.

As Ted left to collect Gunn and his brother, Tom knew now was the time they had to talk to Gunn and find out where he stood.

The four men set about getting a small cook fire started and then preparing a meal of bacon, biscuits from the captured flour, and hot coffee. While the food was being prepared, Tom tried to think about the best way to explain things to Gunn.

"It's time to eat, said Ted and the four of them pulled out their tin plates and let him fill them with bacon and fresh biscuits. Tuck grabbed the coffee pot and filled all of their tin cups. Soon there was silence except for the sound of hungry men concentrating on their eating as the most important task they had before them.

When they had finished, Gunn volunteered to take the cookware to a nearby stream and wash them. When he was out of sight, Tom turned to his brothers.

"I'm gonna talk to Gunn. I'm gonna explain to him our plan and find out if he is in with us or not," said Tom

"Whichever way it goes, I won't blame Gunn if he says no," said Ted. "He's turned out to be a damn good soldier and a good friend. I trust him."

"So do I," said Tuck. "I hope he says yes, 'cause I think we need him. He can shoot like nobody's business."

"He's a free man, and he don't owe us nothin'" said Tom. I'd love to have him along, but I can't blame him if he says no. This ain't his fight."

"He's comin' back," whispered Ted.

Gunn walked around the cook fire and handed each brother their now clean cookware. He had also filled all their canteens and handed then out as well.

"Have a seat, Billy," said Tom. "We need to have a talk with you."

"Sure thing," said Gunn and he took a seat on the ground with a puzzled look on his face.

"You heard the sergeant tell us that we're moving out in about an hour to try to make it back to the Union lines up north," said Tom.

"I heard him, same as you did," said Gunn.

"Well, here's the thing. We ain't going with him," said Tom.

Gunn looked thunderstruck. Then he regained his senses and said, "Why the hell not?"

"It ain't no accident that the three of us wound up in the 22nd Illinois. We joined up with them when we found out they would be part of Sherman's army and knew the regiment would be part of the war in Georgia," said Tom.

"I don't understand?" said Gunn.

"Do you remember when Tuck told you that our Pa was from Illinois and he went back there to enlist when the war broke out?" asked Tom.

"Yes, I do remember," said Gunn.

"Pa joined up with the 88th Illinois Infantry. They made him a captain. The 88th Illinois served under Sherman at Chattanooga in Tennessee. During that fight he got captured by the rebels," said Tom.

"He got captured?" asked Gunn.

"He got captured and is now bein' held prisoner at Camp Oglethorpe in Macon."

"He's in Macon?" said a stunned Gunn.

"Last we heard he was still there. We aint' going back with the major. We're going to Macon and break our Pa out of that damned rebel prison."

"How the hell are you goin' to do that?" said Gunn.

"We plan to follow the railroad tracks from here to Macon. From what I heard, it sounds like Stoneman won't be able to get over the river to Macon and he will be trying to get back north. Every damn rebel in Macon will be following him and trying to catch up with Stoneman."

Gunn looked at Ted with unbelieving eyes, but he kept his mouth shut.

"We plan to slip over the railroad bridge at night. The prison is in an old warehouse on some fairgrounds on the east side of Macon. The three of us will slip past the guards and get into the warehouse and find our Pa. We'll get him out and put him on a spare horse that we are about to steal," explained Tom.

"Steal!" exploded Gunn.

"Them horses are rebel stock and in my mind we're just stealin' from the rebs."

Unconvinced, Gunn continued to listen.

"If you remember, the original plan was for Stoneman to get over the Ocmulgee river to the west side and ride up to Jonesboro and meet General McCook there."

"I remember that was the original plan," said Gunn.

"Then you also remember that Stoneman found that there were no bridges over the Ocmulgee at Seven Islands or anywhere near there. The only way across was three small ferries. Because of that he was stuck on the east side and then headed south to Macon. There ain't no bridges over the Ocmulgee River at Macon except for a railroad bridge. Whether Stoneman can cross the river to Macon or not, when he is done he has to head back to the Union lines."

"Stoneman and his men will be heading north, but they will be quite a bit east of the Ocmulgee. The major will be taking a route that is even further east than Stoneman. We plan on sneaking out of Macon and following the railroad to Atlanta on the west side of the Ocmulgee River. That puts the river between us and most of the rebels who are chasing Stoneman and Carlson. We ride cross country at night and hide during the day, just like we did in Indian country back in the Colorado Territory."

At first Gunn was too shocked by what he was hearing to even think straight. As Tom's plan unfolded, he had to agree that it was possible that the brothers might be able to bring off the rescue of their Pa.

"What about food?" asked Gunn. "You're talkin' about around a hundred and twenty-mile trip, more or less. If you're moving only at night, the trip could take up to a week. Plus, what if your Pa is too sick or weak to travel. From what I bin hearin', them rebels is none too generous in feeding Union prisoners."

"What you say is true, Billy. But we got only this one chance to get our Pa back. To be this close and turn back now would be a disgrace to our family."

Gunn was thinking hard and he said nothing.

"We can forage for food and all three of us are damn good at livin' off the land. All of us have had hard experiences staying alive in the Colorado Territory. After dealin' with Cheyenne and Sioux, I think we can handle moving over a hundred miles and stayin' hid from the rebels," said Tom.

"Why are you tellin' me this?" said Gunn.

"We want you to go with us, Billy," said Tom. "We need you to hold the horses when we get to the prison and we need someone to cover us if we have to get out of there in a hurry."

"You know this is deserting," said Gunn.

"Not to my way of thinkin'", said Tom. "We're just making our own way back to the Union lines. If we go with the major and we get into a fight with the rebs, we'd all get split up and be making our own way north as best we could. Once we get back to the Union lines, we get help for our Pa and we rejoin our regiment. That ain't desertion in my book."

Gunn's initial shock at Tom's plan was wearing off. He was weighing the plan in his mind as he listened to Tom. Finally, he reached a decision.

"So you three boys want to sneak into Macon and free your Pa from a rebel held prison and then tear through all the rebels in Georgia for over a hundred and twenty miles back to the Union lines. Is that right?" Gunn asked.

"That's pretty much the plan," said Tom.

"Count me in," said Gunn a grim look on his face.

CHAPTER THIRTY-ONE

A wave of relief ran through Tom's body with Gunn's response. Tom, Ted, and Tuck each took turns thanking Gunn before Tom got them settled down and back on the plan.

"Show Billy what you found in the train depot in Gordon," said Tom to Tuck.

A smiling Tuck produced a folded document from his jacket pocket. Tuck unfolded the document he had torn from the depot wall. Lying open on the ground in front of the four men was a detailed map of all the railroad tracks in the state of Georgia. The map included all of the cities, towns, villages, and train stops on all of the railroad routes.

"I think this gives us a pretty good advantage over either Stoneman or Carlson," said a grinning Tuck.

Gunn was impressed. Being behind enemy lines was bad enough when the enemy knew the territory well and you didn't. Knowing where you were and not getting lost would be crucial to the success of Tom's plan.

"We ain't got much time before the major will want us to move out, and we got a few things that need doin," said Tom.

"Tuck will be getting' us some supplies, but each of you is to pack all the food you can in your saddlebags. Ted will be getting' a spare horse with a saddle. Billy, you and I will head out like we're gonna scout ahead and then we'll circle back. Tuck and Ted will slip back separately. We'll meet by the railroad tracks on the west side of Gordon. Is that clear to you, Billy?" asked Tom.

"Yes, Tom. I got a couple of questions, though."

"What are they?" asked Tom.

"How far is Macon from here and is there anything between Gordon and Macon?" asked Gunn.

"On the map it looks to be about twenty-five miles and about halfway to Macon is a little town called Griswoldville. We'll skirt around the town and keep goin' till we reach the east side of Macon and the railroad bridge."

Gunn nodded his understanding.

"One more thing, Billy," said Tom. "You're gonna need this," Tom said as he reached behind him and tossed Gunn a tied roll of heavy cloth.

"What's this?" said Gunn as he held up the cloth roll to the firelight to get a better look at it.

"Back on the ranch we called them dusters. I don't know what the hell they call them down here. They're long coats we'll use to cover our uniforms when we go into Macon," explained Tom.

"Got it," said Gunn.

Gunn got to his feet and then realized Tuck and Tom had already left to complete their preparations for the ride to Macon. He took a deep breath and made a silent prayer to God that he was doing the right thing.

Tom and Gunn went to the picket line and saddled their horses. Gunn tied the rolled up duster behind his saddle bags. Then he filled the saddle bags with small sacks of coffee, sugar, bacon, and hardtack. He made sure he had plenty of spare ammunition for his Spencer and his Colt. Satisfied with his preparations, Gunn mounted his horse and joined Tom on the road at the east end of Gordon.

Tom soon reined in his horse next to Gunn, and they sat there in the dark night. It wasn't hot yet, but Gunn found himself sweating like it was high noon in Georgia. After a few minutes, Sergeant Mann rode up and reined in his horse in front of them.

"Anxious to get started for home?" asked a smiling Mann.

"Yes, Sergeant," came the reply from the two troopers.

"Me too," said the sergeant. "Tom, you take your scouts and head out and make sure no rebs are waiting for us."

"I thought I'd just take Gunn, Ted, and Tuck. We move faster and we make less noise with only four of us," said Tom.

"Whatever you think best, Tom. See you boys down the road," said the sergeant and then he wheeled his horse and returned back to Gordon.

Gunn felt guilty they had to lie to the sergeant, but he had made his decision. He knew what he would have done if it were his father who was imprisoned at Camp Oglethorpe. Somehow he knew the McMaster brothers would have come with him just as he was going with them. He trusted them, and he knew he could count on them when the going got hard. On this day they were the best friends he had.

Tom and Gunn rode their horses at a trot for almost a mile. Tom and Gunn reined in their horses to a halt, then Tom slowly rode to the right side of the rode and into the surrounding woods with Gunn following closely behind. Soon the two riders crossed over the railroad tracks and once on the other side of the tracks, they halted and listened carefully to the sounds on the night air. They heard nothing unusual. Satisfied, they turned their horses and headed west at a walk.

Neither man spoke and the only sound was their horses' hooves on the soft ground and the hiss of brush and tree branches as their horses passed through them. As they got nearer to Gordon, they could hear the voices and noises made by men as they prepared for a long ride.

They rode silently past the town and soon were at the west end of Gordon. Tom led the way as they crossed back over the railroad tracks and onto the road. The two riders dismounted and led their horses around a small grove of large bushes shielding them from anyone passing by on the road.

They waited in silence for about fifteen minutes, but it seemed much longer to Gunn. He was nervous and still somewhat unsure about their mission.

The silence was broken by the appearance out of the brush behind them of Ted and Tuck walking and leading their horses. Ted was leading a spare saddled horse.

"Did you get everything?" whispered Tom.

Both of his brothers nodded their heads up and down. Tom mounted his horse, and the other three men mounted their horses. Tom indicated by hand signals he wanted Ted to take the lead. Ted handed the reins of the spare horse to Tuck, and Ted rode out to the road. The others followed him in single file.

The four horsemen rode their horses at a walk. Ted set the pace. They would ride at a walk for fifteen minutes and then ride at a trot for fifteen minutes before returning to a walk. By alternating the pace, they kept the horses fresh and made relatively good time

After almost two hours of riding, they could see some lights further down the road.

"This must be Griswoldville," whispered Tom. He motioned for Ted to move back next to him. "Go ahead and scout out the town and find the best way around it," Tom whispered. Ted nodded his head and rode ahead of the others. After about ten minutes, Tom put up his right arm to signal a halt. Then he dismounted and motioned for the others to do the same. The three horsemen led their horses and the spare mount off the road and into the trees bordering the road.

The silence of the night was broken occasionally by sounds coming from the small town. Someone in the town was up and active and all three men hoped it wasn't the sound of Confederate troops on the move toward them.

Ted rode out of the darkness and pulled his horse up next to Tom. "The town is pretty quiet. A couple of railroad workers are loading some supplies onto a flat car. Other than that, nothing is stirring. The town is almost all on the north side of the tracks. We can walk our horses back over the tracks and get around the town on the south side without bein' seen," said Ted.

Ted nodded his agreement, and he and Tuck and Gunn mounted their horses. The horsemen crossed the road and then rode over the railroad tracks to the south side. Once there, they dismounted and followed Ted single file through the trees and brush.

They moved silently on foot until they were almost past the town. Suddenly Ted held up his right arm as a signal to stop, and he pulled out his Colt. The other three men held their breath as they tried to see what had alerted Ted. Then they saw him holster his Colt and start to walk forward again.

Once they were well past Griswoldville, Ted mounted his horse and soon all four men were mounted and riding slowly through the brush. Ted led them back over the railroad tracks and onto the road. Once they reached the road, Gunn rode his horse up next to Ted.

"What was that back there?" asked Gunn.

Ted turned to look at Gunn and he smiled. "It was a damn raccoon," said Ted.

Despite the tenseness of the moment, Gunn had to fight to keep himself from laughing out loud. The only thing to challenge them on this dark night had been a damn 'coon."

They rode in silence, keeping their horses' pace to a steady walk. Then Ted raised his right hand and the tiny column came to a halt. Tom rode up next to Ted.

"What is it?' asked Tom.

"I smell the river," said Ted.

"It must be the Ocmulgee River," said Tom. "It turns south after it passes by Macon. We're getting close."

"I'll go ahead and take a look-see," said Ted. "You and the boys stay here."

Ted didn't wait for an answer from his older brother. He rode ahead into the darkness for about fifty yards and then he halted his horse and dismounted. Ted took the horse's reins and led him forward down the side of the road. Tom, Tuck, and Gunn dismounted and led their horses to the right and off the road.

As they waited, Gunn noted that the once dark skies were now grey with the light hint of early dawn. He had hoped they would get over the bridge in the dark, but perhaps they were too late.

About twenty minutes has passed before a strange sight appeared before them. Ted came walking down the road leading his horse. Ted was prodding a man with his Colt to keep the man walking in front of him.

When Ted and his unwilling companion reached Tom and the others, they could see the man was actually more of a boy. He was dressed in a rag tag combination of butternut colored clothes, and he was barefoot.

"What have we here, Ted?" asked Tom.

"This young lad is some kind of courier for the rebels. He came thundering down the road right at me. When I stopped him, he had no idea I was a Yankee. To add to his surprise, I relieved him of his gun and his dispatch pouch."

"Where's his horse?" asked Tom.

"I left him grazing by the side of the road. I only got so many damn hands, Tom," said a slightly irritated Ted.

"Did you take a look at his dispatch pouch?" asked Tom.

"Nope. You know I ain't much for readin' and such," said Ted.

Ted handed Tom the dispatch pouch, while Gunn took the frightened young rebel and tied him to a nearby tree.

Tom opened the pouch and pulled out several papers. He struck a match to a couple of dry twigs and made a small torch out of them. Using his improvised torch, Tom read the papers. When he was finished, he walked over to the young courier.

"Why were you carrying messages, son?" asked Tom.

The young courier was obviously scared to death, and he stared at Tom as though he was looking at the devil.

Tom was patient and waited. Finally, the young courier began to speak. He started talking so fast at first that Tom couldn't understand him.

"Slow down, son. We ain't gonna hurt you," said Tom.

The frightened young man seemed to relax slightly at the sounds of Tom's words. He took a deep breath and then began to speak.

"Mah name is Freddy. The telegraph line was out, so they sent me to Gordon with the dispatch pouch."

"Do you know what's in the pouch, son?" asked Tom.

"No suh," replied Freddy.

"What's goin' on back in Macon, son?" asked Tom.

"The whole town is celebratin'," suh," Freddy answered.

"What are they celebratin?" asked Tom.

"We done whipped the Yankees, and they's headed back up north," said Freddy.

"Who's defending Macon?" asked Tom.

"Just some of the home guard and militia. Most everyone else is out chasing after the Yankees," said Freddy.

"How many Yankee officers do they have in the prison at Camp Oglethorpe?" asked Tom.

"I ain't rightly sure, suh. I know they shipped some of them to Charleston by train two days ago when they feared the Yankees might get into Macon and free them from the prison," replied Freddy.

Tom's heart sank at the news that some of the officers held at Camp Oglethorpe were no longer there.

"Thank you, Freddy," said Tom. "Would you like some water, son?" Tom asked.

"Ah'd shore be thankful to you, suh," said Freddy.

Tom gave Freddy a drink from his canteen and then walked back to the road where Ted, Tuck, and Gunn were waiting.

"I got good news and bad news, boys," said Tom.

"Let's hear the bad news first," said Tuck.

"The kid told me that they shipped some of the Union officer prisoners by train to Charleston two days ago," said Tom.

"Shit," said Ted.

"What do we do now?" asked Tuck.

"We keep to the plan. If Pa ain't there we go on without him. There's still a chance he could be there," said Tom hopefully.

"What's the good news?" asked Gunn.

"The good news is the rebels stopped Stoneman from getting into Macon, and he's headed back north with every rebel they can muster in hot pursuit," said Tom.

"So how is that good news?" said Tuck.

"It means that there's damn few rebels left guarding the town and the prison. Most of them are chasing Stoneman north on the east side of the Ocmulgee River. That's just like we hoped for," said Tom.

235

"So we go ahead with the plan to sneak into the prison?" asked Ted.

"Is anybody opposed to staying with the plan?" asked Tom. None of them spoke.

"How about you, Gunn. Are you still in?" asked Tom.

"I think the plan is still good and the risk is worth it. I'm still in."

"All right then," said Tom. "Let's get closer to Macon and figure out how to get over that railroad bridge."

"What about Freddy?" asked Ted.

"I think Freddy will be fine just where he is. Someone will come along before too long and find him," said Tom.

"What if he talks and gets rebels on us before we can complete the plan in Macon?' asked Gunn.

"I'll have a little talk with him to make sure that don't happen," said Tom with a grim smile.

Tom walked over to where Freddy sat on the ground tied to the pine tree. Tom took the dispatch pouch with him and laid it on the ground next to Freddy. Tom kneeled down and bent over to whisper in his ear. When he finished and got to his feet, Freddy had a look of absolute fear on his face.

Tom returned to the others, and they mounted their horses and began their approach to Macon.

Ted pulled his horse next to Tom's and leaned over towards his older brother. "What the hell did you say to that boy?"

"I told him that if he ever uttered a word about us, I'd return and find him and shoot his dick off," said a smiling Tom.

Ted laughed and took his place at the head of the four riders.

The sun was just beginning to rise in the east. That was both good and bad for the four horsemen. The sun behind the four rider and silhouetted them, but it also blinded anyone they were approaching.

The men had stopped and hidden themselves in a grove of pine trees near the top of a small knoll. Ted and Tom had crawled through the trees to the top of the knoll and the spot gave them a good vantage point to see much of Macon.

They could see the ruins of the two wagon bridges over the Ocmulgee River and the still standing railroad bridge. The town appeared to be undamaged. There was no movement on the road on their side of the river and none on the railroad bridge.

The east side of Macon was closest to them and they could see an open area with a long, warehouse type building in the center of it. The open area was surrounded by a twelve-foot high board fence. Tom estimated that the fence enclosed an area of about three acres and that included the long warehouse and some other buildings.

"How many gates through the wall do you see?" asked Tom. Ted had the best eyesight of all three brothers. He was always the first to spot game when they had gone hunting on their ranch.

"I see a main gate and then I see two smaller gates. They look more like doors. The main gate faces west toward Macon. The doors are on the east side and the north side," replied Ted.

"How many guards do you see?" asked Tom.

"I see about two guards outside the closed front gate. I see two more over by the warehouse building. I don't see any at the two doors, and the one facing the river seems to be open," answered Ted.

"Do you see anyone around the open door?" asked Tom.

"I don't see hide nor hair of anyone around the open door to the river," replied Ted.

"What looks like the best way to get into the prison walls to you?" asked Tom.

Ted thought for a minutes and then he answered his brother. "We ride the horses over the bridge wearing our dusters to hide our uniforms. We don't wear our kepis. Once over the bridge we dismount and lead our horses to the east side of the prison wall."

"Why the east side?" asked Tom.

"The east side is hidden from the town. There are no guards up on the wall to see us. We have Gunn hold the horses there. We enter the prison wall through the open door on the north side facing the river. We act like we've been sent to relieve the guards at the warehouse. The prisoners have to be held in that warehouse building. It's the largest building and the only one that has guards."

Ted paused to think some more. "We take out the two guards at the warehouse. We leave Tuck outside the warehouse as a lookout, and you and I go into the warehouse and find Pa. If he's there, we grab him and come out the door where Tuck is waitin'. If Pa can walk we help him out. If he can't walk, you and I carry him out with his arms over our shoulders. We take him to the east door in the wall with Tuck covering us."

"Why the door on the east wall? The north wall facing the river is the one that's open." asked Tom.

"The doors look to be barred or locked from the inside of the fence. We can unbar the door on the outside when we move down to the north side open door. When we got Pa, we go to the east door and unbar it from the inside if it's locked. Then we take Pa out to where Gunn is waiting with the horses. We put Pa on the spare horse and we slip around to the south side of Macon and once past the city, we cut back to the railroad and follow it north," said Ted.

"Sounds like a good plan to me," said Tom.

"It's the best I can come up with," said Ted.

The two brothers turned on their bellies and crawled back into the cover of the grove of trees.

After a few minutes of crawling, Tom and Ted were below the exposed portion of the knoll and soon they were in the cover of the grove of high bushes.

Tom motioned for Tuck and Gunn to join them. The four men were seated on the ground in the middle of the grove of bushes. Tom explained the plan he and Ted had discussed. He swept away the grass, leaves, and twigs on the ground and used his knife to draw a crude man in the bare dirt. He pointed to each entry in the stockade wall to illustrate his plan.

When he was finished, he looked up at his brothers and Gunn and asked, "You boys got any questions?"

"I do," said Gunn.

"What are they?" asked Tom.

"I see a couple of problems."

"What problems?" asked Tom.

"First of all this in July in Georgia and wearing them duster things is gonna look strange in all this damn heat," said Gunn.

"I don't know how we get around that," said Tom. "We need to cover up our uniforms, or we don't fool anybody."

"The rebs might not notice the dusters if they were distracted by something else," said Gunn.

"What have you got in mind, Billy?" asked Tom.

"I think a good distraction would be if you were bringing in a captured Yankee to stick him in the prison," said Gunn.

"What do you mean?" asked Ted.

"I think you and Tom go in wearin' your dusters with Tuck in uniform with his hands loosely bound lookin' like he was your prisoner. From what I hear them guards search all the new prisoners and steal everything they have. I bet them two militia guards would be so focused on Tuck, it would be easy to conk them on the heads and put them out of commission," explained Gunn.

"I like the idea," said Tom.

"Me too," echoed Tuck.

"Makes good sense to me," said Ted.

"Then it's a plan," said Tom. "When we cross the bridge, shouldn't we all wear dusters?" asked Tom.

"We don't want to draw any attention until we get into the stockade, so it's a good idea," said Gunn.

The four horsemen returned to their tethered horses and stuffed their kepis in their saddlebags. Then they unrolled their dusters and put them on. The dusters went down to their boots and covered any sign of their Union uniforms.

The McMaster brothers and Gunn each checked their weapons and tightened their saddles. When they were all finished, they mounted their horses and headed down to the river and the entrance to the railroad bridge over the Ocmulgee.

CHAPTER THIRTY-TWO

The sun was up over the eastern horizon and the four riders were silhouetted against the early morning sky as they rode down to the entrance to the railroad bridge.

They neither met nor saw any other people as they made their way to the bridge. They rode in single file and Ted lead the way onto the bridge as though he had done it every day for the past month.

There had been no rebel guards on the north end of the bridge. The Central Railroad had a junction with the Macon and Western Railroad at Macon and the Central Railroad then went south over the Ocmulgee River and past the east side of Macon.

The foursome slowly made their way over the bridge, their horses picking their way over the wooden railroad tires placed on the wooden bed of the narrow bridge. Tom held his breath as they rode. Being on a high bridge over a river was something he would usually choose to avoid if he could. Today he had no choice.

The bridge began to slant slightly downhill as they approached the south end of the bridge. Ted could see a lone sentry seated on a wooden box by the side of the railroad tracks. The sentry looked to be home guard. He was dressed in civilian clothes, and he had an old shotgun resting across his knees. The sentry had placed an old parasol next to him to provide him with shade from the unrelenting sun. The man appeared to be at least seventy years old.

"Mornin' suh," said Ted in the best southern accent he could muster when he reached the spot where the sentry had made his resting place.

"Mornin' to you, suh." Responded the sentry without even moving his head up. "Nother hot one, today."

"Sure is, suh," responded Ted and he slowly moved past the old gentleman, strongly resisting the urge to put his heels to the ribs of his horse and disappear in a gallop as soon as possible. Instead Ted had his horse maintain their slow pace. Once off the bridge, Ted eased his horse down the railroad bed and over to the road paralleling the railroad tracks on the east side.

Tom, Tuck, and Gunn followed at the same deliberate pace behind Ted. The old sentry didn't even look up at them.

There were roads on each side of the tracks because there were houses on the other side of the roads. On the east side road, there were only one row of houses. Tom took that to mean they represented the far east side of Macon. Rather than ride behind the houses, they kept to the road. Tom thought it might look suspicious to be riding around the back of the last row of homes in the city. This way they were taking the road directly to the prison at Camp Oglethorpe.

They slowly rode about seven blocks to the south until they saw the entrance to the prison on the west stockade wall. They saw no one on the road. Indeed, they saw no activity at any of the houses they passed. Ted led them past the entrance to the prison. As they rode slowly past they could see the two guards lounging against the closed front gate to Camp Oglethorpe.

Once past the stockade, Ted led them off the road and to the east so they passed by the south wall of the stockade, keeping a distance of about one hundred yards between them and the stockade wall.

After they passed the east end of the south stockade wall, Ted began to make a wide turn north toward the river. When he reached a large clump of cottonwood trees he rode his horse behind them and reined to a halt. The others were soon halted next to him.

"This looks like a good place to hide the horses," said Tom. Ted nodded his agreement. The four men dismounted, and the McMaster brothers handed their reins to Gunn.

Tuck took off his duster and tired it behind his saddle. He retrieved his kepi and put it on his head. He handed his Colt to Gunn.

"Take care of this for me, Billy," said Tuck.

"Me, your Colt, and your horse will be right here waitin' for you, Tuck," said Gunn.

Ted produced a short length of rope, and tied Tuck's hands in front of him. He secured the rope with a loose slip knot that will separate when Tuck pulled his hands apart with any force.

All four men pulled out their Colts and checked them. Gunn checked his Spencer as well.

Tom came up to Gunn. "We're countin' on you, Billy. I don't know if there'll be four of us or three of us, but without them horses we're shit out of luck." Tom put out his hand and Billy took it and the men shook hands with a hard grip.

"Good luck," said Gunn

"Good luck to you, too," said Tuck. "We're all gonna need all the luck we can get before this day is over."

Gunn shook hands with Tuck and Ted, and then the three brothers walked out of the large clump of cottonwood trees and headed for the corner of the stockade wall.

Tom and Ted walked slowly with their Colts drawn with Tuck walking in front of them like he was not happy about where they were taking him. Considering the circumstances, Tuck's improvised unhappiness was probably not too far from how he really felt.

It took the three men about ten minutes to talk to the corner of the stockade. Gunn watched them from behind the trunk of a large cottonwood tree. He had his Spencer in his hands, and he kept the muzzle sighted just over the three brothers' heads.

As they walked to the corner of the stockade, Ted looked carefully at the door on the east wall of the stockade. The door did not appear to be locked or barred from the outside. That meant they would need to unlock the door from the inside of the stockade to make their escape.

When they turned the corner of the stockade, they could see the door on the north stockade wall was still open as it had been when Ted and Tom first saw it from the knoll across the river.

As they neared the open door, all three brothers seemed to take a deep breath and then Ted appeared to be prodding Tuck through the door and into the stockade.

The inside of the stockade appeared to be deserted. The only occupants they could see were the two militia guards by the entrance to the long warehouse. Ted could neither see nor hear any activity from the other outbuildings. If some of the Union officer prisoners had been moved, it must have been men from those buildings as none of them were guarded.

The three men walked across the dusty parade ground that was once the fairgrounds for the city of Macon. The two militia guards had taken notice of them as soon as they came through the north door and entered the stockade.

The two militia guards were men in their fifties. One was short and stocky and the other guard was tall and thin. They wore mostly civilian clothes, but each man had a grey kepi on their heads. They both carried long muzzle loading rifles with bayonets attached. As the McMaster brothers got closer, it was obvious Gunn had been right. Both guards' eyes were focused on Tuck in his blue Union cavalry uniform.

"Well, well, what have we heah, Jethro," said the short guard. "Looks like we got some Yankee fresh meat."

"Yessur, Corbin, it sure do look thet way," said the tall guard.

"Wher'd you all find this Yankee?" asked Corbin, never taking his eyes off Tuck.

"Hidin' outside of Gordon," said Tom with as much accent as he could muster.

"Did you all search the blue belly?" asked Corbin.

"We took his gun," answered Tom.

"Well, we'uns are happy to take this blue belly off your'n hands, and we'll give him a proper searchin'," said a grinning Corbin.

Jethro and Corbin stepped forward to take Tuck by the elbows. At the same time Tom and Ted reversed the Colts in their hands and each man used the butt of his Colt to knock both of the guards unconscious.

As soon as the guards hit the ground, Tom and Ted each grabbed one by the collar and pulled them into the entrance to the warehouse.

As they did so, they were surprised by a third militia guard they had not seen who had been standing just inside the warehouse.

"What the hell is goin' on here?" said the surprised guard.

He didn't have time to say anything else before Ted had used the butt of his colt on the guard's forehead. The militia guard slumped to the floor with glassy, unseeing eyes.

Ted quickly pulled him over to the side of the warehouse entrance to join his fellow guards, where they couldn't be seen by anyone from the outside.

Tuck took Ted's Colt and positioned himself just inside the warehouse entrance where he could easily see anyone who might be approaching.

Ted and Tom immediately took stock of the situation in the warehouse. The building was about seventy yards long and about thirty yards wide. They could see dust covered windows at the top of the walls of the building. The windows were there to provide some light and ventilation to the building. But the windows were caked with dirt, and looked like they hadn't been opened in years.

In the middle of the warehouse, in line with the entrance, was a sizeable fire burning in a large fire ring of stones. The fire provided the only significant light and probably the only heat for the building during the winter.

Ted moved to the right of the warehouse and Tom to the left. In the shadows and darkness of the warehouse interior, they could see dark figures moving around. Tom didn't want to create an alarm among the prisoners. He couldn't see how many officers were being held in the building, but he did a visual count and estimated at least five hundred were still guests of the Confederate Army in Macon. Then he had an idea.

He motioned Ted to join him. Since both of them were still in their dusters, the prisoners had no idea they were Union soldiers.

Tom yelled out to the prisoners with as much authority as he could muster.

"I have orders to seize a Captain Timothy McMaster and take him to the infirmary. Where is Captain McMaster?" said Tom.

There was no answer and so Tom spoke again, this time yelling as loudly as he could. "Where is Captain McMaster?"

A voice from the far end of the building floated out to Tom and Ted.

"I'm Captain McMaster. What is your business with me?" said a tall, thin man dressed in a ragged blue uniform bereft of any ornamentation.

"Come forward, suh," said Tom, trying hide the excitement in his voice.

Captain McMaster came forward to the two armed soldiers with as much dignity as he could muster. He was dirty. His boots were ripped. He looked thin and emaciated to Tom. Tom thought his Pa had lost about forty pounds.

As soon as the captain was in front of them, Tom and Ted each took him by an elbow and quickly escorted him out of the warehouse and to the entrance where Tuck stood guard.

It was obvious the captain was weak. He blinked his eyes at the unaccustomed sunlight, and then stared at his escorts. Suddenly recognition came into his now focused eyes.

"Tom? Ted? Tuck? What's going on here?" asked a bewildered Captain McMaster.

"We're takin' you to an infirmary, Pa," said Tom. "Only the infirmary we got in mind is up north."

With that Ted took one arm of the captain over his shoulder, and Tom took the other. Then they headed for the door in the east wall of the stockade as fast as they could shuffle. Tuck ran ahead and unbarred the door and pulled it open, keeping the Colt in his hand up and ready for action as he covered his brothers and his father's escape from Camp Oglethorpe.

Gunn could see them when they exited the stockade door. He immediately mounted his horse and took the reins of the other four horses and moved his horse forward at a trot to meet the escapees so they did not have to struggle all the way to the clump of cottonwoods.

Gunn quickly arrived with the horses. Tuck took a spare duster out of his saddlebags, and he and Tom got it on their

Pa. Tim McMaster was gradually coming out of the shock of suddenly being freed from prison by his sons. Tom, Ted, and Tuck each took turns hugging their father who had tears in his eyes. He started to ask questions, but Tom put a finger to his father's lips.

"We can talk later, Pa. Right now we need to get the hell out of here," said Tom.

His father nodded that he understood. Then Tom and Ted helped their Pa into the saddle. Tuck grabbed his duster and put it on. Then they all mounted their horses and Ted was leading them back through the clump of cottonwoods. Once past the cottonwood trees, Ted slowed them to a fast walk. He did not want to draw any attention to a group of grey clad horsemen by riding too fast and raising a cloud of dust.

CHAPTER THIRTY-THREE

Ted rode his horse to the south, away from the prison and away from the east end of Macon. The others followed close behind in single file with Gunn bringing up the rear.

Within minutes they were out of sight of the few houses on the far east side of Macon. Ted came to an open meadow where cows were grazing. He kept to the edge of the meadow where they would be hidden by a long line of bushes and small trees.

It was now morning and the sun was up and he could hear sounds of human activity floating over the morning air. All of the sounds were behind him and slightly to his right on the other side of the meadow. All of the horsemen were attempting to be as silent as possible. Tom and Tuck had their Pa riding between them so they could keep an eye on him. They were concerned about his ability to stay in the saddle, but he seemed to have a firm grip on the saddle horn and was moving well with the motion of his horse. Their Pa's years as a rancher with long hours in the saddle made riding a horse second nature to him.

After two hours, they halted when Ted found a small clearing in a heavily wooded area. A small stream flowed near the edge of the clearing. Ted signaled a halt and the horsemen complied. Ted and Gunn dismounted as did Tom and Tuck, who helped their Pa off his horse. Gunn then took the reins of all the horses and led them over to the stream to water.

The McMasters made themselves comfortable as they sat in the shade of a stand on pine trees. Tuck took their canteens and filled them with fresh water from the stream. He returned to the pine tree stand and passed out canteens to his brothers and his father. All of them eagerly drank heavily from the canteens. Tom sat next to his father and asked him questions about how he was feeling. Then Tom checked him over for any wounds or open sores. He was pleased to find none. Tim was weak and suffering from loss of weight and strength from a poor prison diet. Otherwise, he appeared to be fine and he kept telling Tom that he was anxious for them to keep moving and put as much distance as possible between them and Camp Oglethorpe. Feeling better after drinking his fill of fresh water, Tim McMaster struggled to his feet and went to each of his sons, hugging each of them as tightly as he could. When he finished, Tim had tears streaming down his face.

Gunn returned from having picketed the horses near the steam so they could water and graze. Tom introduced Gunn to Tim and explained who he was and why he was with them. Then Gunn gratefully took a full canteen from Tuck and drank from it.

Ted went over to the horses and pulled some jerked meat and hard tack from his saddle bags and passed them out. The men sprawled out on the ground in the shade of the stand of pine trees. The emotional strain of the escape from Camp Oglethorpe had taken its toll on all of them. While they lay under the pine trees, Tom did his best to explain what they had done and were planning to do to his father.

After they had eaten their cold lunch and washed it down with cold stream water, Tom gathered them together.

"Where do we go from here, Ted?" Tom asked.

"I'd say we ride south for another hour and a half and then find a place to hide out. We try to get some sleep until it turns dark. Then we start moving to the west to get past Macon. We stay off the roads and move parallel to them, staying in the trees and brush for cover," explained Ted.

"Anybody have any other ideas?" asked Tom.

No one had anything to add, so Gunn went back to the stream and brought the horses back to the grove of pine trees. Minutes later all five of them were mounted and Ted was leading them south through heavy brush and trees.

An hour and a half later, Ted had found a small clearing in heavy brush and the horsemen dismounted. The riders unsaddled their horses, and Gunn led the horses a short distance away and used picket pins to secure the horses where they could graze easily. He then returned to where camp was being set up.

The men spread their blankets and dusters on the ground and used their saddles as pillows. The McMaster brothers and Gunn kept their Colts and Spencer rifles next to them.

Although the bright sun was overhead, the trees shaded the men from the brightness, but even in the shade it was still hot. Gunn took the first watch and within ten minutes the others were all fast asleep.

It was just getting dark when Tom shook Gunn's shoulder and awoke him. Gunn immediately got to his feet and looked around him. Tuck, Ted, and their father, Tim, were in the process of getting up as well. Gunn stood and listened. He could see nothing, but his comrades. He sniffed the air and smelled the scent of dew on the grass and bushes. He could also smell the horses. He listened and then he heard what had disturbed the others. A bugle call floated over the light evening breeze. It seemed to be coming from the direction of Macon. Everyone sat perfectly still and no one seemed to move a muscle for about fifteen minutes. After the bugle call they could faintly hear the sound of horse's hooves and the creak of leather along with bits and pieces of voices in the dark. After half an hour the sounds disappeared and Ted stood up. He motioned for everyone else to stay put and he slipped between the trees and out into the surrounding darkness. He returned about twenty minutes later.

"It's all clear," Ted whispered to Tom. "It was a patrol heading back into Macon. They're movin' away from us."

Everyone seemed to breathe a sigh of relief. All of the men got to their feet and prepared to leave. Gunn holstered his Colt and pulled on his boots. He then walked to the horses and brought them back to the makeshift camp.

Soon all the horses were saddled. Ted handed a chunk of jerked meat and a hunk of hard tack to each man. "Eat it while we ride," whispered Ted. All of the horsemen donned their dusters.

Ted then mounted his horse and led the way into the darkness that surrounded the small camp. The others mounted their horses and followed Ted in single file. Ted set the pace as a slow walk. They rode in the same formation as the day before. Ted in the lead, followed by Tom, then their father Tim, and Tuck with Gunn bringing up the rear. Each rider followed the man in front of him as closely as he needed, to keep him in sight in the darkness of the night.

The night sky had a few clouds, but the moon and many of the stars were visible. They provided enough light to help Ted pick his way through the heavy timber. He rode for about half an hour and then began to curve his way to the west.

After about four hours of riding, Ted signaled for a halt by raising his right arm. The other riders reined in their horses and dismounted. Gunn stretched out his back by putting his arms out to a nearby tree and pushing back against his boots.

His whole body felt stiff. As he looked around, it was obvious that everyone else was having the same problem.

Ted went from man to man and asked how they were doing. As he left each rider, he gave then a piece of jerked meat. Gunn chewed the jerky and took a swig of water from his canteen. What he wouldn't give for a cup of hot coffee. He knew that was out of the question, because any kind of a fire gave off light and smoke that might give them away.

After fifteen minutes, Ted climbed back into the saddle and signaled the others to do the same. Soon they were on the move again. Gunn strained to listen to the sounds of the night. Other than the horses' hooves on the ground and the creak of leather from the saddles, he could only hear the occasional song of a night time songbird. He could smell the horses and the stink of a mixture of dirt and sweat from the riders. Those were all smells he had become accustomed to since he had joined the army.

Ted led them through the woods for another four hours. At one point Gunn pulled his horse up next to Tuck. "How does Ted know we're heading west?" he whispered to Tuck.

"He's usin' the stars," whispered back Tuck.

Gunn looked up at the starry sky and was silently thankful that it was not a cloudy night.

The ride went without interruption except for one incident when two small deer were startled by their presence and bolted out of some brush and crossed in front of their tiny column. The sudden appearance of the deer got everyone's heart racing, but soon they were back to their steady pace of a slow walk. When the faint light of approaching dawn appeared, Ted began to look for a good place to camp. He found a spot on top of a small knoll surrounded by a thick band of pine trees.

They made their second camp on top of the knoll. Gunn picketed the horses a short way into the surrounding woods and the men made their beds under the pine trees that bordered the knoll. Supper was jerky, hard tack, and water. Spartan as the meal was, the men were glad to get it and the small meal was quickly wolfed down. Gunn again took the first watch, and his friends were sound asleep in minutes. About half an hour later, the still of the night was interrupted by loud snoring from Tuck. Gunn walked over to Tuck's sleeping form and lightly shook his arm. Tuck did not awaken, but he did roll over and the snoring ceased.

After almost two hours had passed, Gunn was looking forward to some sleep. He sat on the ground with his back against the trunk of a pine tree. He was close to nodding off when he heard it.

He distinctly heard voices, although they did not seem close. He grabbed his Spencer and slipped his way through the band of pine trees in the direction of the voices. When he made his way to the outside edge of the bank of trees, he stopped and listened again. Sure enough, he could hear two voices. As he peered around a tree he could see further down the knoll was a well-worn path they had not seen in the darkness, when they were looking for a place to camp.

Walking along the path to the north were two older women. A white woman was leading the way and a slightly younger Nero women was leading a mule pulling a two-wheeled wooden cart. The cart was filled with fresh vegetables. It dawned on Gunn the women were probably taking them into Macon to sell. He maintained his position behind the pine tree until well after the women and their cart had passed by. When he was sure they were gone, he retraced his steps back up to the top of the knoll.

When Gunn returned to the top of the knoll, he saw his two hours on watch were up and then some. He went over to Tom and shook him silently awake. When Tom got up, Gunn whispered to him about the cart path down below them. Tom acknowledged this with a nod of the head and Gunn lay down on his blanket and duster and was promptly fast asleep.

Gunn was nudged awake by Tuck pressing his hand against Gunn's shoulder. It was dusk and though the air was slightly cooler than it had been, it was still heavy and muggy. Gunn thought he smelled wood smoke. He looked over and Ted had created a small, hidden, cook fire. He had used branches forced into the ground and then covered with their dusters to shield the fire from any observation. He had dug a small pit and lined it with stones. Then he had gathered an armload of small dead twigs from the ground under the pine trees. To that he had added pine cones he had shredded.

Gunn put on his boots and rolled up his blanket. When he was finished, he walked over to where Ted was cooking something. When Gunn got closer, he could see that Ted was making a soup out of some of the jerked meat in a small pot. To the meat he had added some pine nuts and some salt. Although the fire emitted some smoke, it amounted to very little as the fire of dry wood was also very small.

Ted looked up at Gunn's approach. He answered Gunn's question before he could ask it.

"Pa is having trouble keeping the jerky down. Some soup ought to help him and get his strength back. What we don't eat now, I'll put in one of my canteens so he kin have more in the mornin'," said Ted in a whisper.

Gunn nodded his understanding and went to bring in the horses. After gathering up the picketed horses, Gunn led them back to the campsite.

Once there, he and Tuck proceeded to saddle the horses. "It'd shore be nice if we had some vegetables to put in that soup," said Gunn.

"Who knows what we might find out there today," said a smiling Tuck with a twinkle in his eye. Tuck was becoming notorious for his light fingered abilities. A skill that was not only handy, but very helpful when you are trying to escape from over one hundred miles behind enemy lines.

Ted waved his hands over his head and signaled all of them to sit down to breakfast. Breakfast was soup, hard tack, and water. Ted poured an equal portion of soup into each man's tin cup. Gunn tentatively took a sip. The soup was delicious and after this long without a hot meal, it was welcome as well.

Breakfast eaten and utensils cleaned and put away, the five men mounted their horses. Tim McMaster seemed to be more lively after more rest and food than he had seen in over a year. He was able to mount his horse unassisted.

Ted led the way down the knoll through the thick stand of pine trees. When he reached the edge of the trees, he reined in his horse and carefully scanned his surroundings. He listened carefully and sniffed the air. Nothing seemed out of place and so he led the small column out of the trees and onto the small path Gunn had seen the two women and their cart on.

Once there, Ted halted and looked at the night sky. The stars were beginning to show themselves. Once he found what he was looking for, he moved out, leading them in a westerly direction.

They had been riding for over an hour at a slow walk through a mixture of forest and brush filled openings, when they all heard it. A train whistle. Ted brought the column to a halt. They listened carefully, and they could hear the sounds of a passing train off to their right.

Ted waited until the train had passed. He knew they were headed in the right direction. He needed to keep paralleling the Macon and Western railroad tracks, while keeping a safe distance of at least two hundred yards. Once the train noise had faded, Ted moved forward and the rest of the men followed in single file.

They rode for another hour and came to a stream. The stream was about ten feet wide, but was shallow, and they could see the bottom of the stream was lined with gravel. Ted signaled a halt and the horsemen dismounted. They led their horses to the stream to drink, and then Tuck took their canteens and went a little upstream to fill them. The water was cold and tasted good to the hot and thirsty men.

Their thirst slaked, they mounted their horses and followed Ted as he rode to the west of the stream. About three hours later, Ted came to another small stream and again called a halt. They watered their horses and picketed them so they could graze, while the men had a brief lunch of jerky and water. Ted gave his father the rest of the now cold soup from his canteen, and he washed it down with water.

Shortly they were mounted and back on their self-made trail. After about half an hour, Ted gave the signal to halt. He dismounted and handed his reins to Tom. Without a word, Ted disappeared into the woods on foot. He was back in less than ten minutes. He walked up to Tom and whispered to him. "There's a small place up ahead. Looks like a small farm with some animals and a big garden. We'll dismount and move around it on foot."

Tom nodded and motioned to the other riders to dismount. When all of them were dismounted, Ted began to lead them forward, moving slightly to the left of where they had been riding. They moved Indian style, making as little noise as possible. Gunn was bringing up the rear, and he was surprised when Tuck stopped and moved his horse slightly off the trail Ted had made. When Gunn drew abreast of him, Tuck put his finger to his lips and motioned to Gunn to move ahead of him. Gunn shrugged and moved up behind Tim.

It took them about thirty minutes to circle around the farm. They could hear the sound of cows and pigs and chickens. They could smell the manure from the animals. They did not see any people, nor any lights on in the small farm house, but they continued to stay alert. They had no desire to be discovered by anyone.

Once they were well past the small farm, Ted mounted his horse and as soon as the rest of the men were mounted, he began riding at a slow walk to the west. The trees were less dense at this point and making his way through them had become easier.

Gunn felt movement next to him and looked to see Tuck riding past him to retake his normal place in the single file column. Tuck said nothing, nor did he make any sort of sign to Gunn. Gunn moved his horse slightly to the right to give Tuck room, and they kept moving in single file.

Ted continued to make his way west. In the next three hours, they heard at least two more trains passing by on the railroad tracks to their left. Each time, Ted brought them to a halt, and they remained there until the trains had passed.

Ted was doing this because the sound of the trains drowned out any other noise. Ted did not want to be surprised by some rebel troops or civilian southerners because the noise of their approach was drowned out by the sound of the passing trains.

The faint light of an early dawn began seeping through the trees. Fifteen minutes later, Ted found what he was hoping for. He found a small clearing in a grove of pine trees and brush. At one end of the clearing was a large pile of rocks and at the bottom of the pile was a small spring. Ted made the signal to halt, and then he rode slowly over to the spring. He dismounted and walked over to the spring. He knelt and scooped up a handful of water from the small pool the stones had created. The water was cold and tasted good.

Ted got to his feet and motioned the rest of the party to join him. They made camp and after they had unsaddled the horses, Gunn and Tuck led the horses to the spring to water. Then they led the horses to the edge of the trees bordering the clearing and picketed them, where the horses could graze.

Ted was building another small concealed cook fire when Tuck went up to him and whispered in his ear. Ted smiled. Tuck went over to his saddlebags and came back to Ted carrying some tomatoes, peppers, carrots, and an onion.

Tom took all this in and whispered to Tuck, "Where the hell did you get them?"

Tuck whispered back to his older brother. "From that farm. Don't worry, I just took a few and not more than one from the same patch. I also brushed out my footprints, big brother."

Tom just shook his head at the audacity of his little brother.

Ted made good use of the vegetables, adding some of them to the soup. Each man also got a fresh tomato and a carrot. The resulting vegetable and meat soup was delicious. Tom made as much soup as he could, and the surplus was stored in canteens.

Their stomachs full for a change, they made their beds and quickly went to sleep. Tuck took the first watch. He carefully extinguished the small, concealed cook fire. Then he sat with his back to one of the big rocks by the spring with his Spencer across his lap. The rising sun felt warm on his face.

CHAPTER THIRTY-FOUR

Gunn had the third watch. The sun was high overhead and the day was hot and muggy. He had also chosen to sit with his back to the large rock next to the spring. He could hear the faint gurgle of the water coming out of the spring, and that seemed to have a calming effect on him. A combination of the heat of the sun and the sound of the water soon caused his eyes to droop and he soon slipped into sleep.

He awoke with a start as he felt something wet and strange on his face. He opened his eyes and was staring directly into the face of a small goat. The goat had been licking his face. He looked around and could see a small herd of about twenty goats were gathered around the small spring as they drank their fill. Gunn jumped to his feet, forgetting that he had his Spencer on his lap and the rifle fell with a thump to the ground.

Not wanting to awaken anyone else and not wanting anyone to see that he had fallen asleep on watch, Gunn began waving his arms and moving about to try to herd the goats away from the spring and out of the clearing. He might as well have been trying to herd cats. The nimble goats just danced around him like they were playing some sort of game of keep-away. Finally, Gunn realized his efforts were futile, and he just sat there and watched the goats as they drank at the spring.

Before long, the goats had managed to drink their fill and they wandered out of the clearing as if they were finally bored with the whole affair. Gunn breathed a sigh of relief and resumed his watch while under the shade of a nearby pine tree. For the next hour he kept alert and watchful. Having a herd of goats sneak up on you did not say much for his guard skills.

Gunn was only too happy to wake Tom to take the last watch. He and the McMaster brothers shared the watch duty as none of them felt Tim McMaster was up to it.

Gunn had just laid down on his blanket when Tom shook his shoulder. "What are all these small hoof prints next to the spring, Billy?" he whispered.

"We had a visit from a herd of goats," mumbled Gunn in reply.

Dusk came too soon for a still tired Gunn. They ate a cold breakfast of jerky and water, while Tim had some cold soup. They were soon mounted and waiting for Ted to take the lead. He was standing in the clearing, studying the sky. There were a few clouds, but after a while he could make out enough stars to tell him what he needed to know. Ted mounted his horse and then led them out in a direction he felt was west.

They had only ridden for about half an hour at a walk when Ted held his arm up in the signal for a halt. Sure enough, they could hear the sound of a train whistle and soon all they could hear was the sound of a passing train. Again the train seemed to be about a couple of hundred yards to their right. The men smiled. They were still on the right course.

After the train passed, Ted began to move forward and the rest of them followed in single file with Gunn in his familiar spot bringing up the rear.

After about four hours of riding, they came to a good-sized stream and stopped to water the horses. Ted passed out chunks of hard tack, and they chewed on it and washed it down with water. Tim again had some cold soup.

Gunn thought Tom must have forgotten about the incident with the goats because no one had mentioned it at breakfast. He was wrong. When Tom passed him his chunk of hard tack, he looked at Gunn and said "Baaa." Then he laughed. Gunn couldn't help but smile. It had been funny.

They rode at a slow walk for almost four more hours. Once again they stopped when they heard nearby trains. This happened four times. Gunn thought the trains had to be moving troops either to Atlanta or to Macon. He had no idea of which direction the trains were heading. He could hear them, but because they kept at least two hundred yards between them and the railroad tracks, it was impossible to see the trains with the limited moon and star light available.

Ted had them halt by a small stream and the men dismounted and watered their horses and filled their canteens. Ted gave his reins to Gunn and he slipped into the woods on foot and soon disappeared.

The horses watered and the canteens filled, the men mounted their horses. They had no sooner done so than Ted reappeared out of some nearby brush. He took the reins from Gunn and led the riders around the same brush he had appeared from. They made their way through some heavy brush including some with thorns that tore at their clothing. Soon they were in a very small clearing surrounded by heavy brush. The dull light of an early dawn had replaced the moon and star light.

Ted dismounted and motioned for the others to do the same. Ted, Tom, and Tim cleared away some dead brush to make room for them to bed down. Tuck and Gunn unsaddled the horses and picketed them where the grass was most plentiful in the tiny clearing.

Once again Ted made a small, concealed cook fire and this time he reheated the soup, and also made a small pot of hot coffee. He knew he was taking a chance, but he was using very dry and very small wood and as soon as the soup was hot and the coffee made, he doused the fire with dirt.

The men sat down on the ground and ate their soup out of tin cups and then refilled them with hot coffee for the first time in days. As they sat there savoring their coffee, Ted brought out the railroad map that Tuck had found and laid it down on the ground. As he did so the others gathered around so they could see the map.

"I ain't sure where the hell we are, but I think we are somewhere around here," said Tom as his placed his finger on a spot on the map near the railroad tracks that was south of Lovejoy Station and almost due west from Jackson. "What do you think, Ted?" asked Tom.

Ted studied the map and looked at the curves the railroad tracks of the Macon and Western railroad made. "I think you are pretty close. We made a turn from headin' northwest to more north about an hour and a half ago," said Ted.

"Well, we sure as hell don't want to go into Lovejoy Station," said Tom.

"Where do we go from here, Ted," asked Gunn.

"I figure we parallel the tracks for another hour tomorrow and then we turn dead west. We should hit Fish Creek in a day or two. When we do, we cross it to get on the west bank. Then we parallel it north till we git to Line Creek. That'll be the first fork of the creek to the northwest. We stay on the west bank of Line Creek and parallel it till we hit Lower Newman Road. We cross over the road and keep runnin' parallel to Line Creek till we get to Palmetto. Just before we hit Palmetto we should cross the railroad tracks of the Atlanta and West Point Railroad."

"Do we go into Palmetto?" asked Tuck.

"Palmetto's likely to be full of rebels. We circle to the west around Palmetto. Once we git past Palmetto we parallel the road to Rivertown. We'll have to bypass Rivertown and then it's about five miles to Smith's Ferry."

"Where's Smith's Ferry?" asked Tom.

"Smith's Ferry is on the Chattahoochee River, right across to the Union lines," said a smiling Ted.

"That's still a far piece from where we are," said Gunn.

"That it is, Billy boy, but It's a damn sight closer to home than we were three days ago," said Tom.

Tom folded up the map and after they had secured their cookware, they moved to their blanket beds. Gunn had drawn the first watch. The sun was coming up and the day was already getting hotter. Gunn amused himself by clearing a space in front of where he sat. He used a stick to try to recreate the map they had studied. This time he used only the way points Ted had mentioned. It kept him busy until his watch was up. He was relieved by Tuck. Gunn laid down on his blanket and rested his head on his saddle. Minutes later he was fast asleep.

At dusk, all of the men were awake. They had a cold breakfast of jerky, hard tack, and water. They gathered up their gear and saddled their horses. Soon they were on their familiar way of paralleling the Macon and Western Railroad tracks.

After a little over an hour of riding, Ted turned his horse about ninety degrees to his left and halted. He searched the night sky until he found what he wanted and then he began moving forward again at a walk. The rest of the party followed in single file. Gunn again brought up the rear.

The further they rode, the less dense the forest became. The area was still forested, but it now also contained large spaces of brush and high grass. The next four hours they rode without a break as they were no longer close enough to the railroad tracks to hear any trains.

Ted stopped them under the shade of a grove of pine trees. The riders dismounted and picketed the horse. They walked around and stretched their legs and tried to get the stiffness out of their bodies. Then they drank some water and ate some jerky. Much of their food was now gone, but Ted and Tuck had done a good job of procuring as much food as possible when they had been in Gordon. They still had a fair supply of jerky and less of hard tack.

After twenty minutes, Ted got to his feet and went to fetch his horse. The others followed and soon the five riders were mounted and heading west behind Ted. The night sky was cloudy and the light available was spotty, but the ground was a good deal easier for Ted to follow and he led them at a fast walk.

They rode for almost three hours when they came to a stream. Ted signaled a halt and the men dismounted and watered their horses and filled their canteens.

"Is this Fish Creek?" whispered Tom to Ted.

'Naw. This stream is too damn small to have a name, and it's too close to the railroad tracks we had bin followin'," said Ted.

The horses watered, the men mounted up and Ted led them out as they resumed their nighttime journey. Ted kept them at a fast walk pace for another two hours. Then Ted signaled for a halt. He sat in his saddle sniffing the air.

"What is it, Ted?" whispered Tom.

"I smell water. It almost smells like river water," whispered Ted.

"How far?" whispered Tom.

"Not very far. Keep alert, Tom," replied Ted.

Ted motioned them forward, and he took the lead as they moved on to the west. After about fifteen minutes, even the horses could smell water and they began to quicken their pace.

They rode for a short while and again Ted gave the signal to halt. Tom reined in next to him.

Both men sat in their saddles and listened. They could hear the sound of water flowing over rocks. They could also hear the sound of night birds in the humid air.

Ted dismounted and handed his reins to Tom. Then he moved forward on foot, being careful to move Indian style and make as little noise as possible. He soon disappeared into the gloom of the darkness.

Within minutes Ted reappeared. He stepped up to Tom and took his reins from him. Then he vaulted into the saddle of his horse.

"Fish Creek?" whispered Tom.

"You bet," replied Ted with a wide grin on his face.

CHAPTER THIRTY-FIVE

Ted led the way as they moved single file through the now dense cottonwood trees. They quickly reached the banks of Fish Creek. The creek was larger than the streams they had crossed, but it was only about twenty feet wide and although swiftly flowing, did not look to be very deep. Ted dismounted and handed his reins to Tom. Then he moved upstream on foot looking for a good place to cross. He came upon a game trail and followed it to a point where it crossed the creek. He could see a gully on the other side of the creek the game trail seemed to access.

He returned to the waiting riders and took the reins from Tom and mounted his horse. He led the way upstream along the east bank of the creek. When he came to the game trail, he followed it down into the creek. Before Ted crossed he could see the creek bed was heavily lined with gravel. The water was about eighteen inches deep and his horse had little difficulty navigating the stream. As soon as Ted reached the west bank, he followed the gully up to the top of the bank.

Ted turned his horse and waved the rest of the riders across. One by one, they successfully crossed Fish Creek and joined Ted on the west bank. As soon as everyone had crossed, Ted led them north along the bank of the creek. They rode for about twenty minutes before Ted called a halt. The pale sunlight of dawn was slipping through the leaves of the cottonwood trees overhead.

Tom moved his horse up until he was next to Tom. "What is it, Ted?" whispered Tom.

Ted didn't answer. He pointed ahead of him to a point where the creek made a sharp curve. Tom followed his pointed finger until he understood why Ted had halted them. About fifty yards ahead where the curve of the creek straightened out was a cluster of large crows. More crows were flying overhead in a slow lazy circle.

Ted motioned for Tom and the rest to stay where they were. He dismounted and handed his reins to Tom. Then Ted moved forward as quietly as he could manage. When he reached the spot where the crows had congregated, he stopped and slipped down the bank to the creek and out of sight of Tom and the others.

After a few minutes, Ted reappeared at the top of the creek bank and motioned the others forward. When they reached the spot where Ted was standing, they dismounted and walked to the edge of the creek bank. Below them, lying in grotesque shapes were the bodies of two Union cavalrymen. The bodies were caught in a combination of rocks and brush. The skin of both soldiers was a deathly white, devoid of any sign of life. The chests of both men were torn open where they had been shot several times. The creek water was gradually washing away the blood from their soaked uniforms.

"Shit," said Tom. Ted motioned to Tuck and Gunn and they handed the reins of their horses to Tim and made their way down the bank to the edge of the creek. It took a little time, but they managed to drag the bodies up the creek bank and then paused as the physical and emotional effort had drained all three men. Within an hour they had dug crude graves and gently laid the dead soldiers down to their final resting place. They filled in the graves and then placed rocks over the newly turned dirt to prevent animals from digging up the bodies. Tom had gone through their pockets and in his hands he held what amounted to the earthly possessions of Privates White and Turner of the 17th Ohio cavalry. Ted put the letters and the rest of the contents of the dead men's pockets into his saddle bags. When, and if, they made it back to the Union lines, Tom would see to it that the families of the men knew the true fates of their loved ones.

When they were finished, they mounted their horses and followed Ted for another half an hour. Ted led them into a small clearing about forty yards from the creek and halted. The men dismounted and unsaddled their horses. Gunn and Tuck took the horses down to the creek to water and filled all of their canteens. When the horses were done drinking, they were picketed in the clearing near plentiful grasses. The men spread their blankets and saddles.

Ted walked down to the riverbank with some line and a hook. He found a suitable live willow branch and cut it off and fashioned it into a pole. He attached the line and hook and placed a bit of jerky on the hook. He then proceeded to walk down the creek to a place where the creek had a short drop-off creating a tiny waterfall.

Ted tossed the baited hook above the waterfall and let it drop naturally down into the pool of water created at the bottom of the falls. Within minutes he had a bite and pulled in a sizeable bass. Ted continued his fishing efforts until he had a dozen bass of various sizes lying on the bank next to him.

Satisfied, Ted gathered up the fish line and hook and placed them in his pocket. Then he got a forked stick and slipped all the fish on it, hooking them through the gills. He walked back to the campsite and tossed the stick full of fish at Tuck's feet.

"I caught 'em, you clean 'em," said Ted.

Gunn joined Tuck in cleaning the fish. By the time they were done, Ted had prepared another concealed small cook fire. This time he cooked the fish by placing sharpened to a point green willow branches through the fish and then forced the ends of the branches into the soft ground. He did this at an angle placing the impaled fish just over the small cook fire.

About fifteen minutes later, Ted announced dinner was ready and each man got a freshly cooked bass for his tin plate. The hungry men dug into the fresh fish and washed the meat down with water from their canteens.

After the meal was finished, the cookware and tin plates and cups were washed in the creek. Tom gathered everyone together under the shade of a huge cottonwood tree.

"I bin thinkin' about our plan. We know we're settin' on the west bank of Fish Creek. We kin follow the plan and follow the creek upstream to Line Creek and head for Smith's Ferry." Tom paused to let that plan sink in. "Or we could continue west until we hit the Atlanta and West Point railroad line and follow it up to near Palmetto." Tom pulled out the folded map of railroad lines Tuck had obtained in Gordon. He used his finger to trace out both of the routes so the difference was clear to everyone.

No one spoke at first. Tom was pretty sure they were thinking about the difference in the two proposed routes. Then Gunn spoke up. "If we head west to hit the railroad tracks and follow them up to near Palmetto, we got to go around Newman, Palmetto, and then Rivertown. Goin' that way adds about ten to fifteen miles to our trip. I ain't sure your Pa is up to traveling any further than needs to be."

Tom knew Gunn was right, but he wanted to make sure everyone was agreed on the best route to make it back to the

Union lines. His Pa had gotten somewhat stronger, but he was still weak. Tim McMaster had not voiced so much as a single complaint since they snatched him from Camp Oglethorpe, but Tom knew that the trip had been painful and hard for him.

Tom looked over at Gunn, his brothers, and his Pa. All of them looked tired, dirty, and worn.

"How's our food supply lookin', Ted?" asked Tom.

"We're runnin' low, Tom. We got enough for one more day, maybe two," answered Ted.

"Would it help if we had fish for breakfast?" asked Tom.

"It would help, but it would delay us gettin' started tomorrow night," said Ted.

"We could fish late this afternoon and cook them over an hour before we normally saddle up," said Gunn.

"That would work," said Ted.

"We may pass some cabins or farms on our way up river, and we could look to forage some food," suggested Tuck.

"We could, but we can't take the chance on gettin' caught. We've come this far. Now is not the time to take chances or get careless," said Tom.

"The question is which route do we take?" asked Tom.

"Let's take a vote," said Tuck.

"All right," said Tom. "Everyone in favor of the river route raise their hand."

Everyone, including Tom raised their hands.

"The river route it is," said Tom. "Let's get some sleep so we can get started as soon as it's dusk."

All the men got to their feet and headed to their blanket beds except for Gunn, who had the first watch. When everyone was bedded down in the shade of the cottonwood trees, Gunn took Tom's makeshift fishing pole, baited the hook with a bit of jerky, and made his way down to the edge of the creek where Tom had been successful earlier.

Thirty minutes later he had managed to catch five decent sized fish. Gunn used a short length of rope as a stringer and slipped it through the gills of the fish and tied a stick to one end to keep the fish from sliding off the rope and tied the other end to an exposed root at the edge of the creek. That left the fish lying in a small pool of water at the edge of the creek. Satisfied with his work, Gunn climbed back up the bank and settled himself in sitting under a large cottonwood tree with his back resting against the trunk of the tree.

Gunn rested his Spencer across his knees and listened to the sound of the rushing water of the creek. He could also hear the songbirds in the branches and reeds along the creek and the sound of the wind in the leaves in the cottonwood tree above him.

When Gunn was relieved by Ted, he told him about the fish on the stringer. Ted nodded and pointed in the direction of Gunn's blanket bed. Gunn obliged him and was soon fast asleep.

Gunn woke up to the sounds of Ted whispering to someone. He sat up and looked around. Ted and Tom had made a concealed cook fire and were cooking the fish Gunn had caught on the same poles they had used when they made camp in the morning. Now it was noy yet dark, but Gunn could see the faint light of dusk seeping through the leaves of the cottonwood trees.

He arose immediately and rolled up his gear. He and Tuck then took the horses down to the creek to water them. When they returned they saddled the horses and by the time they had finished, the fish were done. All five of them men took a pole and slipped the fish on it onto their tin plates. They ate in silence and washed the fish down with water from their canteens. Tuck and Gunn took the cookware and dishes to the stream to clean them and to fill the canteens with fresh water from the creek.

As soon as they returned to the camp and packed everything away, the men mounted their horses and Ted led the way north along the west bank of Fish Creek. Gunn rode at the rear of the small column.

Ted halted them after two hours and they dismounted, watered the horses, and stretched their legs. They were soon back in the saddle and making their way upstream. The bank of the creek was fairly clear of brush and other obstacles, and Ted kept them at a fast walk pace.

They rode for another three hours before making another stop to water the horses. This time Ted went to each rider and gave them a piece of jerky. "Make it last," said Ted to Gunn when he gave him his piece. Gunn chewed the dried meat as slowly as he could, but his stomach began to rumble after another hour had passed.

They had only ridden for a little over an hour when Ted suddenly raised his hand as a signal to halt. Tom reined in his horse next to Ted. "What is it?" whispered Tom.

"I smell wood smoke," whispered Ted. He handed his reins to Tom and slipped out of his saddle. He took his Spencer and moved forward on foot until he disappeared from Tom's sight.

Ted was gone for almost twenty minutes. Tom began to get worried. Then he could see Ted hurrying down along the creek bank.

Ted took the reins from Tom and slipped his Spencer into its holder. He mounted his horse and motioned for the others to ride their horses up and close to him.

"About a mile or so up ahead is the bridge of the Lower Newman Road. We must now be on the west bank of Line Creek," said Ted.

"Where's the wood smoke comin' from?" asked Tom.

"That's the bad news," said Ted.

"How bad?" asked Tom

"There's a freight wagon parked on the west side of the bridge. There's three rebel soldiers stopped there for the night. They built a fire and look to be having supper."

"Just three of them?" asked Tom.

"Looks like a driver and two men on horseback. Wagon's bein' pulled by two mules," said Ted.

"That don't sound so bad," said Tom.

"They got two Yankee cavalrymen as prisoners. They got ropes around their necks and the ropes are tied to the back of the wagon. They's towing them like cattle. Looks like they took their boots as the two cavalrymen are barefoot," said Ted.

"What kind of shape are the cavalrymen in?" asked Gunn.

"They don't look wounded, but it looks like they bin beat up some," said Ted. "They're still tied to the back of the wagon and they're layin' on the ground.

"What's in the wagon?" asked Gunn.

"I ain't exactly sure. Looks like guns and gear they took offa Yankee prisoners. They's headed south, likely to Atlanta. My guess is they caught them two boys trying to sneak back to the Union lines just like we are," said Ted.

"If we wait, they'll finish their supper. After we're sure they're asleep, we can pass under the bridge without bein' seen," said Tom.

No one responded to Tom and when he looked at them, they were all staring at the ground.

"What's wrong with you?" asked Tom as he looked at his four companions.

"I reckon it's time I spoke up," said Tim McMaster. "You know them boys are headed to Andersonville. After almost a year in prison in Camp Oglethorpe, I wouldn't wish Andersonville on a dog. It don't feel right to me that we let them boys go to prison, while we sneak by."

"So what are you sayin', Pa?" asked Tom.

"What if it was you and Tuck trussed up like darkie slaves and being taken to Andersonville?" said Tim.

Tom had no answer for his Pa.

"I think we kin go git them boys and make it look like the wagon and them rebs just plumb disappeared," said Ted.

"Just how do we do that?" snorted Tom. "Any shots get fired and we're likely to have rebel cavalry down on us in minutes. Then we all get to see what Andersonville looks like."

"I don't plan on makin' no noise, said Ted, as he reached to his belt and drew his Bowie knife from its sheath on his belt.

"You mean we do this just like the Sioux?" said Tuck.

"Sioux or Cheyenne, take yer pick," said Ted.

"You boys are gonna have to explain this to me," said a puzzled Gunn.

"We use the same trick we used on the guards at the prison," said Ted.

"Tuck and I slip over the creek with our horses. We get south of them rebs, and we come down the road. Tuck in his uniform with his hands tied and me behind him with my Colt on him. With my duster on, I look like a reb. Them rebs will be concentratin' on Tuck, not me," said Ted.

"While this is goin' on, me and Gunn climb up on our side of the bridge and slip up behind the wagon. While them jaspers are intent on robbin' Tuck, we take them out with our knives," said Tom.

"I ain't got no knife," said Gunn.

"You do now," said Ted as he pulled his Bowie knife out of the sheath on his belt. Ted tossed his Bowie knife to Gunn, butt first. Gunn caught it in the air and looked at it carefully. It was the largest and longest knife he had ever seen. He touched the edge with his thumb. The edge was razor sharp.

"Pa, you stay here with the rest of the horses," said Tom.

Tim nodded his understanding. He had a grim smile on his face.

Tuck took off his duster and grabbed his kepi out of his saddlebag. He put the kepi on his head, handed his Colt to Ted, and mounted his horse. Ted took a short length of rope and loosely tied Tuck's hands in front of him.

Ted then mounted his horse and he and Tuck carefully rode their horses across Line Creek to the other bank. Once across they made their way up the bank and rode through the trees. After about ten minutes they emerged on Lower Newman Road. They turned north on the road and Tuck rode slowly in front of Ted, who held his Colt in his right hand and his reins in his left.

They looked exactly like a reb soldier bringing in a Union cavalry prisoner.

Meanwhile, Tom and Gunn had moved quickly on foot upstream and had slipped under the bridge without being seen or heard. They went all the way under the bridge and then proceeded to climb the bank up from the creek to the road, keeping the bridge between them and the three rebels sitting around their little cook fire having supper.

Once Tom and Gunn reached the edge of the bridge, they crouched there in the darkness, waiting for Ted and Tuck to make their appearance.

They didn't have to wait long. The three rebels heard the horsemen before they saw them. All three got to their feet just as Tuck came into view with Ted right behind him.

"Well, well, what we'all got here?" said one of the rebel soldiers, as he and the other two soldiers rose to their feet. Tuck brought his horse to a halt right in front of the three rebels with Ted reining in his horse right behind him.

"Looks like we got us another blue belly. We keep this up we gonna have a whole company of them rascals troopin' behind our wagon," said a second rebel.

All three rebel soldiers had focused their attention on Tuck and virtually ignored Ted. Tom and Gunn took this opportunity to slip past the end of the bridge and up to the back of the wagon where the two Union prisoners were sprawled out on the ground. Both of them looked up in amazement at Tom and Gunn. Tom had his finger to his lips and the two prisoners remained unmoving and quiet in response.

"Let's see what trinkets this Yankee boy has on his person, Harley," said the first rebel.

"Hold on boys, this here is my prisoner," said Ted, his Colt still in his right hand.

"We's just takin' this Yankee offen yer hands," said the rebel called Harley. "Nothin" fer ya'all to fret about."

Harley was standing close to Tuck's horse and was holding the horses reins in his right hand. Ted looked over the heads of the rebels at Tom and Gunn, who were silently moving up in the dark to get behind the other two rebels. When Ted felt they were close enough, he swung the Colt down hard and hit Harley in the head with the barrel of the pistol. Harley dropped to the ground like a sack of potatoes.

Both of the other two rebels looked at Ted, frozen with shock. Then Tom and Gunn grabbed each rebel by his long, greasy hair and pulled their heads back. Two large Bowie knives flashed in the moonlight and both men's exposed throats were slit. The only sound was the bodies hitting the ground.

Ted turned and untied Tuck's hands. Tom searched all three of the rebels lying prone on the road. He checked on Harley, but he had no pulse as Ted's blow had crushed his skull.

"What do we do with the bodies?" asked Gunn.

"We toss them down into the creek and then drag them under the bridge, where they can't be seen from the road," said Tom.

"What about the wagon and the mules?" asked Gunn.

"Check the wagons for anything we can use. Then we push the wagon over in the creek as well. We turn the mules loose, and we use the two reb horses as mounts for our two new guests.

Tom, Ted, and Tuck dragged the bodies of the three rebels over to the edge of the bridge and then tossed them over into the creek below.

Meanwhile, Gunn untied the two Union prisoners. "Who the hell are you?" asked the dark haired trooper who looked to be the older of the two.

"Troopers of the 20th Illinois Cavalry," replied Gunn. "Who are you?"

"I'm Abel Cox and this hear is Jake Cogburn. We was with the 17th Ohio. Our outfit got shot up at Sunshine Church, and we escaped. We got all the way up to Palmetto and got caught by a rebel patrol. We thought for sure we was headed to Andersonville. Thank God for you boys."

Gunn shook hands with the two troopers and tossed then a canteen. Then he took a look inside the freight wagon. It was full of Spencer rifles, Colt revolvers, boots, gear, horse tack, and wallets, watches, and Union greenbacks. It looked like loot taken from Union troopers taken prisoner. Gunn also found some bacon, coffee, and hard tack. He grabbed an armful of bacon and hard tack and tossed them down to the ground.

Gunn turned back to Cox and Cogburn. See if you boys can find your boots in here. While you're at it, get yourself a Spencer and a Colt and some ammo.

The two troopers needed no more urging, and they climbed into the wagon and soon found their boots and slipped them on. Soon they had each outfitted themselves with Spencer rifles and Colt revolvers.

Gunn was done searching the wagon when he spied a long leather case wedged on the side of the wagon by a couple of saddles. He managed to pry the case loose and pulled it free of the wagon. Gunn jumped down from the wagon and took the case off the wagon seat. He took the case over to the side of the road and knelt down and opened it.

Tom, Ted, and Tuck appeared after climbing up the bank from the creek and walked over to the wagon.

"What was in the wagon?" asked Tom.

"Loot taken from Union prisoners. I found some bacon and hard tack and tossed them over there," said Gunn pointing to a small pile of food by the side of the road. "These two boys are Abel Cox and Jake Cogburn. They was with the 17th Ohio and Stoneman. They got beat by the rebs at a place called Sunshine Church and they escaped. They got caught by the rebels up near Palmetto," replied Gunn.

Tom jumped up on the wagon and looked inside. He grabbed a Spencer and a Colt and jumped back down. "I think Pa can make good use of these," said Tom.

Ted gathered up the bacon and hard tack and placed them in his saddlebags.

"What you got there, Billy?" asked Ted.

Gunn had opened the case and removed the contents. He was holding an 1853 model Sharps Rifle. The case also held a cleaning kit and a cartridge box containing twenty rounds.

"Holy crap, Billy, that there is a damn Sharps buffalo gun," said Ted.

"I've heard of them, but I ain't never seen one," said Gunn.

"You kin shoot damn near a mile with one of them," said Ted.

"Should we take it with us?" asked Gunn.

"If you don't take it, I will," said Ted.

Gunn replaced the rifle in the case and retied the straps holding the case closed. The case had a long leather strap attached.

"Come and give us a hand," said Tom. He and Tuck were trying move the freight wagon to push it over the bridge and into the creek. With the help of Ted, Gunn, and Able and Jake, they forced the wheels of the wagon over the bridge and the wagon tottered for a second and them fell over the edge and plunged down into the creek with a loud crash.

By now Tim had arrived leading Tom and Gunn's horses. Ted kicked loose dirt over the spots on the road that had been soaked with the blood of the dead rebels. Then he covered the small cook fire with dirt to extinguish it. When he was satisfied there was little sign of what had happened, he mounted his horse.

Gunn slipped the strap on the gun case over his saddle horn and mounted his horse. Soon all of the men were mounted. Ted leaned forward in his saddle and he sniffed the air. He could smell nothing out of place and he could not hear anything other than the movements of his friends.

"We been up here long enough," said Tom. "Let's cross over the bridge and get over on the west bank of the creek where we can hide in the woods."

The seven horsemen rode over the bridge with Ted in the lead. Once on the north side, Ted led them single file over to the west bank of Line Creek and into the woods that bordered the creek. Gunn brought up the rear of the small column.

Once they were safely in the woods, Ted set a pace of a slow walk and led them upstream and away from the potentially dangerous Lower Newman Road.

Ted led them for about two hours. He wanted to put some distance between them and the road. Sooner or later someone would discover the wagon and the bodies and that would only mean trouble for any Yankees unlucky to be in the area. The incident with the rebels had taken almost an hour. It was still dark, but dawn was not far off.

Ted brought them to a halt when he found a small clearing about a hundred yards from the west bank of Line Creek. The men dismounted and Gunn had Able and Jake help him take the horses down to the creek to water then and to fill the canteens.

When they returned to the campsite, they picketed the horses in the area of the clearing with the most grass and unsaddled them. They carried the saddles and gear over to the shady side of the clearing and each man found himself a bed site and made it as comfortable as possible.

"This here is a cold camp," whispered Ted. "No fires, no cookin' and no talkin'." He handed out small pieces of jerked meat, and the men chewed on the tough meat and washed it down with water from their canteens.

Tom decided watch duty would be shared by himself, Ted, Tuck, and Gunn. His Pa and the two young troopers from Ohio needed all the rest they could get. Gunn took the first watch and by the time he had found a comfortable place to sit with his back to the trunk of a tree, the rest of the riders were sound asleep.

CHAPTER THIRTY-SIX

Ted had the last watch, and he waited until it was actually dusk before he began to wake the others. He took Tom aside and whispered to him. "I'm goin' on ahead and scout the way. I think we got to be close to Palmetto and the road to Smith's Ferry. You get everyone ready, but you keep them here till I git back. I may be gone a spell, so don't you go getting' all nervous."

"Will do," Tom whispered back. Ted got to his feet and walked away into the growing darkness as he headed back toward the west bank of Line Creek.

Tom held off waking everyone up for at least half an hour. A little extra rest could only be good for them. Finally, he went among the sleeping men, quietly nudging each of them awake. Soon, everyone was up and busy packing away their blankets.

Gunn and Tuck retrieved the horses and took them down to Line Creek to water. When they were finished, they returned to the campsite and all of the horses were saddled. Ted handed out a small bit of jerky to each man and they all chewed on the tough meat, washing it down with water from their canteens.

Tom whispered to each man, explaining they were to wait for Ted's return before they started out.

Ted had been gone for almost three hours, and Tom was starting to feel worried about his brother. He knew Ted had the best tracking and woodcraft skills of all the brothers, but he was still nervous.

Ted appeared out of the growing darkness. He had been moving fast and he was covered in sweat and breathing heavily.

Tom waited for his brother to catch his breath. After a few seconds, Ted looked up and signaled for everyone to gather around him and Tom. When everyone was seated on the ground around Ted and Tom, Ted began to talk in a very soft and low voice.

'About half an hour ahead of us is the Atlanta and West Point railroad tracks. Just past the tracks is the town of Palmetto. It looks like we can circle around Palmetto to the west and stay out of sight. The town has a lot of rebs in it. Looks like they're the main camp defending this side of the Chattahoochee River."

"Once we're past Palmetto, it's about an hour to the village of Rivertown. There is an outpost just the other side of Rivertown. Looks to be manned by about twenty rebs. The village is real close to the river. The rebs have removed all the brush and cover between Rivertown and the river where the ferry is located. I can't see no way to sneak past that outpost."

"Where is the ferry boat located?" whispered Tom.

"The ferry boat is on the Union side of the river. They got control of it," whispered back Ted.

"How do we git around the outpost without bein' seen?" asked Tom.

"We don't," whispered Ted. "I saw a corral of cattle just this side of Rivertown, and I think we can use them to get to the river," said Ted.

"How does that help us?" whispered Gunn.

Ted looked at Gunn and grinned. "I forgot you ain't no cowboy, Billy. But after tonight you will be."

"I still don't get it," whispered Gunn.

"When we git to the edge of Rivertown, we sneak over to the corral and we open the gate to let all the cattle out. Then me, Tom, Tuck, and my Pa drive them to the edge of town. Once we got them on the road, then we stampede them through town and on to the outpost," explained Ted in a low voice.

"Them cattle will smash the hell out of that outpost and them rebs will be runnin' fer their lives," explained Tom.

"Thet should give us a clear shot to the river," said Tuck.

"Once we get to the river, how do we get the Union boys on the other side to send us the ferry boat?" asked Gunn.

"Them Union boys is likely to think we are rebs in the dark," said Jake. "How do we let them know we're Union troopers?"

"I think I got somethin' that might help them boys figure out we're Yankees and not rebs," said Tom. He got to his feet and walked over to his horse. He opened his saddlebag and pulled something out. Then he returned to the small circle of seated men. In the dark it looked like he had a small square of cloth in his hand. Then Tom opened up the square. The cloth took shape and the men were staring at a three foot by two-foot American flag.

"How long you bin carrin' that flag, Tom?" asked Tuck.

"I've had it since we left Illinois, Tuck. I had a feelin' we might need it in a pinch," replied Tom. "I figure we attach this flag to a five-foot pole. One of us carries the flag when we stampede them cattle and charge through Rivertown and down to the river"

"I think that man should be you, Billy," said Tom as he handed the flag to a surprised Gunn.

"It's time we moved out," said Ted. "We've lost a lot of night cover. We got about enough time to git around Palmetto. Then we'll hide out in the woods tomorrow. Let's get mounted."

Soon everyone was mounted and Ted led them down closer to Line Creek and then headed north with the others following in single file. Once again, Gunn was the last man in the column.

Ted led them in a slow walk. He would stop almost every fifteen minutes to listen and sniff the night air. After almost an hour, the still of the night was broken by the shrill sound of a train whistle. Ted brought the column to a halt. Soon they could hear the sound of the passing train. No one spoke or made any noise as they waited for the train to pass. When they could no longer hear the train, Ted waited another ten minutes, and then he led them forward at a slow walk.

Ted had changed his route, as he moved slightly to the left of their previous path. Within twenty minutes they were crossing over the tracks of the Atlanta and West Point Railroad. As they rode over the tracks, the riders could see some faint lights to their right, just above the train tracks. Gunn knew he was looking at the lights of the town of Palmetto. He remembered from Tuck's map the train tracks passed right through the center of the town.

Ted continued to lead them through the darkness of the night. The trees had become thicker since they left the banks of Line Creek and they moved slowly, as they carefully made their way closer to the outskirts of Rivertown.

After an hour and a half, Ted put up his right arm to signal a halt. He listened to the night air for sounds and sniffed the air. He motioned for Tom to join him. Tom came forward and reined in his horse next to Tom.

"I spect Rivertown is less than an hour ahead," whispered Ted. "I'll look for a good place to camp. We're about to lose the darkness, anyhow."

Ted nodded his agreement with his brother. It took Ted about fifteen minutes to find a clearing in the woods. Ted led them into the clearing and used hand signals to indicate this was their campsite. The men halted their horses and dismounted. The horses were quickly unsaddled and picketed in a grassy area of the clearing. The men spread their blankets under the shade of the pine trees bordering the clearing. There was no fire, no food, and just water from their canteens. They would have to stop at the first stream they found to water the horses. Gunn took the first watch as the men bedded down on empty stomachs.

Gunn found a good vantage point under the shade of a large pine tree and sat with his back against the tree's large trunk. He placed his Spencer on his lap and watched the surrounding pine trees for any unusual movement.

As the sun came up, the muggy night air became hotter and more miserable. Gunn was tired, dirty, and hungry. Yet, he knew that the next day would bring probably the biggest challenge of his young life. He understood the theory of Ted's plan, but how could they be sure what direction the cattle would stampede? What if they went in another direction? He was glad they had the flag to help the Union troops on the other side of the Chattahoochee River identify them, but it would still be dark and they could wind up traveling all this way to get shot by their own soldiers.

There seemed to be a lot to worry about, and Gunn spent the two hours of his watch doing exactly that.

When his watch was complete, Gunn moved silently over to Tuck and gently shook him awake. Tuck opened his eyes and nodded at Gunn. Tuck arose and picked up his Spencer as Gunn made his way to his blanket and saddle. Gunn laid down and tried to get comfortable under the shade of a large pine tree. He lay silently on his blanket on the ground, but sleep seemed to evade him. Finally, he drifted off.

CHAPTER THIRTY-SEVEN

It was dusk when Tom started to wake everyone up. Blankets were rolled up and gear was packed in almost absolute silence. No one spoke or made any kind of unnecessary noise. It was apparent to Tom each man understood how important this night was to their survival and their future.

Ted surprised Tom by building a concealed tiny cook fire. Once he had fire hot, Ted cooked some of the bacon Gunn had found on the rebel freight wagon. The men had hot bacon and hard tack dipped in bacon grease washed down by water from their canteens. As soon as the meat was cooked, Ted extinguished the small cook fire and buried it with dirt.

"A last meal for the condemned?" whispered Tom to his brother Ted.

"Them boys are gonna need all the energy they can get if all of us are to survive this night," replied Ted in a low voice.

The horses were gathered up and saddled with a minimum of noise, and soon they were all mounted and ready to ride. Ted led the way into the gathering darkness as they rode slowly through the pine trees.

After about an hour of slow riding, Ted called a halt. He motioned to Tom and Tuck to join him. Both men rode up and reined in their horses next to Ted.

"Me and Tom will go ahead on foot and do a little scoutin'. You stay here with our horses, Tuck," whispered Ted.

Both men nodded their understanding, and Tuck took their horses' reins while Tom slipped out of his saddle. Ted and Tom moved ahead on foot and disappeared into the pine trees and the surrounding darkness.

Ted led the way. He moved Indian style through the dark woods. Tom began to wonder if Ted was lost after it seemed like they had been walking in the woods for a long time.

Ted put up his right arm as a silent signal to halt. Then he motioned toward the ground with his hand as Ted dropped to his knee. Tom quickly went to his knee as well. Ted turned to Tom and whispered, "We crawl from here." Tom nodded his agreement.

Ted began crawling forward for about thirty yards. The ground seemed to be sloping higher as they crawled. Finally, Ted stopped just below the top of a small rise. Ted motioned for Tom to join him. Tom crawled up next to Tom. It was dark, but he had been in the dark long enough his eyes had adjusted.

Tom peered through the darkness, but he could see nothing. He looked over at Ted and gave a shrug of his shoulders. Ted smiled and pointed to his nose. Tom sniffed the air and detected the unmistakable scent of fresh cow manure and the smell of many cows.

Tom again peered in the direction his nose had indicated cattle, and soon he could make out the dark shadows of large animals milling around in a big corral. Just beyond the corral, he could see the faint twinkling lights of the small village of Rivertown.

"You stay here," whispered Ted. "Cover me"

With that Ted, crawled over the top of the rise and slithered into the tall grass beyond. At first Tom could detect

Ted by watching the tops of the tall grass waving when there was no perceptible wind. Then he could no longer determine where Ted was. Tom drew his Colt and prayed for his brother.

After about twenty minutes, Tom could see the tops of the grass in front of him moving, and then Ted slid out of the grass and back over the top of the knoll.

"What did you find?" whispered Tom.

"Looks to be about four hundred head of cattle. I saw no guards and the gate opens to the road leading through town and on to the river. I think you, me, Tuck, and Pa can handle this. We'll have Billy and them other two Ohio boys follow us," whispered Ted.

"Let's head back," whispered Ted. Without another word, Ted turned around and began crawling back to the trees. Tom followed right behind him. When they reached the relative safety of the tree line, Ted stopped crawling and got to his feet. Then he began to carefully and silently make his way back through the pine trees to where the others waited. Tom rose to his feet and followed.

Soon they were back with the others. Ted gathered them together, and he and Tom had them sit down on the ground in a circle. Tom cleared off the ground in front of him so there was nothing but loose dirt. He took a stick and made a small "x".

"This here is where we are now," Ted said. Then he took the stick and drew a large four sided square. "this is where the corral is located. It's holdin' about four hundred head of cattle."

Then he drew the two parallel lines next to the corral and leading further north. "This here is the road to Smith's Ferry." Then he drew two long narrow box shapes on either side of the road. "This is the village of Rivertown."

Ted extended the road a little further and put an "x" across it. "This is where the rebel outpost has the road blocked."

Ted then took his hand and made a wide swath in the dirt that crossed the end of the road like a "T". "This is the Chattahoochee River." He drew a small box shape on the far side of the river. "And this is the ferry boat on the Union side of the river."

Ted passed the stick to his big brother, Tom. Tom looked at each of the men seated on the ground and paused for a few seconds. Then he took the stick and pointed to the corral. "Me, Ted, Tuck, and Pa will ride down to the corral. Gunn, you and Abel and Jake will wait in the tree line. You boys got that?" asked Tom.

Gunn and the two young troopers from Ohio nodded their heads in understanding.

"Pa will open the gate and Ted and Tuck will slowly ride their horses into the corral and get to the back side of the herd. I'll be next to Pa. Then Ted and Tuck will begin to move the herd out of the gate of the corral. I'll be on one side and Pa on the other to keep the cattle moving to the road. When we got them cattle moving to the road, you three come out of the woods and get behind the herd," said Tom as he pointed at Gunn and the two Ohio troopers.

"When we got the herd to the road, we'll turn them and head them on the road and into Rivertown with you boys right behind us," said Tom.

"When we get to the edge of the village, we'll fire off our Colts and start yelling to get the cattle to stampede. You boys stay behind the herd and do the same," said Tom.

"We're gonna ride like hell with that herd of cattle through that town. It's the middle of the night and it ain't likely we'll get much trouble, but we might. You boys will be right behind the herd and if you see someone trying to take potshots at us, shoot the bastards. Understood?"

Gunn and the two young troopers nodded they did.

Tom continued with his instructions. "Me, Pa and my brothers have done this plenty of times, and we'll be riding on the flanks of the herd. We'll keep them on the road, and it's just a short distance to the rebel outpost. Them cattle should blow through that roadblock and any rebels stupid enough to get in their way. The stampede should be enough to scare the hell out of them and make the scatter. Even so, some might hold their ground. If you see a rebel, shoot him," said Tom.

"Once we're past the outpost, we'll let them cattle scatter and we ride like hell for the river and Smith's Ferry. Billy, you need to find a stout limb to tie that flag to. We need you and that flag to get down to the edge of the river and let them Union troopers know we're not rebels. If for any reason Billy drops the flag, the next man has to pick it up and get it down to the river. Anybody got any questions?" asked Tom.

"What do we do if we get to the river and nobody brings the ferry boat over?" asked Abel.

"Then you force your horse into the river and swim for it and hope for the best. Either way some of us may need to stop at the river and give the rest cover so they can cross."

"Who do you want to provide cover?" asked Tuck.

"We'll cross that bridge when we come to it," said Tom with a slight smile on his face.

"Any more question, boys?" asked Tom.

There were no more questions.

"Let's mount up and get moving," said Ted.

The seven men mounted their horses for what promised to be the most important ride of their lives.

Ted led the way through the woods and there was no talking and as little noise as possible as they made their way in single file to the tree line above the corral.

Ted raised his right arm in a silent signal to halt them when they reached the tree line. Then he, Tom, Tuck, and Tim rode their horses toward the top of the small knoll.

Tom halted his horse before he got to the knoll. He turned his horse and rode back to the tree line where Gunn and the two young troopers waited. Tom reined in his horse and looked at the three young men.

"See you boys at the river," said Tom and he touched the brim of his kepi with his right hand. He and his brothers and Gunn had shed their dusters. This was one time they wanted there to be no doubt they were Union cavalrymen.

Gunn dismounted and found a nearby tree with a stout branch close to the ground. He cut it off and then cut off the branches, giving him a serviceable flag pole. Then he attached the flag to the pole and wound the flag around the pole. Satisfied with his work, he mounted his horse.

Tom rode to the top of the knoll where the other three riders were waiting for him. Once Tom reached them, the four of them turned and rode slowly down the hill to the corral full of cattle.

Tim rode to the gate of the corral and dismounted, handing his reins to Tom. It took Tim only a few seconds to unlock the gate and pull it open. Then Ted and Tuck slowly rode their horses inside the corral and worked their way carefully to the back of the corral. Nervous cattle shuffled and bumped into each other as they sought to get out of the way of the intruding horses.

Once the two brothers had reached the rear of the corral, they began waving their arms and using their horses to force the cattle to move before them. Soon the cattle discovered the open gate and began pouring out of the corral. A mounted Tom was on the north side of the gate and Tim on the south. They forced the cattle exiting the corral to keep moving toward the road.

Finally, Ted and Tuck had emptied the corral, and they took their places on the flanks of the cattle herd to slowly move them to the road. Gunn and the two Ohio troopers left the tree line and rode down the hill at a trot. Soon they reached the back of the herd and as the experienced cattle drovers from the Colorado Territory turned the herd, Gunn and the two troopers put pressure on the rear of the herd. Soon all the cattle were moving slowly down the road to the south end of Rivertown.

There were only a few flickering yellow lights coming out of some random windows in the little town. There were no people or rebel troops on the street running through the middle of town. Once Tom had the cattle herd halfway into the village where the buildings on both sides acted like very tall fences, he drew his Colt and began yelling and waving his arms as he fired the revolver into the night sky. Ted, Tuck, and Tim immediately joined in and in an instant, the cattle herd went from a slow moving mass to a stampeding avalanche of meat and hooves. The bawling of the cattle mixed with the thunder of their hooves on the road and the yelling and shooting of the troopers to make a nightmare of noise shattering the still of the quiet night. Gunn and the two Ohio troopers rode hard at the rear of the stampede and added their yelling and shooting.

As the cattle herd thundered through the village with Gunn, Jake, and Abel riding at the rear, Gunn saw a rebel run out onto the roof of a building on Gunn's right. The rebel was carrying a rifle and he swung it up to his shoulder to bring it to bear. Gunn switched the flag pole to his left hand, used his right hand to draw and aimed his Colt and pulled the trigger. The rebel threw up his arms and dropped the rifle, and fell from Gunn's sight. Gunn holstered his Colt and switched the flag pole to his right hand.

By now Gunn, Jake, and Abel were riding as hard as they could and hanging on for dear life. They were also engulfed in a huge cloud of dust that seemed to black out even the darkness of the night. The dust made it difficult to see and hard to breathe.

Tom and Ted were each riding on the outside edge of the herd. Tom was on the left and Ted was on the right. Both men were experienced drovers, but racing along the outside edge of the stampeding herd was difficult at best. Each rider had to hold his horse in line and keep from getting crushed against the frame buildings they were passing within inches of.

It was less difficult for Tim and Tuck as they were on the outside edge of the middle of the herd, but no less dangerous. When the herd burst clear of the confines of the small town, Tom and Ted had to keep the lead cattle moving down the road and avoid having them make a turn. Fortunately, it was only less than half a mile to the Confederate outpost. Both Tom and Ted road fearlessly at the front edge of the stampeding herd. The herd maintained their course on the road and thundered toward the outpost.

Tim and Tuck were also clear of the town and doing their best to keep the stampede moving by waving their arms and shouting. They had holstered their Colts for fear of dropping them as they needed use of both arms and hands. Gunn, Jake, and Abel were doing their best to stay right behind the herd, but with all the dust in the air, they were unable to see each other, let alone the stampeding cattle herd.

CHAPTER THIRTY-EIGHT

Amos Watters had just finished taking a leak in the bushes near the roadblock he and his squad were manning just outside of Rivertown. The quiet of the night had been broken only by crickets since he came on duty. He was tired and hungry, and he would be happy when his shift was over and he could climb into his blankets and sleep.

Suddenly, he heard gunshots and yelling coming from the direction of Rivertown. As he buttoned up his pants, he could not imagine what was going on. No Union troops had passed their positon, so it couldn't be a raid. The ground between the outpost and the river had been cut clear of all brush and anything else a Yankee might hide behind. No one could approach the outpost from the river without being seen. The men at the outpost had a clear field of fire all the way to the river.

Then Amos felt something he had never experienced before. The ground began to shake. It was like the ground under his feet was actually moving. He actually knelt down to touch the ground with his hands, and he could feel the ground moving. Then he heard what sounded like thunder along with some strange noise he could not place.

Overcome with fear, Amos ran to the roadblock where the rest of his squad had been seated around a small campfire.

He found them standing and looking around in fear and confusion. He ran to one of the nearby trees and grabbed on to the trunk with both his hands. He could feel the tree shaking. He didn't know what else to do, so he started praying.

Back in Rivertown, the Confederate troop of cavalry stationed there had gotten over their initial shock of waking up to a stampede of cattle down the main street of town. Confederate troopers, some in their long johns, had pulled on their boots and were saddling their horses. Within a few minutes, at least a dozen troopers had mounted their horses and galloped off in pursuit of the stampeding herd of cattle and whoever had been shooting off guns as they rode through town.

As the stampeding cattle approached the rebel roadblock, Tom and Ted began to drop back further along the edge of the herd. Tim and Tuck made the same maneuver and put more cattle between them and the rebels at the roadblock.

The rebels initial fear and shock had worn off and they were scrambling to get out of the way of the oncoming stampede. Some climbed trees, and some dove into ditches. A few poor souls had been frozen in place by their fear. The stampeding herd crashed through the road block, smashing the wooden barrier to splinters and overturning a small freight wagon. None of the rebels who had not run, survived the onslaught. Some of the rebels who did run did not survive either.

Two rebels who had sought shelter in nearby ditches were trampled to death.

Amos Watters was almost ten feet up in a pine tree, and he hung on for dear life as the herd thundered under and past him.

As the herd passed the rebel roadblock they began to scatter and as the cattle became winded, the stampede began to slow down. Tom and Ted raced their horses past the slowing cattle and headed down the road to the river and Smith's Ferry.

Not far behind them were Tim and Tuck who were having to turn their horses to dodge straying cattle. Gunn, Jake, and Abel were almost two hundred yards behind Tim and Tuck. A combination of the heavy dust cloud and the darkness of the night had kept them further behind the stampede. Now they were also dodging groups of cattle who were heading off on compass points known only to them.

Tom's concern about getting the attention of the Union troops on the other side of the Chattahoochee River was unfounded. The combination of the noise of gunshots and the thunderous roar of the cattle herd stampeding had awakened many Union soldiers. By the time Tom and Ted were galloping down the sloping road to the ferry location, there were almost three hundred armed Union soldiers lining the north bank of the river. They formed a skirmish line on the north bank of the river. There they awaited what they thought might be a night time raid by Confederate cavalry.

Gunn slowed his horse slightly as he unfurled the small American flag and held it upright. Even so, he was still about twenty yards ahead of Jake and Abel. When Gunn turned in his saddle to see where the two Ohio troopers were, he could see about a dozen other riders about two hundred yards behind them. He knew those riders had to be rebels.

Then Gunn heard gunshots and he could hear the sound of bullets whizzing over his head. Gunn heard a loud scream from not far behind him. Gunn reined in his horse and turned to face the oncoming rebels. Abel had been shot and was on the ground. Jake had reined in his horse next to the fallen Abel. Now rebel bullets were zipping into the ground next to them.

Gunn could tell Jake was terrified and uncertain of what to do. "Take this and ride to the river, Jake," said Gunn as he handed Jake the now unfurled flag. Jake grabbed the flag and galloped off toward the river. Gunn dismounted his horse and grabbed his Spencer and the leather case hanging from the saddle horn. He forced his horse down on its side and laid down behind it for cover.

Ezra Crook found himself in the lead of a dozen Confederate cavalrymen pursuing the Yankees. Crook was a sergeant and as near as he could tell, no officers were riding with him. Ezra had managed to shoot one of the Yankees out of the saddle. Due to the darkness, Ezra could barely see two more Yankees halted by the fallen man.

Gunn realized he could not stop a dozen rebel riders. He decided to try to confuse them and make himself look like several shooters instead of just one.

Gunn quickly opened fire on the rebels with his Spencer. In his first three shots, Gunn dropped two rebel horsemen from their saddles. This caused the other rebel troopers to rein in their horses. The rebel troopers were surprised at Gunn's stand, and were having trouble seeing him in the darkness. They were unsure of how many Yankees they were up against because of the number of times Gunn had quickly fired at them.

Gunn thought quickly. He would not have time to reload the Spencer if he ran out of bullets and that was more than likely as there were still at least ten rebel troopers out there. Plus, he knew there would be more on the way. He took advantage of the short lull while the rebels were deciding what to do next, by opening the leather case and taking out the Sharps Rife. He loaded the Sharps and laid it on the ground next to him.

The rebels overcame their initial confusion and spurred their horses to come at Gunn again. This time he dropped two more rebels, but fired off four more rounds. Now the Spencer was empty. The rebels had halted again and were sitting on their horses about a hundred and fifty yards away. Gunn laid the Spencer down on the ground.

Ezra had halted his men when they suddenly faced heavy fire from a concealed position in front of them. He could not tell how many Yankees were shooting at them and he had watched at least five of his men get shot out of their saddles. He decided to pull the rest of his men back to a safe distance that he knew would be out of the range of the Spencer rifles the Yankees used. Ezra led his men back to a distance of about three hundred and fifty yards. He was pretty sure that more of his cavalrymen were on their way and then they could overwhelm the Yankee positon.

After taking a quick look at the rebel horsemen moving to a position out of range of his Spencer, Gunn picked up the Sharps rifle. He flipped up the tang sight and lined up a rider. He took a deep breath and let most of it out. Then he carefully squeezed the trigger and the powerful Sharps barked and Gunn could feel the intense recoil in his shoulder. The rider he had placed his sights on flew off his horse like he had been pulled off with a hidden rope. The other riders looked around in confusion.

Gunn reloaded and fired a second time, sending another rebel trooper airborne from his saddle. Now the remaining rebel troopers wheeled their horses and retreated until they were about five hundred yards distant. Then they turned their horses around to face Gunn from a positon they were safe from the Yankee rifles.

Gunn reloaded and lined up a rider who appeared to be in charge of the rebel horsemen. He carefully squeezed the trigger and sent the man cartwheeling off his horse. The rest of the rebel troopers turned their horses and bolted back in the direction of Rivertown.

Gunn rose to his feet and pulled his horse up by the reins. He slipped the Spencer back in its mount. Then he mounted the horse and rode back toward the fallen Abel. His ears were still ringing from firing the Sharps and he didn't hear anything, until he became aware of riders to either side of him. Gunn looked and he could see Tom and Ted riding stride for stride with him. Tuck was right behind them and he was carrying the small American flag aloft he had taken from Jake.

The four men quickly reached Abel, and Gunn dismounted, handing his reins to Tuck. A quick inspection found Abel had been shot in the shoulder. Gunn tore off part of the bottom of his shirt and stuffed it over the wound and used Abel's cavalry jacket to hold it in place. Gunn got Abel to his feet and Tom reached down and helped Gunn get Abel mounted behind Tom on Tom's horse. Then Gunn mounted his horse and the four horses turned and raced to the river. Jake was waiting for them about fifty yards from the river and when they rode past him, he joined them.

The Union soldiers had brought the ferry boat over to the south bank of the river and almost one hundred blue-clad Union infantrymen had come over the river and made a defensive line along the river bank. When the small mounted squad with the tiny American flag rode toward them, the Union infantrymen broke into cheers. When the riders reached the Union line of infantry, the soldiers opened their line to let the cavalrymen pass through to the bank of the river. Soon all seven men and their horses were halted on the river bank.

They dismounted and led their horses on the ferry boat. Four infantrymen carried Abel onto the ferry boat and laid him down carefully on the wooden deck. Soon the ferry boat was in motion and Gunn felt a huge sense of relief. He felt like his heart had stopped and now it was safe to begin breathing again. He looked around the ferry boat. All the McMaster family had huge grins on their faces as did young Jake. Then realization swept over Gunn.

"Shit, I left the Sharps back there," he blurted out.

"You did, I didn't, said a grinning Ted as he pointed to the leather case hanging from the saddle horn of Ted's horse. Once again, Gunn felt a sigh of relief. Within minutes, Gunn, the McMasters, Jake, and Abel were on the Union side of the Chattahoochee River and safety.

Once on the north bank, they were met by a major in charge of the infantrymen. He had a long black beard and wore a fairly new blue uniform. He was a stark contrast to the seven cavalrymen who were filthy dirty, dressed in ragged and torn uniforms, with haggard looks on their faces.

"I'm Major Hopkins," he said. "What unit are you boys with?"

"Captain Tim McMaster," responded Tim, "Recently of the 88th Illinois Infantry. These four gentlemen are troopers from the 20th Illinois Cavalry, and these two young gentlemen are troopers from the 17th Ohio Cavalry."

The major turned and looked at the six troopers. "I assume you boys were under the command of General Stoneman on his raid to Macon?" asked the major.

"Yes, sir," responded all six troopers.

"Did you escape from the battle at Sunshine Church?" asked the major.

"Yes sir," responded Jake and Abel.

The major looked puzzled. "What about you four men from the 20th Illinois?" he asked, looking straight at Tom because he wore corporal stripes on his uniform.

"We were with Major Carlson on the raid on Gordon, Major," responded Tom.

"So you managed to make your way here from clear down in Gordon?" asked the major.

Tom looked unsure of how to answer the major and his father, Tim McMaster decided it was time to speak up and clear the air.

"Major Hopkins. As I told you, I'm Captain Timothy McMaster of the 88th Illinois Infantry. These three troopers are my sons. Trooper Gunn is the fourth member of their squad. After the raid on Gordon, they elected to move west to Macon, where they managed to assist me in escaping from the Camp Oglethorpe prison. We made our way here by moving north and staying to the west of the Ocmulgee River. We traveled at night and hid during the day. While we were traveling north, we encountered these two young troopers from the 17th Ohio Cavalry as prisoners of three rebel soldiers. We freed the prisoners and had them accompany us north until we reached your lines," said the Captain.

The major's face was a combination of shock and amazement. "Good lord, sir. How long were you a prisoner at Camp Oglethorpe?"

"Almost a year, Major," replied Captain McMaster.

The Major recovered from his surprise and turned to his aide. "Lieutenant, take Captain McMaster to the Colonel's quarters. Have the company clerk take down the details from these troopers and make sure this wounded trooper gets to the infirmary immediately."

Within an hour Captain McMaster had been escorted into Colonel Vonalt's tent. When the captain was only partway through his story, the Colonel stopped him and poured both of them a drink of fine bourbon. The Colonel turned to his aide. "Lieutenant, get this man something to eat and make it quick," he said.

While the captain was being questioned, Gunn, Tom, Ted, Tuck, and Jake were taken to a nearby mess tent and allowed to eat while they were being questioned by a captain, as a company clerk took notes.

After almost two hours of questioning, the McMaster brothers, Gunn, and Jake were escorted to the wash tent and each man enjoyed a lukewarm bath and were issued new uniforms and boots. The orderly used a long stick to gather up their old uniforms and take them to the burn pile.

After they had been cleaned up and outfitted in new uniforms, the five troopers were taken to a vacant squad area. Stacked next to a large wall tent were all of their horse tack and their Spencer rifles along with the leather case containing the Sharps. The troopers were allowed to climb into vacant cots in the tent. Soon the air around the area was filled with the sounds of loud snoring.

Late that morning their sleep was interrupted by the arrival of Captain McMaster. He too, had enjoyed the luxury of a bath and had been issued a new uniform and boots. He brought news.

"Apparently we are but one of many small groups who made it back to our lines from General Stoneman's defeat at Sunshine Church. I was told Major Carlson's raiding party suffered losses attempting to return to the Union lines, but they were mostly successful. I was given the impression no unit returning to our lines did it in as a dramatic manner as we managed to accomplish," said the captain as a slight smile crept into his face.

"Trooper Cox will survive his wound and will be kept here in the infirmary until he is fit to travel. I will be traveling to General Sherman's headquarters. He wishes a firsthand account of my experiences in Camp Oglethorpe as well as the method of my escape. When the interview is concluded, I will be granted two months leave to return home to my ranch and recuperate," explained the captain with a big smile on his face.

"Any news about what happens to us?" asked Tom.

"You boys are to be returned to duty with the 20th Illinois. Apparently they lost a good number of troopers on their raid, and they need replacements. They will be more than happy to see the four of you," answered Captain McMaster.

"Jake will also be returned to duty with the 17th Ohio, who are also in need of replacements."

"When we will be returning to our units?" asked Ted.

"The Colonel told me an escort will be here this afternoon to take you boys back to your units. An escort will also be here shortly to take me to General Sherman's headquarters," said the captain.

"So this is good-bye for a while?" asked Tuck.

"Yes, son, this is good-by for a while," said the captain as he tried to keep the tears from his eyes. One by one Tom, Ted, and Tuck hugged their father. Then Captain McMaster turned to Gunn. "Billy, I can't thank you enough for agreeing to accompany my sons on what was most certainly a crazy scheme. That took a good deal of courage, and I appreciate everything you did. I was not at all surprised when you turned back at the river to save Abel. You're a good soldier, Billy, and as far as I'm concerned, you will always be treated as a member of my family." With that the captain shook hands with Gunn and then gave him a strong hug.

The captain had a few words for Jake and then shook hands with him and wished him "Good luck and God speed."

Then Captain McMaster turned and walked over to a lieutenant who had been patiently waiting over on the edge of the squad area. As soon as the captain joined him, the lieutenant escorted him away.

"What the hell do we do now?" asked Tuck.

"I ain't sure about you, little brother," said Ted, "but I'm headed to the mess tent. My stomach tells me I got a lot of catchin' up to do." The rest of the troopers joined Ted in a laugh and followed him to the mess tent.

CHAPTER THIRTY-NINE

It was almost three days before an escort showed up to take Tom, Ted, Tuck and Gunn back to their regiment. They all shook hands with Jake and wished him good luck. Then they were saddling their horses and packing some newly obtained possessions in their saddlebags. Gunn made sure he did not forget the Sharps and slung the long strap of the leather case over his saddle horn.

They left their rest area about mid-morning under the heat of the August sun. As they rode along with road parallel to the Chattahoochee River, Gunn thought back to their one hundred and ten mile ride from Macon to the banks of this river. They had been very lucky. Gunn had seen too many friends and others die since he had enlisted in the army back in Illinois. He wondered how his father, uncle, and brother were doing. Hopefully they had their crops in, and they were doing well. Gunn vowed to himself if he survived this terrible war, he would go back to farming and never harm another soul.

After about a two-hour ride, Gunn began to recognize landmarks along the river. He had been here before.

Shortly thereafter, they arrived at the encampment of the 20th Illinois Cavalry. Their first stop was the corral where they unsaddled their horses and had them fed and watered. They wiped their horses down and used curry combs on them.

Gunn couldn't help but notice there were a lot less horses in the corral than he remembered.

When they had finished with their horses, the four troopers gathered up their horse tack, gear, and their Spencer rifles and started walking back to their squad area. They passed the mess tent, which seemed unusually deserted. As they passed squad areas, they noticed the large number of empty tents. None of this was a good sign, thought Gunn.

When they finally reached their squad area, they found their tents just as they had left them, over a week ago. It was like the entire raid, rescue, and escape had never happened

The troopers had no sooner put their gear away when Major Carlson and a lieutenant they did not recognize appeared in front of their tents.

The four troopers came to attention and saluted the major. He returned their salute.

"At ease, gentlemen," said the major.

The troopers assumed the at ease positon and waited for the major to speak.

"I cannot tell you how happy I am to see all of you back here in one piece. I was not very pleased when Sergeant Mann informed me you had decided to make your own way back to our lines, but I cannot help but applaud your choice to free your father from Camp Oglethorpe prison in Macon. Your rescue of the captain and subsequent escape back to our lines is an impressive achievement," said the major.

The major paused and looked carefully at the four troopers. Then he spoke. "I would like to suspend military decorum here. I'd like to hear your story and having you do it standing out here in the hot sun is not what I had in mind. Let's adjourn to the shade of that grove of trees and talk like soldiers." With that he led the way over to the shaded area and the major then sat down on the ground.

Robert W. Callis

"Please sit, gentlemen, sit. I mean what I said. I wish to know every detail about your assault on the prison and how you managed to escape. You must understand, our raiding party did not do as well as you did. We ran into three different ambushes and lost too many men who were killed, wounded or captured," explained the major.

The four troopers sat on the ground and looked awkwardly at the major. He sensed their discomfort and spoke.

"Corporal McMaster, please tell me what happened and please do not spare any details," said the major with a smile.

Tom looked at his brothers and at Gunn. He then looked at the major and saw in his eyes the major was sincere in wanting to know what had happened to them.

Tom swallowed and then began to speak. He told the major they decided in Gordon to make their own way back to the north and that included going to Macon and trying to free their father. As Tom told his story, the major leaned forward as he listened intently. Tom talked for almost half an hour. When he finished his story, Tom looked up at the major.

"Major, sir, I want you to know if there are any charges involved for what we did, this entire thing was all my idea. I convinced my brothers we could free my Pa, and then we managed to talk Gunn into going along with us. If anybody is guilty here, it's me," said Tom.

The major smiled. "Corporal McMaster, there are to be no charges of any kind. When General Stoneman gave me the order to attack Gordon, he gave me no other orders. My only choice was to have my men make their way north. You did that. In addition, General Stoneman was attempting to attack Macon and to free the Union officers held prisoner at Camp Oglethorpe. He failed, but you did not. In addition, you rescued two other Union cavalrymen held prisoner by the rebels and you managed to bring everyone under your command back to our lines. Corporal, I salute you for that and I welcome you back to the 20th Illinois. We are in need of all four of you. We have suffered serious losses in this last raid. We need veteran troopers like you four to help the new recruits when they arrive as replacements to the regiment," said the major.

"New recruits are arriving every day, and they need training and the guidance only veteran troopers can provide. Rumors tell me General Sherman is on the verge of taking Atlanta. Once that's accomplished, the 20th Illinois will be a part of his effort to sweep through the Confederacy and help bring an end to this war."

The major looked at Tom and broke into a grin. "Please stand up, gentlemen," ordered the major.

When the four troopers were standing, the major motioned to the lieutenant, who had been standing patiently nearby. The lieutenant handed the major a small open envelope.

The major then addressed the four troopers. "Corporal McMaster, you are now Sergeant McMaster," said the major as he handed the chevrons to Tom.

"Trooper Theodore McMaster, you are now Corporal McMaster, said the major as he handed corporal stripes to Ted.

"Trooper William Gunn, you are now Corporal Gunn," said the major as he handed corporal stripes to Gunn.

"Last, but not least, Trooper Tucker McMaster, you are now Corporal McMaster," said the major with a grin as he handed corporal stripes to Tuck.

Then the major and the lieutenant saluted the four newly promoted troopers. Tom, Ted, Tuck, and Gunn returned the salute.

When the major and the lieutenant had left, Gunn turned to Tuck with a grin on his face. "Your name is Tucker?" he said laughing. "All this time I thought Tuck was your real name."

Tuck blushed. "Tucker is my real name, but all it did was get me in fights, so I shortened it to Tuck."

"You're still Tuck to me," said Gunn with a grin on his face.

The troopers were busy sewing their new chevrons on their uniforms when they were interrupted by the appearance of their old troop commander, Captain Dexter.

"Glad to have you boys back," said the captain as he shook hands with each one of them. "Congratulations on your promotions. They're well deserved."

"Where's the rest of I Troop?" asked Gunn as he pointed to the empty tents around them.

"Some of them are at the rifle range, some are still in the infirmary, but the truth is we lost a lot of them killed, wounded, or captured. Sadly, we came back with only about half of the men we started out with," said the captain.

"What about Sergeant Mann?" asked Gunn.

"I'm sorry, son, he didn't make it back," said the captain.

Tom, Ted, and Tuck each asked about other troopers they had known, and Captain Dexter had bad news about almost all of their inquiries.

"Do you know if Trooper Barnes made it back?" asked Gunn. He waited for the captain's answer with a sense of dread.

"Trooper Barnes was wounded, but he saved the lives of the other three troopers in his squad and all of them made it back. I believe Barnes is still in the infirmary," replied the captain.

After Captain Dexter left, the four troopers decided to head down to the mess hall for supper. When they reached the mess hall, they found it about half full of troopers they knew. When the four troopers entered the mess tent, the other troopers took notice and they all rose from their seats as one and cheered the newcomers. There was a lot of hand shaking and back slapping as the men of I Troop welcomed back the four troopers.

The next few days were full of activity as Tom, Ted, Tuck, and Gunn assumed their new duties as non-commissioned officers and were assigned to train the new replacements, who kept arriving every day to swell the ranks of the regiment.

Chapter Forty

The major's word proved to more true than false. In the next few days Atlanta fell to Sherman's troops. Then Sherman surprised everyone on both the Union and Confederate sides, by cutting his supply lines and taking his army of almost sixty-five thousand men and disappearing into the piney woods of Georgia.

Sherman marched south in two long columns of troops with his cavalry scouting ahead and screening his troop movements from the Confederates. The 20th Illinois Cavalry was kept busy scouting ahead of the general's troops.

Sherman and his army emerged from the piney woods of Georgia at Savanah by the sea. They took Savanah and then marched north into South Carolina. They captured Columbia, the capital of South Carolina and burned it to the ground. They then marched east through the state and entered North Carolina. They were still marching when the war ended in 1865.

Captain Timothy McMaster returned from his two months leave only to find Sherman and his army along with the 20th Illinois had vanished into the woods of Georgia. McMaster was promoted to Major upon his return and assigned to troops under General Thomas defending Franklin, Tennessee. Major McMaster led his troops in turning back the last invasion of Tennessee attempted by the Confederates.

Tom, Ted and Tuck McMaster survived the war, as did Gunn. Ted was slightly wounded in the battle of Bentonville, North Carolina, but the wound was superficial and healed quickly. The end of the war found the four troopers and the rest of the 20th Illinois Cavalry in Raleigh, North Carolina.

With the war officially over, Tom, Ted, Tuck, and Gunn marched with the rest of the 20th Illinois from North Carolina to Washington, D.C. On the way they took a short side trip to allow them to march through Richmond, Virginia, the former capital of the Confederacy. The march to Washington D.C. took them twenty days, arriving in the nation's capital on May 19, 1865.

Once in Washington, the regiment went into an encampment along with the rest of Sherman's Army of the West. Sherman's troops learned they were there to march in a grand review in front of the Capital building and the White House. The review would be in front of all the political officials and generals in the Union, including the newly installed President Johnson.

The grand review was to last two days. The first day was to feature the Army of the Potomac. This was the Army of the East. The soldiers who had fought all the battles on the eastern side of the country against Robert E. Lee and his Army of Northern Virginia. The Army of the East were resplendent in their bright new uniforms and shiny gear. They marched in step in a parade lasting all day.

On the second day, May 24, 1865, Sherman's Army of the West marched in review. Sherman's soldiers had no new uniforms. They were dressed in worn and sometimes ragged uniforms. Some of the men were barefoot. Nevertheless, they marched proudly as they passed in review. They maintained perfect discipline in their march. All eyes were fixed straight ahead. Every man marched in perfect step and timing. The stride of the soldiers of the Army of the West was long and sweeping, just like it had been for their thousand-mile march from Atlanta. These were the heroes of Vicksburg, Shiloh, Atlanta, Savannah, and Bentonville.

It was a sight never seen before and likely never seen again in the history of the United States of America.

In addition to the political leaders, government officials, and generals, thousands of citizens lined the streets of Washington to see the grand review.

Tom, Ted, Tuck, and Gunn rode side by side in this their last act as troopers of the 20th Illinois Cavalry. As they rode slowly down Pennsylvania Avenue, Gunn felt a sense of pride for himself and his three friends, and the rest of his regiment. He would never forget them or what they had endured together.

When the review was over, the four troopers were mustered out of the army. They were to proceed to Camp Douglas, just outside of Chicago to be officially discharged from the army.

Gunn gave up his horse, compete with saddle and tack with a thickness in his throat. He stroked the horse on the neck and bid it good-bye. He paid a small fee to the army keep his Spencer and his Colt. He also kept the leather case containing his Sharps rifle close by his side.

Then the four troopers boarded a train for the long ride back to Illinois. It was a long trip, and Gunn stared out the window as the train headed west. He watched the countryside slide by and at every town, large or small, groups of people and children had gathered to wave tiny American flags and to cheer their heroes.

The sun went down and the train continued on into the night. Gunn, Tom, Ted, and Tuck slept as best they could on the hard wooden seats.

Dawn found the train pulling into Pittsburg, Pennsylvania. The area around the train depot was like a park. The train came to a stop and orders were issued for the troops to disembark for two hours. Gunn and the McMaster brothers stepped down from the train glad to have a chance to stretch their legs. They were soon surprised to be greeted by groups of women of all ages welcoming them to Pittsburgh and leading them to long tables heaped with all kinds of breakfast dishes. There were eggs, bacon, sausage, flapjacks, cinnamon rolls, and breads of all kinds with butter. There was hot coffee, cold milk, and buttermilk. No Union soldier went hungry. When the troops had finally vanquished all the food in sight, they boarded the train and were soon on their way east to Chicago.

They arrived at Union Station in Chicago at midnight in a pouring rain. There were no crowds to greet them, no lovely ladies and no tables of food. Just other soldiers directing them to wagons that were to take them to Camp Douglas. Luckily the wagons had canvas tops that kept most of the rain off the soldiers.

Gunn, Tom, Ted, and Tuck were confined to Camp Douglas for four long, boring days. Finally, they were ordered into a line where they were officially separated from the Union army and given all of their back pay, mustering out bonuses, and their separation papers. Once they had exited the line, the four of them were no longer soldiers. Gunn knew the McMaster brothers had a long trip home ahead of them, and he was sad to say good-bye to men who had become more like brothers than just friends. After they were finished with the handshakes and the hugs, Gunn managed to get a ride with an army wagon back to Union Station. There he obtained a ticket to Galesburg and boarded the train. He received a few stares from fellow passengers because of the Spencer Rifle and the Colt, but because he was still in uniform, the glances quickly turned away to other interests.

Gunn sat back in his seat as the train pulled out of Chicago. The scenery changed from the often dirty and crowded portions of the city to the corn fields of the country. He felt excitement growing in him as the train neared the outskirts of Galesburg. When Gunn stepped down from the train onto the station depot platform, he resisted an urge to kneel down and kiss the ground. He shouldered his gear and his weapons, and he began walking out of Galesburg and down the dirt road leading to Altona. Altona was about fifteen miles from Galesburg. No one knew Gunn was coming home, so no one had been at the station to greet him. None of that mattered to Gunn.

As he walked along the dusty road, he could feel the warmth of the sun above him. The sun was warm, but somehow felt good to him, unlike the oppressive heat he had known in Georgia.

As Gunn walked along the road, he could hear meadowlarks in the nearby fields. He met an old farmer on the road. The old man was driving a wagon load of grain to Galesburg. Neither the old farmer nor Gunn knew each other, but they exchanged greetings like they were old friends. The old farmer acted as if meeting an armed, uniformed, Union soldier on the road happened every day. A sense of warmth and belonging surged through Gunn's body.

When he finally reached the outskirts of Altona, Gunn drank in the sight of familiar homes and buildings. He began to walk faster. Soon he found himself on the stone walk to his father's front door. When he got there, he hesitated. Should he knock on the door or just let himself in. Gunn decided the man returning home was not the same man who had left. He knocked on the door and was greeted by his surprised and delighted father. Gunn's father hugged his son and cried, "Thank God, Thank God."

William Gunn had returned home.

CHAPTER FORTY-ONE

September 1, 1865

Gunn gave the reins a little snap to encourage the two horses pulling his rented buggy. The road out of Atlanta had gotten progressively worse the further he drove from the city. Although it was now September, the air remained muggy. Gunn smiled to himself as he felt the heat of the Georgia sun. The last time he had felt that sun he had been in uniform and was fighting for his country and his friends.

A lot had happened since he was mustered out of the Union army back in June. Shortly after he had returned home to Altona, Illinois, he had begun to look for a farm of his own. In less than a month, he had purchased a three hundred and twenty acre farm just outside of Altona. Gunn had saved almost all of his army wages as well as his enlistment bonus and his mustering out bonus. That enabled him to make a down payment on the farm. The farm was a little run down, but with the help of his father, his uncle, and his brother, they had made repairs and improvements. He had worked especially hard to repair and clean up the farmhouse before he left on the train for Atlanta.

After several hours, he came to a small stream and he guided the wagon next to the stream so his horses could drink. While the horses were being watered, he removed his Stetson hat and wiped sweat from his brow with his shirt sleeve. Gunn paused and looked at the cream-colored Stetson cowboy hat. The hat was a gift, mailed to him by the McMaster family in the Colorado Territory. He looked inside the hat. There on the sweatband was his name in gold letters. "William Gunn, Cowboy."

Gunn smiled and returned the hat to his head. He flicked the reins, clucking to the horses, and soon they were back on their way. He met several fellow travelers on the road and most of them were heading toward Atlanta, not away from the city. Those travelers saw nothing unusual in a young man wearing work clothes, boots, and a Stetson cowboy hat driving a two-horse buggy, unless it was the Colt revolver in a holster on his side.

Gunn had heard rumors of what the southerners called Carpetbaggers running around the South. These were northern men, who were drawn to the opportunity to take advantage of the defeated southern people like moths to a flame. Gunn no longer carried the Colt back in Illinois, but he had a feeling that it might come in handy during his return to the South.

Gunn stopped in a small town and bought lunch from a small shack by the side of the road run by a couple of enterprising darkie women.

He took the lunch in a sack and ate it while he traveled down the road. It was late afternoon when he reached Latimer's Crossing. He reined in his team and looked around. The place looked even more run-down than it had when he and the McMaster boys had last ridden through it. Gunn snapped the reins and his team responded. They were headed north on a narrow dirt road full of memories for Gunn.

As Gunn neared his destination, he brought his team to a halt. He took a handkerchief out of his back pocket and carefully attempted to wipe away all the sweat and dust from his face. He replaced the handkerchief and clucked to the team. The buggy advanced and soon Gunn found himself at the entrance to the dirt drive leading to the small farmhouse belonging to the Calhoun family. As he drove the buggy down the drive, he could see two saddled horses tied to a bush in front of the house. As Gunn drove closer, he could hear voices coming from the rear of the house. The voices sounded loud and agitated.

Gunn got down from the buggy and tied off his team to a nearby tree. As he walked to the rear of the farmhouse, he could see Mrs. Melinda Calhoun standing next to a tall, gaunt man. The tall man was dressed in the butternut remnants of a Confederate uniform. Across from them were two rather fat men, dressed in beaver high top hats and checkered suits. The two fat men were arguing with the tall, thin man.

When he was about thirty feet away, Gunn was unnoticed by any of the four people. Gunn halted to listen to what was being said.

"You better take our offer, mister," said one of the top hatted fat men. "If you don't, we'll just buy this place for the back taxes you owe at the next tax sale."

"I tole you this place ain't for sale," said the tall man with an intensity that was unmistakable.

"You ignorant cracker. You ain't got a lick of sense. We'll buy them taxes and I'll take great pleasure in helpin' the sheriff kick you and your family off this place," said the other fat man.

Gunn stepped forward with his right hand resting on the butt of his Colt.

"Good morning, gentlemen, Mrs. Calhoun," said Gunn, as he doffed his cowboy hat.

All four turned and looked at Gunn with surprise. Melinda Calhoun's face went from anger to pleasant surprise.

"Mr. Gunn!" said Mrs. Calhoun. "What a delightful surprise."

She grabbed the tall, thin man by the hand and led him over to where Gunn was standing.

"Sam, this is William Gunn, the Union soldier I told you about," said Mrs. Calhoun.

"Mr. Gunn, this is my husband Samuel Calhoun, late of the Confederate army and now home to his family," said Mrs. Calhoun with a broad smile on her face.

A light of recognition seemed to go on in Samuel Calhoun's eyes as he held out his hand to Gunn. The men shook hands.

"I owe you all a debt of gratitude I can never repay, Mr. Gunn," said Calhoun. "What you all did for my family is something I will never forget. When my wife told me what happened, I took back every mean thing I ever said about Yankees."

"Please call me Billy," said Gunn. "That's what my friends call me, Mr. Calhoun. I was glad I was able to help out when your family was in trouble," he said.

"Then call me Sam," said Mr. Calhoun.

"Sam it is," said Gunn.

One of the two fat men had recovered from his surprise at Gunn's sudden and unexpected appearance. "I don't know what the hell you are doin' here, mister, but you're interrupting our business deal with these people," he said.

Gunn turned and looked directly at the two fat men. Then he spoke softly to them.

"I don't think you boys have a deal. The Calhoun's ain't interested in your offer. If you know what's good for you, you'll get on your horses and ride on," said Gunn.

The fat man started to protest, but his partner had taken in the Colt at Gunn's hip, and the hard look in Gunn's eyes.

He grabbed his partner by the arm and quickly led him to the front of the house where their horses were tied. Within minutes, the two fat carpetbaggers had fled down the road.

Gunn turned to Sam. "How much are the back taxes, Sam?"

"They say we owe seventeen dollars and we ain't got it. I got a crop in the field and by the end of November I'll have it sold and then I'd have the money, but it's due now."

Gunn reached in his pocket and pulled out a small leather wallet. He extracted seventeen dollars in Union greenbacks and handed them to Sam.

"I appreciate the offer, Billy, but I don't take charity, even from you all," said Sam.

"It ain't charity. It's a loan. Pay me back when you can," said Gunn.

Both Mr. and Mrs. Calhoun were overwhelmed, and Mrs. Calhoun began crying.

Mr. Calhoun took her into his arms, and he too had some tears in his eyes.

Gunn hated to interrupt them, but he had come a long way for a very specific reason.

Gunn cleared his throat. Both Mr. and Mrs. Calhoun looked up at him.

"I've come a long distance, Mr. and Mrs. Calhoun. I'm here to ask for your permission to marry your daughter, Anna. If she'll have me, of course," said Gunn.

"It's fine by me," said Mr. Calhoun, "but in my family that's up to my daughter.

"She's inside. I'll go get her, said Mrs. Calhoun, who was still crying. Whether those were tears of joy or not was uncertain, but she had a huge smile on her face

Gunn stood there and wiped his hands on his pants. His heart was pounding, his mouth was dry, and his breath was short. It was exactly the same feeling he had experienced when he had last visited the Calhoun farm.

Anna Calhoun burst through the back door. She had been cleaning, and her apron was streaked with dust and grime. Her hair was askew and her hands were dirty. Gunn didn't care. To him she was the most beautiful thing he had ever seen. His heart raced and his body tingled.

Anna ran to him and almost jumped into his arms in a very unladylike fashion. Anna and Gunn held each other as tightly as they could, seemingly unwilling to let go of each other. Finally, Anna slipped out of his arms and looked up into his eyes.

"I said I'd be back," said Gunn.

"I said I'd wait for you," replied Anna.

EPILOGUE

The first signs of dusk were seeping through the windows of the parlor. Tom McMaster tapped the now dead ashes out of the bowl of his pipe into his open hand. After dropping them into a nearby ash tray, he looked up at the half circle of William Gunn's family who sat before him.

"Five years after the war, I got a letter from Billy," he said. "In the letter Billy asked about buying some of our calves and having them shipped to the farm where he could fatten them up on his grain when grain prices were down. I agreed to sell him all the calves he wanted, on one condition. He had to come out to our ranch in the Colorado Territory and see the calves and our operation, first hand. He agreed, and he came out on the train and stayed for five days. We had a great time ridin' horses and tourin' the ranch. It was the last time we were to see each other."

Tom paused, as if to catch his breath, and he looked down at the floor. When he raised his head back up, his eyes were wet.

"Over the years I sold many calves to Billy. We never signed a contract or an agreement. Our entire deal was based on a handshake. I never had any regrets over a single sale, and I'm sure he didn't either.

Tom looked directly into the eyes of every one of William Gunn's children and grandchildren. They all returned his gaze with looks of intensity. They had been hanging on every word he had spoken.

"The most valuable thing in the world to me is a good friend, who I can trust. Billy Gunn was such a man. All of you should be proud to be his kin. He was like a brother to my family."

Tom again paused to wipe some unwanted moisture from his eyes.

"In the cavalry, one of every four cavalrymen is designated as the horse holder. His job is to hold the horses while the rest of us dismount to fight on foot. It's not an easy job. With all the gun fire and cannon shells exploding, the horses are frightened and try their best to get away from all the noise. Whether we need to move forward or to fall back, we count on the horse holder to have our horses for us when we need them. The horse holder has to be someone we can entrust our lives. Billy Gunn was the best horse holder I ever knew. My family owes the life of our father to Billy."

Tom stood up and placed his now empty pipe back inside his coat pocket. Ted and Tuck also stood.

"I reckon I've said enough. It's time for us to go," said Tom.

All three brothers hugged Anna and said their good-byes to the rest of the Gunn family. As they made their way out the front door of the Gunn farmhouse, they passed by an old walnut coat rack.

Hanging on the top rung was a well-worn cream-colored Stetson cowboy hat.

THE END

ACKNOWLEDGEMENTS

My great-grandfather, William Main, served as a private in Company I of the 102nd Illinois Infantry in the American Civil War. He enlisted at age eighteen in 1862 and served under General Sherman for the entire war. He was never wounded, but more amazingly he never went on sick call.

I read the history of his regiment published in 1865 from official reports and diaries of the officers and non-commissioned officers of the regiment. My wife Nancy and I flew to Atlanta where we rented a car to retrace my great-grandfather's footsteps from Atlanta to the Sea. It was a moving experience. Later I read a book, *Sherman's Horsemen*, by David Evans. While reading this book, I learned about the great cavalry raids made by Sherman's men to cut off supplies to Atlanta and hurry the surrender of the city. I also learned of General Stoneman's failed attempt to take Macon and to free the Union officers imprisoned there. I had never heard of Camp Oglethorpe as a prison for Union Officers. That led to other research and the result was this work of fiction about some of the men who participated in that raid.

This is my fifth novel, but my first stand-alone story and a piece of historical fiction at that. I hope you enjoyed reading this story as much as I did writing it.

Please let me know how you felt about the book by writing a short review in Amazon at www.amazon.com, or Barnes and Noble at www.bn.com. I learn a great deal from my readers as I continue to try to improve my stories.

Once again I relied heavily on my loving and patient wife Nancy, as my proof reader, critic, and support team. I also received assistance from Kerry Wong, Mary Marlin and my oldest son, Steve Tibaldo, who read segments of the book as they were written. All of them passed along their comments and suggestions to me. Their input was helpful and I utilized much of it.

This story is a salute to my great-grandfather, William Main and his loyal wife Anna. It is also a nod to all those brave Americans, both Union and Confederate, who fought and died for what they believed in during a truly terrible and devastating war.

I am now beginning research on my next novel, which will be the fifth in the series about Carson "Kit" Andrews and his best friend Swifty Olson. Thank you for your patronage, and please keep reading.

You can contact me directly at rwcallis@aol.com.

Previous novels by Robert W. Callis:

1. *Kemmerer*
2. *Hanging Rock*
3. *Buckskin Crossing*
4. *The Ghosts of Skeleton Canyon*